ABIDING EVIL

ABIDING EVIL

Alison Buck

An Alnpete Book

Abiding Evil
First published in Great Britain by Alnpete Press, 2007
An imprint of Alnpete Limited

Copyright © Alison Buck, 2007
All rights reserved

The right of Alison Buck to be identified as the author of this work has been asserted in accordance with sections 77 and 78 of the Copyright, Designs and Patents Act 1988. No part of this publication may be reproduced, stored in a retrieval system or transmitted in any form, or by any means (electronic, mechanical, telepathic, or otherwise) without the prior written permission of the copyright owner. Use of product names or trademarks has not been authorised, sponsored or otherwise approved by the trademark owners.

Alnpete Press, PO Box 757
Dartford, Kent
DA2 7TQ

www.alnpetepress.co.uk

A CIP catalogue record for this book is available from the British Library

ISBN 978-0-9552206-3-0

Condition of Sale
This book is sold subject to the condition that it shall not, by way of trade or otherwise, be lent, re-sold, hired out or otherwise circulated in any form of binding or cover other than that in which it is published and without a similar condition including this condition being imposed on the subsequent purchaser.

This book is copyright under the Berne Convention.
Alnpete Press & Leaf Design is a trademark of Alnpete Limited

This book is a work of fiction. All names, characters, places and events are either a product of the author's fevered imagination or are used fictitiously. Any resemblance to actual events, places, forests, people (living, dead or undead), wandering souls, elemental forces or other spirits is purely coincidental.

Printed by Antony Rowe Limited

For
Alex and Raff

I

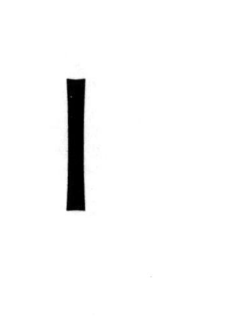

1

Wind whistled through the shack's bleached and broken clapboard walls, chilling to the bone. The lamp's hissing flame, the only source of light, flared and guttered behind its dirty glass, an erratic dance of shadows leaping across the darkened walls.

All in black, sharp face pale in the weak light, a crouching insect of a man sat hunched over a table. With a low grunt of pleasure he leant back and smiled, lifting a small object up into the light. He turned it over and over with his long, bony fingers, silently admiring his own workmanship. It was ready.

Now the game could begin again.

The doll of roughly carved pinewood stared blankly back at him, its eyes, scratched hollows, gouged across the grain. Its wood felt warm in his icy fingers and, as he turned it over, he heard its voice whispering to him,

"Come and catch me. I'm waiting."

The man gasped with pleasure. His black eyes glittered and his thin face creased into a grotesque grimace of greedy anticipation.

2

Emerging from the unbroken dark of rural night, the bus rattled into the slumbering town of Drovers Creek. With a complaining hiss and a shriek of the brakes, it pulled over outside the disused grain depot. Inside, as the engine grumbled and the bus shuddered to an idling halt, sleepy travellers were shaken back to consciousness. They yawned and stretched, rubbing sleep from eyes creased closed, reluctant to open. Moving stiffly, pulling cuffs down to protect their hands, they wiped condensation from the cold windows to peer out into the early morning half-light. Most read the name on the rusting sign and gratefully returned to sleep, shuffling and stretching in their cramped seats. Two, a slightly-built woman in her early twenties and a small boy, both now muffled in layers of thick clothing, dragged their heavy bags to the front of the bus and staggered down its steps.

Leaving the warm, sleepy fug of the bus, they gasped at the sudden chill of the outside air and hugged their coats tighter, trying to still the sudden, violent trembling of their limbs. The driver glanced down at them briefly, disinterested. He said nothing, but grunted at the effort as he wrenched the door shut in their faces. With a hoarse growl and a belch of black smoke, the engine coughed back into life and the bus lumbered off, leaving the two small figures shivering in its wake, alone at the side of the road. The steamy interior lights of the bus, now fading into the distance, were the only sign of warmth in the bleak landscape, a small cocoon of comfort fast receding, soon to be swallowed up by the dark.

Now there was absolute stillness. The woman and child could hear nothing save the ragged harshness of their own breathing. The weak, pre-dawn lightening of the sky gave little illumination to their surroundings. Sufficient though, for it to be clear that there was no life here. The few buildings discernible, darker shapes against the cold sky, had been the grain stores of an agricultural depot, now deserted, dark and empty, padlocked chains hanging loosely across battered, rusting gates.

Without a word, the woman took a tighter grip on the heavy bags, crossed the road and marched off down a dirt track which led across the fields. Also silent, the boy followed. He trudged in his mother's wake, watching as each rasping breath clouded around her head before trailing, swirling, behind her. As she strode on ahead, she seemed to him to move like a powerful steam train rolling down the line, wheels held to the tracks, locked on their predetermined path. And the boy knew that, just like the train, his mother would not deviate from her path, look back, or make a detour for anything. Or anyone. Sighing, he lowered his head and plodded after her, thrusting mittened hands deep into the pockets of his oversized coat.

With the uneven path frozen hard, ridged with sudden ruts and littered with stone-hard clods of soil, the pair made slow and faltering progress. The dull clomping of their stumbling boots and the gasping intakes of icy breath through damp scarves were the only sounds. On all sides, brittle stumps of blackened corn stretched away in rows, disappearing into the gloom; a mist sinking low over the cold, dark earth.

The child's fringe was soon dripping into his eyes. He blinked the sweat away and looked up, straining to see the fading figure ahead. He was anxious, falling behind, but he didn't call out for his mother to slow down; he knew from experience that she would only be spurred on to move more quickly away. He knew that now, as always, he was an inconvenience to her; she never made any effort to hide her feelings towards him. He had never known from her the comfort of a hug or the tenderness of a goodnight kiss. She was simply a part of the pattern of his life as he was of hers. There had never been a love between them so, having never known her affection, the boy had no expectation of it; he accepted the situation without any sense of loss or regret. Their relationship was what it always had been and, for him, it represented normality. So he stumbled on, breathing hard, trying to catch up with her, the only familiar element in this icy, wasted landscape.

It seemed to the boy that the mist cleared suddenly and he all but ran into his mother. She had stopped and was talking to someone. The boy cowered behind her. He knew the routine; keep quiet and keep out of sight. But on this occasion, uniquely, his mother turned and pulled him forward to meet the stranger, an old woman.

"His name's Jon," she said, pulling the scarf from around Jon's head.

Jon recognised the look that flashed over the old woman's face. The instant, instinctive response was always the same; the gasp and the wide, shocked eyes. Most women additionally put their hands to their mouths, but this one reacted as men usually did; setting her jaw and swallowing hard. Jon had produced such reactions for as long as he could remember so he no longer gave it much thought. It was just the way things were. His mother however did still care. This reaction of strangers towards her son never ceased to hurt her, not because it evoked in her any sense of empathy or tenderness towards him, but rather because it reflected so negatively on her. Their shocked reaction was, she believed, an implicit criticism of her for having produced such a malformed child. She hated the criticism and she hated Jon for being its cause.

"You gonna let us in, or what?" she snapped.

With her eyes still fixed on Jon, the old woman grunted assent and stepped to one side, allowing the boy and his mother to pass. Making no move to help lift the bags, the old woman stood watching, frowning, her hands stuffed into the pockets of her oversized dungarees. Scowling, Jon's mother did not ask for help, but grunted as she lifted the heavy bags clear of the ground then struggled, the bags banging heavily into the risers, to climb the steps to the door of a small farmhouse.

Once inside, she dumped the bags and threw herself down into the threadbare armchair. Apparently forgotten, Jon now stood by the door and stared about him. The single armchair was close to a wood stove, which stood against the one stone-built wall. The floor, ceiling and remaining walls were all of rough pinewood, as were the table and chairs that stood over by the window. The table, and the floor below it, were littered with the discarded remains of the old woman's meals. But, apart from these scattered leftovers, there was none of the everyday clutter that would suggest that someone lived here; that the room was a part of someone's home. It was a functional, bare and comfortless space and the low-powered lamp gave out little light. The room looked and smelt dusty; neglected. In this respect at least, it was similar to all the rooms in all the many run-down apartment buildings that Jon had ever known. The boy felt at home.

The old woman had followed them in and now stood, hands still in her pockets, looking from Jon to his mother.

"Is he normal?" she asked.

Jon's mother looked up, disbelief on her face.

"You tell me Ma. He look normal to you, huh?"

"No, no, I mean in the head. Is he like a retard?"

Jon's mother shrugged.

"He don't say much and he ain't never been to school or nothing, but he mostly does what you tell him."

The old woman gave Jon an appraising stare, then nodded as if satisfied. She turned to her daughter.

"So what are you doing? You coming back here now?"

"Well gee, thanks for the welcome home Ma. It's just great to be back."

"I asked you a question, Jeannie."

"Don't call me that," she said, her face sullen.

"Jeannie? Why? What's wrong with that? It's your name ain't it?"

"Not any more. I left that godawful name behind me when I left this dump -"

"And now you're back," the old woman interrupted.

"Yeah," her daughter muttered, crestfallen, "now I'm back."

She turned away, staring into nowhere. Behind her, the old woman chewed her lip, not knowing what to say. She had never been good at talking to people, even her own flesh and blood: especially her own flesh and blood.

She shrugged.

"So what d'they call you now?"

"As if you care."

"Suit yourself."

Her daughter had always been like this, wayward,

moody; downright ornery. The old woman turned her attention back to the boy.

"You hungry, boy?"

Jon said nothing, but looked up at this woman, his grandmother, with pleading eyes. The old woman knew that look.

"Starving huh? OK, go see if there's some bread in the kitchen there. Can you do that?"

Jon nodded and plodded into the tiny kitchen. The old woman was still watching him, fascinated, unconvinced that the boy would be able to do something even as simple as finding and eating a hunk of bread. But find it he did and, squatting down on the grimy linoleum, he ate it, breaking it into manageable pieces before noisily sucking it in through his ragged tear of a mouth.

"How the hell d'he get like that?"

The younger woman sighed.

"He was born kinda odd-looking, and then he fell out the window when he was a baby. Cut his head right open to the bone," she traced a finger across her own face from ear to chin, "They stitched his face back up like that, but they said there weren't nothing more they could do."

"And his father?"

She shook her head.

The old woman nodded.

"Well I gotta go see to the traps. I'll be back at noon. Guess you know where things are. Help yourself."

"Yeah. Thanks, Ma," The younger woman paused a moment, hesitating, then added, "It's Gina, with a G. They call me Gina now. It's like a stage name."

The old woman nodded again, then took up her gun and left without saying another word.

When she came back to the house, the old woman was half expecting her daughter to be gone. But Gina was still there. She had unbuttoned her coat but had not taken it off and she was fidgeting, restless with impatience, but she was there. She looked up as the old woman came in and, straight away, just from that look, her mother knew that she wanted something from her. The old woman waited to see what the something was. Money? Or a place to stay a while?

"Ma?" Gina began cautiously, "I got something to ask you."

The old woman nodded but said nothing. She began to skin the rabbits she had just dumped on the table.

Gina winced with disgust. This is why she had left this place, with its primitive ways and dirt and lack of any ambition beyond simply getting though another day. She looked away, trying to block out the ripping, sliding sounds of skin parting from flesh.

"I've had an offer to try out for a part in a movie. It's such a big break for me, Ma. I'm real lucky they're even considering me for it."

She paused, trying to gauge her mother's reaction, but the old woman merely continued skinning the rabbits. The world of actors and film-making were so far removed from her everyday experience that her daughter might as well have been describing the workings of another planet. The old woman listened, but could make little sense of what Gina was telling her.

"Thing is, Ma, it's a two month shoot, out in California, can you believe it? And see, the thing is, I'm gonna be busy the whole time."

Her mother began to understand. Gina continued,

"I couldn't take Jon with me. I'd love to, naturally, but it just wouldn't be fair on the boy."

The old woman stopped her work and prepared herself. Gina took a deep breath before making her final pitch.

"So I was wondering if he could maybe just stay here with you. Just for two months, three at the very most. I really, really need the work and you could get to know your grandson. He's really no trouble at all. What d'ya say?"

Even having had a few moment's warning of the request, the old woman was unable to find the words to reply and, delighted, Gina took her mother's silence for agreement. She was thrilled; barely able to believe how easy it had been. Her spirits soared. In an instant the dark and heavy shutters that had obscured the way ahead, the way to her deserved success, had fallen clean away. An incredible world of unlimited possibilities opened up for her, a world without that goddamn boy dragging her down, holding her back. After years of demeaning struggle and failure, the prospect of freedom was almost too wonderful and Gina had to work desperately to conceal her sudden exhilaration; to stop herself jumping for sheer joy and relief. She lowered her head and, with apparent concentration, repeatedly smoothed the creases from her skirt while she fought to chase the smile from her face. Eventually she was able to raise her head and speak in a voice that was cheerful and bright, but gave no hint of the wild euphoria she was actually feeling.

"Oh, thank you, Ma, thank you so much. You don't know how much this means to me. This is the break I've been waiting for all these years. I'm gonna make it big, Ma, you'll see."

Her mother continued to stare down at the bloodied carcasses on the table, as if in a dream.

Standing, Gina rebuttoned her coat and began to pull on her gloves.

"His clothes and such are in there," she nodded towards one of the bags. "Thank you so much, Ma. I won't ever forget this."

She came over to her mother and nearly surprised them both by giving her a hug, but the sight of the plump, pale, skinless bodies on the table brought her back to reality in a hurry. Hug this filthy, vile-smelling old woman with her slimy, blood covered hands? Hell no! What had she been thinking? Now with a look of thinly concealed disgust, Gina turned away and picked up her bag.

"You ain't going right now?" the old woman asked, suddenly coming to life, realising what was happening.

"I got to, Ma. Filming starts next week and the bus leaves town at three."

The old woman shook her head, trying to clear her confusion.

"But Jeannie, you...er...you got money for a ticket?"

"Got my ticket right here," Gina smiled, patting her handbag. The old woman knew that the matter was decided. Discussion was over.

Gina walked to the door, a spring in her step; so nearly free.

"Ain't you forgetting something?"

Her mother's sharp tone cut through Gina's sense of elation. She stiffened, frozen, her hand already grasping the door handle. There was panic on her face; she was so close to freedom, just seconds away from the start of a new life. Please God, don't let it go wrong now. Slowly, she turned.

Her mother nodded towards Jon who was huddled in the corner of the room.

"Ain't you planning on saying goodbye to the boy?"

Gina suddenly relaxed, a look of relief sweeping her face.

"Sure I am. Why, what sort of mother do you take me for?"

"Come here boy," ordered the old woman.

Jon came over to her, but kept his eyes down, fixed on

the shiny lilac of his mother's skirt. He knew her: this was not going to be a tearful parting. He had watched as Gina played the role of delicate, vulnerable ingénue more times than he could count, but he was also more than familiar with the desperate and self-centred individual who existed just beneath the veneer of vulnerability.

Gina walked over to her son and stiffly patted him on the head.

"Be good for your grandma. And do like I told you; stay out of sight, away from people. You understand? Good. And don't you worry; I'll be back for you, soon as I can."

All three knew this for the lie it was, but nothing was said to challenge it. Jon had to stand mutely beside this stranger, watching his mother as she walked down the steps, away across the fields and out of his life forever.

For the next ten years Jon lived with his grandmother on the farm, hidden away from the rest of the world. No one in Drovers Creek, or the nearby town of Losien, ever knew of his existence and, living in the remote farmstead at the end of a mile-long dirt track, Jon saw no one but the old woman. In all the time since his mother's departure, no visitors had ever come to the farm and his grandmother, knowing what reception the boy would have been given by the people in the town, determined instead to give the boy the means by which to live as independently as she had herself.

All her life she been a hard-working woman, well used to the demands of farming and, as the oldest girl in a large family, she had been a second mother to her six brothers and sisters. Escaping at barely nineteen from the numbing drudgery at home, she had married and travelled across the country with her new husband to this farmstead where she had spent the rest of her life. Her husband had been a powerful and upright man with clear ideas on the behaviour properly befitting a wife. He would not tolerate being crossed and had once beaten her to the floor for daring to express an opinion in disagreement with his own. She soon learned to keep her opinions to herself and subsequently enjoyed a few years of measured contentment, until the day when her husband dropped dead out in the corn field, leaving her with a farm to run and a child to raise.

Several men from the town had visited the farm in those early days, looking to marry the young widow or to get their hands on her land by some other means. They had sympathised with her, poor Lizzie Benson, a young widow woman without a man to care for her. How could she hope to manage a farm alone? They made offers to buy her land, 'As a kindness, so she could make a new start for herself and her daughter back East'. But Lizzie was nobody's fool and she saw clean through their weasel smiles. And while she may not have had much education, she knew enough to judge that they were offering far too little for the land. So Lizzie got down her husband's old shotgun and ran them off her property, every last one of them. She would never remarry: she would live her own life and speak her own opinions as often and as loud as she liked. And she would work the farm herself, or die in the trying.

Over the years, Lizzie acquired a fearsome reputation as something of a wild woman. She had little time for niceties and dressed in dungarees and heavy working boots. Long days spent working in both the withering heat of summer and the bitter cold of winter soon aged her. Occasionally, at the end of another cruelly exhausting day, bone weary she would allow herself a fortifying swig from her dead husband's stash of Jack Daniels. And when, eventually, the last bottle gave out, she scandalised old man Carney by marching into his liquor store and buying another bottle, the biggest he had. Lizzie no longer had to care what behaviour was fitting for a woman; through sheer hard work and grim determination, she had established herself as a tough-talking, hard-dealing farmer in her own right.

Years later, she realised that this hard-won acceptance had perhaps come at too high a price. Her daughter, Jeannie, had grown up with no father and seeing little of her mother. Jeannie resented her mother's strangeness; her scruffy appearance and her blunt talking. She wanted a soft, womanly mother, like the other kids had. She wanted a mother who fixed her hair, baked cookies and dressed in pretty clothes.

Jeannie's own clothes were always ill-fitting, bought as an afterthought on the rare trips into town for supplies. Everything was bought big to last longer. Her mother always said she would grow into them, but Jeannie was a small kid, and she stayed small. In her long dresses and oversized boots, she was the butt of every joke in the school. The other kids pinched at her. They jeered at her. Some even threw stones and shouted that her mother was an ugly old witch.

For all of this, Jeannie blamed her mother; hating her even though she knew something of the many hardships Lizzie had to endure. Looking to her own future, Jeannie wanted more for herself. She wanted out. And soon after her fourteenth birthday she made her escape, heading off to the city with an itinerant farmhand.

Driven off his own family's land down south by the drought and the dust storms, he had wandered north looking for work. He came to Lizzie's farm offering to help with the harvest. But he left with Jeannie and forty dollars that he stole from her mother.

In the years following Jeannie's leaving, Lizzie became

even more reclusive. She despised and distrusted the townsfolk and they returned the sentiment in full, leaving Lizzie in the total isolation she demanded. It was to be nearly ten years before she saw her daughter again and, now that Jeannie had finally returned, with her new name, and her malformed son, Lizzie saw no reason to break that isolation and invite the scorn of the townsfolk on to the boy.

So Jon never took the school bus he glimpsed far in the distance, away across the fields. He never had a day's formal education, but Lizzie taught him how to set traps and find clean water. She showed him how to make and mend his clothes and cook his own food. She worked Jon hard as a labourer around the farm and taught him how to fend for himself. Between the two of them, they grew or trapped almost everything they needed and, every three months or so, Lizzie would go into town and barter for the remainder. Jon roamed his grandmother's land and trapped and hunted in the vast ancient forest that surrounded its fields and stretched for hundreds of square miles to the mountains in the next State.

Lizzie accepted the responsibility to care for her grandson, but she was not a woman given to gentleness and was quick to threaten a whipping if he defied her. Yet, despite this, Jon respected her and, if there was little love between them, there was at least a closeness. They each knew the boundaries of contact between them and, within these limitations, they shared a sort of gruff affection, the one for the other. The old woman gave Jon a stability that he had never known during his early nomadic years on the road with Gina. He and his grandmother got along together well enough and Jon at last felt he had his place in the world, even if he was not always made to feel so very welcome in it.

Jon's mother had never told him in what year or on what day he had been born, but, looking back later, he guessed he must have been about sixteen years old when his world again changed irrevocably.

It was a warm evening, in early June. Jon came back to the farm after a few days' hunting to find his grandmother sitting, rigid at the table. He took the old woman's hand to rouse her, but she was already cold. The once rheumy blue eyes were dry and partially closed. The thin-lipped mouth had sagged open and the head lolled to one side, dirty grey hair in disarray.

Jon was almost certain that Lizzie was dead, but he had no idea what he should do now. She had always acted as if she would live forever, never admitting to any weakness. It was almost impossible to believe that this indomitable spirit could have ended. It was as if Lizzie's fiery determination and raw, hard work should have guaranteed her endless life and vitality. And yet, here she was, dead, while, around her, everything else had continued, unconcerned.

Death was a part of the life of the fields and forest all around them, yet Lizzie and Jon had never discussed this eventuality. When her old mongrel had died, Lizzie had dealt with its disposal alone. By the time Jon had returned from his day's hunting, the dog was simply no longer there. So, with no experience of funeral parlours or chapels, Jon had an understanding of the handling of death drawn solely from his time spent in the forest. If an animal was dead and it was good, you ate it. If an animal was dead but diseased or decayed, it was not good, you left it to rot and maybe some other animal would eat it.

Neither option seemed appropriate for his grandmother.

Jon didn't like looking at that face, somehow unfamiliar now the life had left it, so he took the sheet from his grandmother's bed and covered her with it. He stood for a moment, undecided, hands rammed into his pockets, just as his grandmother so often had. Then, with a shrug, he went off to his own bed as usual.

By the next morning the body had slumped forward onto the table. Jon skirted around it as he prepared his breakfast before a normal day's work, but he was concerned. Was the body supposed to be able to move like that? Was that right? He had no idea. He lifted the sheet, reached out and touched the old woman's hand. At the cold, unnatural waxiness of her skin, he reflexively pulled his hand from hers. He couldn't bear to lift her head and look again into those dry eyes, but he felt there was no need to; she had to be dead. Moved or no, she had to be dead. So, what was he to do? What should he do? Still unsure, he decided to go hunting. He should have been working in the vegetable patch near the house that day but, under the circumstances, he reasoned that Lizzie was unlikely to raise an objection to his change of routine.

Jon spent the whole day out in the forest. Here he felt comfortable. He had everything he needed and the trees provided a soothing shade from the warm summer sun. He stayed away until late in the evening.

By now, his grandmother's body had started to smell. It was unmistakable and hit Jon as he opened the door. He winced, but was relieved. At least now he could be absolutely sure that Lizzie was dead; he knew the smell of decay. Gathering up his blanket and a lamp, he prepared to spend the night in the barn.

The next morning he moved his few personal possessions and all the tinned foodstuffs, hunting knives, gun and cooking utensils and so on, out into the barn. Then he spent the next few days tending the vegetable patch and avoiding the house altogether. He tried not to think of his grandmother sitting there at the table. He couldn't help but feel that he should do something special with her body; but what? Stirring the embers of his fire on his third evening living in the barn, he had an idea that he could perhaps burn the body, but he couldn't be sure that was the right thing to do. The problem was gnawing away at him.

He decided to get away for a long hunting trip and put the worry behind him. Having packed some gear he trekked for eight or ten miles into an unfamiliar area of forest before making camp in a small cave above a clear running stream. The weight of worry soon dissipated and he spent several days as happy as he had ever been. He felt an acceptance here in the forest and found solace in the peace surrounding him. He was relaxed; at home here, not in a house.

And not in a barn.

With that, his thoughts went back to the farm, and his sense of duty decided him to go back. He ate, then packed his bag with a heavy heart.

Jon knew something was wrong while he was still some way off. There was a dark rectangle where the farm door should have been. He discarded his gear and ran the last few hundred yards to the house, leaping the steps to the door in one bound. The door was swinging open and he had an immediate impression of the room being in disarray. Then, disturbed by his sudden appearance, a cloud of flies rose up and buzzed around him. He stopped dead. Near his foot, on the floor just inside the door, was a scrap of his grandmother's shirt. It had a mass of something brown and fibrous on it.

Flesh.

Swatting at the flies that were obscuring everything

with their constant movement, Jon forced himself to go over to the table. His hand trembled as he grabbed at the sheet and he had to swallow hard to quell his stomach when he pulled it away. What remained of his grandmother's body was shocking. An animal, or animals, had partially dismembered it, removing many areas of flesh and gnawing at the exposed bones. Jon was appalled. He swayed slightly.

Some of the flies had now settled, making it easier for Jon to see the rest of the room. Dried up trails of blood laced the floor, linking larger stains where something had presumably ripped apart pieces of his grandmother's body. Jon could take no more. He had to get out.

Retching, he slumped down outside the barn; unable to think clearly. The buzzing foulness of the room stayed at the forefront of his mind and its stinking air still filled his lungs. He shook his head. His grandmother should not have ended like this. No matter how fierce her outbursts of anger had been, or how harsh her occasional beatings, Lizzie had deserved better than this. And Jon knew it was his fault. He could not have shut the door properly when he went on the hunting trip. But, even if he had secured the house, he knew it had been wrong to go off, leaving her body like that. He should have done something. But what? What should he have done?

The horror of the room now decided his actions for him. He certainly could never live in that house again. He would return to the welcoming safety of his forest cave and make his home there.

Soon he was making the first of many trips into the forest, carrying supplies and utensils, clothes and tools from the farmstead. He had to be thorough, taking everything he might need, because he knew he would never be coming back. He stashed everything in a hollow about a half mile into the trees, covering it all with a tarpaulin. He would move everything to the cave by the stream, once his task here was completed.

He made his final journey back to the farm and climbed the steps to the door, but he did not go in this last time. He had earlier poured kerosene around the room, soaking it into the armchair. Now he made a silent farewell to the old woman, opened the door and hastily threw in the lighted rag. With a dull 'woomp', like something heavy being dropped into a sack of flour, the fire took hold, immediately engulfing the room. With sudden roaring ferocity, a wave of hot air forced Jon back down the steps.

He retreated and watched from the edge of the trees as the house burnt, quickly leaving no more than a few charred fingers smoking into the appropriately blood red sky. In the distance, lit orange by the setting sun, Jon saw puffs of dust rising from the farm track. Someone from town must have noticed the smoke and come to check on the wild old woman. But Jon didn't wait. These people were nothing to do with him. His time spent on the edge of their world was ended. From this point on he would live in the forest and he fully expected never to have to deal with another human being ever again.

3

Suzie walked confidently towards the corner at the end of Main Street, head held high, shoulders back. Stopping, she checked herself in the window of Mercer's Hardware and smiled with satisfaction. Superimposed over the hammers, nails, brooms and pots of paint in the window, her reflection looked radiant. She wore her red cotton shirt, her new, matching, shiny red slippers and had her cardigan draped over her shoulders like the ladies in Paris, France. Her sister, Mona, who worked as a beautician, had back-combed Suzie's blond hair and set it with choking clouds of hairspray so that it stood up, framing her pretty face in a stiff halo. Suzie turned from side to side. She was looking good and she felt like a movie star. A million dollars.

But Danny was late. They had agreed to meet at seven and it was already a quarter after. As the minutes dragged by, Suzie became increasingly self-conscious. She began to wish she hadn't dressed with such care and to such stunning effect. She was sure it must be plain to anyone passing by that she was waiting for someone special, and it would soon be equally plain that her someone special had decided not to show. Suzie saw understanding in the smiles on passing faces and read sympathy in their acknowledging shrugs. She felt her own face warm and redden with embarrassment and, looking down, she pretended to search for some dropped item. In this way she managed to avoid meeting their eyes.

The sun had set, the sky was darkening and there were no street lights here on the edge of town. Suzie couldn't wait any longer. Biting her lip she looked up the street one last time. To her surprise she saw someone suddenly wave to her from further out of town. Danny? What was he playing at? She called to him, startling an old lady who was walking past. Mumbling an apology, Suzie waited a moment for the woman to walk on by, then she called out again. But he merely beckoned to her from the shadows on the far side of the road. It must be some kind of game.

Now that Danny had finally arrived, Suzie felt no anger towards him for having made her wait here for so long. He would have no idea how foolish she had felt because it was, she thought, typical of a boy to be completely unaware of time. Suzie felt an almost maternal indulgence towards his thoughtlessness. She loved him and, though she might chide him, she had in fact forgiven him already. Her embarrassment was forgotten and even her slight irritation at the hiding game he was now playing was pushed to the back of her mind. If it had been her choice, she would have had him stop the games and come right over to Mercer's to meet her. In the weak light still filtering out from the back room of the store, Danny would then have been able to see how gorgeous she looked. He would have seen the care she had taken to look great for this their first date and then she could have pretended that it was nothing, that she always dressed like this out of school. Over there, in the shadows Danny wouldn't see that her shirt and slippers were almost a perfect matching red and he wouldn't see how beautifully Mona had set her hair. But none of that was important.

All that mattered was that she and Danny were on a date. She, quiet little Suzie, had a boyfriend. She could scarcely believe her good fortune.

Smiling happily, Suzie stepped out into the road.

A week later, in the local press, disturbing articles speculated on what had happened to her:

THE LOSIEN GAZETTE, APRIL 15, 1957

POLICE TO SEARCH WOODS WITH BLOODHOUNDS

```
Police are still no closer to
discovering the whereabouts of
local girl Suzie Bower, 17, first
reported missing by boyfriend,
Danny Rivers, also 17, on the
evening of Thursday last.
Beechers Park resident, Mrs
Louisa Hayward, reported being
startled by a young girl matching
Suzie's description on Thursday
evening but there has been no
confirmed sighting of Suzie since
that time. Extensive searches of
the Bower home, and interviews
with family and friends have so
far revealed no clues and Sheriff
Mason Daniels has called for
anyone with information regarding
Suzie's disappearance to contact
his department.
```

Over the long summer months there were more grim

headlines:

THE LOSIEN GAZETTE, JUNE 21, 1957

A SECOND CHILD DISAPPEARS

The Sheriff's Office has announced that a second boy has disappeared from the Lakeside area of town. Little Joey Harper, aged 7, was last seen playing near Spirit lake, but was found to be missing when his friends prepared to return home. Joey is described as small for his age, with dark hair and blue eyes. He was wearing a red and yellow shirt and blue jeans.
Joey's disappearance comes only twelve days after that of 9 year old Tony Fisher, who was also last seen in this area. There is no news as to the whereabouts of either boy at this time.
Sheriff Mason Daniels has confirmed that his men will again be dragging the lake.

By the fall of that year, the town was in deep shock; the townsfolk dazed by the tragedy relentlessly unfolding in their quiet town:

THE LOSIEN GAZETTE, SEPTEMBER 21 1957

EDITORIAL

As rumors circulate that the FBI is to become involved in the case we, the citizens of Losien, are warned to stay indoors and keep our children close. But how long can this continue? So soon after the disappearance of 17 year old Suzie Bower, we have in our midst a monster capable of stealing our children away from their loving families. What kind of person does such a thing?
Look out for your neighbors. Keep a watch. Report anything unusual to the Sheriff's Office.
Sheriff Daniels told our reporter that his department is doing everything possible to find the missing children but they have no definite leads at this time. We must all therefore dedicate ourselves to finding the person responsible; we owe that much to the suffering families of Suzie, Tony, Joey, Hannah May and most recently little Julie Hardy.
Our prayers are with them all.

4

Another doll was clothed and put up on the shelf.
 Bony fingers began to carve the next.

5

THE LOSIEN GAZETTE, OCTOBER 7, 1957

SUZIE BOWER SIGHTED

After nearly six months with no news, Lilli and Michael Bower, distraught parents of missing teenager Suzie, 17, have had their hopes raised by a reported sighting of their daughter.
Maria Bianchi, 10, of Ellis Heights, identified Suzie as being the young woman who spoke to her on her way home from school yesterday. Maria claimed that Suzie asked her to come play, but having been warned to go straight home, Maria refused. Maria described Suzie as looking sad but well. She said that Suzie told her to hurry on home.
Sheriff Byron Mitchell has stressed that, as yet, there is no evidence to support young Maria's claim. But, faced with

increasing calls for results from Losien residents, newly appointed Mitchell told this reporter that the search for Suzie and the other four missing children will continue with all the resources at his disposal.

6

Jon heard a crash. Something quite large was moving quickly through the trees some distance away. Jon had been living in the dense forest for over a year now but he hadn't heard an animal moving like this before. Scattering dirt over the embers of his fire, he gathered up his gear and cautiously moved in the direction of the noise.

This was no animal.

Jon called on his few remaining memories of his mother and recognised this as a young woman but, even to Jon's inexperienced eyes, she was acting strangely. Unseen, Jon tracked her for some time, observing her closely. She was moving quickly, seemingly in headlong panic, heedless of cuts and scratches as she tried to run through the broken branches and clamber over the fallen trunks that littered the dark floor of the forest. She had a blond tangle of hair, which now had twigs and pine needles caught up in it. Clearly she had been unprepared for this venture into the forest; her thin red shirt was ragged and her feet were bare. Also, she was carrying nothing: no supplies, no water, not even a knife. And evening was closing in fast; the air already becoming chill. How did she hope to survive the night?

By now there was very little light down here below the

trees, the girl was tiring, stumbling more frequently and whimpering quietly between snatched gasps for air. Finally, she allowed herself to stop. She was bent double, trying to catch her breath, when suddenly she sensed something. She froze, obviously terrified. After several minutes of silence, she risked raising her head and looked around. The gloom was intense, but she peered forward at something lying on a fallen tree only a yard away from her. It was a small pile of wild berries and dried meat that Jon has just placed there for her. Hidden in the darkness, he smiled as she took a hesitant step forward, clearly unable to believe her good fortune. All at once she grabbed at the food, cramming it into her mouth, chewing frantically and moaning with pleasure.

Jon recognised that hunger. Last winter, his first in the forest, had been the worst in the area for a century and he had come desperately close to starvation. When, in that terrible, icy wilderness, he had found anything edible, he had torn into it in the same frenzied way as this poor girl was doing now.

She wiped her mouth with the back of her hand, breathless after the burst of activity. Slowly, she drew herself upright.

There was a sudden, wet thud on the ground beside her. She quite literally leapt into the air, her eyes wild with fear, and when Jon cleared his throat to speak, she collapsed to her knees, her arms bent protectively over her head. She was shaking with terror.

Jon was alarmed and he wanted to reassure her, but he hadn't spoken to a fellow human being for so long that he was unsure how to start.

"Water," he muttered, "You should drink."

She lowered her arms a fraction.

"Who's that? Who's there?"

"I won't harm you."

"Are you with him?" she asked, both fear and anger in her voice.

"Who? No, only me."

"Then what are you doing out here in the dark?"

"I...live here."

They both paused for a moment, taking stock.

Still not making a move towards the water pouch, she said, "Let me see you."

Jon was uncertain. He hadn't expected this. He had all his life avoided human contact. First his mother and then his grandmother had stressed again and again that he must keep away from people. Now faced with this frightened girl's unprecedented request, he was nonplussed.

"Drink."

"Not until you show yourself."

Another pause.

"I am ugly," said Jon quietly, "You'll be afraid."

The girl's face registered surprise and then concern, but now it was not solely concern for herself.

"I'm already afraid and, believe me, I've seen so many terrible things that nothing could make me any more scared than I already am," her voice was low; weary, "Please, let me see you."

Again Jon hesitated.

"Please," she sounded close to tears, "I could really do with a friendly face right now."

"Here."

Jon had walked forward, until he was near enough for her to make out his face. She gasped and her hand went to her mouth. Her instinctive reaction brought back an instant flash of recall from Jon's earliest years. Living apart, he had till this moment forgotten how people used to react when they saw him. He had forgotten how truly hideous he must be.

"I say I'm ugly," he said flatly.

"No, no. I'm sorry I made you do that, but I just had to be sure."

"Sure?"

"I've run away from someone; a man. He took me to a cabin somewhere here in the forest, back upriver, near some cascades. He said if he hurt me that no one would hear me scream, not even if they were right nearby, because of the thundering of the water over the falls. I was so scared," she paused, her shoulders sinking, "He made me help him do some terrible, terrible things. I didn't want to, but he hurt me so bad that I brought those poor little kids to him. But I don't care what he does to me any more. I won't help him do it again. He's evil."

"Can I help?"

"You already are," she said, finally picking up the water pouch, "Can I?"

Jon nodded.

The young woman gratefully drank most of the contents of the pouch. When she realised how little remained, she offered it back to him with a shy, apologetic smile. But Jon merely shrugged.

"Finish. I'll get more later."

"Thanks. I'm so thirsty I could die."

She downed the rest of the water.

"D'you know a way out of the forest?"

"A road twelve, fifteen miles there," he motioned to the south, "You want me take you there?"

"Oh God, yes. I just wanna go home."

Her reserves of strength failed her and all at once, she broke down and began to cry. Jon felt awkward, standing over her, not knowing what to do.

"Stay here…," he muttered, "Your name?"

"Suzie," she managed, through choking sobs, "You?"

Her question took Jon by surprise. He paused a

moment before replying.

"Jon. Name is Jon."

The words sounded strange to him, as if he had forgotten ever having a name. He shook his head and worked to form the unfamiliar spoken words. His speech was still hesitant and clumsy but he could feel the pattern of the words returning slowly as he spoke.

"Stay here, Suzie. I will go, get more water. Not be long, then we'll start. I know the forest so good, so we can go by night."

Suzie could barely contain her gratitude for the kindness he was showing her. Several months spent living in constant fear had stretched her ragged nerves close to breaking, and here was a gentle stranger lifting the crushing terror from her shoulders and offering hope. She struggled to reward him with a smile.

"Want me to come with you?"

"No. You rest. Water on the other side of ridge here. Dangerous to climb in the dark. Stay here. Rest. Stay hidden. I'll be back very soon."

With the water pouch refilled, Jon was scrambling back down the rocks. But he held back, stopped in mid-stride halfway up the ridge. Something was wrong. He strained forward, trying to see further into the darkness. A branch snapped close by, just to the north of his hiding place. Something large was creeping through the trees, trying to make as little noise as possible. Jon scanned the area but saw nothing, until a subtle shift in the background darkness suddenly caught his eye. A tall dark figure was moving slowly by, its lank black hair just a few arm lengths below him. Jon froze, heart thumping, holding his breath until it had crept past. Jon had no doubt that this was the man from whom Suzie had escaped. There was palpable menace in his slow, deliberate movements and, in all his time in the forest, Jon had never felt a chill like the one he was experiencing now, just having been near him. Jon knew now why Suzie had been so frightened.

He heard a cry.

It was Suzie. And then, much lower, another voice, a cold, hate-filled voice. Jon couldn't make out what the man was saying at first, but then the voice grew louder. He was coming back, pulling Suzie after him. Jon was desperate to avoid being seen by the man, but he wanted to help Suzie. From his vantage point he watched the two go by below him. Suzie was strangely compliant, not struggling but apparently resigned. Jon decided to follow at a safe distance and rescue Suzie as soon as her captor dropped his guard.

Jon tracked Suzie and the man for several hours. It was quite easy since, having recaptured Suzie, the man was no longer making any attempt to move stealthily. He obviously felt secure out here in the vastness of the forest; confident that he could move freely, without any fear of capture. Jon, on the other hand, was taking immense care not to make a single sound.

It was getting close to dawn before the man allowed Suzie to sit down and rest. Jon moved closer to watch and listen.

"Five minutes. No more," the man was saying. His voice was deep and powerful; at odds with the brittle thinness of his frame.

Suzie looked exhausted, defeated. She hung her head.

"Let this be a lesson to you, Doll," he went on, "There's no escape. You'll never get away. You belong to me."

He bent, leaning forward, moving his head closer, his hollow, death white cheek next to hers.

"So don't you ever try to run away again," he hissed,

"or you know what'll happen."

Suzie stared ferociously ahead, trying not to allow him the satisfaction of seeing her react. He continued, still speaking through clenched teeth.

"You'll go back there and this time you'll bring her back, else I could get angry, you understand? If I don't get to play I could get real angry," he gripped her chin and forced her face towards his, "Such a shame if I had to teach you another lesson, Doll. You got such a pretty face. Wouldn't be so pretty then, huh?"

She said nothing.

"I just asked you a question, Doll."

Suzie shuddered, wincing at his foul breath on her face.

"You know what you gotta do?"

Suzie's reply was almost inaudible,

"I won't," she whispered, shaking her head free of his grip, "I won't do it again."

"What did you say bitch?" he spat, his face still only inches from hers, "Did I hear you right? What did you say?"

He raised his hand, ready to strike.

Her whole body shaking, Suzie forced herself to reply,

"I don't care what you do to me. I won't help you do what you do to those poor kids."

Suzie shut her eyes, obviously expecting him to explode and vent his fury on her. She braced herself for the blow. But instead, the man lowered his hand and straightened slowly. He contorted his mean face into a smile; pale, bloodless lips parting to reveal bone-white teeth.

"Come on, Doll," he said, his lowered voice now sounding earthy, familiar; almost reasonable, "I don't want to hurt you, Doll, you know that. But I need them. And they wanna play with me...O yeah, they wanna play.

I need them, Doll, but they mean nothing to me, none of them, you know that; you're my particular favourite," he drew a thin finger across her cheek, "I just need them. You understand that, right Doll?"

Suddenly, with an incredible, unexpected burst of movement, Suzie sprang to her feet and sprinted away. For a moment the man looked stunned, but he recovered quickly and leapt after her, howling and cursing. Ignoring the branches hammering back at his face, he charged through the trees with terrifying speed. In seconds he was upon her. He caught her arm and smashed his other fist down on her head. Suzie's head snapped forward onto her chest with the force of the blow and her body crumpled. He let go and she dropped, falling into a heap on the ground.

Jon gasped, horrified, unable to believe what he'd just seen. He watched, eyes wide, body frozen, as the man lifted and shook Suzie's unresisting shoulders. Her head lolled lifelessly and thin lines of blood trickled from her mouth and nose. The man spat an incoherent curse and roughly pushed Suzie's rag doll form back to the ground, a dead weight.

The man strode away and, all at once, Jon's tensed muscles relaxed. He fell back against the trunk of a huge tree and stared up through its branches at the glimpses of paling sky above. But his brain was not conscious of what his eyes were seeing. His mind was reeling, trying to make sense of the inexplicable violence he had just witnessed. It made no sense. Suzie was so much smaller than the man; she was no threat to him. And, as she had had no chance of out-running or harming him, there had been no need to kill her. His attack was senseless.

All Jon could think of now was stopping this man; putting a stop to this brutal, unnatural behaviour. But how?

Could he brave going into town and get help, or should he act alone? There was not really any option for him; unnerved though he was by this killer, Jon knew that he would have to deal with him alone. After a lifetime in seclusion Jon would do anything rather than face going into town.

A soft thumping sound brought Jon back to his senses. The man had returned and was digging in the soft earth with a long-handled shovel. Jon watched him, intrigued, carefully making his way closer. Now he could see that the man was digging a long, shallow trench. He was cursing Suzie as he worked, showing no remorse for the attack. At length, he threw down the shovel and straightened. Jon watched him go over to Suzie's body and stiffly bend to pick her up.

Jon saw his chance. He eased forward and, using a fallen branch, drew the shovel closer. It was almost within his reach when he had to pull back under cover. The man was returning. He dropped Suzie's body to the ground and then rolled it over and into the trench with a kick of his foot. She lay there, her pale hair a tangled mess covering most of her face and her clothes in tatters. She looked broken and ragged, like a scrawny fledgling fallen from its nest. Seeing her lying there, pathetic and lifeless in the dirt, Jon was overwhelmed with a feeling of grief unlike anything he had felt at either the departure of his mother or the death of his grandmother. They had felt a duty towards him and each, in their own way, had cared for him. Their goings had marked the endings to different parts of his life. They were there and then they were not, and Jon had moved on. But Suzie was someone who had turned to him for help. She had looked at him without revulsion and she had trusted him. It was his duty to help her and he had utterly failed her. Now, for the first time he was feeling loss, and the emotion was the more intense and painful for being so unexpected. He had known Suzie for only a matter of hours and yet he felt bruised, his spirit wounded by her death. It was a huge shock of emotion to cope with, all at once and unprepared.

The man drew something from his back pocket; a black metal pair of shears. He knelt, leant forward over the grave and, smiling with pleasure, began carefully to cut a piece of material from the little that remained of Suzie's red shirt. He pulled something from his pocket and wrapped the scrap of worn cloth around it. Concentrating on his task, he seemed oblivious to the discarded body, as if he had already dismissed Suzie from his thoughts; she had ceased to serve any purpose and was of no further interest to him. His attention was wholly consumed by the object that he turned over and over in his thin, spiderlike hands. He was savouring this moment, almost salivating with pleasure, the sharp-toothed smile never leaving his face.

At this final, callous desecration, Jon's anger erupted. He leapt forward, grabbing up the shovel. In a single swift movement, he raised it high above his head and brought it down again with all his strength. In the instant before the cold metal crashed into his skull, the man looked up and saw Jon. In that second, his face registered total, wide-eyed surprise.

The shovel hit his head with a wet 'crump'. Jon felt the immediate loss of resistance as the skull shattered, yielding the soft tissue of the brain to the shovel's full, destructive force. The man's head snapped back and his body swayed a second or two before he fell forward into the trench, on top of Suzie. Her body flexed at the impact and her wild hair flew away from her face.

Jon fell to his knees, his body trembling with nervous

tension. He gulped a deep breath, trying to calm his racing heart, and looked down at Suzie.

She seemed to him to be smiling.

Justice had been done.

Jon threw down the shovel and heaved the man off her, roughly pushing him aside. On the ground where the man had fallen, lay a rudely-carved wooden doll wrapped about with a shred of red cloth. With some hesitation Jon picked up the doll. The red scrap was the piece that had been cut from Suzie's shirt as she lay dead. This doll was now a link to her and Jon would not leave it here in this terrible place, with that terrible man. He tucked it into the bag at his shoulder.

Then, with great tenderness, he lifted Suzie out of the trench and gently laid her on the ground. Smoothing her hair, he searched her face for any sign of life. He spoke to her and rubbed her chilling hands, but he knew that she had gone. Slowly, he rose to his feet, staring down at her poor scratched and dirty face. He couldn't leave her like this. He had to take her away from this place. But first he had a task to complete. Grimacing with the effort, he rolled the man's body into the grave in Suzie's stead. The thin face and long fingers looked bleached white against the black of his clothes and the deep, rich browns of the earth. But, even in death, his was not a face at peace. The sight of him was still chilling.

Jon scuffed some earth over the dry, black folds of the man's clothes, but paused, steadying his nerve, before kicking dirt over that gaunt, white face. He half expected the man to react; the eyes to snap open, but the dirt hit the pale skin and slid into the creases, pooling in the circles of the eyes, without a reaction or any sign of life. Hugely relieved, his heart still thumping wildly, Jon backed away and sank down next to Suzie's body, kneeling motionless until his heart became calm once more. He eased his hands under the fragile body and lifted her, holding her to his chest as he rose.

Carrying her, he followed the river upstream, back to the cascades that Suzie had described and beyond them, to the cabin. He lay Suzie's body carefully out of sight amongst the trees and crept cautiously towards the building, across the low scrub of the clearing. From what Suzie had told him he was fairly sure that the man had worked alone, but he needed to be sure. He sidled up beside the window and glanced in. There was no one inside the single room. He tried the door. It opened easily enough and he stepped inside.

Jon had been used to frugal living during the years on his grandmother's farm, but even that humble farmhouse seemed comfortable, almost welcoming, in comparison to this desolate hovel. There was no stove, just an empty hearth, a black kettle and a filthy cooking-pot. A pile of blankets lay in a heap against one wall, opposite a long table with a single chair. Above the table was a shelf on which were a series of figures. As Jon's eyes grew accustomed to the gloom, he realised that they were four roughly carved wooden dolls, each dressed with a small triangle of cloth. The first was dressed in blue, the second in a material with a red and yellow pattern. The third doll was in pink and the fourth in green. Various wood-chisels, hammers, saws and axes hung neatly from hooks below the shelf and a number of cut logs were stacked in a basket under the table, presumably awaiting carving. The table top was covered in fresh wood shavings. Jon didn't understand what all this meant and he didn't care to. He swept his hand across the table and blew the remaining wood shavings onto the floor.

Backing the door open, he carried Suzie's body into the room and laid her out on the table with great gentleness. Wanting to make her look pretty again, he gathered some grasses from just outside the cabin, arranging them around her on the table. He wanted in some measure to atone for having failed to save her. If nothing else, he would ensure that her body would be treated properly, with care, with love. He removed the dirt and twigs that had become embedded in the mass of hair around her face and tried to straighten her ragged clothes. In doing so, his hand lingered on her shirt and he frowned. The man had used the shears to cut a small triangle from Suzie's shirt.

Jon looked up at the figures on the shelf, then again at Suzie's pale, lifeless face, and shook his head. He knew that both his experience and knowledge must be lacking due to the isolation of his existence, but he also knew with certainty that what this man had been doing here was not in the normal run of things. Something very wrong had taken place in this forlorn and dingy shack. Despite the fresh-cut aroma of the grasses, and Jon's loving care for this poor, dead girl, a palpable evil still hung around them, lurking in every dark recess of the room.

At length Jon decided that he should burn the cabin, as he had his grandmother's house. No animal was going to get at Suzie and no vestige of the evil in this place would be allowed to remain. He began to gather fallen branches and twigs, stacking them outside, against the walls.

Returning from the forest, arms laden with wood collected for the pyre, Jon suddenly dropped to the ground. A woodsman was hesitantly approaching the cabin. Some ten years older than Jon and stockily-built, the man grunted as he climbed up to the door. He looked around, but saw no one; Jon staying low in the waist-high ferns at the edge of the clearing. The man removed his wide-brimmed leather hat and leaned close to peer through the grimy window panes before opening the shaky door. Jon tensed; his immediate thought that this was an accomplice of the man he had killed. But within seconds, the man came rushing out, vomit splashing noisily onto the steps. Obviously horrified merely by the sight of Suzie's body, he surely could not have had anything to do with the evil thing that Jon had killed. Jon stayed hidden as the man stumbled away into the trees.

Jon waited a while, against the woodman's return, then continued to gather kindling. By evening, the pyre was completed, but Jon was reluctant to light the fire. For reasons he did not fully understand, he felt the need to stay here, guarding Suzie's body through the night. He would set the fire in the morning. He spent most of the night awake, sitting with his back to the door of the cabin, only drifting into an uncomfortable sleep as the sky began to lighten into dawn.

The sun was higher in the sky when Jon awoke. He stretched and rose stiffly, rubbing warmth back into his painful muscles. In waiting with Suzie through the night, he felt he had shown her the respect denied her by her killer. Jon now felt able to let her go and return to the quiet routine of his solitary life.

But, before he could set the fire, Jon had to run for cover; a terrible noise was coming in his direction and soon the ground was shaking with the deafening thunder of helicopters thumping overhead. Lizzie had told Jon about airplanes, but he'd only ever seen the tiny sunlit specks flying high and silent in the sky. He'd certainly never imagined anything so alien and terrifying as these machines. Their noise was appalling and the saplings around him were whipping back and forth in the downdraft. Jon's hair stood on end. It was like being in the eye of a terrible storm. He threw himself to the ground and stayed there even when the noise abated. All too soon, having disgorged their passengers, the helicopters started up again, with a whine rising to thunder, before lifting out of the clearing. As Jon raised his head to watch, the helicopters dipped forwards, like animals lowering their heads to charge, then raced away, skimming just above the treetops.

The terrible machines and their noise had gone, but the area was now alive with uniformed people carrying backpacks full of equipment. Retreating, Jon had to watch their purposeful comings and goings from the safe distance of the opposite bank of the cascades. They were shouting to one another, organising their search, but the roar of the waterfalls drowned the sense of their words. Jon could only guess at what was happening. He saw mystifying flashes of light inside the cabin and, soon after, two men went in and came out carrying a large bag on a stretcher. Lights were set up around the clearing then, as evening came on, the helicopters returned and most of the people left.

Jon decided to return to the seclusion of his cave. He needed rest. He had not slept properly in over forty-eight hours and his head ached with too many images. So much had happened in so short a time that he almost doubted it had happened at all. But, doubts or no, he couldn't shake the memory of Suzie's face from his mind as he crept on through the trees, crossing the river some distance downstream, safely out of sight of the people guarding the cabin.

Once across the river, he came to the place where he had killed the man. Jon's first inclination was to go by without dwelling on what had happened here, but he forced himself to look. He stopped in his tracks; immediately alert.

The trench was empty.

The body had gone

All Jon's senses were alive and straining for any

warning sound or movement. He dropped to a crouch, feeling for the first time in his life exposed and vulnerable here amongst the trees. In the fading light, he searched the ground around the trench for any signs of animal activity, but found none. He knew that the people from the helicopters hadn't explored this area yet. But, if they hadn't moved the body, and no animal had been this way, then there had to be a chance that the man was still alive. Jon couldn't believe that anyone could have survived that blow to his head. He had heard the man's skull crack and felt the brain beneath yield to the force of the shovel's blade.

But, incredible or not, the body had gone.

Jon was unnerved, completely confused. He tried to think. He reasoned that, though mortally injured, the man might have survived just long enough to drag himself out of the trench, in which case he had probably soon died somewhere nearby, amongst the trees. And, if the man were somehow still alive and able to walk, he would probably have made his escape from the area as soon as he heard those monstrous aircraft arriving at the cabin. Either way, his path was not likely to cross Jon's again, in this life at least.

This thought should have comforted Jon, but it did not. He desperately wanted to be reassured but, at the back of his mind, two other thoughts jostled for his attention. He knew that the man had seen him, in the second before the shovel smashed into his skull. If he had survived, then a fierce hunger for revenge would surely drive him now and could perhaps be strong enough to overwhelm the terrible pain of his injuries. But, most disturbing of all, was the fact that Jon had examined the area closely. He had been tracking animals for as long as he could remember and could read the smallest of changes in the soil, the undergrowth and even on the rocks. He knew that no one had been dragged, or had dragged himself, out of that trench. There were simply no fresh signs of disturbance anywhere around it.

The body should still be there.

Jon could make no sense of what had happened and the gathering darkness seemed to echo his own rising fear. There was nothing he could do here now, in the dark, and all he could think of was to return to the reassuring familiarity and safety of his cave. But the urge to hurry home was tempered by the pressing need to avoid pursuit. To this end he travelled along the river for several miles in the darkness, the flowing water carrying his scent away. It was a route that took him far out of his way, to the east and he only resumed his path south-west when, after many hours, he felt it safe to leave the protection of the steep river valley and move carefully across country again. He saw this diversion, which cost him an additional uncomfortable and wearying day, as a necessity. He had killed a man, the body had gone but Jon was certain that the man must be dead. The people at the cabin must by now have found his body and their dogs would have picked up Jon's scent, followed it and tracked him down had he not taken the detour. While he might have been willing to face justice for killing that killer, Jon doubted that anyone would believe he had not also killed Suzie, so it had been vital to hide his tracks.

But, even as he told himself this, he knew it to be a fruitless exercise in self-deception. Jon's real dread, the cold fear that clutched at his heart, was not of those people or their dogs, but of being tracked down by the dark-clothed killer whose brittle, white skull he had so assuredly smashed with that shovel.

7

THE LOSIEN GAZETTE, OCTOBER 10, 1957

SUZIE DEAD! BODY FOUND IN FOREST.

Sheriff Byron Mitchell today confirmed yesterday's reports that the body of teenager Suzie Bower has been found. Woodsman, Eric Spielman, 28, made the grim discovery when he was exploring an area of forest approximately ten miles east of Losien. Spielman found the body in a deserted cabin and immediately alerted the authorities. Suzie had died as a result of a powerful blow to the head and it appears that her killer had made some attempt to destroy the evidence of his crime.

Police Chief Mitchell, extended his sympathy to Suzie's family for their loss and urged townsfolk in Losien and the surrounding county to remain vigilant until this killer is caught.

Sheriff Mitchell also confirmed that his men are currently searching both the cabin and the surrounding area. However, he would not comment on whether he was linking the still as yet unsolved disappearance of the four Losien children to Suzie's murder.

THE LOSIEN GAZETTE, OCTOBER 12, 1957

MORE BODIES FOUND IN FOREST.

Sheriff Byron Mitchell today told reporters that the discovery yesterday of a fourth body in the vicinity of the so-called 'Cabin of Death' had brought to an end the search for the children abducted in Losien during the summer. The four bodies have now been confirmed as being those of Tony Fisher, Joey Harper, Hannah May Bunce and Julie Hardy.

At this time Sheriff Mitchell is not releasing any details as to the way in which these children met their deaths.

8

For nearly twenty years no more dolls were made.
   Evil was biding its time.

9

Jon was older now. By his own reckoning he was probably in his mid-thirties; his hair showed touches of grey, but his body was still lean. He had long ago settled into his solitary life in the forest and the passing of time now held little meaning for him. His ordered routine was governed by the turn of each day and the rolling change of the seasons; moments slipping away imperceptibly into his past.

Today he had wandered far from the safety of his cave by the stream. He had avoided this part of the forest for many years, initially fearing discovery by the people hunting Suzie's killer and thereafter in dread of an encounter with the shadowy figure he had seen smash the life out of her. To this day Jon remained fearful of the creeping evil that still haunted his nightmares. He wasn't sure what had drawn him back again now but, since the dark days of this last winter, he had felt a powerful but inexplicable need to return to where he had laid Suzie to rest.

So it was that he was now crouched at the edge of the clearing, his hand firmly gripping the handle of his knife and his eyes alert for any hint of danger. He had been watching the area since early morning, but all seemed quiet. In the many years since he was last here, the clearing had become overgrown and the shack dilapidated. There was no sign of life.

Since turning his back on the farmstead pyre, Jon had lived by his skill at hunting, the keenness of his senses and his knowledge of the forest. In that time he had dealt with terrible winters, forest fire and flash floods. He had survived illness and accidents and even, on one occasion, the ferocious attack of a female bear protecting her well-hidden cubs. And yet returning here, to the edge of this pool of sunlight, Jon was uncertain and afraid. The dark, stooping insect of a man had been unlike any of the other dangers that had threatened Jon's life down the years. There was a cruelty, a darkness about him, that was quite unlike anything else Jon had encountered. The bear would probably have killed Jon had he not managed to throw himself into the fast flowing river to escape her. But there had been no malice in her attack. Her fury had been understandable, her actions reasonable; in her eyes Jon represented a threat to her young. Suzie, however, had represented no threat whatsoever to the shadow man. He had killed her in anger, and that was beyond Jon's comprehension. It was simply wrong. Strangely perhaps, Jon felt no remorse for having then attacked the killer when his back had been turned. The man was bad, manifestly evil, irredeemably corrupted. He had to be destroyed. And Jon had killed him; smashed his skull with a shovel. He had been dead. He must have been dead.

And he should have stayed dead, where Jon had left him, in the trench.

With a final last look around the clearing, Jon rose to a crouch and moved towards the shack. He straightened somewhat to climb the steps, then opened the door quickly, before he could change his mind. The tiny room was even more desolate than it had been years before. It was more gloomy now, as the window panes were filthy and several had been broken. The resulting holes had over time become stuffed with dried grass and dirt, tangled in a network of cobwebs. In the consequently dim light, Jon could see that there was no sign of any recent use of the hearth. The table and chair were still there, albeit dry and brittle with age, and there were thick, grubby cobwebs strung between them and the walls. The desiccated husks of long dead insects hung, cocooned, from the webs; the dusty grey pendants of macabre necklaces. The room was silent, muffled in its thick layer of dust and dirt.

The shelf was still in place. It was empty now and hung with dirt and cobwebs like the table, but Jon's attention immediately fixed on the tools, still hanging from their hooks beneath it. He crossed the darkened room to look more closely, for, unlike everything else here, the tools were shiny, oiled and razor-sharp. Jon's flesh began to crawl. He glanced down. There was something lying on the deep and otherwise undisturbed layer of dirt on the table.

A doll.

Jon felt an awful, sinking sense of recognition. Like the dolls he'd seen here years before, this had been roughly carved from pinewood. Jon leaned closer. There was a dreadful, disturbing familiarity in this wooden effigy. The same hand had carved this. The same blades. Jon had seen all this before. History was being repeated.

Jon was trembling, unable to stop. The tools and the doll meant that, despite the absence of any other indications of life, someone had been here, recently. Someone, or something, had carefully sharpened these blades and carved this thing. But the only footsteps in the dirt on the floor were Jon's own and there was no sign of these boards having been trodden by anyone, or anything, in years. Jon shivered, filled with the creeping dread that he was not alone in here.

He had to get out of this place. He turned to leave.

Something stood rigid, stiffly folded, as if hanging from the hook on the back of the door.

Something sinister. Something dark.

Jon's blood ran cold. The figure was unmoving, but Jon knew it was alive and aware of him. It was waiting, biding its time.

Jon's heart was thumping but his body refused to move. He was frozen, wide-eyed with the same certainty of inevitable fate that he had witnessed so many times in cornered animals.

The smothering silence of the room was scratched by the slightest rustle, as of dried leaves. The shadow was waking, stirring. The tiny, rasping sound filled Jon's head. He was paralysed with fear.

Its dark head raised and the black eyes sparkled with cold recognition. The sharp teeth parted as the pale, dry skin pulled back in a terrible smile. The figure seemed to unfold, growing larger as it slowly raised its brittle arms.

Suddenly it burst forward, lunging at him.

Jon screamed and his body finally reacted to the threat with a lightning-fast dash, past the grasping arms and out of the door.

In absolute terror, he ran, hurtling down the steps and across the clearing, plunging into the densest growth of trees, desperate to be hidden from that dark thing behind him. He didn't look back. He couldn't. Evil was at his heels.

Jon's headlong flight from the cabin was short; ending abruptly when he tripped and fell down a steep escarpment.

He lay gasping, trying desperately to keep his mouth

closed and his breathing quiet. He expected, at any second, to be engulfed by the evil that had chased him from the cabin. But everything remained quiet. In time, his breathing calmed and he was able to lie in absolute silence, listening hard. Still nothing. He was baffled. How had he managed to lose that creature? Jon had run as far and as fast as he could and in his blind panic he had acted with uncharacteristic disregard. As his mind threw aside all his hard-learned forest sense, Jon had risked an injury, perhaps even a broken leg. Gingerly, he now felt along his legs and arms, touched his ribs and gently moved his head from side to side. Unbelievably, he had no broken bones. His fall had left him winded and his ankle was weak and painful, but nothing more. He had been incredibly lucky and, had he not still been terrified of attracting attention to himself, he would have laughed with relief, loud enough to shake the trees.

He lay there, listening, for several hours, reluctant to risk any movement. Despairing thoughts turned over and over in his mind. He had come to this terrible place seeking peace, a final closing of the door, but instead, the killer had jumped forward from its prison of the past, to loom, huge, dark and terrifying, in the here and now. No longer confined to nightmares, the insect man was still alive.

Only when dusk was falling did Jon get stiffly to his feet, brush the dead leaves from him and look around. He hadn't been at the foot of these rocks before, but the position of the evening stars overhead gave him his direction home. He needed to go south but, in his panic, he had fled north from the cabin which now represented a terrifying obstacle between him and the distant safety of the cave. In spite of the pain in his ankle Jon decided to cross the river and make a wide detour to the east before resuming a more direct path. Cautiously and with uneven, painful steps, he set off.

After about two miles of slow movement through the trees on the far side of the river and with many stops to rest his aching ankle, Jon risked crossing back. By his reckoning he should be at least a mile south of the cabin by now. There were no easy crossings of the river here, no boulders dividing the fast-moving sheet of water. He clambered along the bank until, at a slight widening of the flow, where the speed of the water slackened, he carefully lowered himself into the river and waded across. After this, sodden and shivering, he made even slower progress, but trudged on with single-minded determination to reach the sanctuary of his cave.

Once there, Jon remained; grateful for the need to rest his ankle. What had happened in the shack had been so real and the terror so intense that, try as he might, Jon could not dismiss what he had seen. He continued to try to reassure himself, knowing that the senses could play tricks. He tried to explain the experience rationally, but he had been brought up hearing the folk myths and stories of this forest from his grandmother. Those tales had never been entirely forgotten, remaining in some corner of Jon's adult mind, informing his view of the now.

Lizzie had been a great storyteller. If, on her return from her infrequent visits to town, she was satisfied that she had traded for a good price, she would allow herself a few deep, celebratory gulps from a large, dusty bottle of Jack Daniels. She would savour every drop, wipe her mouth dry with the back of her hand, and smile a rare, contented smile. Jon then was permitted a glimpse of a side of his grandmother that was at other times totally hidden from the world; under the loosening influence of the drink, the normally taciturn Lizzie became loquacious; an unexpectedly gifted teller of tales.

On one such evening Jon had crouched, warmed by

the stove, grasping at every word, as Lizzie conjured images of the long-dead tribes: old and mysterious peoples who had once called this forest their own. Though overrun by white settlers, and succumbing to disease and starvation, they had never lost faith in the redeeming certainty that they and the spirits of their ancestors, driven from their beloved forest in life, would return here in death. This belief offered these last scattered remnants of a venerable lineage, their only comfort and, of all their rich heritage of stories and myth, this had been one of the few they had passed on to those who had displaced them. Perhaps the vanishing tribes had intended this as revenge, so the white invaders should always know that they were surrounded by the souls of those whose line in history they had ended.

Hearing this as a wide-eyed child, Jon had shivered. For some weeks after, he would dread going to sleep: his dreams being mournful with the drifting, sorrowful ghosts of exiled tribes. With the help of Jack Daniels, Lizzie undoubtedly unlocked an instinctive feel for the telling of a story but, sadly, the bottle did nothing to enhance her ability to empathise with a young boy. Jon remembered his grandmother laughing at him. The ghosts of a few Indians were nothing to fear, she'd said; in life they'd just been folks struggling to live their lives, like us. What harm would they do us in death?

Perhaps, had the old woman stopped there, Jon would have been comforted. But oblivious and insensitive as always, Lizzie had continued. She never did explain to Jon how she came to know the Indians' stories but the fraction of their age-old folklore that had survived she retold, with spell-binding mastery. This was an ancient forest, she told him, dark and deep since the beginning of time. This vast, wild place had no need of man. It had its own untamed life and had its own ancient spirits; dark, evil shadows that had existed since long before even the Indians had come to this land.

If you want to fear something boy, she'd said, fear those dark, ancient spirits, not a few lost Indians' souls.

Then Lizzie, seeing how Jon was hanging on her every word, suddenly laughed out loud at the foolish boy's gullibility and cuffed his head with the palm of her hand. Jon remembered running to hide in his meagre bed, pulling the scratchy blanket tight around his ears to block out his grandmother's scornful laughter as it filled the small house. Looking back now, he was sure that his grandmother had believed none of the old tales. To her they were just stories, elaborated and twisted over the centuries, containing no more truth for being ancient than did any modern day piece of fiction. To her they were all make-believe. Nothing more.

Now, hiding in his cave, Jon tried to force himself to think as Lizzie had, but Jon had seen too many things during his time in the forest and he had certainly seen too much back there at the shack. He couldn't dismiss the memories. And he couldn't shake off the fear.

He still felt that he belonged here, in the forest. He still felt at home, but he no longer felt at ease.

He belonged here, but so too did many other souls.

Several weeks passed before Jon felt able to range any distance from the cave. With time though, and with the warmth of lengthening summer days, both his strength and his confidence began to recover. By day, the terrible memories of the cabin no longer flooded into his every moment, since he had to attend to the mundane requirements of his everyday survival in the forest. Gradually the fear faded from the forefront of his imaginings.

At night however his dreams still shook him awake.

Sweating in terror he would lie trembling, not daring to make a fire or any reassuring light for fear it might attract attention to his hideaway. Another month would pass before the rhythm of peaceful sleep returned and Jon no longer woke in the dreadful dark hours of the night, but with the first hopeful light of dawn warming the sky.

10

A woman was shouting over the din of a washing machine.

"Laura, you get back here! Laura?"

Her husband touched her arm, a calming gesture,

"Karen, let her go. She's growing up. She needs to win some of the battles."

"Some? Are you kidding? She wins all of them and right now we really do need some help here."

"I know, I know. Give her time to cool off. She'll help. She's a good kid."

"I know she is, but she could do with some discipline."

"Oh, come on -"

"No Jack, she's gotten so headstrong and," she searched for the word, "argumentative."

"And who do you think she gets that from?"

He gently touched the side of his wife's face.

"I'll go speak to her, OK?"

Karen merely shrugged.

Jack put down the basket of washing and wiped his hands dry on his jeans as he climbed the basement stairs. His daughter was in her bedroom, prostrate across the bed, crying passionate tears into her pillow. Jack sat on the edge of the bed and waited for the tears to subside.

"Laura? Laura, tell me what's wrong."

"I wanted to finish reading Wuthering Heights and then I wanted to go see my friends."

"But we do need your help, Laura."

"You always need my help. I never get to do what I want to do. I don't have any life here. And Mom won't let me go see my friends," she gulped dramatically for air, "She doesn't want me to have any friends."

Jack let his daughter get all this out and then spoke quietly.

"Now Laura, you know that's not true. Your mom's happy you've made friends here. And who was it drove you to the mall last weekend when she had a real bad headache?"

Laura couldn't really argue the truth of this; it was usually her mother who drove her into town. But she still felt aggrieved, so she half-heartedly persisted with a final question

"Then why won't she let me go see them now?"

"You know why. Like she told you, we do need your help here today. We've got to finish making up the beds and cleaning the rooms before lunchtime."

Laura knew she was beaten and that she'd been acting selfishly. Her parents really did need her help and they didn't pull this 'all hands' routine very often. They really weren't so bad. If only her mom would relax and not get uptight over the least little thing. Dad often said she and her mom were alike, but Laura couldn't see it.

She decided she would help out her parents now, then one of them would be able to give her a lift into town later and she could still meet up with her friends at the mall. She wiped away the hot tears and sniffed. Her father smiled indulgently at her, encouraging her.

"That's my wonderful girl," he said tenderly, proffering a handkerchief, "Now, will you help me make up the beds?"

Laura and her father worked together for several hours.

When all the beds were made and the rooms finally finished, Laura and her father went down to the kitchen in the basement for a Coke and a beer. Jack called up to Karen to join them. She came into the room looking exhausted.

"OK, that's everything ready, at last," she said, collapsing into a chair.

"Laura was a great help, Karen," said Jack, smiling at his wife, "She cleaned the top floor all by herself. No way would I have had the rooms finished without her."

Karen knew when praise was due and Jack was right, they were lucky to have such a great kid.

"Thanks Laura," she said, getting up from her chair to give her daughter a gentle hug, "and I'm sorry I lost it earlier. You do know it's the worry of our first bookings, right? I'll be OK after this week. I'll be back to my old, easy-going self."

Both Jack and Laura laughed out loud.

"What?" said Karen, with feigned indignation, "Are you saying I'm **not** easy going? Heck, back East they used to say I was one cool, laid back chick."

"Who's 'they'?" asked Jack.

"People," she smirked.

"People who'd never met you, maybe."

"Hey, I don't have to stay here and take this abuse," she looked wounded, " Heck, I could - "

She stopped mid-sentence at the sound of the bell on the reception desk.

"They're here! They're early! And I haven't had a chance to freshen up."

"Don't worry. I'll go," Jack said, straightening his collar and smoothing his hair. He took a deep breath. "Do I look OK?"

"You look just fine," said his wife, "Go get 'em."

73

Laura suddenly spoke up.

"What about my ride into town?"

Her father looked apologetic.

"Sorry, Laura. What can I say? They're early. I can't leave now and your mom's got to make the midday meal for the guests."

"But Dad!"

The bell jangled again, insistent. Jack looked anxious, torn.

Karen felt her temper rising.

"We can't take you now," she said firmly, "Don't you get it, Laura? This is how we make enough money to live, so you can have the stuff you need. We've got to make this work. We can't just take off and be your cab ride whenever you want."

"But you promised."

"I didn't promise anything," Karen snapped.

The bell rang again, louder and longer than before.

"I've got to go," Jack said, "I'm sorry Hon. Explain it to her, will you Karen."

Laura was furious. She watched her father leave the room and was overcome with the injustice of her treatment. She had worked really hard all morning and this was the thanks she got.

"Laura?" her mother started.

"Oh forget it Mom. Why should I get to do anything I want? I'm just the help."

"Laura come back."

"I'm going out."

"It's too far to walk into town."

"Tell me something I don't already know. Of course it's too far; I'm a prisoner here. Stuck out in the middle of nowhere, with nothing but trees, trees and more stupid trees as far as you can see."

"So, why not stay here with me? We could do

something together if you like."

"Yeah, like getting the food ready?"

Her mother's face was pained. She knew how hurt Laura must be feeling. In so many ways she saw her own younger self in her daughter's tempestuous and gregarious nature. Karen remembered her own teen years. How important it had been to be 'where it was at', to be one of the 'beautiful people' back then. They had all seemed wonderfully exotic; the way they dressed, even the expressions they used were so new and exciting. But for Karen it had seemed that the world was changing for everyone but her. She wasn't in that world; she had to stay in and do schoolwork. She couldn't listen to the music she wanted and she would never have dared to try any drugs, even if she had known where to go to get them. How easy it had been to imagine everyone else was living the new age of Aquarius, while she had to stay home and do chores. Karen ached for her daughter; they were so alike. But, right now, there really was work to be done and the mall had to wait. Karen tried conciliation.

"Well, Honey, I do have to make a start on the meal soon, but we could maybe spend some time together first. Just you and me. If you'd like."

Expecting anger, Laura was touched by the tenderness in her mother's tone. She looked up, saw the love in her mother's face and felt her own anger begin to melt away. She didn't want to be the cause of that distress. With depressingly familiar regret, she wished she had perhaps not said some of the things she had. She never meant to get mad, but it seemed to happen too easily and too often. Many times, she found herself in the middle of a heated argument, usually with her mom, without any clear idea as to what had sparked it off. In more lucid moments, when she could view the problem calmly, she would resolve to curb her temper and be more patient, especially with her mother, because she understood something of what her parents were going through. She knew how difficult it had been for them to start their lives over. Her father had lost his job in the city and her mother had quit her part time job so they could sell up and move here. They had put everything they owned into this place. Harsh necessity had forced her parents to leave behind everything they had known since childhood: family, friends and the neighbourhood they had grown up in.

Of course, Laura had also had to deal with the change and upheaval, but, for her, the sadness of leaving behind old friends had been offset by the thrill of adventure. To her mind, with an imagination fed over the years on a diet rich in romantic historical novels, she and her parents were off to start a new life out in wild frontier lands. Initially the remoteness of the small hotel they had bought, and the long journey to it, following dark and mysterious forest roads, had been a source of huge excitement to her. Exploring their area of forest and discovering the river flowing close by had been magical. To a dreamer like Laura it had seemed that she was a living character from one of her novels.

It was only with the familiarity of passing days and weeks that the wonder had begun to dull; the deep, majestic presence of the forest gradually diminishing, to become merely a backdrop to the family's domestic routine. Then Laura took to wishing that something would happen; anything, to break the monotony of their backwoods existence. Only the swirling pools of the cataracts along the river retained their deep fascination; casting a spell over Laura, with the waters' endless, eddying dance soothing and calming her frequent hot-headed outbursts. The long forest road into town no longer seemed magical. It now represented only a barrier, delaying her getting to school or to the mall to meet with her new friends. But Laura had to admit to herself that her mother and father had, on many occasions, dropped what they had planned to do in order to drive her to town. And had then made the long round trip again to pick her up when she was done.

Laura again looked into her mother's face. Full of remorse, she hugged her mother close. Her parents had both worked so hard to get the hotel ready and today was the big day, the start of their new life; the first guests had arrived. And, instead of helping willingly, instead of recognising that anxiety was the cause of her mother's short temper, she'd behaved like a spoiled brat. She turned away.

"I'm so sorry Mom."

Her mother put out her arms and drew her daughter back.

"Hey, Honey, it's OK. I'm sorry too; I get a bit crazy sometimes," she hugged Laura, rocking her gently and stroking her hair, as she had when Laura was a tiny child afraid of the dark. "This has all been so hard on you, hasn't it; leaving your old friends and starting over? And being a teenager is never easy," she looked at Laura intently, "Believe me I do understand, really. And we will make it up to you. We love you so very much."

"Love you too Mom."

They both wiped away some tears, laughing at their own sentimentality.

"So," said Karen brightly, "are we gonna have us some quality time?"

"Thanks, Mom, but I think I'll go down to the pools, if that's OK. That's if you don't need me to help you with anything here for a while?"

Her mother shook her head.

"Thanks, I won't be long."

"No problem. But please don't wander too far. We

can go explore more of the woods together next week, when this lot check out, OK? Till then, don't go any farther will you? I'm sorry to play the over-protective mom, but what can I say? I'm typecast for the role. Can't help myself."

"It's OK Mom," Laura smiled, "I'm used to it."

"Great. So you won't mind putting this on?" Karen handed her daughter a garish sweater from the pile of dry laundry, "It can get cold in the shade of those trees."

Laura pulled a face, but then acquiesced with good humour and a drawling Southern accent.

"Why I'd simply adore to, Honeypie. And not just on account of how it's you asking," she pulled the fluorescent yellow sweater over her head, "but also 'cos this shade so closely matches my oh so beautiful eyes."

Laura posed with a radiant smile, batting her eyelids like a Hollywood starlet. She was rewarded with her mother's laughter.

Karen shook her head, this daughter of hers was the most amazing kid; a real joy. As Laura walked across the clearing, she turned and waved to her mother standing, still smiling, at the kitchen door.

"Bye Mom. See you later."

Karen hugged herself in the warmth of her daughter's affection and waved back.

"Love you."

From the clearing, Laura followed the narrow path and was soon in deep shade. Out of direct sunlight, the temperature had dropped appreciably and she was thankful for the sweater, though it glowed a rather incongruous neon lemon in the dim light under the trees. Laura looked around her and smiled; she might long for the faster pace and modernity of the town, but this place really was special. The dreamer within her imagined a welcome in the cool stillness here amongst the trees, as if the forest was protectively hugging her to itself. She loved the soft bed of needles and dried leaves underfoot which cushioned her steps and muffled any sound. And she loved the dusky twilight that wrapped itself around you even on the brightest of days.

There was peace here.

The path drew her towards the river. Laura had walked this way with her parents, exploring, on their first day here. And they had all been dizzy as kids at Christmas when they discovered the waterfalls and pools just over the rise. In the months since then, Laura had made this walk whenever she wanted some quiet time to herself. This was her special place, the perfect retreat. She had spent many hours sitting on the rocks reading, or simply watching the water tumble over the falls and swirl in the pools below. The never-ending movement would cast its spell; carrying away her worries and freeing the imagination. It induced an almost trance-like calm.

The stream's course through the forest was accompanied by a thread-like break in the tree cover, which allowed sunlight in to sparkle on the clear, fast-flowing water below. Laura topped the rise and saw the ribbon of sunlight twinkling through the trees ahead. She scrambled down onto a large, flat rock which overhung the stream as it left the plunge pool of the second fall. The rock had been warmed by the sun and Laura stretched out lazily, like a cat on a sunny window ledge. She let her hand slip into the water and gasped in shock at the icy cold. But she persisted, lifting a cupped handful of water into the air, to watch it sparkle, falling back into the racing stream.

She was totally absorbed in this way for over an hour, her mind roaming freely and her body completely relaxed. Eventually though, she drifted back to reality and decided it was time to head back home. Her mom could probably do with some help now; clearing away the meal and resetting the tables. With slow, reluctant movements, Laura got to her feet and was about to turn away when something caught her eye. Something small and pale had just tipped over the rim and dropped down the face of the first fall. Intrigued, Laura waited for it to come spilling out of the first plunge pool and over the second fall. And there it was. A small figure.

A doll.

It seemed to be made of wood, but it was being dragged under and around the pool by the rolling currents. Laura strained to see it in the churning water. She wanted to get it out, but it was almost impossible to predict where it would surface next. Too late she decided to concentrate just on the water leaving the plunge pool. She crouched low over the exiting flow just in time to see the doll being swept past her under the surface, its blank eyes staring up at her. With a cry of irritation, Laura jumped back to her feet and set off along the bank of the stream, scanning the water, searching for the doll. She ran alongside as the stream widened and the flow gradually slackened, but she couldn't see it. Eventually she stopped and was about to give up on the chase, when the tiny figure suddenly bobbed back up into view. It was now being gently rolled over and over, bumping along the pebbly bank on the opposite side. Laura grabbed a fallen branch and heaved it across the stream, poking at the doll, trying to drag it towards her. She succeeded in hooking it on the branch and pulling it away from the bank. But the stronger current in the middle of the stream tugged the doll free and began to carry it further downstream. The branch was too heavy to carry any distance so Laura threw it aside and ran, following the now floating figure, further and further down into the forest.

As she approached some impressively roaring water falls, a clump of dense, overhanging trees made it difficult for her to stay near the water. She had to scramble further up the bank to get around the thicket and by the time she was able to come back down to the water's edge, there was no sign of the doll. Laura paced back and forth looking for it, but to no avail.

It had disappeared.

She kicked a stone over the falls in frustration, then, resigned, sat down on the mossy earth to catch her breath before beginning the journey back upstream. Calming, as her breathing slowed back to normal, she began to feel rather foolish. What had possessed her to chase a doll - a kid's toy and a scruffy, roughly-made one at that - this far into an unfamiliar area of the forest? Best not to tell mom, she decided.

Getting to her feet, she dusted herself down and frowned, realising that the return journey would be uphill all the way. She clambered back up the bank, around the densely growing trees. Glancing to one side, her eye was drawn to a pool of sunlight a short distance to her left. She hadn't noticed it earlier, in her haste as she scrambled downstream, but she saw now that there was a scrubby clearing, fringed with dark pines. Leaving the roaring of the falls behind her, to take a closer look, she could now make out a very decrepit shack, slumped in the centre of the open space.

When Laura and her parents had first moved here, they had been warned to keep the clearing around their new home cut low, in case of forest fire.

The old timers who sat outside the general store all day, watching the world go by, had nodded sagely as Mr Bowen, the storekeeper, explained to Laura's parents how they might have need of that fire break one day. Of course, old man Bowen might just have been selling them a line so they'd buy the scythes and cutters they needed from him, but her father had taken no chances. He had followed the advice dutifully and kept the clearing around their new home very much under control. But the clearing here, surrounding this desolate shack, was under three or four foot of new growth, with taller, spindly saplings jostling for sunlight and air. There couldn't have been anyone living here for years. Laura was intrigued. She glanced at her watch. It wasn't too late. If she ran most of the way back, she would have time enough to check out the ruined shack first.

Laura stepped a few paces forward to the edge of the trees and looked about. There was no sign of life. Hesitating a moment, feeling both nervous and excited, she then stepped out into the glare of sunlight in the clearing. As soon as she felt the warming sun, her spirits lifted, the tension was broken and she started to run through the waist-high scrub, laughing. She stopped in the shadow of the listing shack and shivered, feeling suddenly chill in its shade. The decayed, bleached wood seemed incongruously lifeless at the centre of all this vigorous, green regeneration. There were gaps between some of the planks of its walls and tangled clumps of dead leaves and grasses had become wedged in the cracked and shattered panes of the grimy windows. The whole was hung with an air of sorrowful desolation that put Laura in mind of the gothic haunts of her beloved victorian literary heroines. Letting her mind wander, Laura imagined with sadness the person, perhaps the patriarch of a pioneer family, who had first carved out this clearing in the ancient forest. Why had he and his family chosen this place? And what had become of all the enthusiasm and ambition, the hopes and dreams that must have fired them? Had they been happy living here, or was the sorry state of the clearing perhaps eloquent evidence of difficult times and hard years spent in fruitless labour? Laura's was a romantic notion of pioneer life and she touched the grey wood of the shack as if to connect herself with its past. Feeling the bone dry, aged planking, she could almost summon up a glimpse of those early settlers building this, their new home, in the wilderness. The sun would have burned down on them too, as they toiled, backs bent, to clear the land with no more than axes and long, two man saws. Their task would have seemed almost overwhelming and the effort exhausting. Laura sighed. The empathy she felt towards these long dead hopefuls was such that her imagination could almost reach out to them across the years of lonely dereliction here.

"Hey you!"

Laura leapt as a man's voice rang out across the clearing. She spun round and saw a stocky man standing at the edge of the trees.

"What you doin'?" he yelled.

Still stunned, Laura opened her mouth but no sound came out.

In her many trips into the forest, she'd never met another living soul and she was shocked to have done so, this far from home. She simply stared at him, breathing deeply, trying to calm her rising panic. Although she knew that only about fifteen acres came with their hotel, Laura now realised that she had come to regard the whole forest as private to her. But maybe this odd looking man owned this place. Without intending any wrongdoing, she might now be trespassing on his land. And he didn't look like the understanding type.

He was wearing a greasy, misshapen leather hat pulled down low. His barrel-like chest strained to burst out of a dull-coloured check shirt and he had an axe resting over his shoulder. Laura gasped as a notion flashed through her mind that time might somehow have slipped. Was it possible that the history of this place was still alive and just a breath away from the now? Could this man be the pioneer who had first cleared this land? If so, who was out of time? Was he a ghost in her time, or was she an echo of the future in his? Laura had wanted so much to glimpse the past of this place, but now she was afraid.

Be careful what you wish for.

Her mind was moving fast. She had to get back in control. Shutting her eyes she turned back towards the shack. She forced herself to reopen her eyes and was hugely relieved to see not a newly built cabin, but the same decrepit grey shack in its forlorn state of collapse. Reality fell back into place. This was now; 1978, her time, not the past. She looked back. The man was still there, but now it seemed to her that he looked very much alive and far too solid for a ghost. She began to relax.

Then the man said something strange.

"You real?" he asked uncertainly.

'Real?' Laura thought, 'What sort of question is that?'

She frowned, then nodded.

The man stayed at the edge of the clearing, making no attempt to come any closer. He looked uneasy, as if he didn't want to come out of the shade into the sunlight.

"What yuh doin' here?" he shouted, "This 'ere's private property."

"I'm sorry. I didn't know. I was only looking."

"Come here."

Laura stayed where she was.

"I said come here."

Still Laura kept her distance. It was strange that the man seemed so reluctant to come into the bright sunlight of the clearing. Laura fought off another irrational notion that he might be a vampire, but vampires were rarely this rotund and, though he might be unwilling to come into the light of the clearing, vampires were never as suntanned as this guy already was. Laura made a mental note to stop watching the late night horror movies. No, this was just some loner who probably lived out here in the forest because he liked his own company and wanted to be left alone. And, if he was living a solitary life out here, her sudden appearance had probably given him a greater shock than he had her.

Laura felt in control now and moved a short distance towards the man while remaining alert and ready to run at the first hint of any danger. She wasn't frightened exactly, after all, she was thirteen, young and fit whereas this man was middle-aged and, though obviously strong, was clearly not built for speed. She was confident she could outrun him if the need arose.

"What do you want?" she called.

"Just wanted to get a good look at yuh. Yuh don't belong here," he frowned intently at her. "This 'ere's private property."

He tilted his head and she glimpsed the round, ruddy face beneath the rim of the misshapen leather hat. His skin was leathery and lined and, as he screwed up his eyes the better to focus on her, he displayed an amazingly uneven set of tobacco-darkened teeth. It was impossible to guess the man's age from his appearance. Prosaically, he could simply be prematurely aged by the hardships of an outdoor life, but alternatively, he could be an old, old man who had walked this land for decades, centuries perhaps, heedless of the passing years. Naturally, Laura decided on the latter.

All of this was going through her head as the man stared at her. Just as she began to feel irritated by this scrutiny, he suddenly shrugged.

"OK, yuh can go. But don't yuh come back here. This' ere's private property. I see yuh round here again,

I'll get my dog and I gotta gun. Now get!"

Offended by his tone and determined not to appear afraid, Laura turned slowly and began to walk away across the clearing.

"I said get!" the man bellowed.

"I'm going, I'm going," said Laura, utilising the innate ability of teenagers everywhere to irritate their elders.

She smiled, not needing to turn back; she could easily imagine the irritation he must be feeling at her leisurely departure, but she felt he deserved it. She was annoyed at his rudeness; she had given him no cause to speak to her in the way he had. Her trespass had been an honest mistake and, he needn't worry, she didn't want to come back to his part of the forest ever again. Still smiling, she paused to annoy him further by stopping to pick a single weed. She snapped the stem and held it lightly, twirling the tiny flower head slowly with thumb and forefinger.

She could almost feel the man bristle with fury.

But there was another observer of the scene. Hidden from her view, at the far side of the clearing, a dark figure watched Laura with a cold, hungry intensity.

"Get!" the old man shouted again, his patience near its end.

Laura made no move to hurry; she was going to drag this out until she felt he had paid for his rudeness.

"I'm going, I'm going," she drawled.

She walked with a lazy swaying motion, sauntering as if out enjoying the warm sunshine without a care in the world.

This was too much. The man had had enough and he moved with startling speed for a man of his build. He didn't cover much ground, but the sudden noise of his charge was enough to make Laura scream. She bolted, running as fast as she could, as if her life depended on it, crashing into the cool darkness under the trees bordering the clearing. She kept on running even as the man's raucous laughter rang out behind her.

Slowly, making no sound, the dark figure moved from its hiding place and began to stalk Laura, a smile of sharp, white teeth terrible in its thin, sunken face.

11

With the full glory of summer lighting the forest, Jon felt all his old strength restored. He now ranged far from the cave, often covering fifteen or twenty miles in a day, but he would leave the cave at first light and turn for home no later than noon. Night still brought the uncontrollable return to his dreams of the horror of that creature in the cabin, and to endure the wearying, trembling hours between fitful shreds of sleep, Jon still needed the safety and familiarity of the cave around him. By day, though, the great forest beyond the cave was his trusted friend once more. By day, Jon was able to push away his nightmares and walk the forest with all his former wonder and take pleasure in its beauty and quiet grandeur.

On one such journey, along the ridge of low hills to the north, Jon could see the buildings of Losien in the distance. The town held no fascination for him. He felt no longing to go there. Quite the reverse; he took pride in his independence from the town and its people. Losien, to him, was an alien structure in the landscape; totally foreign and of little interest. Jon had looked down on the town from this ridge many times, each time grateful that the townsfolk seemed rarely to venture into the forest, into his world. On this journey, however, he saw signs of human activity along the dirt road from town.

Jon had watched the people working at the road's end in the forest over several recent trips. He had seen a family working to clean and repair a large, disused building. He had watched the father cutting back the scrub and saplings to re-establish the clearing. Over time, Jon had come to feel that he understood these people. He admired their hard work and dogged persistence. To his surprise he also came, grudgingly, to acknowledge an unexpected yearning: he felt drawn towards them. Having been alone for so long Jon was surprised at this sensation. He had never wished for company and felt in no need of the safeguard offered by mutual support, so why did he keep returning to this family? Intrigued, he had trekked the many miles to observe them far more frequently than was warranted by their activities in the forest. Finally, however, he had accepted this need within him; this would be his last visit here.

Soon Jon was heading back to the cave. Again he had taken a route that swung wide of the cabin; he would never go near that place again. Taking his bearings, he followed the crest of a spur that took him down from the ridge. He was back in the cool of the trees, taking a meandering route as dictated by the lay of the land, but basically heading south. Jon felt good, at ease. He had travelled some twenty miles already today but his body made no complaint; his muscles were strong and his spirits high. He would be back at the cave well before the setting of this long summer's day and, with no need to rush, Jon maintained a steady, unhurried pace. Some distance on, however, he came to a sudden halt. This break in the trees was familiar. He knew this place.

He shuddered. His path had brought him to the spot where, years before, he had smashed that thing's skull. This was the place and over there was the shallow open grave into which he had kicked that awful body. Jon looked over and froze; the strength and self-confidence draining from his body. Something was lying there.

What was it?

Despite his mounting terror, Jon felt drawn towards the trench. What was in there? Could that shadow thing have found him? Was it in there ready to strike? Terrified; feeling utterly vulnerable and exposed, Jon spun from side to side. Knife in hand, he was ready to strike at every tiny sound: the fall of a twig or the rustle of dry leaves lifted into swirling life by a breath of wind. Tense and alert, heart racing, eyes darting to left and right, Jon moved slowly over to the trench. He had to tear his eyes away from scanning the trees to snatch a quick look down, but what he saw there held his gaze against his will. He couldn't look away.

A girl, not Suzie but young like her, lay cradled in the rich, brown earth. Her hair had fallen across her face and was clotted with blood. The gash on her forehead was garish against the waxy pallor of her skin. Her hands and arms had been cut many times; her sleeves stained brown, slashed and torn. Jon's life had taught him to read such signs. This girl had put up a desperate fight; had tried to protect her head and face from her attacker.

She had lost a shoe, leaving exposed a small, bare foot, which was dirty and bruised. That missing shoe gave her the air of a small, lost child, and awoke in Jon the same feelings of tenderness that he had felt for Suzie. He had no doubt that this poor girl had fallen victim to the same killer.

The monster was very much alive.

Jon's gaze travelled up the broken body and took in the final proof; a small, ragged triangle had been cut from the fluorescent yellow of the girl's sweater. The monster was still alive.

And still killing.

Numb with sadness, Jon knelt beside the girl's crumpled body. Tenderly, he leant forward and moved aside the clotted mass of hair that had partially covered her face. She was beautiful, or rather she had been beautiful. Looking down at her bruised face, Jon was suddenly gripped with the awful realisation that he knew her. She was the girl from the big building. He had watched her frequent visits to the falls. She would come to the water and spend long hours lying on the rocks nearby, dreaming. Unobserved, Jon had smiled at her obvious enjoyment of the pools and the sparkling waters. It was clear that, like him, this girl had accepted the forest's gentle welcome: a welcome quietly extended to any who needed it. She might live in the renovated building but Jon knew that, like him, she felt truly at home here, in the forest. He had finally come to understand that this girl was the reason he had continued to observe the family, the reason he had felt compelled so often to return. He felt he shared with her a common understanding of the wonder of this place. It was the closest he had come to human companionship since his brief time with Suzie.

Jon had last seen this girl at the falls near the building only a few hours ago. Having determined to make that his last trip to the family, he knew he would miss her and he had brought her a parting gift. She had such pale skin and, though her hair was dark while Suzie's had been fair, this girl had reminded him very much of her, so the gift had seemed appropriate. In any case he had little else that he could have given. In planning this farewell he had once, fleetingly, considered speaking to the girl, but had backed away from such directness. He had been content to silently wish her well and remain unobserved. Seeing her this morning, lying in the sun, Jon had placed his gift to her into the stream above the falls and turned to leave, a contented smile lighting his face. That had been only a few hours ago. She had been a radiant, wonderful creature.

And now, here she was, dead. Abandoned, left lying in the cold earth.

She had been partially covered with branches and earth, but most had already been scratched or dug away. Shaking himself out of his stunned stillness, Jon began quickly to gather ferns and other greenery with which to completely cover her again. Then he heaved heavier branches across the top, in an effort to protect her body from scavengers. Throughout all this frenzied effort, knowing that her dark killer might still be close by, Jon kept watch, frequently looking over his shoulder. It was hard to believe that the creature would not hunt him still. The sun was sinking lower and, as the shadows lengthened, Jon worked with increasing, anxious haste. He knew what had done this to her. On that terrible day, in the shack, Jon had seen what had done this. The evil had killed again and Jon wanted to be away from this place before darkness fell.

He wanted to be far away.

His journey home was terrifying.

Leaving the poor girl there, in the deepening gloom, knowing that what little protection he had been able to give her body would almost certainly not be enough, Jon stumbled through the trees, his eyes burning with tears of bitter frustration. He felt helples; he could not have done more and yet knew that he should have tried. Wretchedly escaping from the pitiful grave, he felt contempt for himself for having done so little. Fear had directed his actions, taken over and made him weak. He was no longer the man who had survived the dangers and privations of years in the forest alone, resourceful, alert and undaunted. He was a pathetic husk, running scared, desperate to get back to the shelter of his cave; no different from any of the animals he had hunted and killed over the years. His mind was overwhelmed with images of the thing that had leapt at him in the cabin. His skin crawled with the scratching of those sharp, grasping claws. Most terrible, in every dark hollow and space between the trees, Jon saw those dark, greedy eyes staring out at him, wickedly savouring his terror. As he staggered onwards, his legs increasingly weak and shaky beneath him, Jon fully expected an attack at every step.

The sky was just beginning to lighten as he finally clambered up the slope above the stream and fell, trembling, into the darkness of his cave.

Jon hid in the cave for several days. He had taken a long detour on his way back here, following the stream as he had all those years before, when Suzie had been killed, and for the same reason. But now even this sanctuary seemed insecure. His mind, denied the peace it craved, turned events over and over. In returning to the cabin he had retraced his steps of nearly twenty years ago and found history being horribly re-enacted.

And now another young woman lay dead in the dark earth.

But, for Jon, the awful image of that poor girl's dead body kept slipping from his mind; it could not over-lay, or eradicate the earlier, terrible events in the shack which were now back at the forefront of his mind. The man, or whatever it now was, the killer, had leapt at him from the shadows. It had looked right at him. And Jon had no doubt that it knew him.

He shivered.

12

Again the bone white hands fell still.

Another twenty years would pass before the blades were sharpened and the wood selected from which to carve another doll.

II

13

The Chevrolet Suburban, all doors flung open, stood within a circle of holiday clutter as if it were somehow repelling the boxes, bags, fishing lines, boots and other assorted necessities that lay about it on the drive. 'Works like a magnet in reverse.' thought Jeff, surveying the scene.

 A tall, sandy-haired man, Jeff was still lean although pushing forty-five. He was dressed now in the linen shorts, cotton polo shirt and canvas shoes of the sport-loving, but decidedly non-sports-playing, professional man of middle years. He liked to dress this way, in what he supposed was casual clothing, but in truth this outfit was as much a uniform as was the tired grey suit he wore to college every working day. Musing as he began to heave suitcases into the car, Jeff thought that his students should perhaps get to see this informal side to his nature. It would help them to regard him more as one of their number rather than as the remote, intellectual figure; the inspirational, if somewhat intimidating guru. One summer, he decided, he would organise an end of semester picnic, or a barbecue, or something: it might help to dispel the deference and admiration which he fancied his students felt for him. In this view of his students, as with his studied casual clothing, Jeff was hopelessly wide of the mark. Thankfully however, the distance that his students rigorously maintained allowed Jeff to continue in this self-delusion; he remained blissfully unaware of just how very far from reality was his lofty view of the regard in which the student body held him.

Accurate or otherwise, these thoughts of awed respect and attendance on his every word had to be put from his mind for a while: today was the start of Jeff's family holiday so there would be little chance of his being held in respect, awed or otherwise, for its duration.

"OK you guys," he shouted, "let's get this lot stowed away properly."

"We'd have been done hours ago if **you** hadn't made us take everything out again."

The voice was a teenage whine belonging to his daughter, Emma. She was leaning against the wall of the garage, arms folded and face set in a scowl. When he looked at her, Jeff had to strain to remember the gorgeous little poppet this pale-faced, Adams family lookalike had once been. And not so long ago either. Em was still only just thirteen, though she did look older, he had to admit that. She looked older, yes, but beneath all the attitude she was still just a kid. Only two years ago he had still been her darling Daddy and she his little princess. These days she dressed completely in a black that looked dull grey even when it was brand new and wore an habitual look of bored disapproval relieved only by sustained bouts of total indifference.

Jeff had read all the books. He knew the theory. But he was tired of Em testing the boundaries and asserting her independence; he just wanted his little girl back. Sometimes he would reject outright all the books' accumulated words of advice. On these occasions he would fall back on simply blaming his ex-wife, Julie, for the change in their daughter. It didn't strike him as inconsistent that he had never felt the need to credit Julie for Emma's former charming sweetness of character and he didn't see any contradiction in this. In fact he rarely saw things logically where they concerned his daughter. He had long harboured a vision in which the adult Emma, by then an accomplished woman in her own right, would accompany her venerable father to the launch party of his latest book, smiling and laughing indulgently at his sparkling conversation. In this daydream Emma would be dutifully impressed by her much-respected father's pre-eminence in his field, since he would by then be world renowned and well used to receiving the plaudits of his academic peers. And, in this dream, Emma would share his thoughts and ideas, naturally concurring with his views on everything.

One day, perhaps. One far off day.

Fate had possibly given Jeff's dream a boost. Julie had had to go into hospital for some minor cosmetic surgery with the result that, while Julie convalesced, Jeff was to have Em for more than just the weekend visits. Today was the beginning of a week of togetherness and father-daughter bonding. He aimed to start her return from Goth rebel to loving daughter over the next few days.

To achieve this he knew he would have to try not to let her goad him. He must stay cool; be firm, but keep calm.

"I'm not going to explain again," he started, before immediately going on to explain, for the fourth or fifth time, "We are giving Annie, Bill and the kids a ride, so we need to clear the seats."

"If you need the space that much, why won't you let me stay here. I don't want to go to some hick hotel in the middle of nowhere."

"You'll love it when you get there."

"Oh yeah? And just how d'you know that? You ever been there?"

"You know I haven't," he said, affecting measured calm, "You saw the pictures on the internet, same as me," he caught her eye, hoping to get an acknowledging shrug, but the blank face remained indifferent. He forced a smile, "C'mon, it'll be great; there's forests and lakes and loads of other really cool stuff."

As soon as he said the word, he knew that 'cool' had been a mistake. He was too old and forty-something for 'cool'. Emma's sneer reached new levels of disdain and Jeff blundered on, pretending he hadn't noticed, trying to mask his embarrassment.

"We'll go rafting and fishing and maybe camp out in the woods."

Emma was stifling a yawn and devoting all her attention to clearing something from under a fingernail.

"Are you listening to me?" Jeff asked, though of course he knew the answer already and instantly regretted asking the question.

As expected, Emma ignored him completely.

He wrestled with the irritation. Must keep calm. Must keep calm.

No chance. Jeff's irritation wrestled his calmer self to a submission, and he snapped.

"Emma," he shouted, "I'm talking to you! Are you listening?"

Slowly Emma nodded, again stifling a yawn. Jeff strode over to her, determined to make her show some respect, though how exactly he was to achieve this was unclear, even to him. Thankfully at this point, his wife Rita stepped between them and intervened to deflate the situation. She held her hand gently against his chest and turned to Emma.

"Emma," she asked lightly, "could you go inside and

check you haven't left anything you'll need in your room? And don't forget your boots. The forecast said there was a good chance of snow over the next few days."

Emma shrugged, "Yeah. Whatever."

Jeff watched as Emma slouched back into the house.

"Ree? How do you **do** that? You ask her one thing, one time and she does it, right off, no bitching, no complaints. But for me? Nothing. She ignores everything, and I mean every damn thing I say."

"It's because she loves you. You're important to her and I'm not. I'm just someone who's around a lot, an observer: unimportant and uninvolved."

"No. You're wrong," Jeff interrupted, "Em loves you."

"No, Jeff, she doesn't. But that's OK; I don't expect her to. I'm not her mom. We get on just fine being friends who happen to live in the same house. And I think she's a great kid. Y'know she could have made life hell for both of us when we got together, but she didn't. She and I get on OK, but she doesn't need my approval or my love; I'm just not that important to her. You are. Plus, she knows you and she knows exactly how to get a reaction. She's just a kid, hungry for attention, most especially from her father," she smiled at him, "I think it's sweet; quite flattering in a way."

Jeff looked at Rita in disbelief. But, though he shook his head, he knew that she was right. He would just have to try to go with the ebbs and flows of Emma's headlong dash into adulthood, keep on being patient and be there, ready, if and when she finally decided that maybe, just maybe, her father might have something useful to contribute. But it wasn't going to be easy.

He sighed and Rita rubbed his arm comfortingly.

"She's a teenager, she's your daughter and she does love you."

"Yeah, sure!" Jeff pretended to dismiss the idea, but he liked to hear it said just the same.

They had just finished repacking the car when a taxi pulled up across the street. Bill and Annie had arrived. Jeff looked on in mounting disbelief as the cab disgorged its contents; first Annie, then Bill, then their children, Lisa and Michael and finally a mountain of luggage. Annie, flamboyant as ever, ran over to him.

"Hey," she gushed, "isn't this going to be great; all of us together again? I can hardly wait and the kids are just thrilled."

Jeff looked over to the kids and saw in little Lisa the first tell tale hint of a raised eyebrow, a proto-look of disdain. 'Thrilled?' he thought, 'I don't think so. Ah, how early it begins.' Lisa could only be eight, or nine at most.

Michael, Lisa's six year old brother, looked to be equally unenthusiastic. In a cab ride of only twenty minutes across town, he had already vomited down his front. 'Ah, yes,' thought Jeff, remembering a particularly unpleasant picnic trip with Michael the previous summer, 'Mikey's motion sickness. Great!'

Meanwhile, some sixty miles away, a man was standing, waiting, outside an elegant and expensively understated apartment block near the city's business district. Dave was dressed somewhat inappropriately for his surroundings, in jeans, check shirt and hefty hiking boots. From a distance, an observer might have been forgiven for thinking that he was perhaps a farmer, or a lumberjack, newly arrived in the big city. But close up, the pristine, gleaming newness of the boots, the stiff creases down the shirt-sleeves and the artfully faded stone-washed effect of his expensive new blue jeans betrayed his true origins; Dave was a city boy.

Dave was in advertising, but today he had tried to buy

into a look; the rugged adventurer, the man who could tame the wilderness, the man who could live off the land and be at home far from modern creature comforts. He had just spent a small fortune purchasing the necessities to cover all outdoor living eventualities. The items included: a hugely expensive jacket (bright orange and absolutely guaranteed waterproof); packs of survival rations; water purification tablets; cans of maximum strength insect repellent, a mosquito net; socks guaranteed to protect from ticks; a multiblade army knife; a GPS receiver, with built-in maps and colour screen and a flashlight which had been billed, 'As seen on TV' and was, according to the sales assistant, the model used in the X Files. Having helped Dave to select these and the many other essentials for surviving seven challenging days in the woods, the wonderfully helpful sales assistant had swiped his credit card with eager anticipation. Her face had then lit up in utter bliss as the confirmation came through from the card company; her thoughts were already on her commission and the new large screen TV her kids had been pleading for. Dave had been a little unnerved by her beaming smile. Who enjoys working in the service sector that much? True, he'd been impressed by the level of service and her commitment to customer satisfaction, but this woman had to be bucking for employee of the year, if not of the decade.

But, contrary to his earlier expectations, Dave had actually enjoyed shopping for all this exotica. He had anticipated a poor selection of drab, unflattering clothing and dull, utilitarian equipment, but had found to his delight that colour and gloss had found their way into the outdoor clothing sector. He had never dreamed that so much gadgetry and decadent luxury was available for the modern man in search of the simple life. Dave had returned, laden, to his apartment, content that he now had the wherewithal to deal with whatever the upcoming week held in store. He wasn't going to look like some soft city boy. Changing into some of his new gear, he admired the pleasingly handsome effect in the full length mirror. The rest of his new buys he crammed into his one large backpack and a medium-sized suitcase. The suitcase, he decided, was really too good for the no doubt fairly rough conditions he was going to have to endure for the next week; he should really have bought another backpack. But there wasn't time to go back to the store now.

Having staggered, dragging his luggage, out into the bright sunlight on the sidewalk, Dave had expected to be waiting only a few minutes. But Neil was late.

Looking rugged and manly out in the wilderness was one thing, but standing here, right outside his own apartment building and just two blocks from his office, Dave soon began to feel uncomfortable. Being in advertising he understood the supreme importance of image, and it concerned him that people, seeing him dressed like this, might think he actually was some hick backwoodsman. Of course, though he did not know it, he need not have worried on that score; the just-bought newness of his entire ensemble suggested only too clearly that this man's wardrobe had never before contained such exotic wear. Indeed, the starched perfection hinted that the wearer had probably never so much as spent a night under canvas at Summer Camp. In fact, truth to tell, Dave regarded even the city's well-manicured central park as Nature in the raw.

It comforted him that, with his new purchases, he was now as ready as he would ever be to cope with life in the wilds. But, as the minutes dragged by, Dave was keenly aware that he was wearing clothes that were definitely only intended for use outside the city boundaries. What if someone he knew happened to pass by? What if they didn't just dismiss him as a country bumpkin lost in the big city but recognised him, even dressed like this? It would confirm every prejudice they'd ever harboured concerning the sartorial habits of gay men.

Thankfully, so far, no one he knew had passed by, but Dave did have to suffer, with stinging embarrassment, the amused glances of strangers, the young, sharp-suited men and women, who smirked as they walked by and saw him. Resenting their sniggering condescension, Dave made defiant eye contact with them and they quickly looked away, just as Dave himself had done so many times; flinching from the direct, intimidating stares of itinerants and bag ladies. Dave now felt some guilt for having acted like that then, but, dammit, he wasn't homeless, he wasn't a beggar, he was a sophisticated, professional man and he resented like hell being viewed as one of the city's crazies, like the wild-haired guy who talks to himself and always sits much too close on the subway.

Dave paced back and forth, marking time, feeling ever more conspicuous and feigning interest in the stark metal structure that dominated the area in front of his building. According to the sign at its base, the edifice represented, 'Mankind's Search for Hope'. By now, Dave had read the inscription at least twenty times, and paced around the ugly pile of recycled junkyard trash for what felt like an age. In that time he had come to the definite conclusion that, if this was a fair representation of mankind's search for hope then the human race had better give up right now and ring down the shutters.

At last a huge, black SUV pulled over. A pane of tinted glass slid down and Neil called out to him.
"Hi. Come on. Get in."
No apology.
While Dave dragged his luggage to the car, Neil made

no attempt to help, but continued in a loud voice, all the while checking his perfect teeth in the rear view mirror.

"I had to meet with a new client. The man kills his business partner in front of witnesses and knows that only the very best lawyer in the state can keep him off Death Row so, naturally, he comes to me. Says he's willing to pay whatever it costs. I tell you, it doesn't get much better than this!"

With a final sweep of his tongue across his dazzling smile, Neil turned to Dave and noticed, for the first time, that Dave was moving unusually slowly,

"Come on, I want to be out of town before the interstate gets choked."

As usual, Dave passed no comment on Neil's self-obsessed insensitivity. With no more than a resigned shake of his head, he heaved the back pack and suitcase up onto the rear seats and opened the passenger door to climb in. Neil stared at him, a quizzical eyebrow raised.

"Interesting lumberjack thing you've got going there. Almost wish I'd had enough time to buy some new gear myself."

"What? Are you planning on roaming the woods in the Armani?"

"Didn't really give it much thought. Like I said, I had to meet with this new, and very lucrative, client. I just had time to throw a few things into an overnight bag. But I have no intention of going native out in the backwoods; I've seen Deliverance. Thanks, but no thanks."

Dave felt crushed. In the light of Neil's lack of preparation, his own shoppingfest now seemed rather foolish.

"I just thought I'd like, get a few essentials because you never know what you might need, and we could be like, miles from civilisation."

Neil merely nodded, his attention on the congestion

which had so far prevented them pulling out into traffic. Dave shrugged. He never stayed down for long and, sure enough, a moment later, his dejection had lifted; he had remembered the fun he'd had choosing and buying all his new gear.

"Man," he said, "you would not believe the stuff you can buy; I've got gadgets that do everything! They're amazing, really amazing. And the clothes, wow, they are so cool. And the outdoor thing is a really good look for me. Just take a look at these boots, man," Dave hoisted one Nubuck-booted foot onto the dashboard, "Rugged or what?"

Neil barely glanced at them.

"Yeah, sure, very impressive. Now will you get your foot down off my dash."

Dave removed his foot.

"You think I wasted my money buying this stuff, don't you?"

"It's your money."

"Yeah, but you don't think I'll need any of it. I mean like, you're taking one overnight bag."

"Who knows, maybe you'll turn out to be the smart one here. I mean, the weather could turn, there could be an earthquake or a flood, or a forest fire. Who knows when we might need the services of a really well-dressed lumberjack."

"You're mocking me again."

But Dave was smiling. He was no longer downhearted. He would enjoy the fantasy that he was to be a macho, backwoodsman for a week and he'd actually be quite happy if he never had to use any of the survival gear in anger.

"OK, so maybe I went a bit overboard. But if we're not roughing it, are we going to a fancy hotel?"

"Fancy? No. Hotel? Yes. Well at least they call it a

hotel, but it's small and out in the middle of nowhere. It'll be basic."

"How many stars?"

"None."

Dave didn't care. Determined to enjoy this, their first holiday together, he bounced back to his usual enthusiastically cheerful self.

"It'll be cool! And no stars, means it's star-lite. Get it, like starlight?" as Dave chattered on, he began to let his imagination run free, "Hey, I could use that; I could hang an ad on that. And think of the graphics; starlit skies over the brooding forest, cool aurora, northern lights, all that kinda stuff. Yeah, you could like accidentally mention to the people at the hotel that I'm in advertising and then you could suggest that y'know like they should have me do an ad for them. I could really put 'em on the map. It'd help if they'd agree to change the hotel's name to 'Starlight', but, hey, I'm a persuasive guy. And it'd be fun; something we could work on together, y'know like, when the others are out trekking and doing, oh I don't know, forest stuff.

"Or were you planning on just chilling out? Man, that's cool too. Yeah, we could catch up on some reading. Reading's good. You got any books in that overnight bag of yours? I didn't pack any, but hey, have you read the latest Peter W-"

Neil was used to the mile-a-minute delivery. Dave could go on for quite some time before realising that he was the only one making any noise, but now his voice faltered. He had noticed Neil's frown.

Neil waited for a few seconds of silence.

"Are you done?" he asked dryly.

"Sure. Sorry man. Talking too much again, huh?"

"Always." Neil sighed.

"I'm sorry man, but I'm so pumped about us going

away together. Aren't you?"

"Aren't I what?"

"Excited, that we're going away together for the first time."

"Yeah, sure."

"You don't look like it to me."

"Well I've got a lot on my mind right now."

"What, the corporate killer?"

"Yeah."

"Forget him, we're going away."

"Dave, this will get me the partnership. When I get this guy off, the firm will give me anything I want."

"Get him off? You said he killed the guy!"

"Didn't I tell you I'm the best lawyer in the state? In the country?"

Dave shook his head in mock despair.

"Neil, you are a very, very bad man."

Dave's smile broadened and his laughter filled the car.

They wove smartly through the traffic, heading out of town.

14

"Ah, I knew I'd forget something," said Jeff, "The cell phone; I left it on the table by the door."

"Hey, don't worry about it," said Rita, lowering the map to smile at him, "We're on vacation. We won't need to call anyone. We're going to have a really restful time. It's going to be so great."

Somewhere, in the cramped conditions at the back of the car, Emma snorted derisively and Jeff found himself guiltily pleased that this small sign of rebellion was, for once, directed at Rita rather than himself.

Annie, half-hidden under a large sports bag, joined the conversation, agreeing with Rita.

"Yeah. It is going to be wonderful. I've been looking forward to this for ages. D'you know, we haven't all of us been together like this since before most of the kids were born. Remember?"

"Yeah," said Rita, "and that was before Phil and Lou got together. Have you met her yet?"

"No. You?"

"Only briefly. They were in town one time, shopping, and they had a baby, a boy I think, but they were on their way somewhere so they couldn't stop. She didn't say much but she seems, y'know, OK. A lot younger than us though."

"Oh yeah? How much younger?" asked Annie.

"Oh I dunno, mid twenties."

"The bitch! I hate her already," Annie shouted, suddenly laughing.

Sitting next to her, Bill said nothing, but he nudged his wife and inclined his head, warning her not to say too much in front of the three children sitting behind them. Annie shrugged his hand from her arm. She knew she should have chosen her words more judiciously. She had simply forgotten that the children were there and now she was embarrassed, but also irritated, at the way in which Bill had reminded her, as if she were a child herself. She turned to the window and stared out in sullen silence. Bill awkwardly withdrew his arm and quietly turned to stare out of the window on his side of the car. Behind them, Emma looked from one to the other and shook her head. 'Adults!' she mused, 'When do they get to grow up?'

Jeff glanced in the rear view mirror and took in the scene. The journey already seemed to be taking its toll and Mikey hadn't even started throwing up yet. Jeff could hardly wait! He glanced across at Rita and her eyes met his. She pulled a face. She had obviously come to the same conclusion.

It was going to be a long drive.

Several comfort breaks later, the Suburban pulled off the interstate. Rita pored over the hand-written instructions that had been sent with the booking confirmation.

"It says to continue along this road till we get to a place called Losien. Says it's the nearest big town."

About ten miles further on, a sign at the side of the road informed them that they were now in Losien, an 'Historic town of great charm and interest.'

Annie was not impressed.

"This is the 'big town'?"

Looking around at the dilapidated buildings and boarded-up shops, Jeff couldn't help himself.

"I'd say it's about as big as it is historic and charming."

Rita shushed them both.

"We take a right off Main Street, just after the church."

They saw the church. The area around the building showed someone's devoted care; the lawn neatly trimmed and a few late flowers still in bloom around the foot of a simple wooden cross. But even this quaint old building looked in grave need of a fresh coat of paint. As they turned off Main Street everyone felt their spirits lift; relieved to be driving out of town.

The unmade, dirt track was now rising through wooded country, the trees gradually becoming more densely planted and the road narrower. Eventually they crested a rise and the whole of the forest lay spread before them, seemingly unbroken, melting into the far distant blue-grey horizon. Rolling gently to a halt, they all gasped at the sheer expanse of dark green; its scale too much to take in. It was as if an entire world had been laid out below them with countless miles of untouched, primordial habitat. Even Emma was lost for a sarcastic comment.

"Shit," she whispered softly, eyes wide in amazement.

"Em!" Jeff quickly hushed her, "Don't talk like that around the kids."

He looked up to give her a warning look in the rear view mirror, but saw that the younger children were both fast asleep, their heads pillowed on Emma's lap. Immediately, his look softened. Rita had been right; Em was a good kid. And even the scowl his daughter now gave him, as she noticed his dopey smile, couldn't dent the love he felt for her at that moment. His sweet, gentle little girl was still in there somewhere. There was hope.

The road dipped down from the ridge and took them into the deep darkness beneath the trees. The thick cover seemed unbroken except, every now and then, where the winding road crossed a small stream. Crossing the rattling bridges, Rita could see the crystal, sunlit water edged with deep green cushions of moss and fern, as far as the first bend in each stream. Beyond that, the streams were hidden from view, lost in the smothering trees. These infrequent and enticing glimpses of dazzling light, in the otherwise overwhelming dark of the forest, were wholly enchanting. Rita, drowsy from the long journey, fell to daydreaming; imagining the shades of ancient peoples who might for centuries have offered worship to their gods at magical places such as these.

Jeff glanced across at his wife. It was good to see the smile on Rita's face. She was already happy and they hadn't even got to the hotel yet. He knew this was going to be a great holiday.

A few miles behind them, Neil and Dave were driving into Losien. In his haste to get to the meeting with the new client, Neil had left his copy of the instructions back in his apartment. Dave had tried calling Jeff, but Jeff wasn't picking up. Luckily the name of the town had stuck in Neil's mind and had got them this far, but now they needed to find someone local to give them directions to the hotel itself. Unfortunately, the streets of Losien seemed devoid of any life, local or otherwise.

They drove quietly into town, past the derelict stores with their whitewashed windows and perfunctory graffiti. Neil was at the wheel, but driving so slowly that he had time to look carefully to left and right. Searching for signs of life, he peered forward over the wheel.

"Where the hell is everyone?"

"Look around you. Does it look like anyone actually lives here?"

"Well, better just hope there's a gas station here

somewhere. We're running low."

Dave shrugged in reply, untypically lost for words.

"There'll be a gas station," said Neil, "Hell, they have gas stations out in the middle of the desert. Even if no one still lives here, there'll be a gas station."

"Wouldn't bet on it man."

"There will be. And we can ask them for directions to the hotel."

"First, find your gas station."

"We could use your new satellite positioning thing."

"No. Battery's got to charge up first."

"OK. So we just keep looking."

They motored slowly on.

"Man, this place is a ghost town."

"Yeah, like in the movies, with the tumbleweed rolling by."

"Man, that's right," said Dave, "there's always tumbleweed rolling across the deserted, dusty street, just so's you know it's a ghost town. There's gotta be like, some guy out in California making a living, rolling up balls of tumbleweed for the movies. Some niche market, huh? Any money in it, you reckon? No? You sure? 'Cos like, every godforsaken Wild West town has tumbleweed. First, the tumbleweed blows across the scene. Then cut to a low angle shot from just behind the bad guy, as the new sheriff slowly steps out to face him, knees knockin' and sweat pouring down his face. The gunslinger flexes his hand near his holster. There's a sound like, oh I dunno, a burst of loud acoustic guitar strumming, and terrified townsfolk rush to close the drapes, pull down the shutters. And, oh yeah, one guy always tries to hide by diving head first into an empty barrel outside the livery stable."

"This Wild West town of yours seems kinda busy for a ghost town."

"OK, so it's not always a ghost town, but the tumbleweed? Man, that's a given, there's always tumbleweed; sets the scene; lends authenticity. You see tumbleweed and right away you know you're in some desolate, one-horse town in Arizona or New Mexico."

"Whereas, in reality, you're in Spain or Morocco."

Dave held up his hands in mock surrender.

"OK, well maybe the guy in California exports the stuff. What do I know? Me, I'm just making conversation here so's we don't focus too much on the fact that we're lost. We're in the middle of nowhere, in a ghost town, we're totally lost and we're nearly out of gas. Just thought I'd make some conversation to lighten the mood."

"Like you ever needed an excuse to talk."

"Oh man, that hurt," said Dave, all mock indignation, "OK, I'll keep quiet…Won't make a sound…You'll see…Not another word…Nothing…Zip…Nada."

"OK, enough," Neil protested. "Look, there's some cars parked up ahead."

"Oh praise the Lord! Some small pocket of humanity has survived the apocalypse. How many d'you think? Enough to rebuild civilisation, or what passes for it in these parts? God, I hope so, else we'll have to selflessly put aside the fact that we're both so very queer and do our patriotic duty to help repopulate the earth. Eugh!"

"Are you done?"

"Well, can I say once again and this time with feeling, eugh!"

Neil raised an eyebrow.

"OK. Sorry man. I'm done," said Dave with a shrug, "It's just I get really, really bored on long car rides. My brain has to have something to do."

"Nature abhors a vacuum huh?"

"Something like - hey, wait up. Are you suggesting

my head is empty?"

"I'm a lawyer, so I'd naturally need proof. But can you prove to me that it's not?"

"Ouch…Tricky…OK yeah, how's this? I'm a good, and I mean a spectacularly good, ideas man. Ad campaigns don't make themselves y'know. So there you are. That's all the proof you need," Neil didn't look convinced. Dave capitulated, "No? OK, then you got me," he feigned a blow to the chest, "and that hurts me man," Dave paused, for dramatic effect, before he brightened up, "FYI, you should know that I can only tolerate these cruel truths because I love you man?"

Neil said nothing. He was manoeuvring the SUV into a space outside a dilapidated five and dime. Rather disconcerted, Dave tried again,

"Hello? Are you listening? I said that I love you."

Again Neil appeared not to have heard him.

"That would be where you get to say, 'I love you too' man."

Dave's face showed no sign of hurt, but the hint of uncertainty in his voice begged for reassurance.

As always, Neil was noncommittal, almost insulting, "Yeah. Sure. Whatever."

But Dave was happy to accept even this meagre acknowledgment. He made very few demands on Neil, because he really did love him. He loved Neil probably more than Neil would ever know and certainly far more than he deserved. Perhaps naïvely, Dave simply assumed that his love was being reciprocated.

The two men climbed down from the vehicle, yawning and stretching, legs stiff from several hours of inactivity. They made an odd-looking couple; Dave in his spanking new woodsman gear, and Neil in his now rather creased business suit. But there appeared to be no one about to notice or pass comment, no sign of the drivers of the other parked cars.

The bell above the door jangled as they entered, but otherwise, the store was quiet save for the angry buzzing of a large fly. Waiting for the store owner to appear, Dave watched the insect repeatedly fly at the large window, fall, then fizz around in a frantic dance on its back. There were already several other flies lying dead and undisturbed in the dust at the bottom of the glass, composing what seemed to Dave to be a bizarrely bleak window display. He wondered if such neglect drew many passers by into the store. Surely, even in a town with as little to offer as this, you had to make some effort to pull in the customers, so perhaps the dusty dead flies explained the emptiness of the place. It was several minutes, during which Dave and Neil wandered the small store, checking out the shelves, before they heard a bead curtain abruptly clatter. A woman entered from a back room. She was perhaps in her late twenties and quite pretty, but her eyes were dull. She looked utterly bored.

"Can I get you fellas something?"

"Yeah, sure," said Neil answering for them both as usual, "We'd like a map of the area."

"Don't have none. No call for'em round here. Nobody comes here who don't already live here."

"Well, **we**'re here and we could do with some assistance so, if there's no map, could you tell us where the Whitewater Hotel is?"

The woman didn't even pause for thought.

"Nope."

"You sure? The Whitewater Hotel? You've no idea where it is?"

"Like I said, nope."

Neil was beginning to get annoyed. As with everything in his life, he took the woman's disinterest personally. Dave recognised the warning signs and quickly insinuated himself between Neil and the woman.

"Do you know of anyone else who might know the hotel? Someone else we could ask?" he asked, smiling hopefully.

"Nope."

"Well, thanks for your help," Neil snapped. He walked away, "Come on, we'll go find someone else."

He was already leaving the store, but Dave hung back.

"While we're here I could get you some more suitable gear. OK?"

Neil paused for a second, but didn't look back.

"Knock yourself out."

Dave could tell that Neil was annoyed with him now. Wanting to make a dramatic gesture, sweeping out of the store and probably slamming the door behind him, Neil would be angry that Dave's delay had ruined the effect.

Having bought a few items and thus all but clearing the clothing shelf in the store, Dave emerged and carried his bag to the SUV. Neil was not in the car. Dave eventually found him in a diner, hidden away down a dusty side street. Neil was sitting at a table by the window, but made no response when Dave waved at him. He was still angry. Dave knew he'd have to soothe Neil's injured pride, but he was used to that; Neil was given to sulking whenever things failed to go his way. To most it would seem a tiresome habit but, in Dave's eyes, it was quite endearing, the one childish aspect of an otherwise very cool-headed and rational individual. As with all of Neil's faults, Dave found a way to excuse or ignore his sulkiness, loving Neil regardless; seeing worth where others saw only self-absorbed superficiality.

Dave took a deep breath as he pushed open the door of the diner but, always easily distracted, his intention to placate Neil was forgotten the instant he saw the décor. The interior of the diner looked to have changed little in fifty years. From the faded red cushioned bar stools at the rounded counter, the black and white chequered linoleum floor and the sun clock with its chrome rays, the look was straight out of American Graffiti. Full of enthusiasm, Dave hurried over to Neil's table.

"Man, just look at this place! Talk about your timewarp. This is your actual retro, the real deal. None of this is repro. How cool is that?"

Neil looked away.

"Oh yeah," Dave suddenly remembered. Dragging his enthusiastic gaze away from scanning the room, he forced himself to focus on Neil, "Sorry about that."

"Sorry about what?"

"You know, back there, in the store."

Neil shrugged.

Dave shook his head indulgently, "C'mon man, I know you were set to make one of your big exits, and I blew it. So I'm sorry."

"Whatever. Drink your coffee. It's getting cold."

Dave had barely raised the cup of cooled coffee to his lips when Neil got to his feet and turned to leave. Dave quickly replaced the cup, grabbed some notes from his pocket and scattered them onto the table.

"Money's there," he called to the waitress. She nodded indifferently and, though hurrying to catch up with Neil, Dave felt obliged to say something more, "That was great coffee by the way. Great coffee. Thanks."

The waitress watched the flustered city boy hurry out, in his spanking new clothes and pretty yellow boots. Slowly she shook her head. You could never understand city folks. They were just different is all. Why, that young man hadn't had but a drop of his coffee and anyhow, she knew for a fact that that it was godawful coffee; she wouldn't drink it. And the other man had wanted to know the way to the hotel they'd made from the old workers' building out in the forest. She'd never been to the place herself but she was pretty sure that the Whitewater wasn't the sort of fancy hotel he'd be used to staying in. That guy had money. The sharp suit told you that much. Clearing their cups from the table, she peered out at the two men; Dave scampering after Neil, and he striding purposefully on, ignoring Dave's calls for him to wait up.

City folks! Are they weird or what?

"Are you sure we should listen to that waitress?" asked Dave, "She didn't look all there to me."

"She got us here didn't she?"

The SUV roared into life and they lurched away from the town's gas station.

"OK, but the gas station was like, just round the block. You sure she knows where the hotel is?"

"Yeah. She said it's right at the end of a track that they built way back when they were going to build a dam and flood the forest."

"There's a flooded forest?"

"No, the dam was abandoned, never finished. Back then, the hotel was an accommodation block for the workers."

Dave laughed.

"A block? And near a half-built dam? Sounds peachy. Why, the name 'Whitewater' hardly does it justice. Surely something like, 'The Bunkhouse', or even 'The Doghouse,' would better conjure up that certain ambience that we aesthetes so crave in our holiday accommodation."

Neil ignored the irony.

"She said the hotel doesn't get many visitors -"

"No shit?"

"She said it doesn't get many visitors. But could just

be that it's selective, you know, exclusive. Could be one of those places that people get to hear about it through personal recommendation only. You do a hard sell on a place like that and, bingo, the place loses its prestige."

"So I can forget the Starlight campaign?"

Neil glanced at him, but didn't bother to reply.

"No campaign then. Don't want any visitors swamping the place."

"So it's quiet. So what? We don't like crowds."

"No, only the most selective and exclusive bunkhouses for us."

"It'll be fine," said Neil, becoming exasperated, "and it's only for a few days."

Dave smiled.

"It's OK, man. I'm just messing with you. I mean, how bad can it be, right?" Dave was already moving on, "It's going to be so great meeting up with your friends. I want to get all, and I do mean all, the dirt on your past. There must be some good stories; you can't have been so middle aged all your life."

"I'm not middle aged. I'm jaded, what can I say?"

"Yeah, yeah, I know; you've seen it all, you've been everywhere, done everything and bought the Brando. I know."

"Brando?"

"Yeah. Streetcar named Desire."

"You're weird, you know that?"

"No. It's the T shirt," Dave grinned, "Just a fantasy of mine. Go on."

Neil gave Dave a quizzical look.

"You are weird. But, let me tell you, I am not middle-aged. I've just seen it all in my time. Nothing much impresses or excites me any more."

"I'd keep that one to yourself if I were you. Don't think you'll stay at the top of the greasy legal heap with that attitude."

"Firstly, no one describes heaps, legal or otherwise as being greasy. Poles or ladders maybe, but heaps, no. And, second, thank you, but I can still function perfectly well as a brilliant lawyer. I may not be impressed by anything anymore, but I can fake impressed with impressive sincerity."

Dave looked across at Neil, wondering for a fleeting moment just what else in Neil's life might be a fake. For the briefest of instants, Dave even allowed himself a tiny doubt as to Neil's feelings for him. In insecure moments like this it seemed to Dave that Neil could be altogether too rational and detached than was good for either of them.

15

Jeff turned off the engine and sank back in his seat, glad that the long drive was over. His passengers were slowly rousing themselves; the adults with much stretching and yawning, the children with instant, wide-eyed excitement. As they clambered out, they had their first chance to check out the hotel. The building was low, only two floors, and was constructed almost entirely of wood. It was surrounded by an area of open grass, straw-pale and dry after the long, hot summer. With delighted shrieks, Lisa and Michael ran across the grass to the play area with its wooden climbing frame. Emma hung back with the adults, the recent glimpse of her gentler nature once again hidden beneath her more familiar scowl.

Annie picked up her bags and swept into the hotel, the doors banging noisily behind her. Bill hung back, obviously uncertain about leaving the kids out of doors and unsupervised. He caught Rita looking at him, smiled and shrugged,

"You go on in," he said, "I'm just going to stay out here for a while, with the kids."

Rita and Jeff exchanged questioning looks.

"Go on," Bill insisted, "You must be beat; you've been driving for hours."

"OK," said Jeff, turning to his daughter, "You coming

Em?"

Emma shrugged but said nothing.

"Em?"

Still nothing. Tired and irritable after all the driving, Jeff could feel his temper begin to rise.

"Emma," said Rita, intervening quickly, "Emma, I just wanted to say thank you; you did a great job with Lisa and Mikey. It had to be so cramped back there, but you kept those two happy the whole trip. You did a really good thing. Thanks."

Bill nodded in agreement.

"Yeah, thanks Emma," he said, with feeling, "Those two can be hard work sometimes. Believe me, I know."

"So," Rita continued, "why don't you stay out here a while and get some fresh air. Perhaps come on in with Bill and the kids when you're ready?" she looked at Bill, checking this was OK. He nodded, "Great. We'll see you both later."

Behind her, Jeff slammed the trunk shut and grabbed at his bags, frustrated at having missed the holiday's first opportunity to improve things with Em. He was furious with himself for not having thought to congratulate her himself. He wished he'd thought to tell her how proud he felt, seeing her looking after the younger kids. He wanted her to know that he'd noticed how kind and gentle she had been. But it was too late; to say anything now would just look insincere. He was aware of Em looking at him, expecting something, but he turned and followed Rita without a word. Behind him, Em kicked the dusty earth in disgust.

"Yeah Dad, thanks for that."

Alone in the lobby, Annie was waiting at the reception desk. She was drumming her fingers on the polished wood, indignant, shifting her weight from foot to foot like some caged animal; ready to pounce. She was seething, ready to complain forcefully to the receptionist, whenever the unfortunate made his or her appearance.

Jeff and Rita came in.

"I've rung the bell already," Annie said, "but the place is deserted. Well, I guess this is what you get if you book into some dump out in the backwoods of Hicksville."

She paused, frowning; Jeff and Rita had both suddenly looked away. Why? Oh, damn! They'd chosen the venue for this reunion hadn't they? Damn, damn, damn!

"Sorry," she said apologetically, trying to retrieve the situation, "No, really, I am sorry. This place is great, and the scenery round here? Wow! Fantastic, magnificent, I mean, really spectacular. Lots of, you know, trees. I like trees."

'Damn', she thought, 'that was lame', but she battled on.

"We are all going to have a really, really great time here," she turned back to the desk, "That's if someone will just come and give us our damn keys."

Jeff and Rita nodded their forgiveness. They were used to Annie speaking impulsively without the prior engagement of her brain. She was volatile, unpredictable and somewhat self-absorbed, but that had always been part of her make up, part of her particular charm. While Rita waited for Annie's patience to fail again, she took in their surroundings. The room was homey rather than grand; a lobby designed not to impress, but to welcome. The walls, floor, chairs and desk were all made from a smooth, golden wood and, over the stone-built fireplace, a large, hand woven rug added rich reds and yellows to the palette. A family portrait; smiling mother, father and pretty, teenage daughter, hung next to the door behind the desk. Rita liked this place. It felt good.

Patience exhausted, Annie was just about to ring again,

when, with a gentle click, the door opened and the father from the portrait came through, to welcome them all to his hotel. His smile was so genuine and his manner so apologetic, that Annie's anger simply dissipated.

"I'm so sorry you were kept waiting," he said, nodding to each in turn, "but I'm afraid my wife is very sensitive, very easily distressed, and she's always anxious when guests are arriving. I was just persuading her to go have a rest for an hour or two. I do hope I didn't keep you waiting too long."

"Waiting? No. No problem," said Annie expansively, signing the register with a flourish.

Behind her, Rita and Jeff shook their heads in disbelief.

"In my business," Annie continued, "there's a lot of hanging around, waiting for things to happen. You just have to take it. No sense in getting stressed over it."

Rita and Jeff exchanged amused, knowing glances, as the hotel owner obligingly picked up Annie's implicit invitation to ask more.

"What business is that, Miss…er," he looked down at the register, "Clearwater?"

Annie waited a second, but the name obviously didn't mean anything to him. He merely held her gaze and continued to smile expectantly. Normally this lack of recognition would have rankled, but Annie reminded herself that the man lived out here in the middle of - well, not even in the middle of, but miles outside of - nowhere. How could he be expected to know about an upcoming singing star? She decided to bestow on him one of her most glowing smiles.

"I'm a singer," she said simply, "some jazz, some blues. I've been very lucky and the people seem to like what they hear."

She was well used to the response that these few,

affectedly casual words normally provoked; it seemed that everyone, no matter their age or status, thrilled at just being close to, actually talking to, someone in show business. It gave them a glimpse beyond their everyday lives, a glimpse of something altogether more wonderful and desirable, and, for them, wholly unattainable. Being with Annie was their chance to shine, if only with reflected glamour. With suitably self-effacing humility, Annie would let them know that she was one of the charmed, golden few, then she would wait for the lips to form the 'Ooo' and the eyes to open wide with excitement. For her part, she delighted in their reaction, basking in their childlike adulation. She couldn't get enough of it. Recognition and applause had become like drugs to her.

Pleasingly, even this hotel owner, who lived about as far from the centre of all things cultural as Annie reckoned it was possible to be, was not beyond the seductive reach of show business glamour. He looked gratifyingly impressed and asked her to tell him more about her work. Annie was happy to oblige, warming to her favourite topic of conversation: herself. Jeff and Rita signed in almost unnoticed, save for a cursory smile and nod from the man as he handed them their keys.

Once in their room, they fell laughing onto the bed.

"God!" said Rita, first to recover, "Lil' Annie just lurves that star treatment. But, and this is what I think makes her so very, very special, Annie always has time for the little people. Y'know, it is truly educational watching her work her charm on them."

"Educational. That it is," said Jeff coughing with the last of his laughter, "but it's harmless enough. She needs reassurance from them and they just want to be associated with greatness."

"Greatness? Excuse me, but have you heard that lady sing the blues?"

"Oh, c'mon now," Jeff protested, "she's good at what she does."

"You reckon?"

"Sure."

"Then how come she's still playing such small gigs?"

"Dunno. But she did say she has a dedicated fan base."

"She should see a proctologist about that."

Laughing, Jeff threw a pillow at her and they fell into each other's arms. Their exhaustion from the journey soon forgotten.

16

The final members of the reunion party had not yet reached Losien.

Their car was moving slowly along the highway, forcing all in the long line of cars behind them to pull out one by one to get past. In the front passenger seat sat Phil; a large man, muscular rather than overweight, with small grey eyes, a heavy, square jaw and close cut, greying hair. He was frowning out at the scrub and trees lumbering slowly by and his glowering expression was not improved when, yet again, the occupants of one of the overtaking cars hooted derisively and gestured obscenely before speeding away. Phil couldn't take much more of this.

"Lou, for the love of God, will you stop the car and let me drive?"

Lou, a rather beautiful young woman, kept her eyes fixed firmly on the road ahead as she answered.

"There's no need, Honey, I'm fine. I'm not tired at all."

"Did I ask you if you're tired? Do I look like I care if you're tired or not?"

Lou allowed her eyes to flick across to his for just a second.

"Well thank you Mr. Congeniality."

"The answer is no, I don't care," Phil's fists were clenched, "What I do care about is you driving so freakin' slow. If you don't put your foot down we are never gonna get there."

"Oh you silly thing. Of course we'll get there and more importantly, we'll get there in safety."

"You can overdo the safety thing," said Phil quickly, "and right now I'm all for screwing safety. I'd rather just **get** there."

"Shh. Why don't you try to relax, maybe take a nap?" said Lou, smiling, soothing. Irritating.

That was it.

Phil hated that tone, the measured, patient tone that told him Lou had not the slightest idea of how much she was bugging him. She was really bugging him, and not for the first time. Over the years Phil had come to realise that being oblivious to the way you were irritating other people was a trait common to all the women in his life. That's a problem with these good looking babes, he thought; because they expect life to go their way, they just have no clue about the real world and how to deal with people. Lou thought the world should be pretty and sweet, so she just poured honey onto everything till it fitted into her way of seeing things. She thought that sugary tone would calm him, make him forget the last three hours spent crawling along, suffering the abuse of other road users. Three hours of getting nowhere, painfully slowly. Phil tried hard to keep the irritation out of his voice.

He failed.

"I don't wanna take a nap. I don't wanna relax," he spat through clenched teeth, banging his fist on the dashboard, "I just wanna get to this freakin' hotel before next freakin' year!"

Lou was outraged.

"Phil! Ethan!" she hissed, "Don't talk like that in front

of him."

"The kid's asleep, for chrissake, so I'll speak anyway I choose. Now, will you please pull over right now and let me drive?"

For a moment more, Lou dug her perfect, pretty nails into the wheel and wondered whether she should refuse to acknowledge such boorish behaviour. It would go against all her instincts for correction and self-improvement if her distaste of further unpleasantness were to allow Phil to have things his way. And besides, he wasn't a particularly good driver himself. He was the one who had reversed into the trash cans this morning. And then there was Ethan, gorgeous little Ethan, currently asleep in his car seat behind her. Ethan had to be protected from all danger, and that obviously included fast cars. However, Lou could also see that Phil was working himself into one of his moods. If she made him promise to drive carefully, she reasoned, it would probably be OK.

"Alright. But you must promise to drive carefully. Dr. Hoffmeyer writes about the long-term psychological impact of even mild physical trauma in infancy. I've got his book here in my suitcase, if you'd like to read it later on."

"Lou, he's in a car seat for chrissake. Strapped into a freakin' car seat. So Hoffmeyer can just go fu -"

"Phil, that's enough! OK, I'll pull over."

As Phil, still scowling, pulled out into traffic, Lou checked back on Ethan, sleeping contentedly in his car seat. She smiled. Her son was the very centre of her life. She was daily overwhelmed with wonder at him and she could hardly remember a time before she'd had him. Looking at him now, his head back, hot, rosy cheeks pressed against the side pillow, little plum mouth open wide, and his whole body relaxed and peaceful, she felt that smile, close to tears, lighten her face. As always, she tried to fix this image of him in her mind, knowing that he would be growing up, and away from her, all too soon.

She sighed and turned back to Phil, her head still awash with warm, peaceful love for her son. Almost drowsily, she asked,

"You will drive carefully, won't you Sweetie?"

That tone again!

Phil slammed his foot down on the gas and the car leapt forward, pushing them both back into their seats. Lou gasped.

Grim-faced, Phil had had enough.

Dave and Neil had arrived at the hotel. For a few moments they contemplated the building in silence. Neil was obviously unimpressed, but Dave was determined to be positive.

"OK," he said, "it's not the Hilton, but it's not Grizzly Adams' cabin either."

"No, Grizzly's place would at least win one star for authenticity."

"Oh, come on man. It's rustic, it's charming, it's..."

"Yeah?"

"...only for a week."

"I guess."

"Come on, let's go see what pleasures await us within."

Dave was already out of the car and wrenching his luggage from the back seats.

"Dave, are you on something?"

The manager greeted them in the lobby.

"Some of your party are already here, sir, but there's no one in the lounge yet, so I imagine they're still in their rooms. Could I ask you to sign in please?"

Neil down put his cell phone and picked up the pen to

sign in for both of them.

"I'm afraid you won't be able to use that here, sir. There's no reception this far away from town."

Neil fixed the manager with an angry glare.

"If I lose the murder case because the firm can't contact me this week, someone will pay."

Dave tried to placate him.

"Come on man, we're on our holidays; who needs a cell phone? But I'm sure," he said, looking to the manager for confirmation, "there's a phone here in the hotel for emergencies."

The manager was happy to concur.

"Certainly is, sir. Just through this door. In the office."

"How charmingly last century," Neil muttered, sweeping up his useless cell phone.

Dave smiled apologetically and led Neil away.

Once in their room, Neil unpacked his overnight bag while Dave agonised over what to wear.

"Wear whatever you like," said Neil unhelpfully.

"What are you wearing?"

"I'll wear one of the shirts you bought me at the five and dime."

"You like them? Oh great. I was worried because their range was limited and the shade...Not too dull?"

"No. Dull is fine. Thank you."

"OK, if we're going native then..."

Dave was soon sporting blue jeans and a bright orange shirt.

"You paid money for that?" Neil asked, in obvious disbelief.

"The saleswoman said it's a hunter's shirt."

"So give it back to the hunter, it's godawful."

"No, it's supposed to be this bright. It's so's you don't get yourself shot by accident."

"Oh yeah? Well don't worry about that, you won't be shot by accident; you'll be shot by someone with good dress sense, aiming very carefully."

"Oh ha ha. Very droll. Thank you so much."

"Here," Neil threw Dave one of his own new shirts, "wear this."

"I don't wanna," said Dave, playfully throwing it back.

Neil grabbed it out of the air and held it scrunched in his fist.

"Wear it!"

"No, it's OK man, I'm beginning to quite like this," Hands on hips, Dave gave a catwalk model flounce, "Come on tell me, you think orange could be the new black?"

Neil didn't even look up.

"Just get that thing off," he said, "and wear this."

Dave was beginning to feel pressured. Why was Neil making such a big deal out of this?

"No man, I don't want to wear your shirt. I'm cool in this."

"Just wear the fuckin' shirt! I don't want to introduce you to my friends all dressed up like some fuckin' fruit."

Dave was stunned. Where had that little explosion come from? What the hell was up with Neil? Slowly, Dave reached out and took the shirt, then he stood for a moment, staring down at it.

"If it means that much to you…" he muttered.

"It does."

There was an awkward moment of silence between them, then Dave said,

"OK man, I'll wear the shirt."

Dave didn't look at Neil as he turned away. He'd been stung by Neil's sudden outburst but he didn't want him to know how much his words had hurt. Much as he loved him, he didn't want to give Neil that satisfaction.

Phil, Lou and little Ethan had finally reached Losien.

Phil was sitting at the counter in the diner, stirring a cup of coffee. He'd been slowly stirring it for at least three minutes, his mind elsewhere. After all this thought, he had decided that Annie's idea of getting everyone together for this reunion week had been a mistake. Or, at least, his bringing Lou and the kid had been a mistake. They were in the washroom now and Phil was sitting on a stool from which he could see the washroom door, but he knew Lou wouldn't be coming out any time soon. This was the fourth stop they'd had to make since he'd taken over the driving. Ethan was too hot. Ethan was too cold. Ethan was hungry. Ethan was thirsty. Jeez that kid was a royal pain in the ass. And right now Lou was probably breastfeeding him too. She'd promised she'd stop that, hell, the kid was two years old! But Phil was sure she carried on when he wasn't around to see. The bond between those two was way too intense. That kid was going to turn out weird. No question about it.

Phil should have left them back at home for the week. Yeah sure, like he had a choice. Hell, he might as well be married for all the freedom he had. And it's not like the kid was even his.

His spoon ground harder into the base of the coffee cup.

Phil was feeling very low, life had dumped on him again. Intent on wallowing in self-pity, he conveniently chose to forget that Lou hadn't actually wanted to come on the trip. 'Go have a great time,' she'd said. 'We'll be just fine,' she'd said. But Phil had wanted her there with him, this beautiful young woman, a real babe, on his arm. That'd show the rest of them, with their careers and their big houses and their goddam happy freakin' families. But then the kid had to come along too. Always the kid, with his crying and his puking and his stinking diapers.

Goddamit, he hated that kid.

He continued stirring the cooling coffee in stony silence.

The woman behind the counter was drying some glasses with slow thoroughness, occasionally holding one up to the light. But all the while, out of the corner of her eye, she was watching the guy with the coffee. She didn't like the look of him; he looked moody and powerful, angry, and his eyes were way too small. And that coffee stirring? How irritating was that? She watched Oprah; she knew about obsessive-compulsives, and this guy sure fitted the bill. But she'd missed the end of that particular show, so she now had a nagging worry that it might have concluded that obsessive-compulsives go on to become psychotic. But no, looking at him again she decided, based on nothing more than a hunch, that he was just a big lug, probably harmless enough. And not too bright. She'd stiffed him with his change when he paid for his coffee and though he'd frowned for a moment, staring at the notes in his palm, he hadn't said a word.

And they say that living in the city makes you sharp! A few more customers like this one and she could make a living wage.

17

There had been a knock at the door, but Jeff and Rita hadn't heard. So when, seconds later, the door suddenly opened and Emma stood there staring at them, utterly appalled, they were taken completely by surprise. They simply froze and stared right back at her. Jeff was the first to snap out of it. He pulled a sheet across to cover his bare buttocks and tried to get up, but his pants were bunched around his feet and he fell towards Emma, sprawling headlong onto the floor. She shrieked and quickly stepped back, out into the corridor. Still backing away, she mumbled some hasty apology then fled.

From his prone position on the floor, Jeff stretched an arm to push the door closed, then let his head sink to the floor.

"Oh God," he moaned, "Oh God."

Feeling as embarrassed as he had ever been in his life, he lay there, a sad crumpled, faintly ridiculous figure, wrapped and tangled in the sheet like an overgrown chrysalis unexpectedly fallen from its branch. But, in the depths of his personal hell, Jeff was amazed to hear giggling. What? He struggled clumsily to his feet, tripping repeatedly on the knotted sheet. What? Rita was giggling! Jeff was hugely indignant; what the hell was there to laugh about? Desperate to retain some dignity, he tried to pull up his pants whilst also attempting to keep the bed sheet tight around him. It was hard work. And, all the while, Rita giggled helplessly. She had fallen back into the pillows, trying to stop the noise by covering her face with her hands. But it was no use, she simply had to laugh. If you couldn't undo or take back what had happened, you might just as well try to see the funny side of it.

But, to Jeff, the funny side of this particular situation seemed a very long way off. And still Rita laughed.

"Will you please stop," he begged.

Rita sat up and nodded furiously, holding her hands still tighter over her mouth. But the giggles continued. Jeff pulled himself up to his full height and wore his most serious face; the one that he imagined lent an air of authority to his delivery when he was lecturing. He cleared his throat to speak.

"Rita, I see nothing even remotely funny in this situation."

That was too much. The sight of her husband trying to be pompous whilst wrestling both with his half-mast pants and a tangled bed sheet, was too much for Rita. She fell back and erupted with renewed laughter. Jeff hobbled to the bathroom.

By the time he came out, Rita was calm once more.
"You OK?" she asked.
"Me? Me? You're the one who was manic."
"Sorry, but you must admit, it was very funny."
"No, Ree. It was not funny."
He pulled on a sock.
"Where are you going?" she asked.
"To find Em of course."
"To say what?"
"God, I don't know. But I've got to say something."
"OK, just give me a minute, I'll come with you."
"No," he said quickly, "You stay here. I want to speak

to her alone."

Rita had paused as she got out of the bed. Sitting at the edge of the bed, she absorbed what Jeff had said and then settled back into the pillows, pulling the sheet up over her.

"OK. Good luck."

"Sure, thanks."

"Jeff?"

"Yes"

"What **are** you going to say to her?"

"I've told you, I don't know. I'll think of something. See you later."

Annie looked up from her armchair in the lounge and saw Neil and Dave standing at the door, looking like extras from the Python's lumberjack sketch.

"Neil?" she shrieked, "Neil, is that you?"

Dave noticed an almost imperceptible shiver pass through Neil's body.

"Yes, Annie, of course it's me," said Neil, his voice giving away none of the distaste that Dave had read in that shudder, "Who else would it be? Hi...Is Phil here yet?"

"No, not yet. Come on over," she whined childishly, patting the seat next to hers, "I've got no one to talk to."

Reluctantly, Neil walked over, but Dave hung back, unsure of the dynamics at play between these two.

"And who's this?" said Annie spotting him. She beckoned for Dave to come over. Neil looked back.

"Oh yeah. This is Dave."

"Well, hello Dave," said Annie, lavishing one of her most radiant smiles on him. She loved meeting Neil's latest pretty boys. And this one was very pretty. Such a pity, she thought, ruefully, that all the best looking guys were gay. She smiled at Dave again and saw him awkwardly return her smile. He was naïve this one, she thought, not the self-possessed, Teflon egos that Neil usually attracted. He looked vulnerable somehow. It was with a momentary twinge of regret that she wondered how long this one would last.

Annie was distracted from this line of thought by Neil asking her how her music was going. Neil then sat back and let the tide of Annie's self-obsessed chatter wash over him. For the next half hour or so, he had little cause to say a word; simply raising an eyebrow from time to time seemed sufficient encouragement for Annie to continue. And Dave, normally so talkative, was all but silent as Annie enthused and expounded on her soon-to-be glittering singing career, without any apparent need to pause for breath. Dave shifted in his chair, waiting for the topic of conversation to change. Even had he been able to interject, he could have contributed little to Annie's monologue as he'd never heard of the mid town venues she mentioned and, perhaps against type, he had never cared for the music of the great jazz divas. But, much as he wanted to divert the conversation, Dave wasn't yet sufficiently sure of this friend of Neil's to interrupt her. What Dave couldn't understand was why Neil wasn't saying anything. Why wasn't he bursting to tell this woman about the two of them and their new life together? In fact, rather than wanting to tell Annie about the new love in his life, surely his biggest piece of news since they'd last met, Neil seemed to have forgotten that Dave was even in the room.

Eventually, Annie and Neil barely noticing, Dave excused himself and left. If the rest of Neil's old friends were like this one, Dave wasn't sure he'd be able to cope with the week. Back home, in the familiar surroundings of the ad agency and the vibrant city that was the background to his world, Dave felt, and exuded, an easy, extrovert confidence. But here, away from the city, in the company of Neil's oldest friends and the echoes of his life way back before Dave, the situation was proving very different. Here, Neil was Dave's sole familiar point of reference and Dave realised that he was totally dependent on Neil in a way that he never had been before.

Soon after meeting Neil for the first time, just three months ago, Dave had come to believe that they were made for each other, needed each other and would be able to give each other all the support and reassurance they would ever need. Yet even then, Dave had always been confident in his own separate role, his own abilities and his own, individual place in their world. Until now, he had always managed every situation. At the agency, he was respected; he was good at what he did and he knew it. So, for Dave, this feeling of being out of his natural environment, and alone, was horribly unsettling.

He decided to take a walk, to clear his head.

Bill was still outside, watching the kids playing on the climbing frame. They seemed oblivious to the chill in the air but Bill, who had on a thick jacket, was stamping his feet to keep warm. Looking up, he nodded at Dave, inadvertently obliging him to come over and introduce himself, though he would rather have had a few quiet moments alone.

"Hi."

They shook hands.

"Hi. I'm Bill."

"Hi. Dave. I'm… I'm here with Neil."

"Oh, where is he?"

"He's inside, with Annie," said Dave, "…so he could be some time."

"Talking is she?" said Bill with a smile.

"God, is she ever. Does that woman ever stop?"

Bill smiled again.

"Believe it or not," he said, "her talking hides a lack of confidence."

"Certainly hides it well," said Dave, "I tell you, she was non-stop."

Bill decided he'd better stop Dave before he dug himself too deep a hole.

"Annie's my wife," he said simply.

Dave winced with embarrassment and raised his hands apologetically.

"Man. I'm sorry."

"Don't be," Bill smiled again, "It's OK, really."

Now Dave didn't know what to say.

"You see," Bill explained, "Annie has to believe in herself. She's trying to make a career in a really tough business and she has to fight every step of the way. But deep down...deep, deep down, the poor girl is full of self-doubt. Try not to be too hard on her."

"Yeah man. I'm sorry."

"Don't worry about it."

"Yeah, but-"

"No. No buts. It's OK. Annie can sometimes be a little overwhelming, believe me, I know."

"Thanks man," Dave paused, "Think I'll take a walk now. Catch you later?"

"Sure, later," said Bill, still smiling.

Jeff was outside Emma's room, knocking on the door for a third time.

"Em," he pleaded, in an urgent, shouted whisper, "will you please let me in? Em, we should talk."

There was still no response and the door remained locked. He considered getting the manager to use a master key to open it, but no, he'd rather deal with this himself. There was no need to get anyone else involved;

he was embarrassed enough as it was. He listened in vain for some word, or any sign from the other side of the door, but there was nothing. He gave up and returned to his room.

From the edge of the clearing Dave wandered into the forest, following a narrow path that rose ahead of him. It might be cool out in the open, but under the trees the air was noticeably colder. He began to walk more quickly to keep warm. As the path crested a ridge, Dave looked down at a series of waterfalls and pools.

"Cool!" he whispered, something of his usual enthusiasm returning, "Now that is cool."

"Who's there?"

Dave was startled. Who had spoken? It sounded like a girl's voice.

"Hello?" he said, looking around.

"Who are you?"

"Dave...Dave Lowell. I'm staying at the hotel."

"How long have you been here?"

"We arrived this afternoon."

"No. I mean how long have you been here, in the woods?" asked the voice.

"I just got here."

"You weren't following me?"

"What? No," said Dave, confused, "Why would I be following you?"

He was sure the voice was to his left, so was again startled when a girl stepped from behind a rock directly in front of him. Dressed all in black, her face very pale, it was Emma.

"Don't know, but something started following me after I got into the trees," she said, "It kept creeping towards me," she shuddered, "I ran away, but it just came creeping after me. I was so scared. I just ran and hid here. Then you came," she stepped closer and looked up at him, "Can I walk back to the hotel with you?"

"Sure," said Dave, alarmed at what she was telling him, tensing as he scanned the rocks and undergrowth for any movement, "What was it, d'you know?"

"Jeez, I don't know; a wolf, a bear? Maybe a stalker. I don't know. I didn't see it. I only heard it. But it was big, I know that much," she tugged at his sleeve, "Please, can we go now?"

Em was shaking and obviously very frightened. Her fear was infectious and, beneath his borrowed shirt, Dave could feel the hairs on his arms and at the back of his neck begin to tingle. He looked around, listening carefully, wary, as he offered Em his hand and helped her scramble back up the ridge. As they made their way back along the path every snapping twig and creaking branch had them both jumping, panicked, nerves alert to any sign of pursuit. They didn't stop to investigate any of the sounds, but hurried on as quickly as possible, almost running until they burst through the trees at the edge of the clearing.

Once back in the weak sunlight, they slowed down and Emma began to relax a little. She let go of his hand.

"What did you say your name was?"

"Dave."

"Thanks for the rescue Dave," she said, with a weak and unconvincing laugh. She felt foolish now for having let herself get so frightened back there in the forest, "Guess I must have imagined it, yeah?"

"You think so?"

"Yeah. Yeah, sorry. Please, can we forget it? I'm Emma, by the way. I'm here with my Dad."

"Is your Dad still in the forest? Should we go find him, let him know you're safe?"

"No, he's back in the hotel," said Emma, her face

falling into a sullen glower, "humping my stepmom."

Dave winced. Kids sure were open about things these days. He was lost for words. Had he heard her right?

"I walked in on them," Em continued, "God, it was so gross! And Dad got up but he was all tangled up in the sheets and he fell over right in front of me, right on the floor. Jeez, he's such a dork!"

"Is that why you were out there?"

"Yeah."

"Did your Dad get angry?"

"Yeah."

"And… are you OK?"

Em guessed where the question was leading.

"No, he didn't get angry or hit me or anything. He never does anything like that. My Dad likes to talk any problem through, y'know? He goes on and on and on, saying everything like a million times, just to make sure you've got the point. No, he'd never go ballistic but it was just, y'know, really gross. I was **so** embarrassed. I mean, wouldn't you be, if you walked in on your Dad and his new wife?"

Dave was trying hard not to picture his father doing any such thing. He was feeling out of his depth talking with this girl.

"I…don't know," he mumbled, "I guess."

"I just don't know what I'm gonna do when I see him next, that's all. It's gonna be awful."

Dave was no longer adrift: he could help with this. He found himself repeating words spoken to him, many years before, by his doting and, for the times, very tolerant aunt. His father had exploded in one of his rages, shouting some truly terrible things, but Dave had taken Aunt Sarah's advice then and, sure enough, his father had eventually accepted his only son's way of life. Mind you, this acceptance had taken nearly twelve years of silent patience on Dave's part. That, and his father's diagnosis with an inoperable cancer.

Dave said, "Emma, right now your father probably feels just as bad as you do, if not worse. Just wait; give him a chance to make things right, OK?"

Dave was somewhat disappointed to see that the words seemed to hold far less significance for Emma now than they had for him as a troubled fifteen year old. She simply shrugged.

"Yeah, right. Whatever."

Emma seemed to be completely recovered from her fright and, waving a goodbye to Dave, she hurried off to play with Lisa and Mikey. They welcomed her with joyful shrieks. Left alone, it took Dave a few seconds to shake off the memories of his dying father and of Aunt Sarah's gentle understanding. Then, looking around, he waved an acknowledgment to Bill, but avoided having to go over to exchange words by conveying, with a vigorous rubbing of his arms, that it was turning very cold and he had to go back inside.

Easy going as always, Bill waved a cheery farewell.

18

The sun was sinking below the tree tops before the last of the friends drew up at the isolated hotel.

Phil kicked open his door and climbed out of the car, stretching to release the stiffness from his limbs. Lou remained in her seat. She was still waiting on an apology from Phil for the aggression he'd shown throughout the journey. He was, it seemed to her, the worst of travellers; impatient, short-tempered and inconsiderate. She was only grateful that little Ethan had been asleep most of the time and hopefully had heard none of the appalling language Phil had been hurling towards other drivers at the least provocation. Lou had only known Phil for thirteen months and this trip had shown her a new side to his nature. A side she didn't care for. Indeed, she had already decided that, if she couldn't correct his anger management problem, if he refused to address it, then their relationship was not going to last. His apology now would be a first step along that path, the first hurdle.

Phil was known for not being the most empathic of individuals and yet he had realised that Lou was expecting something from him. If he had been honest with himself, he would even have acknowledged that she was probably waiting for an apology; he had perhaps been a little short with her today and, being the woman she was, she would probably have mistaken his natural eagerness to get here quickly, for impatience, or even anger. He could apologise. He didn't have to mean it and it would keep her happy; she would feel like she'd won the day. And that was the problem: Phil was nothing if not competitive. He was a sportsman, a high school football coach, and he knew that the whole of life was a game; once you started making concessions and letting the other guy get past you, you'd already lost it. He would keep his silence. Sure, Lou would be mad at first, but she'd get over it. Heck, she'd probably have forgotten all about it in an hour or two.

Phil hauled their bags and all the baby gear out of the car. He half-dragged, half-carried them all the way to the steps of the hotel and heaved them up to the doors. Still Lou made no move. Phil waited a moment for her. What was taking so long? Why did women have to take so long to do every little thing? Was it some cosmic law, set in their genes, or did they just do it to annoy him? Most likely the last, he thought with irritation. Shifting the bags to ease the strain on his arms, he decided to go on ahead: the load was too heavy for him to stand around unnecessarily and Lou would not be rushed. With a loud grunt, he wrestled all the luggage inside and let the doors bang shut behind him. At the sound, Lou's exasperation erupted into furious indignation. How dare he just walk off like that? How dare he…and without a word of apology for his appalling behaviour? She was breathing heavily, shaking with anger.

Minutes passed. The car creaked and groaned, cooling down after the day's long drive and, though Lou's face was hot and flushed, she soon began to feel the cold. She didn't want to trail into the hotel after Phil, as if everything was right between them, but she knew she couldn't stay out here either. The temperature was definitely dropping and, though Ethan was warm under his covering quilt, he could wake up at any minute now that the soothing rocking movement of the car had stopped. For his sake she would have to leave the car fairly soon, but she determined to try waiting just a few minutes more. Surely Phil must, by now, have realised that he should come out to check on them. When he did, he would see that she was upset and then he would apologise. That was worth waiting for. Lou could endure the shivering a while longer.

But the last rays of the sun had now gone as evening ebbed into night, and Phil had not reappeared. Lou wiped a window clear of condensation and looked out. Save for the few lights from the hotel, everything was black, a featureless, deep blue-blackness that she had never seen before. In the city there was always some neon or street-lighting, so the sky was never this colour. It was always orangey, a sort of dirty brown; people complained that the light pollution meant never seeing the stars. Looking out into the pitch darkness, Lou thought that, if those people knew how dark night really was, they'd never again complain about a few street lights. Lou leant forward and turned her head so as to look upwards through the cleared patch of glass, expecting to see a sky glittering with brilliant stars, but she saw nothing but more darkness. Another thing those people were wrong about.

It was clear to her now that Phil was not coming back. In the cramped space of the car, Lou pulled on her thick jacket. She fixed her purse over her shoulder and across her chest as she would need both hands free to carry Ethan safely into the hotel. Even warmly dressed, Lou felt the sudden drop in temperature as she climbed out of the car. The fast descending chill caught at her breath and made the skin of her face tingle. She would have to work quickly to get Ethan into the hotel before he was affected by the cold.

The darkness around her was total but she was neither concerned nor afraid until, going to the back to get Ethan, Lou felt something soft but icy cold touch her cheek.

She gasped.

"Phil?"

No response.

"Who's there?"

Her voice, sounding harsh and unexpectedly loud, hung metallic in the air, reverberating about her as if she were trapped in some cold, sealed chamber. And, if sounds were trapped, then no one would hear her if she called for help. Panic rising, Lou struggled to control her breathing, and listen.

Nothing.

Then, without a sound, the icy cold softness again brushed her cheek. Screaming, Lou hit out. Unable to see anything, she had no idea who or what had touched her. It was almost a breath, too light to be corporeal.

Half-remembered ghost stories and bad dreams from long ago came rushing back, convincing her that something malevolent was out here with her. Playing with her. Relishing her fear. This was an ancient forest and who knew what dreadful events could have happened right here? A restless spirit could haunt the place; a wronged ghost staying close to its mean, unmarked grave. Lou's imagination instantly filled with images of many such graves, all around her, perhaps the final resting places of a serial killer's victims. A mass grave could lie undiscovered here for years, centuries. Right now she could be surrounded by a shifting grey veil of wraiths, hidden in the blackness. Her eyes might be unable to see anything, but in her mind Lou could picture their dry, long-dead and sunken eyes staring right at her. Thin, pale faces concealed by the darkness, maybe only inches from her own. Lou could almost feel their wasted breath and their bony touch on her skin. She shivered uncontrollably.

She had to get to the hotel.

Leaping to the car, she wrenched open the door and fumbled blindly with the harness on Ethan's seat, frantically looking to left and right, utterly terrified. Scanning back and forth she glanced up.

At once, her agitated activity stopped. She froze, heedless of the drowsy child now squirming in her arms. Her face still upturned, Lou found herself blinking repeatedly, her eyes and lashes caressed by gently falling flakes.

It was snowing.

Overcome with relief, Lou slumped forward, her forehead melting the fine dusting of snow on the car's roof. She was trembling and laughing with relief, but also hugely embarrassed. She was thankful that no one had witnessed her foolishness. Shaking her head, she let the laughter dissipate the tension.

But then, looking around, Lou suddenly realised that the falling snow was already partially obscuring the few lights of the hotel. In a heartbeat, panic gripped her once more. Fearful of losing the path, she gathered up her son, pulling the quilt tight about him. Then, hunching protectively over him, she turned and stumbled in what she hoped was the direction of the hotel. She was desperate to hurry, but effectively blind in the near total darkness and thickening snowfall. Why had Phil parked so far from the building? Stupid, selfish man! It was vital to get Ethan into the hotel quickly. No one keeps a small child out in the cold: they don't regulate their body heat properly. Lou had read that. She'd read all the childcare manuals. Phil had refused to read any of them.

If he hadn't been so stubborn, he'd have known how

quickly babies can fall ill. Heck, everyone knows that. Everyone but Phil. Feeling increasing resentment towards the absent Phil, Lou was now angrily muttering her thoughts aloud. Disturbed by the noise, Ethan moaned and wriggled.

"Shh, Darling," Lou whispered, feeling her tears begin to form, "Mommy's here. Shh."

Reaching the hotel doors, Lou felt the stress of the long day's emotions overwhelm her: Phil's anger and impatience, his rudeness, all the swearing and shouting, and, above all, her own feelings of helplessness and her inability to make him calm down. All the day's frustrations swept over her as she stumbled into the lobby. She was gasping and crying, in such obvious distress that the man at the desk dropped his pen and ran over to help, putting an arm out to support her.

Lou was still sobbing and felt hugely relieved just to be safely in out of the cold and the dark, so she meekly allowed herself be led to an armchair. The man gently eased her down into the seat. Lou felt her knees bend with stiff reluctance beneath her. Her muscles felt rigid.

"Here, sit and rest a moment," the man said, "Can I get you anything?"

Lou shook her head.

"Are you here with the reunion party?" he asked.

Lou didn't reply immediately. She was beginning to recover and she took her time to consider how she might answer the man's question, given Phil's awful behaviour today. She thought she might tell him she had been with the party, but no longer wanted anything to do with them. Alternatively, she could deny any connection with Phil and his no doubt boorish friends, demand her own room and arrange a taxi for first light tomorrow. That would show Phil! But in the end she decided she was just too exhausted to be cantankerous. Also Phil wasn't around to hear her disassociating herself from him. Time enough for that later. Letting out a long breath, she leaned back into the enveloping support of the soft cushions.

"There's no hurry," said the man, his voice soothing and patient, "Take your time."

"It's OK. I'm OK now. Yes," she sighed, "we are here for the reunion. We're with Mr Calder."

"We?"

Lou pulled back the corner of the quilt to reveal Ethan sleeping contentedly on her lap. The man's face immediately creased into a smile, and that small show of appreciation towards her son was enough to restore Lou's spirits. She took a deep breath and stood up.

The man again reached for her elbow to steady her, but this time Lou eased her arm away. Some of her anger at Phil was coming back and right now she didn't want to accept help from any man.

"Thanks, you've been very kind, but I'm OK now, really. Could I please have my room key?"

The reunion party had booked all of the hotel's six rooms. With no remaining, unallocated bedrooms, Lou had no choice but to share the room she had previously booked with Phil. For the moment, she just wanted to go somewhere quiet to rest and decide what to do. But what if Phil was in the room? What would she say to him? She realised that they could be about to have their first real row. Trying to put that prospect out of her mind, Lou absently watched the man as he walked to the key cupboard behind the desk. Her eyes settled on the family portrait hanging by the door. This man was obviously the man in the photograph, although he now looked somewhat older. With him, in the photograph, were a young woman and a dark haired girl whose pretty faces shared a strong familial resemblance. They had to be mother and daughter.

"Is that your family?" Lou asked.

The man followed Lou's gaze to the photograph and nodded, but said nothing.

"Your daughter's very pretty."

Again the gentle smile.

"Hmm," he agreed at last, "just like her mother."

Lou nodded and smiled, although something of regret or sadness in the man's face made her smile seem inappropriate.

"I'm sorry," she said hurriedly, "Did you tell me your name?"

"John. This is my hotel, and this," he held out his hand, "is your key, Mrs Calder."

In assigning her Phil's surname, John had inadvertently reawakened her annoyance with Phil, but she tried to keep the irritation from her voice.

"Thank you John, and thank you for your help, but it's 'Miss'. And it's not 'Calder'; not now and, after the journey here today, maybe not ever. It's 'Beauchamp'," she added proudly, "And that's French."

The door swung open as Lou pushed her key into the lock. Phil was sprawled on the bed. He looked up lazily.

"Hi Babe, you took your time. Where d'ya get to?" he asked.

Lou, astonished at his casual lack of concern, was momentarily speechless. Then she found her voice, bitter and harsh through clenched teeth.

"I was out in the car, where you left us."

"What?"

"Out in the car, in the dark, without a word."

"What?"

"You left me, and Ethan, out there in the cold and the dark and you didn't come back for us. And now it's snowing, for God's sake."

"Snowing? Cool!"

Phil realised what he had said and laughed at his own supposed wit.

"Hey, how about that? Snowing - cool?"

"Phil!"

"Hey, yeah. Sorry Babe, I thought you came in right after me," he said, bafflement obvious in his dumb frown, "What happened?"

Lou was furious. Did she have to spell it out? He should have known that she was waiting out there for him to apologise for the way he had behaved. Surely that was obvious.

But Phil continued to stare at her, completely blank.

"For God's sake," she hissed, exasperated, "I was waiting for you to say you're sorry for the way you've been acting all day."

"Huh?"

Lou was still standing just inside the door, Ethan in her arms, the words pouring out. And she could feel tears beginning to prick at her eyes.

"Don't you 'huh' me," she shouted, "like you don't know what I'm talking about. You left us out there because you were in a mean mood, selfish, like you've been all day: aggressive, impatient and just plain ornery from the start."

Though justly famed for his insensitivity, Phil at least had the good sense not to smile at the word 'ornery', though Lou was the only person he'd ever met who still used it in regular conversation. Normally it amused him. But now was definitely not the time to smile, that much even he had grasped from the palpable tension in the room. However, he could see no real need for him to apologise; the journey here had been long and tiring and he'd had to be forceful, but no more than that. And it had only been because he wanted to get here before nightfall…as much for the sake of the kid as for himself. Phil was pleased with that last thought. It was inspired. And, if he kept saying it to himself over and over, he knew he would come to believe it was actually true: that the only motivation behind his impatience to get here quickly had been to avoid little Ethan's routine being upset.

Phil considered sharing the thought with Lou. She'd like that. She always softened when he showed some consideration for, or said something nice about the kid. I mean, sure, no way was he going to apologise for no reason, but the lie would be close enough to an apology, without actually being one.

However, before he could tell Lou how selfless his actions had been, he realised that she was close to tears.

Great!

Now, this was a situation Phil knew how to handle. No need to think this one through. With a practised look of apparent concern he took Ethan from Lou's stiffened arms and laid the child, still sleeping, onto the bed. Then, shushing softly under his breath, he put his big, strong arms around Lou and held her close. At first she resisted, but he held her tight, almost crushing her to him and he felt her body relax as he knew it would. She let her head drop forward onto his chest and began to cry, releasing all the emotion of the day, letting it wash away in hot tears. Phil held her for some time, softly whispering platitudes and gently shushing as if to a child, until the sobbing finally subsided.

"That's it Babe," he said, "Just lean on me. Everything's gonna be OK."

Phil loved this feeling. There was no intellectual challenge involved here, no need to try to understand the other person's motives, no need actually to care about the other person at all. It was a feeling of power, and not just the raw power of almost crushing Lou's fragile frame in his embrace, but also the fantastic power of being in total emotional control of another person. Lou was really no more than a child and she needed him. She was so young and weak and helpless. She needed his strength. Phil smiled. He liked his women like this; beautiful but flawed, sexy certainly, but needy and utterly dependent on him. And, right now, he was finding Lou's weakness and vulnerability intensely arousing. He didn't stop to consider her feelings, or question the appropriateness of his timing. He wanted her right now. He leant down and kissed her neck, arrogant, knowing that he had completely won her over. She wouldn't refuse him. He could be as rough as he liked and he knew she wouldn't even feign resistance. Lou turned her tear-stained face up to his and shut her eyes, yielding control to him. Phil lowered her onto the thick rug next to the bed, pushing away her clothes.

Breathless and urgent, they had sex, there on the rug, below the sleeping baby.

Dave had rejoined Annie and Neil in the lounge, but Neil hadn't seemed particularly pleased to see him again. Annie gave him the warmer welcome, patting the chair to her right, inviting Dave to sit. So he sat there, opposite Neil and wondered what to say. For several minutes there was only silence between them and Dave became very conscious of the regular quiet ticking of the clock. Finally Annie spoke, turning to Dave.

"Where did you get to?"

"I went out for a walk. I met Bill and a girl called Emma."

"Is he still outside?" she asked.

"I guess. But it's getting real cold. I think he'll have to come back in soon."

"Emma?" said Neil, with no real interest, "That's Jeff's daughter isn't it?"

"Uhuh," said Annie, "Must be twelve or thirteen by now."

"She looks a lot older," said Dave, "Talks older too. Either that, or twelve year old kids today know a hell of a lot more than I did at that age."

"What do you mean?"

"Oh nothing," said Dave hastily, rather wishing he hadn't said anything.

"Do tell," said Neil, intrigued.

"It's nothing; just something Emma said, about her parents," Dave was having to suppress a smile, "It's not important."

But Annie and Neil both fixed their gaze on him expectantly, eager for something new to talk about and Dave felt a ridiculous thrill at finally being the focus of their combined interest. With only a moment's further hesitation, he determined to hold on to that attention by telling Emma's story and perhaps improving the anecdote with a few embellishments along the way.

A few moments later, Jeff and Rita came into the lounge, attracted by laughter from the trio by the window. Annie looked up, saw them, and nudged Neil and Dave.

"That's Jeff," she whispered to Dave.

They looked up and their laughter immediately died to a splutter.

Jeff felt the colour flood his cheeks. They knew! Emma must have told them and now they were all laughing at him. Beside him, Rita must have come to the same conclusion because she was grinning down at her shoes. Infuriatingly, she still found this funny.

"OK, ha, ha, have a good laugh at my expense," he said, "But, just you wait, Annie; your two will soon be old enough to think the idea of you and Bill having sex is just as appalling."

"Don't worry, dear," said Annie, "I think the idea of me and Bill having sex is appalling."

"Her word was 'gross' actually," Dave whispered.

"Well thank you!" said Annie, indignant.

"No," said Dave, "not you and Bill, I meant Jeff and…"

"Rita," said Rita, extended her hand to Dave, "And that would be me."

Now it was Dave's turn to be embarrassed. He stood up and took the proffered hand, smiling lamely at Rita.

"And you are?" she asked.

"Dave, Dave Lowell. I'm here with Neil."

Somehow he felt self-conscious, saying those words in Neil's presence, as if Neil might suddenly contend the assertion. But Neil merely raised a hand in a limp wave to Jeff and Rita.

"Come children, join us," he said languorously, with another tired but elegant wave.

Jeff was still embarrassed and indignant. He was inclined quite literally to make a stand, but Rita tugged at his hand.

"Oh come on," she said, "lighten up."

Rita let go of his hand and drew two chairs over.

"That's right," said Annie, "you're amongst friends, and at least one parent and fellow sufferer. So come sit, tell us all your news…or at least all that's fit to publish."

At this last, Dave, Rita and Annie began laughing again. Even Neil raised an amused eyebrow. Jeff had reluctantly to accept his being the butt of the joke. There was nothing to do but try to take it gracefully.

"I guess it's good to see you two," he said to Neil and Annie. Then, with more sincerity, to Dave, "And good to meet you at last; Neil's told us all about you."

Dave was intrigued and actually a little surprised.

163

"Oh yes?"

"Sure, you know Neil," said Jeff, his mouth, without much intervention from his brain, making conversation simply for conversation's sake, "He just goes on and on,"

"All good I hope."

"Sure, don't worry, all very complimentary," said Jeff, warming to his subject and digging a deeper hole for himself.

"Well, I've been quizzing Neil here for ages and he told **me** absolutely nothing," said Annie, leaning forward to better hear what Jeff had to say, "so tell all."

That put Jeff on the spot. He and Neil hardly ever spoke outside these reunions and, at last year's, Neil had arrived having just ditched Elmo, the body builder from Queens. What talk there had been had concerned the narrowness of Elmo's guilt-ridden Catholic outlook and the constant, insufferable and messy interference in Elmo's affairs by his large and energetic Italian family. Neil and Dave hadn't yet even met back then. Consequently, Jeff knew next to nothing about Dave, and he now looked to Neil to help him out of this self-inflicted embarrassment. But Neil was smiling at him lizard-like, his eyes glittering with amusement. He was going to enjoy this.

"Well, I think Neil should tell you himself, don't you?" Jeff bluffed.

"Oh no," protested Neil, "you tell such good stories Jeff," he waved graciously, "You tell Annie, I don't mind."

Jeff made a mental note to kick Neil sometime soon. And after that, a second note, to kick himself good and hard for getting into this mess in the first place. He felt the expectation of the others focus on him, causing beads of sweat to break out along his hairline. Then Rita, wonderful Rita, saved him.

"I'd rather hear from the man himself," she said

brightly, "Why don't you tell us all about yourself Dave."

Dave appreciated the welcoming tone in Rita's invitation. And, as he began to tell the friends all about his work, his meeting Neil and the wonderful life they had shared since, he gradually felt their acceptance of him growing. He was becoming a part of the group. It bothered him somewhat that Neil maintained an unhelpful blank stare throughout, but everyone else, especially Jeff for some reason, seemed really keen for Dave to talk. Dave felt his normal confidence returning and, as his speech became more relaxed, it was soon liberally peppered with the ludicrously hip expressions he so loved. He was talking now as he loved to talk: quickly, humorously, with wild gesticulations, and at great length.

Annie eventually stopped him. She felt she had to; not because he was uninteresting, but rather, because she felt something between embarrassment and pity at his many fervent expressions of the love he so obviously felt for Neil. Annie had known Neil since college and she knew that he had never felt love, or anything even close to it, for any of the pretty boys he had attracted over the years. Neil simply had a need for someone beautiful to be there with him. Annie hadn't been at the last reunion, but she could well imagine how very difficult it must have been for Neil to come alone, having impetuously ditched Elmo just days before; inadvertently leaving himself no time in which to secure suitable replacement eye-candy.

Over the years, Annie had seen very many beautiful young men come and go, but this one was going to be hurt when Neil tired of him. Really hurt. And Annie liked this bright, fresh-faced young man. She could imagine how painful his rejection was going to be, so she didn't want to hear him innocently singing Neil's praises anymore. It was too poignant.

There followed a few seconds of silence, then Phil and

Lou came into the room, arm in arm. Neil saw them first. He raised an eyebrow.

"Hell," he said, "what is it with you straight people?"

Rita and Jeff turned to see. Both Phil and Lou had that relaxed after-glow about them. Rita smiled; Neil was right. Phil hadn't wasted any time.

"Hi Phil," she said, standing, "And Lou, remember me? We met in town that time?"

Lou vaguely recalled having met some of Phil's old friends, but her mind had been elsewhere that day; it had been raining and she had been worried about Ethan catching a chill.

"Sure I do," she lied, "you're…?"

"Rita. And this is Jeff. And this is Annie, Neil and Dave."

"Oh yes, Neil and Dave, Phil's told me all about you."

"I'll bet he has," said Neil.

"And I think it's great you being out and proud, y'know, about being gay an' all."

There was a moment's silence, then Neil looked up at her, his lips forming a thin smile.

"Well, thank you so much for your support, my dear," he said, his tone ringing with insincerity, "It's the few, small words of encouragement that make it worth struggling on day after day. Of course, it's never easy being a screaming queen, but thank the Lord there are still a few tolerant folks like you out there to ease this heavy burden."

Annie shot Neil a critical look. He met her gaze and then simply looked away, dismissing her censure with a yawn of boredom. Dave frowned, unsure why Neil had been so patronising to the girl. She looked harmless enough; a young, blond airhead. Neil's irony had been unnecessary and was, in all probability, wasted on someone as naïve and clueless as her.

Neil's remark left an awkward atmosphere in the room. Lou sensed it and smiled timidly at Neil, before lowering her eyes and sinking into the nearest chair. Dave felt for her and looked to Phil, expecting harsh words for Neil. But Phil said nothing and merely took his seat next to Lou. She edged closer to him and he smiled. He was a contented man; again she'd had to turn to him for reassurance, reinforcing her complete dependence on him. Phil felt in total control and faced the rest of the group with the calm assurance of one who knows he rules his world.

Dave shrugged and caught Rita's eye. She raised an eyebrow and that small movement spoke volumes. Jeff shifted uncomfortably in his chair, eyes to the floor.

Neil eventually broke the silence himself.

"Annie, where's the little home-maker?" he looked up, "Well, would you believe it? Here he is, right on cue."

Bill came into the room but stopped before he had even said a 'hello', sensing the awkward atmosphere in the room. Everyone turned and smiled a welcome, but only Neil and Phil looked at their ease. Then Annie spoke, addressing Lou.

"Don't mind Neil, Lou," she said, "He's just an embittered old queer. Sometimes he's not fit for polite society."

In other circumstances, at another time, Neil would have laughed off her remark. He might even have smiled at the truth of it. But this evening he was not in a mood to tolerate any criticism.

"What would you know of polite society, or embittered old queers for that matter?" he asked her coldly.

Surprised by the bitterness in Neil's voice, Annie laughed, but the sound she made was hollow and forced.

"Well?" asked Neil.

"Shut up Neil," said Rita, bored with his rudeness.

Neil held up his hands in mock surrender and eased back into his chair. Rita drew a deep breath and continued more brightly.

"Lou, Dave here has just been telling us all about himself, y'know, what work he does, how he met Neil and so on. Would **you** like to tell us a bit about yourself?"

Lou suddenly looked as if she would like nothing less. Seeing her anxious look, Bill took pity on her.

"Why don't we all introduce ourselves to you first?" he said to her, "Would that be better? Let's see...is there anything in particular you'd like to know about us? We've known each other for a very long time, so we've got some good stories, I can tell you. Perhaps you'd like to know what Phil and Neil got up to in college, eh?"

Lou looked surprised and turned to Phil, who was now scowling. Rita and Jeff both laughed, while Dave, like Lou, was rather confused.

"Oh no," laughed Bill, "It's not what you might be thinking. They were both on the rowing team, nothing more intimate than that, I'm sure. Won cups and everything. A very impressive pairing."

"You never made it to college, did you Bill?" said Phil, nastily, "You weren't even there, so you know squat."

Unperturbed and smiling calmly, Bill graciously gave way to Phil.

"Perhaps you'd like to start then Phil?" he offered.

"There's no point; everybody already knows me," Phil grumbled, unwilling to do anything at Bill's direction.

"Dave probably doesn't," said Jeff.

"Well that's where you're wrong, Jeff," said Phil, "because I knew Dave even before he knew Neil; I kinda introduced them."

"You didn't mention this, Dave," said Rita, teasing.

"As I recall, Phil," Neil interrupted, "you just told me

there was another fag at the club, a really hot guy, and, for a small fee, you could arrange an introduction."

Phil shrugged, not apparently chagrined by Neil's exposé of his mercenary behaviour. Dave looked uncertain; he'd never liked the word 'fag' but, on the up side, there was nothing wrong with the phrase 'really hot guy', especially when it was referring to him. He shrugged.

"So you knew Neil from way back?" he asked Phil.

"Yeah. I first met Neil at college. We kinda kept in touch over the years and, as you know, I work evenings as a personal trainer across town at the Diamond Health Club where, turns out, you're both members."

"Tell him what else you do, Honey," Lou whispered encouragingly.

"Uh, OK. I'm Coach over at the Lanvers County high school and, like I said, I work as a personal trainer three evenings a week. And…er," he felt a sharp nudge in his side, "Oh yeah, sure, this is Lou. And we've been together just over a year."

"Thirteen months and two weeks," said Lou helpfully.

"So how do you know the others?" asked Dave.

"Me, Neil, Annie and Jeff were all at college together."

"But you got to know some of us better than others," said Neil, "Isn't that right Phil?"

Again, Lou's face wore a puzzled frown.

"See what I mean?" said Annie, "He's a bitter old queer. What he's alluding to is just a few perfectly innocuous dates a very long time ago."

Lou looked horrified, and turned to Phil

"What? You and him?" She pointed at Neil.

Phil looked appalled and Neil burst into derisive laughter.

"God no," Neil grinned, "I have some standards."

Annie was also laughing, but without Neil's harshness.

"No Lou," she said, "I was the one he dated. It was Phil and me. We went out on a couple of dates, but it didn't work out. No big deal and a very, very long time ago."

Lou felt her face redden. She hadn't known about Phil and Annie and she should have. Why hadn't Phil mentioned it to her? Sure that she must have slipped back a step in the estimation of the rest of the group, she fell into a sullen silence.

Next to her, Phil glowered at Neil, who returned a careless smile, heartily enjoying Phil's discomfiture.

Dave looked across at Neil and saw someone he wasn't sure he liked. Neil must be feeling tired after the journey, or unwell maybe, to act in this objectionable way to the friends he had come all this way to meet. Dave looked to Annie to lift the mood.

"Annie? How about you, and Bill? How did you two meet?"

"Oh Darling, my agent set me up with Bill on a blind date. Can you believe it? And I have to admit that it wasn't exactly love at first sight was it, Sweetie?" Bill shrugged contentedly by way of reply. He was well used to Annie's sentimental speeches and he'd heard this particular one many times. She might not say it with as much conviction these days, but Bill was sufficiently easy going to smile indulgently at her as she continued, her voice cracking, "But let me tell you, this man is so good for me. Oh yes you are, don't you shake your head like that. I couldn't pursue my career if I didn't have Bill there to support me and make everything happen. He's the most wonderful man, my best friend and my rock. He's the wind beneath my wings." She finished on a quavering high and dabbed at an affected tear.

With a spluttering snigger, Rita, Jeff and Phil began laughing while Neil gave Annie a slow hand-clap of applause. Dave and Lou were unsure how to react and Annie herself looked shocked.

"How can you laugh," she asked, "when I bare my soul to you?"

"The wind beneath my wings?" said Jeff, "Annie please. We're you're friends, you shouldn't throw that crap at us."

Dave looked at Annie, expecting a tearful outburst. But, after a moment's hesitation, her face broke into a smile.

"Oh, OK. You think that's going too far? It went down really big at the last gig I did at Secrets."

"Secrets?" said Dave, "You've sung at Secrets?"

He'd actually heard of the place. It was one of the more elegant of the city's gay bars.

"Sure have. And let me tell you, those guys loved me. They also," she added with a grin, "absolutely loved my 'meeting Bill' story; had them weeping into their pocket books; not a dry eye in the house."

Dave shook his head. These people would take some figuring out.

"Don't worry," said Rita, "You get used to them in time."

"Really?"

"Well, kinda."

"I could get Neil to sue you for misrepresentation of the facts you know."

"OK," Rita laughed, "Now I suppose you want to know about me and Jeff?"

"Yeah. If you weren't at college with the rest of them, how did you and Jeff get together?"

Jeff cut in quickly,

"Rita is my second wife."

"Don't say it like that," said Rita, "You make it sound like she died," she turned to Dave, "Jeff and his first wife,

Julie, were an item at college but, I guess lucky for me, things didn't work out, they split up and I met and married Jeff what, four years ago. We work at the same place, we're very happy and we share Jeff's daughter Emma with her mom. It's all very amicable."

"Says you," said Jeff.

"Uhuh," said Dave, warming to his role as interviewer. "And would I be right in thinking that you, Jeff, are a little older than the rest of the group?"

The others waited to see if Jeff would be offended by the question, but he didn't seem to be.

"Yes, I was a mature student, doing my masters when the others were still lowly undergraduates. But I like to think I'm doing pretty well for my age."

Phil sniggered.

"What?" asked Jeff, "I'm only forty-five. That's not old. You ask any of my students, they think I'm pretty cool," oh no, he'd said that word again and it still sounded ridiculous from his lips. He blundered on, "And anyway Bill's nearly the same age as me."

Dave turned to Bill, taking in his round face and easy smile.

"No. Really?" he asked, disbelieving.

Rita laughed, but Jeff was not so amused.

"Yes, really. Bill's only a year younger than me," he insisted.

Dave put up his hands.

"Sorry man. Didn't realise it was an issue," he smiled, "I'd just assumed we'd all be about the same age, but here I am, surrounded by all you old folks."

He'd intended it as humour, but it was met by resentful embarrassment and silence. His palms became suddenly moist and he looked around frantically for an ally. But Neil merely raised an eyebrow and remained otherwise impassive.

"Oh, come on you guys," Dave pleaded, "it was a joke. Come on."

Annie was the first to break. She burst into throaty laughter and the others followed. Dave had been had.

"You should have seen your face," Jeff chuckled.

Recovering, Dave accepted their laughter with a gracious shrug. He looked across at Neil and saw that he was the only one not sharing the joke. Dave was touched at what he took to be a show of loyalty.

Rita touched Dave's arm, encouragingly.

"Don't worry. Like I said, you get used to them in time."

As the laughter died down a small voice spoke up.

"Actually, you're not the one surrounded by old folks," said Lou, "I am."

"Why Sweetie," said Annie, "how old are you?"

"I'm nearly twenty," said Lou.

In the moment of stunned silence that followed, Rita, Annie and Jeff exchanged knowing looks and Neil raised a quizzical eyebrow. Phil looked down, avoiding their eyes. And only Bill managed to appear relaxed,

"Don't concern yourself Lou," he said, "we're only jealous. Though, y'know, I'd have thought you were older; you seem pretty mature to me."

"Yeah sure, I'd have guessed twenty or even twenty-one," said Neil unhelpfully.

Fortunately, at that moment, a metallic clanging announced the evening meal and everyone rose swiftly to their feet, grateful for the chance to change the subject.

The meal was served by Mr Cousins and his wife. He maintained a quiet conversation with his guests, answering their requests for information about the walks and the trails to be enjoyed in the vicinity. She however said nothing. In answer to all questions, she merely smiled briefly and lowered her head. Soon the questions to her ceased.

After the meal, as Annie and Rita took their coffees through to the lounge, Rita caught sight of a girl standing in a doorway across the room. She was obviously the Cousins' daughter. The girl smiled and mouthed a cheery 'hello' in return to Rita's own, then popped back through the door.

"Well, at least one member of their family is actually happy to have us here," Rita muttered.

"What's that?" asked Annie settling herself into a comfortable sofa.

"Oh I was just saying that at least their daughter has a friendly word for people."

"Whose daughter? Mine?"

"No, Mr and Mrs Congeniality, the owners."

"They have kids?"

"Yeah, a girl. She just waved hello."

"A girl? How old?"

"Oh, I dunno, fifteen, maybe sixteen."

"Well, no wonder that woman is so tired and worn down; she must have been over forty when she had her. A baby at that age? That has to be seriously hard work. It's bad enough when you're young and gorgeous, like us!"

They both laughed.

"But really," Annie stared down into her coffee cup, "I don't envy the poor woman. It must have been hard, especially living out here on the far side of nowhere. And the winters here have to be a bitch."

"Well their daughter looks like she's coping better with the isolation; she's the image of her mom, but it looks like she hasn't inherited the crippling shyness, thank God."

"Yeah, what is it with that woman?" Annie asked with her more usual lack of subtlety, "Is she weird or what?"

"Annie Clearwater, you're a very bad person! One minute you're all sympathy and understanding, next you're calling the poor woman a weirdo."

Annie was unabashed.

"Yeah, whatever."

Annie was irrepressible; it was part of her charm. Rita smiled.

"Don't you remember? Her husband said she was nervous when we checked in. I guess we just didn't get how bad."

"Yeah, maybe that's why they live out here. That woman couldn't survive in a town full of people. I'm not sure she can cope with a hotel full of guests either, for that matter. D'you reckon she ever leaves this place?"

As if in answer to Annie's question, Mr Cousins came into the room at that moment and crossed to the fireside to speak to the two women.

"We'll be going to church early tomorrow morning," he said, "but don't worry; we'll leave the breakfast things out on the heated counter over there before we go, and we'll be back in good time before the mid-day meal."

"That'll be just fine," said Annie expansively, dazzling him with one of her widest smiles, "And Mr Cousins - I'm sorry, John - perhaps you could say a prayer or two for me whilst you're there."

Rita smiled. Annie had the poor man in the palm of her hand; she had the glamour, no question about it and he was completely taken in. That's show business for you. John left the room, promising to pray for Annie tomorrow and indeed every Sunday thereafter.

As soon as the door closed, Annie glanced around quite theatrically, and unnecessarily as they were now alone in the room. She lowered her voice and whispered conspiratorially.

"Can you believe how old that girl of Phil's is?

Nineteen and a mom already for God's sake. What the hell is going on there?"

"I know. I nearly laughed out loud when she told us; I thought it was another joke. I mean, I knew she was young, but I had no idea she was **that** young," Rita gasped, "My God, d'you realise she's exactly half his age? I mean, she could be his daughter. What is he thinking?"

"Phil thinking? Hmm, now there's an image to conjure with."

"Ooh, that's too cruel," Rita admonished, smiling.

"What can I say? Sometimes the truth hurts," said Annie flippantly, "No, but really, y'know what Phil's problem is? He doesn't like to be challenged, and remember I am speaking from experience here. Phil likes to be in total control, decide everything, do all the thinking. Hah! There I go again; I'm sorry I just cannot get my head around it. I mean, can you imagine it, Phil, thinking? If the man actually had a brain he'd be dangerous!"

Rita was smiling, but had found Annie's outburst quite disturbing; behind the light-hearted tone there was hitherto unsuspected venom in Annie's words.

"You really don't like him, do you?"

"He's a jerk. What can I say?"

"So how come you've kept in touch all these years?"

"We didn't really. We got to know Neil through him and we got on OK with Neil; his humour was less cruel back then. Phil was just an outsider who somehow just kinda tagged along. And he's been tagging along ever since."

"For all these years?"

"Yeah, pretty much, but I never really figured out why. He always, and I do mean always, comes to these reunions, never misses a one. But why? It's not like he actually likes any of us. And did you see how stressed he got with Bill back there? What was that about? Problem is, Phil has absolutely nothing in common with the rest of us except that some of us happened to be at the same college at the same time. And even back then he was strange. Like he scraped into college on a minor football scholarship, did no work but then couldn't take it when, surprise, surprise, we all did better than him. I mean duh! But it really bothered him. And, even now, he's still trying to prove he's as good as, if not better than, the rest of us."

"So, what, you think she's a trophy wife?"

"Wife? No, not if she's got any sense."

Rita smiled.

"Annie?" she asked

"Yeah?"

"Why did you and Phil break up?"

"Are you serious? Break up? We only had like four dates."

"But why was it never more than that?"

"Have you not been listening to me? Did you not hear what I said? The man is a muscle-bound moron."

"No other reason?"

"Isn't that enough?"

Rita shrugged, non-committal. Annie paused a moment wondering if she should say more.

"Phil is a bully," she said sombrely, "He hit me one time and let me tell you I was out of there so fast. Oh, he apologised and said it would never happen again, but I never trusted him after that. And, you know what, he tried joking about it one time, just to me, years after; tried to make out like I'd remembered it wrong, like it never really happened. But he hit me all right. So I told him where to get off and he's never mentioned it again."

"Wow, he hit you? I hadn't expected that."

"Really? He's classic wife-beater material; inadequate, resentful and stupid. Plus he thinks a woman's place is only either at the kitchen sink, or in his bed."

"Poor Lou."

"Yeah, poor Lou. The kid deserves better."

"Mmm."

"And Dave's another kid who deserves better. Neil is getting worse isn't he?"

"Well, I haven't known him for as long as you, but that guy's certainly got issues he should deal with. And Dave seems a nice kid; I'd hate to see him get hurt."

There was a long pause whilst the two women, both deep in thought, sipped their coffees and stared into the log fire's dancing flames.

"Rita?"

"Yeah?"

"I never told Bill about what Phil did. He doesn't need to know, and I don't want him to, OK? So please don't say anything about it to anyone, even Jeff. It was nasty, but it was all a long time ago and I'd like to leave it that way. You gonna be OK with that?"

"Sure, sure. I won't say a word."

Later that evening, Jeff and Rita were talking over the day, as they unpacked their bags.

"Why did you say what you did about things with Julie being amicable?"

"Because it's true," said Rita, "I think you and Julie have a pretty good divorce."

"Pretty good for us maybe, but have you seen Emma lately? Without me around to stop her, Julie's turning her into some kind of freak."

"Oh, come on, you can't seriously be blaming Julie for the way Em dresses."

"Who else? I only get to see her on second weekends, so what influence do I have?"

"I don't believe this. Em's a teenager. She's rebelling.

It's what teenagers do, or hadn't you heard? You're being ridiculous."

"We'll see. We'll see. I've got Em away from Julie for a good long break now, so we'll just see what happens shall we?"

"You're setting yourself up for a fall, you know that?"

"You'll see. I intend to make things right between us."

"Then you better start by having that chat. Her finding us in the sack and you lunging at her, butt naked, probably needs a talking through, don't y' think?"

"Oh God," Jeff slumped onto the bed, remembering.

"Hey, I was joking! She's a bright kid and way more mature than you give her credit for. But you haven't spoken to her about it?"

"No, I tried, and again, over the meal, but y'know, everyone else was there."

"For goodness' sake Jeff. Go find her now. Talk to her; she'll be fine."

Jeff didn't look convinced. He procrastinated.

"OK, I'll go when I've finished this."

Rita decided not to push him. She changed the subject.

"What was up with Neil this evening? He was in a mean mood."

"Oh, he just likes to think of himself as some kind of towering intellectual, way above the rest of us, the common herd. He likes to think he's witty."

"Yeah? He drags wit to new depths."

"It's a gift he has."

Jeff was knocking on Emma's door. She took a long time to answer and, when she did, she didn't invite her father in, but talked to him through the half open door.

"Em, I think we need to talk."

"I really don't think we do. Just leave it, will you

Dad."

"No. I just wanted to explain."

She put her hand up.

"Don't go there! Believe me, no explanations needed here OK? Just do me a favour and lock your door next time will you?"

Jeff was pleasantly surprised; this was embarrassing certainly, but not as excruciatingly embarrassing as he'd anticipated.

"You're OK with this?" he asked.

"Uhuh."

"You sure you're OK?"

"I'm fine with it. I'm happy. Really couldn't be happier."

"Em?"

"OK, look Dad, I'm your daughter and what you and Ree get up to in the sack is none of my business. Believe me, I really, really, really don't want to know. So can we please just leave it?"

"OK. But I am sorry Em."

"Sure, whatever. 'Night."

She shut the door and Jeff stood for a moment staring at its wood panelling only inches from his face.

"Glad we had this little chat," he murmured.

He turned to leave and his shoulders, which he now realised had been hunched and tense, began to relax. He was hugely relieved; that could have been an awful lot worse. He rubbed his hands. Life was good again.

He went back to his room and closed the door. And this time, he double-checked that it was locked.

19

The following morning's breakfast was barely over when Lisa and Mikey came running into the lounge.

"It's been snowing!" they shouted, wild with excitement, "Dad said to ask are you gonna come build snowmen or what? Come on," they begged, "please, please, please."

Rita looked up at Jeff and grinned.

"Oh no," said Jeff, "No way."

But Rita had grabbed his hand and was already pulling him towards the door.

"Come on, you guys," she urged the others, "it's stopped snowing. It'll be fun."

Annie shook her head.

"I'd love to, but I can't," she said, "I have to protect my voice from extremes of heat or cold."

Lisa and Mikey looked crestfallen; they'd really wanted their mom to come with them.

"But," said Annie brightly, overcompensating with feigned enthusiasm, "I'll go sit right at the window, so I can watch everything. Would you build the snowmen just outside the window, Sweeties, so mommy can see? Would you do that for mommy, would you please?"

The two children nodded, turned and walked resignedly to the door. They hadn't said anything more, but Annie could feel their sullen disappointment.

"Don't be like that, Sweeties," she said, "You do know mommy has to protect her voice, right?"

Eight year old Lisa turned and gave her mother a look far beyond her years.

"I told Mikey not to bother asking you," she said, "I told him you wouldn't play with us, you never do. But he's too little to understand. Come on Mikey."

Annie stood in awkward silence as Lisa led Mikey from the room. Jeff and Rita exchanged glances.

"OK then," said Jeff, now quite glad to have an excuse to leave, even if it was to build a snowman, "guess we'll see you all later."

Dave looked down at Neil. Did he want to go out? No, Neil was looking bored with the whole business.

"You go," said Neil.

It didn't sound to Dave like permission to go and have fun, but more like an order just to go away. Dave stood, not knowing whether to go or not.

Annie decided him in the way she said, "Don't get frost bite."

It sounded to him like a dismissal, as if the matter was settled.

Opening the door from the honey-toned, comfortably heated corridor was a shock. The air rushing in was biting cold and the children's voices rang sharp and clear, although they were both already out of sight. Dave pulled on his new ski gloves and turned up the collar of his jacket. Only two steps down from the stoop, he already regretted not bringing his new and splendid furry hat. Rounding the corner of the building, he had cause to regret it even more, as a large, wet snowball hit him, splattering on the side of his face. He swore and pawed at his face, as Lisa and Mikey came running over. They danced in front of him, delightedly copying and repeating the new words they'd just heard.

"Shhhit! Holy shhhit!" they mimicked, singing in happy, high-pitched voices.

With the bulk of the snowball melted or wiped away Dave opened his eyes to see not only the kids but also Rita and Jeff laughing at him. Bill however was more sympathetic.

"Hey kids, that was cruel," he said, "You didn't give Dave a chance. Now say you're sorry."

Lisa and Mikey immediately hung their heads; guilty as charged. To Dave's benign and untrained eye, the two children looked the picture of contrition. He even felt bad that they'd been told off. But Lisa and Mikey were slyly peeking at each other, out of the corners of their eyes, co-ordinating the next wave of attack. Too late Rita spotted the snowballs hidden behind their backs.

"Look out!" she yelled, "They've got more. Run!"

But before Dave could gather his wits, Lisa and Mikey had loosed the snowballs at his unsuspecting head and dashed away to safety, laughing and shrieking. Behind them, apparently dazed, Dave stood, unmoving, as the compacted ice melted, burning, into freezing rivulets that coursed, tickling, down his neck. Biting her lip, Rita watched him closely, almost feeling the cold chill of the melting snow on her own cheeks. Jeff was looking equally unsure. They didn't know this guy. Dave was, after all, Neil's partner, and Rita would definitely describe Neil as being 'humour-challenged'; the man seemed never to have fun, or ever really enjoy anything. Perhaps Neil had, in Dave, found someone like himself. If so, this would be a bad way to start the week. Bill too, was waiting expectantly for Dave to react. Even the two children sensed that they might have gone too far this time. They stopped, staring at Dave, anticipating the inevitable punishment.

Rita broke the silence.

"Are you OK?"

Dave said nothing, but slowly turned his back on them all and leant his head against the wall. Thinking he must be hurt, Bill and Rita hurried over. As they came close they could see Dave's face reflected in the glass of the window next to him. Suddenly he caught their eye and winked. They were confused for a second, until they realised that he was sneakily fashioning snowballs from the drifted snow on the window ledge. Bill smiled and Rita composed a rather severe look on her face. She turned to call to the children.

"I think you two had better come over here right now and say you're sorry," she said firmly.

Slowly, Lisa and Mikey came over, nudging each other forward. Dave waited until they were right next to him, heads down and mumbling some words of apology, then he spun round and wedged a snowball down each exposed collar.

Lisa and Mikey were almost incoherent with shock. They frantically wriggled and hunched their shoulders, mittened hands scooping snow from the folds in the scarves at their necks

The adults laughed and scattered, running for cover. Battle was joined.

Hectic snowball warfare continued for a half hour, until everyone was caked in a cracking layer of powdery snow. Exhausted, they all fell together in a laughing heap.

"OK kids," said Bill, "I think that's enough."

The children whined their objections. Rita tried to deflect them.

"You guys, I thought we were going to build snowmen," she said.

"But I want to fight some more," Mikey wailed.

"No, she's right," said Dave, nodding at Rita, realising he'd forgotten her name, "I was enticed out here with misinformation. I was told that we would be building snowmen and, let me tell you, I really wanna build a snowman. Plus I know a pretty sharp lawyer, so, if I don't see some snowman-building pretty soon, I'm gonna sue," Lisa and Mikey frowned at him, "C'mon you guys," Dave pleaded, "it'll be fun."

The children admitted defeat and Dave soon had everyone agreed; they would each build a snowman that looked like someone here in the hotel. He, of course, only really knew Neil, so he built a snowman with a briefcase in hand and a cell phone at his ear. He was proud of his creation, but no one recognised it until he added the final touch; Neil's exceptionally long nose. Shrieking with laughter, Lisa and Mikey both ran to the window, knocking on the glass to attract Annie's attention. They pointed back at Dave's snowman and then inside to Neil. Annie seemed not to understand, but it was clear that Neil saw the likeness immediately, and he didn't look pleased. He caught Dave's eye and stared at him coldly for a few seconds before deliberately turning away.

Dave awkwardly dusted the snow from his hands.

"Don't worry about it," said Rita quietly, "He'll get over it. Never did have much of a sense of humour. Isn't that right Jeff?"

Jeff nodded.

But the fun was over for Dave.

"Think I'll go inside," he said, "I'll see you later."

The children were about to object to Dave's departure, but Rita again distracted them, this time with extravagant praise of their own artistic endeavours.

As Dave walked, somewhat dejectedly back to the hotel, he saw Emma standing alone, watching them all from a safe distance. He called to her, but she feigned deafness, turned and walked away. That's one really strange kid, he thought. In spite of the cold, her face was absolutely white but for the stark black lipstick and thick kohl smudges lining her eyes. And she had managed to buy only black cold weather gear so that, out here in the fresh snow, she almost faded into the background monochrome of trees and snow. He watched her walk away, smiling to himself at the exaggerated way in which she had to raise each heavily booted foot up and clear of the deep snow. It made her gait clumsy and ungainly and Dave was sure that wasn't the look she was striving for.

He felt sympathy for her; being a teenager was never easy. But then, it wasn't always that easy being an adult either.

Emma was struggling to walk quickly, but the snow was making her progress embarrassingly awkward so she decided to duck under the cover of the trees right at the edge of the clearing until Dave had gone back inside. Turning from her hiding place to look, she saw him climb up the steps, pause to stamp the snow from his boots and go in. He hadn't been watching her, spying on her; he'd just called out to be friendly. He was OK.

Still hidden by the trees, Emma brushed the snow from a fallen stump and sat for a long while, watching Jeff, Rita and Bill playing with Lisa and Mikey in the snow. Only a short time ago, maybe even last winter, she would have been there with them herself. But that was then. Such childish activities now seemed a pointless and rather foolish waste of time and energy. She sighed, her breath drifting slowly in the icy air. What was she supposed to do? There was nothing for her here. This place had nothing to offer her and no one to hang out with. She was already bored, and had begun the descent to the monumentally numbing depths of world-weariness to which only adolescents are capable of sinking.

The snowballers were shrieking and laughing. In the clearing, their voices had seemed as clear and brittle as ice, but here under the trees everything was muffled, absolutely still and quiet, as if the whole forest was hushed, alongside her, watching the playing children. She could no longer hear her father's voice. He must have gone back inside. Emma shivered and rubbed her hands together; they were becoming painfully cold even within her thick black gloves. She could go back to the hotel. No. She would go back, but not yet. How long, she wondered, would it be before her father noticed that she was neither out in the snow with the children, nor in the lounge, somewhere silent in the background of the adult conversation? Emma herself had lately become increasingly aware that her place was no longer with either grouping. She was neither child nor adult; she just didn't fit. It was incredible that her father couldn't grasp that, when to her it seemed so obvious.

Emma was reasonably sure that Jeff did try, in his own clumsy way, to understand her, but his efforts were routinely frustrated by his preoccupation with his work and his new life with Rita. That said, Emma occasionally found herself wondering whether she was deluding herself; maybe her father didn't actually care about her feelings at all. After all, living most of the time with her mother, Emma saw her father only rarely, but that arrangement appeared to suit him just fine. And it wasn't as if he were spending time with her here, now that he had the opportunity. Where was he? Most likely, he was now comfortably settled by a roaring fire, not having given her even a moment's thought. She wondered whether she should stay out for a good long time, long enough even for him to notice she was missing. That would give him a fright. That would shake him up a bit; make him pay her some attention. With a wicked little smile of satisfaction, Emma pictured Jeff anxiously running along the corridors, darting from room to room, searching for her. She would let him suffer a while. Then, later, she would appear in the lounge, really cool, acting like nothing had happened.

She snapped back to reality at the sudden breaking of a twig close by. She span around, but saw nothing save the snow-laden branches and the pillows of deep snow beneath them. Nothing was moving and nothing seemed out of place. Frowning, Emma turned back towards the hotel.

And there he was.

Just a few feet away.

A tall, painfully thin man, dressed all in black, stark against the snow.

Muscles flexing automatically, with the shock, Emma fell back off the tree stump and landed in a mound of powdery snow. Gagging and spitting icy mouthfuls, she scrambled to her feet.

"Get away from me!"

The man made no reply. He merely inclined his head to one side and continued to stare directly at her, his dark eyes glittering in the deep hollows of his face.

Emma's heart was racing and any thoughts of teasing her father now fled; she wanted Jeff here with her, right now. But she was alone and this weird-looking man stood in her path, between her and the cheerfully shouting children; between her and safety. She felt a sudden, freezing grip of fear constricting her chest. She struggled for air.

"Go away! Leave me alone," she rasped, her throat suddenly dry.

Again, the man said nothing.

Emma summoned all her courage and poured it into her voice, forcing the words to come out evenly; their apparent strength conveying a confidence she certainly did not feel.

"What do you want? Why d'you keep staring at me?"

Finally, the man stirred. His voice was disturbingly dry and thin, but Emma took a fleeting scrap of reassurance from the apparent normality of conversation.

"Pardon me," he said quietly, inclining his head in the merest hint of a bow, "The snow deadens every sound, every sound. I can move as silent as the grave," he raised his head once more to look at her, his dark eyes sharp as shattered glass, "I've been watching you."

"What? Why?"

What did he mean, he'd been watching her? What the hell?

Emma was almost overwhelmed by the urge to turn and run in blind panic. Her breathing was becoming impossible to control and there was no disguising the rapid, shallow breaths, as the puffs of warm vapour jostled in the icy air.

Then the man smiled, revealing deadly cold white shards, the dreadful sight of which swept away the last reserves sustaining Emma's paper-thin show of defiance. But it was too late. She was now incapable of running; frozen by the cold but also by a paralysing fear. She knew this man meant to do her harm, but she could do nothing but wait for him to strike. But the man made no move. Still staring, unblinking at her, he maintained his awful smile, but spoke slowly and quietly.

"Oh I think you know why I've been watching you, Doll. I think you know. Look at us. You and me, we're not like these others," he slowly motioned with long, thin fingers back towards the clearing, "We're different. We don't fit with their ways. We don't dress the same. We don't look the same. We don't think the same. Know what I mean?"

Emma's mind began to wake from its stupor. Unable to react for a moment, her mind replayed what he'd just said and she found herself smiling weakly in cautious agreement. Had she been wrong about this man? Had she misread the situation completely? Initially shocked by his sudden appearance she had panicked, but now she began to feel ashamed at having been so easily frightened. She felt her cheeks redden; this man must think her such a klutz, such a dorky kid.

She looked carefully at the stranger's pinched face and wondered how old he was, but it was impossible to guess. His skin, which was the palest she had ever seen, wasn't wrinkled, but it didn't have the elasticity of youthful skin either. When he smiled, the skin around his mouth folded back rather than stretching as you'd expect, and it seemed dry, almost flaking. Perhaps it was make-up. That might also explain why his eyes seemed so very dark and unnatural. Or perhaps he was suffering from some skin condition, or some illness that might also explain his skeletal thinness. What was it? Cancer? AIDS?

"Are you sick?" she asked, almost without realising she had spoken aloud.

After a pause, he smiled his thin smile and said, "Some would say so."

"AIDS?" she blundered on, surprising herself with the intrusiveness of her own question.

For a moment the man's ashen face slid into a puzzled frown, then, abruptly, he seemed to lose all interest both in the question and in Emma herself.

"You'd better get back with the other kids, Doll," he said, looking away from her for the first time.

Emma felt crushed. She had obviously hit a nerve or overstepped some boundary, and now she was being shooed away like an irritating child. With his abrupt dismissal, the man, who just minutes before had terrified her and reduced her to petrified helplessness, became immediately interesting; a mystery and an object of fascination. Furious with herself for having asked such a crass question, Emma now wanted to stay and talk, but she could think of nothing to say that would salvage the situation.

The man moved effortlessly to one side to allow her to pass and, realising that their conversation was over, Emma reluctantly walked towards him. As she passed by him, she shivered slightly, as a sudden chill, an echo of her earlier fear, momentarily gripped her. She hurried on to the edge of the trees before looking back.

"Do you live around here?" she called.

He made no reply.

"Will you be coming back this way again?" she persisted.

He turned his face towards her once more and paused, as if reconsidering something.

"I'll be here again this evening, just before sundown."

He was giving her another chance and she was absurdly pleased.

"Then I'll be here too."

"Sure you will."

"No, really, I'll meet you here, tonight."

"Your folks won't let you out that late, Doll."

"It's nothing to do with them," she insisted defiantly, "I do what I want."

"Is that right?" he said, rewarding her bravado with his chilling smile.

"Yeah, I'm not a kid anymore."

She'd responded too quickly and she regretted the words as soon as she said them. Her effort to appear mature had been completely undermined by the clumsy, unprompted assertion. She was hugely embarrassed and her words hung, reverberating, in the ice-cold air.

Assuming that the stranger would now be smiling condescendingly at her, amused by her childish awkwardness, Emma kept herself from looking into his face. She realised that in spite of, or perhaps because of, his bizarre appearance, she found this man uniquely attractive and she desperately wanted to impress him. If only she could think of something intriguing or memorable to say, something witty and apparently spontaneous. But the words wouldn't come. She was utterly tongue-tied, her mind a complete blank. Still, she felt she had to say something. Anything.

"I'm really a lot older than I look," she finished lamely, finally daring to raise her eyes to look at him.

Again, the terrible, humourless smile,

"Is that right?" he whispered.

Emma drew on her pride and tried to inject some defiance into her voice,

"Yes, it is. And if I say I'll be here this evening, then I'll be here this evening."

"Don't go doing me any favours, Doll," he drawled, his menacing smile broadening, "Not yet anyhow."

Emma had nothing to say in answer to that, so she turned and trudged through the knee-deep snow, back out into the bright sunlight of the clearing.

Lisa and Mikey saw her first. They called for her to join them, but she shook her head and walked on directly back to the hotel. At the door she turned. It seemed to her that she could still make out the dark figure standing just beyond the edge of the clearing. But the more she strained to see clearly, the more the dark shape appeared to shift and fade into the crowded tree trunks, until it was lost from sight.

Emma shook off her boots and hurried to her room.

She lay on her bed thinking over what had happened. Meeting the weird stranger was the only interesting thing that had happened since getting here and she knew she had to meet him again but, at the same time, she felt some unease. Obviously she couldn't tell her father that she wanted to go out late to meet some strange guy in the woods. In fact, put like that, she wasn't sure if she was completely relaxed about the idea herself. If she did sneak out to meet him it would be the most outrageous, daring thing she had ever done.

On the other hand, in expecting him to attack her, she had already jumped to the wrong conclusion about the man once. So perhaps she owed him the benefit of the doubt. It pained her that she had been guilty of judging by appearances, just like her father.

Though angry with herself, Emma was momentarily distracted. She smiled, recalling the stunned disbelief on Jeff's face when he'd first seen her wearing her black gear. Then, and since, he'd tried so hard to appear relaxed about it, but he'd failed. The effort was futile; it was plain that he absolutely detested his little girl's new look. Emma had overheard him describing it to Rita one evening. To Jeff, the 'unrelieved black drabness' of Em's clothing was 'evidence of an attitude of complete negativity', which apparently would soon manifest itself in 'an insolent intolerance of tradition, authority, family and all else that America held dear, up to and probably including apple pie!' Rita, clearly surprised by this show of previously unsuspected conservatism in her normally liberally-minded husband, had tried to lift his mood and make light of his concerns.

Listening unseen at the top of the stairs, Emma had heard her father's satisfyingly lurid tirade. And she had been rather pleased. After all, a major factor in her decision to wear the gear had been her desire to generate precisely this reaction. The look was sartorial shorthand; projecting an aura of contemptuous superiority to, and rejection of, everything and everyone around her. At least that was what other people read into her black clothing. These were the judgements people made, without ever actually speaking to the wearer to find out what she was really like. No one was interested in the person. Stuck fast in their dull, suburban way of thinking, people would make assumptions about her, based solely on the way she looked. And Emma reckoned that, if they were so judgemental and shallow, then they deserved to be shaken up a little.

Just then, the image of the stranger in the woods drifted back into her thoughts, interrupting her self-satisfied wallow in righteous indignation. Her smile fell at once.

Dammit!

She had made exactly those same hasty judgements on first seeing the stranger. She had leapt to exactly the same shallow conclusions about him, though she had far less excuse for her behaviour than did the disapproving citizens of middle America. After all, she and the stranger were, as he himself had pointed out, very alike. Like her, he was deathly pale, dressed all in black and like her, seemed to be all alone. She should have recognised him immediately as a kindred spirit.

But there was something about him. He had said he was different, and he was right. He was strange. Was he also dangerous?

Emma bit her lip.

No, surely if he had been intending to hurt her, he'd had ample opportunity and he had done nothing. No, she had misjudged him. Thinking of him now, Emma felt a thrill of excitement, a sense of fear mixed with desire. She recognised that some part of his appeal was undoubtedly the knowledge that her father would utterly disapprove of him on sight. If she did spend more time with her stranger, she would have to wait and choose the right moment to drop him into conversation; her father's reaction was going to be something to behold: seismic! Emma allowed herself a guilty smile at the thought.

But she was getting ahead of herself. She wasn't going to mention the stranger to anyone yet and there was still the small matter of how she was going to sneak out, unnoticed, to meet him at sundown.

Having decided that the sun must set at around supper time, she developed a plan that involved her feigning tiredness and returning to her room before the evening meal. Then, changing into the outdoor clothes that she would have to secrete by the back door in advance, she would slip out while all the rest of the group were together in one room, eating.

That settled, Emma found herself thinking about the stranger again. As she reviewed their encounter, she became aware of something that had only registered subliminally at the time; he had remained all but motionless throughout. Only his head and his left hand had moved at all, and they with only very slight movements. The rest of his body had not seemed to sway, or even tremble with the cold, while Emma, once she'd recovered from her terror, had been stamping her feet and rubbing her hands together for warmth. It was as if he were totally unaffected or unaware of the bitter chill. And when he'd finally left the path to let her pass, he had seemed almost to glide. Unlike her, he apparently had no difficulty with snagging roots or fallen branches hidden under the snow. He hadn't had to wrench each foot out of and clear of the snow's compacted grip. His movement had been effortless and smooth.

Emma puzzled over this for a moment, then let it

drop. She tried instead to picture his features, but could recall clearly only his dark, compelling stare. His thin face had been pale, she remembered that, and his cheeks hollow; symptoms perhaps of his illness, whatever that was.

Perversely, Emma felt an odd thrill at the prospect that he might have AIDS. Having never, to her knowledge, met anyone afflicted with the disease, she felt a certain satisfaction that she was handling this meeting with a possible sufferer with such maturity. From daytime TV movies and waiting-room magazine articles, she'd formed a notion of the AIDS sufferer, not as an ordinary person like herself but as a tragic, almost poetic figure, as much a victim of the intolerance and fear of others as of the disease itself. With this in mind, Emma resolved to rise above such unthinking prejudice and treat this stranger with compassion.

But the sentiment behind her resolve was not pure altruism. The general stigmatisation of AIDS sufferers lent a measure of glamorous appeal to the idea of going against the norm. Emma saw herself as proudly following in the footsteps of the caring celebrities whose beautiful, glossy images so often smiled out from those same waiting-room magazines. These were the stars whose agents, no doubt recognising a bandwagon when they saw one, routinely had them attend charity fundraisers at which they could be photographed looking radiant, yet touchingly sincere, in their designer fashion and borrowed gems. It was surely just a happy coincidence that the selflessness of these beautiful people generated vital column inches of glowing praise.

Like these stratospheric luminaries, Emma yearned to be seen as admirably brave, principled and independent. Unlike them she had no audience to applaud her greatness of spirit but, in her own mind, she was satisfied that she was acting in a way which would have impressed even her parents, had she been able to tell them about it. It really was a shame that she couldn't tell her father about the stranger, because, once he'd recovered from the tremendous shock of seeing his daughter associating with this weird person, Jeff would perhaps have finally come to appreciate how very understanding and mature his daughter now was; he would have to concede that his little girl was growing up.

Emma pulled herself back from her daydreams and reminded herself, with some reluctance, that the stranger hadn't actually confirmed that he did have AIDS, so she shouldn't be assuming that he had. He might of course have cancer, or some other awful illness she knew nothing about. However, there was also the chance that he was just naturally very thin and pale, and didn't have any life-threatening illness at all. For the briefest moment Emma felt slightly cheated at this prospect. Startled at her own selfishness, she hastily pushed the fleeting disappointment from her mind.

Thinking back to their meeting in the woods, she wondered how old the stranger might be. He'd acted with the quiet self-assurance of an adult, but to her eye, his thin, lanky build suggested late teenage or early twenties. She really had no idea. Her prime concern for the moment was the possibility that he might turn out to be much too old for her, not that she had yet decided exactly how old was too old. She supposed that the acceptable disparity in ages would vary depending on the characters of the two people involved, and she wasn't about to start setting any hard and fast rules before even getting to know him. That was just the sort of blinkered thinking she had come to expect from adults. And Emma had decided that, unlike the rest of them, all those old, blinkered, narrow-minded people, she would treat everyone as an individual.

The inconsistency inherent in her view of the world was not, even briefly, apparent to her.

20

"I think you're making way too much out of it," Annie was saying to Neil, "It's only a snowman and yours is actually the best made of the lot."

But Neil was not to be cajoled into good humour.

"Will you just let it go. And come away from the window, you're encouraging them."

Outside, the children, with the enthusiastic assistance of the adults, were cheerfully adding more and more snow in an effort to make the nose of Neil, the snowman, even longer. Inside, Neil, the iceman, was not at all amused. He sat, arms folded across his chest and glowered.

"Do you want me to stop them?" Annie asked.

"And just how do you propose to do that?"

"Well, I could, y'know, wave and do this," she said, knocking on the windows and frowning disapprovingly.

The children carried on regardless. Annie turned and shrugged her shoulders.

"Kids eh? Can't live with'em, can't tie them up and mail 'em to Alaska!"

She sat down next to Neil, but if she thought that her light-hearted remark would have softened his mood, she was mistaken. There followed an awkward few minutes of silence during which the delighted shrieks of the playing children could be heard clearly. At length, Annie was relieved to see white flakes begin to flutter down past the large picture windows. The fall thickened even as she watched. Never having been very comfortable with silence, she was hugely relieved finally to have an excuse to say something. She jumped to her feet.

"The snow's getting heavy again," she said, gesticulating to her children still frolicking out by the snowmen, "Come...back...in," she mouthed to them, slowly and theatrically.

Lisa saw her, but affected not to understand what her mother wanted. She shrugged, waved and ran off into the thickening blizzard.

"That girl!" Annie fumed, "If she doesn't come back in, this instant I'll-"

"You'll what?" Neil cut in irritably, "Huh? Your daughter won't come in because she doesn't want to and she knows damn well that you won't actually do anything to make her. Oh you'll shout and wave your arms about like some demented diva, but she knows that you won't actually get up off your ample butt to go out and get her."

Genuinely shocked and offended, Annie turned to Neil, her face suddenly solemn.

"I have to stay indoors to protect my voice. You know that."

"Oh yes, the voice. We wouldn't want to risk any harm to that. What would all those second rate bars do for entertainment?"

Annie looked him up and down for a moment in silence.

"Y'know, Neil, you're not a nice person anymore," she said at last, "You have a mean streak in you and it just keeps getting wider and wider."

Neil put his hand to his face in mock contrition.

"It's not funny, Neil. Do you see me laughing? I was right, wasn't I? You really are becoming an embittered old queer. Well, OK, that suits you now. But one day you're gonna wake up and find you've got no friends left, because you've pushed all of us away. And by then you'll be too old and too desperate to seduce any more pretty boys like poor Dave."

"Poor Dave! Shows how much you know."

"I know enough, Neil. I know you. And anyone can see that Dave's a nice kid. He certainly doesn't deserve to meet up with someone like you when you're in one of your self-destructive moods. I don't want to see him get hurt."

"Then don't look. Anyway, it's nothing to do with you. Just keep out of other people's business."

"But it is my business. We're supposed to be friends."

"Hah, friendship, now there's an interesting thing. Seems to me like it's just become a licence to interfere and snoop around in other people's lives."

"I'm not interfering or snooping; I'm just being honest. And, honestly Neil, you should stop and think what you really want from your life, before it's too late."

"Oh, thank-you yes, I nearly forgot; to interfering and snooping, please add pontificating."

"Why do you say these things?"

"What? Are we done with honesty already?"

"Neil, why do you try so hard to push people away? Everybody needs someone they can talk to."

"Isn't that a line from a song? Not one of yours I hope."

"I'm serious."

"So am I. So kindly butt out."

There followed a painfully long minute of silence. Neil seemed unconcerned and stared, unfocused, at the continuously falling snowflakes at the window. Annie however was agitated; her mouth trembled, beginning to form words that remained unspoken. Finally, she had had enough.

"I don't think I want to spend time with you anymore," she said with quiet dignity. She rose majestically to her feet and walked slowly from the room.

Behind her, Neil slow hand-clapped his applause.

Crossing the lobby, Annie saw Dave standing at the window.

"Your boyfriend's in there," she said, stabbing her thumb back towards the door of the lounge.

Dave nodded, but stayed where he was. Annie stopped to look at him.

"Don't tell me you're pissed with him too?" she asked, trying to keep an even tone while discretely wiping a tear from her eye.

"Pissed? No. Hey, are you OK? You look like you've been crying."

Annie sniffed, but shook her head defiantly.

"No I'm alright, Sweetie," she touched his arm solicitously, "but how are you? Are you OK?"

Baffled as to why Annie was being so intense, Dave decided to ignore her concerned look and change the subject quickly.

"Sure. I was just wondering if the owners are back yet," he said, "Have you seen them?"

"No, no I haven't," said Annie, reluctantly releasing his arm, "I'm sorry, would you excuse me, I have to get something from my room."

"Sure. Catch you later."

As Annie hurried off along the corridor, Dave was immediately almost bowled over by Lisa and Mikey as they charged into the lobby.

"That was so cool!" they shouted, "We made your snowman even better. When it stops snowing will you come out and see it? Will you? Will you? Please!"

They were each pulling at one of his hands and turning him round and round. Not knowing how to extricate himself from their grip, Dave was going around for a fourth time and beginning to feel distinctly woozy, when Bill rescued him.

"Hey you two, leave the poor man alone. He's suffered enough."

Bill tickled the two children. They released Dave, and Bill chased them both away along the corridor. Behind him, Jeff and Rita laughed at Dave as he stumbled dizzily against the wall. Rita offered a steadying arm.

"You're great with kids," she said, "Do you have any of your own?"

Jeff looked askance.

"Rita," he whispered, nudging her.

"What?"

Jeff raised his eyebrows exaggeratedly, by way of explanation. Rita was no wiser.

"What?" she asked again.

Dave tried to help.

"Rita," he said, "I think Jeff's subtly trying to remind you that I'm gay."

"Thank you," said Jeff.

"And," Dave continued, "he assumes that a gay guy couldn't have kids."

"Thank you again," said Jeff.

"Which, of course," Dave finished, "is nonsense."

"Uh?"

"But, in answer to your question," Dave continued, smiling at Jeff's confusion, "no, I don't have kids. I didn't know I was any good with them till this morning; I've never had much to do with them, not even when I was one myself."

"Well," said Rita, "you're a natural."

"Thanks. It was cool. And the snow was awesome.

Talking of which, have either of you seen the Cousins? Have they made it back yet?"

"I hope so," said Jeff, "I'm starving. I'm going to take a shower and then I'll be ready to eat at least half a cow. I'll see you later. Coming Ree?"

"Yeah, in a minute."

She turned to Dave.

"Is their pickup back?"

"Who can tell in this blizzard?"

"Good point. Have you checked if they're down in the kitchen?"

"Er, no. I was just y'know, wondering."

Dave was beginning to wish he hadn't started this. Rita grabbed his sleeve.

"Then let's find out."

Always one to act impulsively Rita, pulling Dave after her, strode behind the reception desk. She knocked on the door but there was no reply. Opening the door, Rita had another door to her right while, to her left, was a flight of stairs leading down to the basement. The door had a frosted glass panel and Rita could see that the room was in darkness, so she turned her attention to the basement.

"Hello?" she called, descending slowly, "Hello, Mr Cousins?"

Though Dave had been released he followed on behind, but he was uneasy at this invasion of the Cousins' private space.

"OK, they're not here," he whispered, "Can we go back up now?"

"No. I mean, they might be held up for hours in this snow. What time is it? Heck, it's after midday. They're already late, so why don't we show some initiative and make the meal?"

"By 'we', you mean us?"

"Sure do."

"And by 'show some initiative' you mean crash their kitchen and help ourselves to their stuff?"

"I wouldn't put it quite like that. I mean, we'd be eating the food at some point even if they were here, wouldn't we?"

"True, but could we give them more time, please?"

"OK. But, if they're not here by one, we'll make the meal: you and me. OK?"

"I'm not that great in the kitchen. Neil isn't either. We eat out a lot."

"Come on, it'll be fun and we all gotta eat, right?"

One o'clock came and went, with no sign of the Cousins' return from town, so Rita checked the contents of larder and freezer and, with Dave's unskilled assistance, put together a meal for everyone.

"OK Dave, it's nearly ready. Can you go tell the others to get places set for, what are we, twelve?"

Unable to find a bell to announce the meal, Dave went from room to room summoning everyone. At Phil and Lou's door his knock was met first by silence and then by the appearance of a very dishevelled Phil. Dave told him that lunch was ready.

"Lunch?" said Phil, scratching his head, "What time is it?"

When Phil realised that he had slept the entire morning away he merely shrugged.

"Couldn't get the kid to sleep till after five this morning. He slept too much yesterday, just like I told her, and then he couldn't sleep. It was nearly daylight, for chrissake," he yawned and scratched at the stubble on his chin, "Did we miss anything?"

"We had a snowball fight and made a couple of snowmen."

Phil stopped, mid yawn.

"What? You got Neil outside, building a snowm-"

"No, no, Bill and Annie's kids. Neil stayed inside with Annie."

"Lucky Neil," said Phil sarcastically, "or should that be, lucky Annie?"

Dave frowned. He wasn't sure what to make of Phil.

"Yeah, whatever. Anyway, like I said, the meal's ready."

"Thanks. How come you're going round calling everyone? This ain't summer camp."

"Because the Cousins still aren't back from town."

"No? So who cooked the meal? Ah, let me guess, must be Rita, am I right?"

Dave nodded.

"Yeah," Phil continued, "there's a woman who likes to be in charge. You've gotta feel sorry for Jeff, right? Wouldn't wanna be in his shoes; he's nearly as downtrodden as that poor old fool Bill. Now there is one sorry excuse for a man."

Dave had heard enough. He left quickly, before having to say anything he might later have to pretend to regret.

Despite Neil's grumbling at having been asked to help set the table and serve the food, the meal was, on the whole, an enjoyable occasion; only Annie was subdued. Between mouthfuls, in happy, high pitched voices, Lisa and Mikey related every detail of the snowball fight and the snowman competition to their mother, but she merely nodded inattentively.

After the meal, everyone congratulated and thanked Rita and Dave for the food then sat back, replete. Full stomachs had even calmed Lisa and Mikey. Outside, the snowfall was still heavy.

"When do you think the Cousins will get back?" asked Lou.

"Who knows? Could be anytime," said Jeff, "Could be tomorrow. I guess it all depends on the snow."

"Looks like it's easing off a bit," said Bill, rising slowly and walking over to the window.

Lisa and Mikey slid from their chairs and joined their father gazing, rapt, at the cascade of shifting shades of white.

"It's so beautiful," Lisa sighed.

Still transfixed by the tumbling flakes, she called over to Jeff.

"Jeff?"

"Yes?" he answered guardedly, cautious of being drawn into another snowball war.

"Thanks for arranging all of this. And you too Rita. This vacation's the best ever!"

Jeff was taken aback and thoroughly pleased by the unexpected praise.

"The whole reunion thing was originally your mom's idea. And I can't honestly take the credit for the snow," he smiled, cheerfully self-effacing, "But arranging the rest was easy; I found this place on the net. I'm really glad you like it here."

Various adults, prompted by Lisa's unselfconscious thanks, hastily added their own, and Jeff basked in their kind words. He was particularly touched to notice that even Emma was wearing a smile. Maybe his little daughter of darkness was going to be happy here after all. He allowed himself the reassuring belief that he was already making some progress in his quest to become closer to her. Perhaps things were going to be easier than expected. He settled back comfortably in his chair.

Right now, life was good. But his opportunity to savour the glow of self-satisfaction didn't last long.

"How about Jeff and me clear this lot up?" Bill said brightly.

With sudden dismay, Jeff surveyed the cluttered detritus of a dozen meals. Amazing how quickly life punishes smugness, he thought.

But he acquiesced good-naturedly,

"Sure. Dave and Rita did all the cooking so, how about it Neil, you gonna give us a hand?"

Neil gave Jeff a withering look.

"I'll take that as a no," said Jeff, grinning, "but don't worry, you can cook this evening's meal if the Cousins haven't made it back by then."

There was a ripple of laughter, but Neil remained impassive.

"I don't do cooking," he said coldly, "and I don't wait tables either, especially when I'm paying good money to be waited on by someone else. If they don't get back this evening, I'm leaving."

Dave looked surprised, clearly taken aback by Neil's outburst.

"And just how do you propose to do that?" asked Annie.

"The SUV."

"And what about me? I like it here," said Dave defiantly. He met and held Neil's angry gaze, daring him to have an argument right there, in front of everyone.

But that wasn't Neil's way. He turned away without saying another word, but Dave knew he'd have plenty to say later, when they were alone.

"What I meant," Annie continued, "was that the Cousins know the area and if they can't get in here, what makes you think you'll be able to get out. The road must be blocked or something. And it's still snowing, so it's only going to get worse."

"Actually, Hon, it's stopping," said Bill.

Everyone turned. Bill was right. Even as they watched, the total whiteness of the view from the windows began to dissolve, revealing large dusty flakes fluttering down against the sparkling blue-white of the already settled snow. As sunlight edged through the thinning cloud, it revealed a breath-taking scene of dazzling perfection; whites, blues and the palest lilacs, all magically sparkling with thousands of tiny, glittering stars. From those watching, there came a collective sigh of appreciation. No one said a word.

Looking away from the windows, to the faces of those around him, Bill saw smiles and open-mouthed amazement; his friends, jokers and cynics, almost to a man, were, for once, hushed; startled into silence by one unexpected glimpse of perfection.

Phil was the first to break out of the spell.

"OK, if it's stopped, we'll take Ethan out."

"Honey," worried Lou, "I don't think that's such a good idea."

"Are you kiddin' me? If we have another night like last night, I'll be hitching a ride outa here with Neil. We got to get that kid tired enough to sleep, so he's gotta get out there and get some exercise."

"Can we come too?" Lisa and Mikey begged, already jumping with enthusiasm, "Now, now, can we go now?"

"But it'll ruin the snow," said Annie wistfully, "and it looks so still and perfect now…"

She fell silent, at the expressions of complete incomprehension on the faces of her two children.

"OK, OK," she said resignedly, "go on. I guess it'll snow again later and cover up the mess you two hoodlums are gonna make."

"Ych!" Mikey shouted, "Come on Lisa. Let's get ready."

At the door, Lisa turned back briefly, before dashing

out of the room.

"Love you Mom."

Annie smiled.

"Love you too, Sweetie," she whispered.

Bill walked over and stood behind his wife. He put his arms around her and she lent back, letting him hug her close. She was still smiling.

"Makes up for what she said to you earlier, doesn't it?" he whispered.

"Oh," said Annie contentedly, "it makes up for everything."

21

Grumbling, Jeff drained the sink.

"How can they not have a dishwasher?"

"Maybe it takes too much power," said Bill amiably, "Maybe they like the simple life."

"They've got two washing machines, a drier, a deep freeze, two microwaves and a deep fryer. How simple is that?"

"Ah, quit bellyaching," Bill chided, "We're done now. You ready to go outside with the kids?"

Jeff grimaced.

"Do we have to? Haven't we earned a break? How about a game of chess instead?"

"I'm tempted, but as they're my kids I kinda feel responsible for them, y'know?"

"No need; Phil and Lou are out there with them. And it's their turn; we were out in the cold for hours this morning. Come on; the kids won't even notice we're not there."

"OK, I'll just check they're OK and then I'll let you beat me at chess again," Bill smiled, "Jeff?"

"Yeah."

"You do know that I let you win, don't you?"

"Sure you do," said Jeff, "Sure you do."

As he waited for Bill to join him in the lounge, Jeff was still complaining about the absence of a dishwasher to anyone who would listen. Emma was not one of these. She was reading, sitting cross-legged in a high back chair in the corner, and showed little interest in Jeff's sorry tale of domestic drudgery. Indeed, she showed little interest in anything going on around her, and it was all too easy to forget she was in the room at all.

Annie and Dave, however, were gratifyingly indulgent. At Jeff's pointed prompting, they nodded sympathetically and examined his water-wrinkled palms. Neil, however, frowned; he was bored with Jeff's performance.

"You wanted a backwoods hotel and that's what you've got," he muttered, "That's what we've **all** got. Thanks."

Before Jeff could defend himself, Rita came into the room and Jeff chose to ignore Neil's barbed remarks, opting instead for more sympathy.

"Ree, can you believe it? There was no dishwasher. Just look at my hands."

"Yeah, Bill told me. But a place like this has to have one. Are you sure you looked everywhere?"

"Would I have hands like this if they had a dishwasher? Believe me, I looked."

"Ah, my poor, poor baby," said Rita, stroking his face with exaggerated concern.

In her corner of the room, Emma quietly closed her book and rose from her chair. As she left the room, Rita grimaced at Jeff.

"Sorry, didn't see her there. I thought she was outside with the others."

"No, she hasn't been out of the hotel once." said Jeff, "So much for experiencing the great outdoors; we might as well have gone to Disneyworld."

"She has been out," Dave corrected, "She was at the

edge of the clearing earlier. And yesterday, when I was out walking, something had spooked her."

"Spooked her?" Jeff asked, his chapped hands forgotten.

"Yeah. She said she thought something had been following her."

"What?"

Dave shrugged.

"An animal maybe? Who knows? I didn't see anything. And she was fine once we got back to the others."

"So what happened?"

"Nothing really. She said she thought she'd been followed, so we came back into the clearing together and then she said she must have imagined it and she was OK again."

"But she wasn't OK about it, was she?" Jeff said thoughtfully, "She must still have been upset because she came in, probably wanting to speak to me about it, only she burst in on the two of us…y'know."

"No, no, she was outside after that," said Dave, wincing as he realised he had reopened yesterday's embarrassment, "I know, because she kinda told me what had happened."

"Did she?" said Jeff, "Great. Look, I don't know what Em said, but it was just an embarrassing accident; I thought the door was locked."

"Relax. She was cool about it, grossed out, but cool. She's a very mature kid."

"I should go speak to her," said Jeff.

"I thought you did already," said Rita.

"Not about that; about whatever it was that followed her in the woods."

"Jeff," said Rita, "Em could be embarrassed that she got scared, OK? So just ask her if she wants to go for a

213

walk or something, and let her bring the subject up if she wants to, when she wants to."

"I know, I know. I can be sensitive," he caught Rita's raised eyebrow, "What?"

"Nothing," she smiled, "You'll be just fine."

"OK. Thanks for your support. Think I'll go now."

Jeff left the room, passing Bill as he came in.

"Sorry Bill, can I take a rain check on the chess?"

"Sure, no problem. The rest of us can play a game of Monopoly," he rubbed his hands together energetically, "There's a box over there and it's got nearly all the pieces."

Minutes later, Rita was crossing the lobby.

Having loathed Monopoly since childhood, she had managed to excuse herself from the game on vaguely articulated and wholly fictitious moral grounds. She had escaped from the game, but now found herself with a long afternoon to fill, and Rita had never been very good at doing nothing. Absently pausing at the reception desk she found herself rearranging the pens into a neat row. She was already bored. So when, on the spur of the moment, it occurred to her that she might go and see whether Jeff was right, she acted at once. There must surely be a dishwasher in a place like this; Jeff had simply not been thorough in looking for it. He never really searched for any mislaid item and was always calling her to find things he'd lost, that were in fact in plain view, right in front of him. She'd find the dishwasher and then poor, dear Jeff would have to quit his complaining about his washday hands. She could be in and out of the basement in no time and the Cousins still weren't back from town yet, so she wouldn't actually be intruding. It wasn't really trespassing either because she did have a reason to be there, albeit not a very pressing one.

Rita may have reasoned away any objections on the grounds of acceptable curiosity, but she nevertheless checked that there was no one else in the lobby before she slipped behind the desk and quietly opened the door that led down to the basement.

The kitchen was quiet yet Rita felt strange being down there alone. The room was well lit and its brushed steel units clinically utilitarian, but she felt an unusual prickling of her skin; the shivering thrill of being where she had no honest right to be.

Several rooms led off from the kitchen itself: two store rooms, a walk-in larder and a utility room. Rita moved from one to the next, searching for Jeff's missing dishwasher.

Engrossed in her task, she didn't realise that she was no longer alone in the silent kitchen. Pale eyes now followed her progress.

Oblivious to the newcomer, Rita completed her search. Jeff had been right, there was no dishwasher here. Rita closed the utility room door and stood for a moment, mentally checking off each room. Satisfied, she turned to go.

"Jeez!" she gasped, recoiling, "You gave me a shock."

The girl had been standing right behind her, pale eyes regarding her gravely.

Still shaken, Rita leant back against the door for support.

"Phew. I'm not kidding. That was some shock you just gave me."

Still the girl said nothing, but she smiled at Rita sympathetically and Rita began to feel rather foolish. As the shock began to subside, she realised that she knew the girl.

"I'm sorry, I didn't know you were back already. Guess you must have had a hell of a journey with all the snow."

The girl maintained her smile, but her continued silence only added to Rita's embarrassment; she felt as guilty as a schoolgirl, caught playing hooky.

"Look, I'm sorry I came down here," she said, recovering somewhat, "You're not going to believe this; but I actually just came down here to look for a dishwasher."

The girl's large pale eyes flicked towards the tall stack of obviously clean dishes that Jeff and Bill had so carefully constructed. Rita could not but follow her gaze.

"Yeah, I know, silly huh? My husband, Jeff, washed them by hand. He did tell me that you didn't have a machine, but I thought you'd have to have one and so I kinda came down to look for it. But hey, turns out he was right. First time for everything, right?"

She smiled lamely but still the girl said nothing.

"Y'know what?" Rita persisted, "The dishwasher's not important. I'll just go back upstairs. Say hi to your folks for me, OK?"

Not waiting for an answer, Rita walked quickly over to the foot of the stairs. As she placed her foot on the first step she jumped, startled, at the girl's quiet, unmodulated voice.

"It's in the room with the green door, off the dining room."

"What is? The dishwasher?" Rita asked, turning back.

The girl nodded.

"Right. Thanks for that...er...What's your name Honey?"

The girl showed no sign of responding, so Rita tried again.

"I'm Rita," she smiled, "And you are?"

The girl didn't seem to understand. Maybe she was a bit slow. Rita shrugged and again turned to leave.

Once more, the quiet voice, "Laura."

Rita turned back and smiled at the girl.

"Laura? That's a pretty name. Well, thanks for your help, Laura. And I really am sorry about, y'know, coming down here. See you around, OK?"

Laura smiled and nodded. Rita hurried on up the stairs.

"Ree!"

Rita again jumped, startled this time by Jeff's call.

"Sorry. Didn't mean to scare you," he said, "Why so jumpy?"

"Nothing, only I didn't know the Cousins had got back and I was downstairs, looking for your damn dishwasher."

"Aha, been caught snooping have you?"

"Shut up, it's not funny. It was really embarrassing. And it's all your fault."

"How d'you reckon that?"

"Like I said, I was looking for your damn dishwasher."

Jeff wisely resisted the urge to question his ownership of a non-existent dishwasher.

"And did you find one?" he asked.

"No."

"Hah!"

"It's not down there, Mr Smartass, because it's here."

"Huh?"

Rita opened the dining room door and pointed,

"It's in a room over there, through that green door."

"Makes sense I guess; less distance to carry everything. But, if they keep the plates up here, they won't be too pleased that Bill and I stacked them all down there in the kitchen."

"No, it's OK, there's a dumb waiter thing that they use to send the cooked food up. They can use it to get the plates back up here."

"Ah, so you weren't so embarrassed that you couldn't stop to quiz them while you were down there?" Jeff laughed.

Rita returned the smile, but said nothing. She was puzzled. How had she known about the dumb waiter? She hadn't discovered it in her search and she had no recollection of Laura having mentioned it when they were in the basement. And yet now it seemed to Rita that she could recall Laura's dull, quiet voice explaining where the dumb waiter was. Rita knew it was there; she even had a mental image of it in use.

"I think I'll go take a nap," she said, rubbing her temple.

"You OK?"

"Yeah, I'm fine. Oh, how was Em?"

"She's in her room and she doesn't want to talk. But she sounds OK, far as I can tell. I think you're right; I'll let her talk to me in her own time. You sure you're OK?"

"Yeah, really, I'm fine. I'll catch you later."

"Looks like the Cousins have finally made it back," Jeff announced to the group in the lounge.

"Finally," echoed Neil, "Now we can get room service and, thank God, we can look forward to having decent meals made for us, by someone who can actually cook."

"Hey, I think Ree and Dave did a great job," Jeff countered loyally.

"Very impressive," Bill agreed.

"It's OK folks," Dave said good-naturedly, "I can take it."

Neil looked bored with them all. He rose from his chair and announced to the room in general, "I'm going to take a bath and I may dress for dinner."

Dave looked up.

"You feeling OK?"

Neil ignored the question, so Dave got to to his feet and offered his arms for an embrace, but Neil pulled away. The very public rejection left Dave feeling awkward and humiliated. Yet, even as Dave stood in silence, watching him walk away, Neil seemed completely unaware of the effect he had had. Annie, however, thought she caught a momentary glint of pleasure in his eye as he turned away.

The door closed behind Neil, and Dave immediately turned his attention to the floor. His face was burning and he felt ridiculous standing there. Sitting around him, the others also lowered their eyes, sharing his embarrassment. Bill recovered first. He rose and put a consoling hand on Dave's shoulder.

"Don't let him get to you. It's just his way; he can be an A grade shit when it suits him. Takes some getting used to, but he'll be OK later, you'll see."

By the time that Dave was walking slowly back to his room, an hour or so later, he was smiling again. Bill, Jeff and Annie had made a determined effort to cheer him up. They had joked and cajoled until finally Dave felt able to join them, swapping anecdotes, happily relaxed. Out of regard for his feelings, Bill and Jeff refrained from too harsh a criticism of Neil, though Annie made several barbed remarks. For his part, Dave still could not bring himself to think too badly of the man he loved. The others had laughed, but Dave thought it endearing that Neil, the man who had spent the majority of his time here loudly bemoaning the primitive conditions, was even now proposing to dress for dinner as if he were staying at some fancy hotel back in the city.

As he climbed the stairs Dave smiled fondly, deep in thought. Neil was such an engaging mass of weird contradictions. It seemed to Dave that Neil was a man who needed the security of knowing that his life would unfold as he expected. He felt unsettled when actual events deviated from his expectations. With these excuses, and in spite of abundant evidence to the contrary, Dave managed to explain away Neil's frequent bouts of irascibility. He persisted in the belief that Neil turned a face of bitterness to the world solely as a mask behind which he concealed his deep insecurity; the inner anxiety of the lost, frightened boy within.

This misguided belief made Dave resolute; he would care for Neil and be at his side forever, protecting him and providing the security he secretly, perhaps even unconsciously, craved. Overwhelmed by his feeling of devotion to Neil, Dave's spirits rose. He was in love and his face glowed with a contented, loving smile.

The smile however was short-lived and slipped from his face as soon as he opened his door. Neil was pacing the room, clearly agitated. He had already helped himself to several shots from the mini-bar and his face was dark with brooding anger.

Having no idea as to what had given rise to this mood, Dave tried a light approach.

"Hey, what's up man?"

Neil scowled.

"Are you serious?" he snapped.

"Huh?"

"Are you seriously asking me what's wrong?"

"Yeah man, you look really pissed and I don't like to see you this way," Dave's tone was soothing, "What's up?"

"I do not enjoy being laughed at. I will not be ridiculed. Is that so very hard to understand?"

"No. But..."

Dave shook his head, mystified.

"The snowman!" Neil hissed.

"The snowman? What about it?"

"You made me look a fool."

"Oh man, it was a snowman, just to make the kids laugh."

"So what, now I'm a fucking clown; here to amuse Bill and Annie's no-neck runts?"

"Whoa man, chill! It was snowing and we had some fun. No big deal," Dave raised his hands, "And don't talk about the kids like that. They're OK. They had fun. I had fun. It was great. No, really. Maybe you should try it sometime."

"You want to have fun, fine, but not at my expense," Neil's tone was icy, "Just leave me out of it."

For a few moments neither said a word. Then Dave broke the silence.

"Where's all this come from? You were OK when you left the lounge. Hey no, you weren't, were you? You pushed me away."

"I thought I'd made myself clear. I expected you to follow me up. Why did you stay down there so long?"

"We were talking, you know, just relaxed. It was fun. Your friends are OK. I can see why you've kept up with them for so long."

Neil sneered derisively and once again, silence descended between them. Dave watched uneasily as Neil poured another shot and downed it in one mouthful. Then he decided to ask Neil the question that had been bothering him since yesterday evening's conversation in the lounge.

"Why did you come all the way out here if you hate the country and all these people so much?"

"I don't hate them."

"You bitched at them all yesterday evening."

"It's what they expect."

"That's not how I read it."

"Well, I naturally defer to your extensive wisdom on the subject. I guess I've only known all of them since college, whereas you've known them for... I forget... How long is it? Oh, yes, that's right, one day! What was I thinking? Of course you know better than me what goes on in their heads."

"You can deny it all you want, but you were not a nice person to be with yesterday evening, especially when you picked on that poor girl. She was just trying to make conversation."

"Oh yeah," Neil began to imitate Lou's high, thin voice, "I think it's just great that you're happy bein' ho-mo-sexual."

"What's wrong with that?"

"What's wrong is the implicit assumption that it must be difficult, if not impossible, to take pride in being gay because it's such a disgusting and ungodly perversion."

"Oh come on."

"What?"

"She didn't say anything like that."

"Implicit, David, I said 'implicit'. We're talking subtext here."

"You look for insult everywhere don't you? Have you ever stopped to consider that the problem might not be with other people, but with you."

"Oh, spare me the psycho-babble bullshit, please," said Neil, pouring himself another drink, this time a double.

"No, I'm serious Neil," Dave persisted, "I think you're a deeply unhappy person."

"Then why not make me happy again by shutting the fuck up?"

Dave was hurt. But he cared for this man, so he persisted.

"Know what man? You're not always an easy person

to love."

"So don't love me."

"Like I have a choice." said Dave quietly, forcing a smile.

Neil fixed Dave with a cold stare.

"We all have choices."

Phil had decided that Ethan had had enough exercise and fresh air.

"Lou, go fetch him will you? It's getting too cold; I reckon it's gonna snow again."

Lou hurried over to the playing children, gathered Ethan up in her arms then stopped as something caught her eye. A shape was moving just beyond the edge of the clearing.

"Phil!" she called, not quite a shout, but urgent.

"What is it now?"

He followed her gaze to the trees at the edge of the clearing. Nothing. No, wait, there it was; a movement, something moving towards them, but still within the trees.

"Kids," Lou shouted, "come back here. Right now!"

Lisa and Mikey picked up the anxiety in her voice. They moved towards her, then turned to look back towards the edge of the clearing as a man stepped out from the cover of the trees.

He wore a battered, leather hat pulled down so low that the watching group were unable to make out his features until he was only a matter of yards away from them. With a tipping back of his head, he looked up.

"Howdy folks. Thought I'd look in on yuh, seein' as how the road's blocked an' I reckon Jack and Karen are gonna be stuck in town awhile longer. Told 'em I'd keep an eye on you folks if something like this happened. You OK for firewood?"

"What?" asked Phil.

"Firewood, son. You OK for firewood?"

"I guess. I dunno. How should I know?"

The old man fixed Phil with an appraising stare. His face was incredibly wrinkled and his skin brown as tanned hide. He was obviously a good age, but he showed no sign of frailty, with his strong voice and his purposeful manner. His broad chest strained at the buttons of a faded padded jacket which, like him, looked to have seen many winters.

"You should make it yuh business to know, son, 'cause yuh ain't in the city now an' a good wood pile can keep you an' yuh kin alive when winter storms blow in like this. Temperature can drop mighty quick."

"Is that a fact?" Phil resented being lectured to by this old timer and the irritation showed in his voice, "Well, as we're only just into the Fall, I don't think this snow's gonna last. We're not gonna be dying of frostbite any time soon, Grandad."

"Know a lot about life out here do yuh, son?"

Phil stood as erect as possible, arms folded across his chest. He fixed the older man with an obstinate glare.

"Enough."

"Ha!" the old man laughed, obviously unconvinced.

Sensing Phil's rising anger, Lou spoke up quickly.

"Have you come all the way from town, Mr…?"

"Spielman, ma'am, Eric Spielman."

The old man touched the brim of his hat and stared down at Lou.

"No ma'am. I live not far from here. Make a living supplying firewood to the townsfolk, an' here, to the hotel."

"Pleasure to meet you, Mr Spielman, and thanks for looking in on us," Lou proffered a hand, "I'm Lou and this is Phil."

Phil grunted an acknowledgement.

"These yours?" asked Spielman, "Don't mind my sayin' so, ma'am, but yuh don't look old enough for to have kids this age."

"This is my son, Ethan," said Lou, glowing with pride as the conversation turned to her darling son, "Say hi, Ethan," she guided the child's chubby little hand in a clumsy wave, "And these are our friends' kids."

Mikey and Lisa stepped out from behind her. They smiled shyly.

The old man seemed to pause as he looked from Lou to the children.

"Is something wrong, Mr Spielman?" Lou asked.

The old man seemed indecisive for a moment, then he grabbed at Lou's sleeve, the sudden movement taking her by surprise. With an urgency that was not to be questioned, he moved her away from Lisa and Mikey.

Lou resented being pulled along like this, but she'd always been taught to show respect to old people and so felt obliged to accept this strange man's odd behaviour. She shot a glance at Phil to follow, so he trailed after them, still resentful.

"OK, what's going on?" Phil demanded, once they were out of earshot of the children.

Spielman pointedly ignored him and spoke only to Lou.

"You know anything 'bout the history o' this place, ma'am?"

"No. Should I?"

The old man hesitated, as if trying to decide whether to go on. But Lou had to know.

"What history, Mr Spielman? Please tell us."

Spielman sighed.

"Goes back a long way. Some say as it goes back to before any people lived here, white or Injun. But I only know for sure of what happened in my time," he waved his arm, taking in the hotel and its clearing, "This place, the hotel, was built back in the fifties as a bunk house for workers on the dam."

"Dam? What dam?"

"They were set on floodin' the forest for miles. Folks said it would'a bin the biggest man-made lake in the world. Hydroelectric. Men came from all over looking for work on the construction. Heck, Losien grew to the size it is today in no more'n two years. But soon after they started work on fellin' the trees, that's when things started to happen."

"What kind of things?" Phil asked, interested now, in spite of himself.

Again, the old man ignored him.

"Some said spirits of the forest bin disturbed. Some said it was spirits o' the dead Injuns returned for to exact their revenge."

"Dammit, what revenge? What happened?"

With evident amusement at Phil's irritation, Spielman shook his head.

"Was a bad business, a bad business," then he coughed, "But what am I thinkin'? Sun won't be up more 'an a few hours, I'd best go check the wood pile. If yuh do need any more wood, I'll bring some when I come back later."

The look of rising frustration on Phil's face gave the old man a good deal of pleasure, but Lou also wanted him to say more.

"Please, Mr Spielman," she begged, "Please tell us what happened. I really need to know."

Spielman looked down into Lou's anxious face. Annoying that young moosehead, Phil, was good sport, but this young woman's eyes were pleading and fearful, and she so reminded him of another girl, from years before. He couldn't play with her feelings, so at length he relented.

"It was bad," he said, quietly, glancing around to check that Lisa and Mikey were nowhere near, "Kiddies began to disappear."

Phil and Lou hurried the kids back into the hotel.

"Why d'we have to come in?" Mikey whined, dragging his feet.

"Because we do, so get indoors!"

Lisa and Mikey had not heard that sharpness in Lou's voice before. They exchanged glances and shrugged in agreement; adults were strange, it was no use trying to understand them. Resigned, they followed Lou and Phil into the hall. But, once inside, Phil and Lou seemed suddenly to lose all interest in them.

"Go play, you two," ordered Lou, "Phil and I have something we gotta do."

"Great! Come on Mikey, let's go finish the new snowman."

"No, not outside! Go play in your room."

The kids' faces fell, but Lou was not to be swayed.

"Go on. To your room, now."

"Can't we come with you? It's boring just being on our own."

"No, you can't," said Phil, "but you can take Ethan with you."

Phil prised the toddler from Lou's reluctant grasp. She looked fiercely into his eyes, but he dismissed her concern with impatience.

"Will you please relax, what's gonna happen here in the hotel? He'll be fine with them."

Lisa and Mikey led Ethan away and Phil opened the door to the lounge for Lou. She swept past him into the room, pointedly ignoring him, her anger plain to Bill, Jeff and Annie. Bill turned back to the chessboard and asked, apparently casually, if everything was OK.

"No," snapped Lou, "everything is not OK. There've been child abductions around here for years. Did you know that?"

The rook slipped from Bill's hand.

"What? What d'you mean?"

"We met a guy outside-"

"A guy?" asked Jeff, "What guy?"

"A guy who supplies the wood for the hotel."

"Spielman," said Phil.

"He found one of them, for God's sake. He said kids were disappearing since way back."

"The fifties," Phil added.

Lou shot him a glare, and continued.

"I don't care if it was years ago. We should've been told about this. I don't want Ethan to be here. I wanna go home."

There was a moment's shocked silence as the others tried to absorb the news. Rising, Annie put out her arms and hugged Lou to her, as she would a child. She could feel the young woman trembling. Whatever the stranger had said had Lou very frightened.

"Shh now. It'll be OK. Phil, what exactly did this guy say."

"She's told you what he said," said Phil, "Kids disappeared. But it was all a long time ago."

"They caught the killer?"

"Killer?" asked Jeff, "The kids were killed?"

"I guess."

"So who was he, the killer?"

"I don't know. Spielman didn't say, but like I said, it's all over now."

"You saw the way he reacted when he saw the kids," Lou snapped, "Does it look like he thinks it's all over?"

"Lou, if he found one of the bodies, he's bound to be

a bit, y'know, freaked."

"Where's this guy now?" asked Jeff.

"Who, the killer?"

Annie felt Lou shudder.

"No, Phil, this Spellman guy."

"Spielman," Phil corrected, "He's gone to get some more wood. Said he'd be back later."

22

Rita had slept for over an hour. She stretched slowly, in an indulgently feline movement and yawned lazily. Finally, reluctantly, she pushed the quilt aside. She was in no hurry to go back downstairs, especially as the prospect of a long, leisurely and undisturbed soak in the tub now suggested itself. She rechecked her watch. There was still plenty of time before supper. Grinning with pleasurable anticipation, she padded over to the bathroom and poured a generous gloop of bubblebath into the steaming water swirling in the tub. The heady fragrance dispersed in a warm, fragrant mist that filled the small room then curled low, rolling across the carpet, out into the bedroom. Rita let her gown slip from her shoulders and stood, enveloped in perfumed, soothing warmth, savouring the moment, as her reflection gradually disappeared behind the condensation on the mirror.

With the tub full almost to overflowing and clouds of bubbles teetering high above its sides, Rita turned off the water. Just as she slipped into scented, foaming heaven, she heard a voice, shouting, from outside. It sounded like Lisa.

There was nothing unusual in Lisa's tone, no reason at all why Rita should have given it a second thought. Nevertheless she paused. Was everything OK? Lisa and

Mikey weren't her responsibility, but she liked them; they were great kids. It sounded like the kids were still out in the clearing and Rita couldn't hear any adult voices. She wasn't clear about what dangers might be out there. She had a vague and probably foolish notion that there might be bears or other wild animals in the area but, foolish or not, she wasn't happy with the thought of Lisa and Mikey being out there on their own. Was someone with them? Bill, most likely. Sure, Phil might be irresponsible, he would come back in leaving the kids outside on their own and not think to tell anyone, but Bill would have been going out from time to time to check that they were OK. He'd have taken over if Phil had come back in without them. The kids would be fine.

Nevertheless, though she was now immersed in luxuriously deep, hot water, Rita wasn't able to relax; despite her attempts to dismiss it, the worry nagged away at her until, sighing, she got up, out of the tub. It would only take a second to reassure herself that the kids were OK, then she'd be back in the tub and able to properly enjoy the indulgence.

Wrapping a towel about her, Rita tip-toed to the window, dripping a trail of wet bubbles across the bedroom floor. She pushed her face against the glass, which steamed up immediately, blocking her view. Rubbing a circle clear, she looked down and saw Laura smiling up at her from the clearing below, as if she had been waiting, somehow knowing that Rita would come to the window. Rita shivered, not solely because of the chilled air near the window pane, but also from a sudden sense of unease. Laura, however, continued to smile up at her while, behind her, Mikey and Lisa scampered delightedly in the snow.

At that, Rita finally relaxed and smiled. Laura was a strange kid, no question, but it looked like she'd been kind enough to offer to watch over Lisa and Mikey and they seemed more than happy to be out there with her. Surely Laura would know what dangers to look out for; she lived here, for Pete's sake.

From the clearing below, Laura returned Rita's smile, waved once more, and then turned back to the game.

Dave had left the bedroom. He needed to be alone; away from Neil. He stood now at the hotel's opened back door, gasping in the cold air, turning over what Neil had said to him. What choices do we have? What was Neil trying to say? Dave's mind tumbled with thoughts and doubts, so much so that he was unaware of the icy wind blowing over and around him. Only when he was already shuddering uncontrollably did he come to his senses and register the biting cold at his face. Though still unsettled, he knew he'd freeze if he stayed here any longer. He began to turn to go back in.

Something caught his eye; a movement at the edge of the clearing. Dave frowned. He peered out into the gathering darkness, but could see nothing. It must have been a trick of the fading light. Yeah, must have been. He shrugged and shut the door.

There was a movement behind him.

"Dave, at last, I've been looking for you everywhere. Where have you been?"

Dave looked down into Annie's puzzled face and was himself confused.

"Nowhere," he said, "Well, here. I wanted some air."

The door suddenly blew open again, loosing a fresh blast of freezing air. Annie slammed it shut then, turning, touched Dave's sleeve.

"God, you're frozen! Why didn't you wear a jacket?"

She drew Dave's hands together and rubbed them vigorously whilst he simply stood, allowing her to fuss over him without protest, his mind obviously elsewhere.

Gradually though, as warmth flooded back into his hands, he began to recover.

"Why were you looking for me?"

"What?" said Annie, pausing for a moment in her furious rubbing.

"You said you were looking for me."

"Oh yeah, that's right. We're all meeting in the lounge. Lou and Phil met some guy who told them there've been child abductions here and now Lou wants to leave."

"What! Child abductions?" Dave couldn't take in what he was being told, "Here? When? What happened?"

"I don't know any more than that, but we're all meeting to decide what to do. Are you warmed up enough to move? Come on."

"What about Neil?"

"What about him?"

"He won't know."

"About the meeting? Yes he does."

"No, I mean he doesn't know you've found me; he could still be looking for me. Should I go find him?"

Annie hesitated,

"No, Dave, don't worry. He'll be OK."

When Annie led Dave into the lounge, he saw that Neil was already seated in the armchair closest to the fire, looking moodily disinterested in all around him. Neil noticed Dave, but immediately glanced away, making no acknowledgement of him, not even the merest nod of his head.

Dave's spirit was crushed. He realised now that Neil had never been looking for him. Annie had come to find him because Neil simply hadn't been interested in finding him. He knew that Neil had been drinking, but nevertheless he was hurt that Neil had so easily dismissed him from his mind. Dave dropped into a window seat at the end of the room, farthest away from Neil. Annie still held his arm and was about to insist that he move closer to the fire, but she caught his look towards Neil and also saw the scowl on Neil's face.

She'd seen that icy, unyielding look in Neil's eyes before, and she could read the signs; Dave was on his way out. It was a pattern Annie had seen played out many times over the years. From this point on, Neil would show nothing but contempt for Dave, until, unable to take it any more, the poor boy would make a quiet exit. And all the while, Neil would refuse to give him or anyone else any explanation as to why he apparently now loathed the man who had so recently been at his side. Annie's heart sank to a leaden weight within her chest. She hated these situations. They were predictable of course; Neil's rejection followed the relatively short period of attentiveness as surely as night followed day, but the events were no easier to witness for having been anticipated.

Over the many years she had known Neil, Annie had met many of his partners. Not all had been likeable, indeed many had been a match for Neil's self-obsession and casual, thoughtless cruelty. Several, though, had been sweet kids who deserved far more than Neil would ever be able, or willing, to give. But of all Neil's partners, Annie had really liked this one. Maybe it was her age, but she felt something akin to a maternal fondness for him. And, though she was certain that Dave would eventually be happier alone rather than with Neil, she ached for him at his sudden rejection. She squeezed his hand sympathetically. Dave nodded and Annie left him, going to sit next to Bill.

"Everyone here?" Phil asked, scanning the room.

"Rita's up in our room," said Jeff, "She's asleep."

"Don't you think she should be here?" asked Lou.

"I don't really know why **we're** here, and I wasn't about to go wake her and drag her down here to hear some old timer's stories."

"They're not just old stories," insisted Lou, her voice high, clearly distressed.

"OK, OK, I'm sorry."

With reluctant resignation, Jeff eased himself out of his comfortable armchair and walked stiffly to the door.

"I'll go see if she's awake."

Lou, shaking with scarcely controlled apprehension, could hardly bear to watch Jeff's unconcerned lack of haste. Her chest felt constricted, tight with fear and urgency, she couldn't breathe. How could Jeff take all this so calmly?

"Can't you hurry, Jeff, please?"

Jeff, however, felt annoyed that Lou was making some long dead case into such a big deal. Phil had said it was all over years ago, so what was the panic? Still, if it had served no other purpose, Lou's over-reaction had turned Jeff's thoughts to Emma. He decided to drop by her room and check she was OK. Knocking on her door, he was amazed when she called him in, her voice sounding quite like the old Emma; no hint of a sneer or sarcasm. But she was lying on her bed and Jeff was alarmed.

"Honey, are you OK?"

"No Dad, but I think I just ate too much at lunch. I'm gonna give supper a miss if that's OK."

Emma added a weary closing of her eyes to complete the effect and Jeff was completely taken in. He knelt next to the bed and took her hand, speaking softly as he'd used to when she was a tiny child.

"Of course it's OK, Em. You just stay here and rest. Can I get you anything?"

"No, thanks Dad. I think I just need to rest, quietly. I'll be OK in the morning."

Jeff tenderly stroked his daughter's hair and Emma was amazed at just how good this felt. It was wonderfully soothing. Normally she would not have allowed her father to comfort her like this and, in this rare moment of closeness, she almost felt bad at deceiving him. She did feel bad. But she knew she couldn't tell him what she was planning; he wouldn't understand. This was the best way, the only way. And anyhow, she'd be out and back again before he, or anyone else, even realised she'd left the hotel.

Jeff tucked the quilt around his daughter, smiling, ridiculously pleased at this small opportunity to show his love for her.

"Goodnight Love."

"Night Dad."

"Love you."

"Love you too, Dad."

Still smiling, Jeff switched off the light and gently closed the door.

Minutes later, he found himself talking through a bathroom door to a very drowsy Rita.

"Jeff, is that you? Sorry, I must have dozed off. That's weird, I've only been in here about twenty minutes. But I'll be getting out soon."

"OK. Ree, can you come meet me in the lounge when you're ready?"

"Sure," Rita paused to yawn, "I'll be out real soon."

She yawned again, then Jeff heard her run more hot water into the tub. This didn't seem to him to be the action of a woman intending to leave her bath any time soon.

"I'll see you downstairs then, in the lounge? Ree?"

"Yeah, got that. In the lounge. I'll be there."

Jeff left with little expectation that his wife would be appearing before supper time.

"She says she'll be down soon, but I think we should start without her," he announced to those gathered in the lounge.

"Before we do, shouldn't we ask the Cousins to join us?" asked Annie.

Bill let his hand rest on hers.

"I'd rather hear what Lou has to say first, Honey," he turned to Lou, "Do you want to tell us what this guy said?"

"Shouldn't we wait for Rita?" Lou asked.

"Just get on with it, will you," Neil snapped.

His sharpness shook Lou's confidence and she sat down abruptly, looking to Phil to take over.

"OK," Phil began, "this old guy, Spielman, says he's a woodsman. He's got a place out in the forest. Says he supplies the hotel with firewood, though why they can't cut their own firewood when they've got a whole goddam forest all around them, beats the hell outa me," Lou fidgeted, anxious to keep him to the subject at hand, "OK, yeah," Phil continued, "Speilman says this whole area of the forest, for miles away towards the mountains, was going to be flooded by a new dam."

"What's that got to do with anything?" Bill asked.

Phil gave Bill his most withering sneer.

"Can I continue?"

"If you must," Neil muttered.

Phil's rising anger was plain, but Lou tugged at his sleeve.

"Not now Phil," she whispered, "just tell them what he said."

Phil pursed his lips peevishly, but continued.

"This guy Spielman says that when the workers came to work on the dam, kids started disappearing from Losien."

"So it was one of the construction workers?" Jeff asked.

"No one knows. They never caught him."

"You say this all happened years ago?" Bill asked, wanting confirmation.

"Spielman said it started back in the fifties."

"OK. So when did it stop?"

"He got kinda evasive when I asked him that. He said that he discovered the body of one of the girls, back in '57. Came across her body in a broken down shack in the woods and the Sheriff's Department found the bodies of other missing kids buried all around it."

"How many?" Annie wanted to know.

"Does that matter?" Bill said quietly, "One is too many."

She gently squeezed his hand.

"This shack," asked Neil, "tell me, is it now a hotel?"

It amused Neil to see that Lou was visibly shaken by the implication.

Phil fixed Neil with an irritated glare.

"Can you believe it? I didn't think to ask him that one."

Suddenly Lou relaxed.

"No, Honey, it's OK. He said this place was a bunk house for the dam workers."

"Oh, those damned workers," Neil muttered.

"Will you shut up!" Annie had had enough of him, "This isn't the time for you to try to exercise your supposed wit!"

She glared at Neil and had the fleeting satisfaction of seeing his eyes widen in surprise, before he managed to control his reaction and look away.

Bill was similarly surprised by his wife's unusual show of aggression. But Neil could look after himself and there were far more important matters at hand, so he let her outburst pass without comment.

Phil continued.

"Lou's right. Spielman definitely said this place had been built for the workers."

"But I thought you said that the killer was one of the workers," said Jeff, "so I guess he could have stayed here."

Again, Lou shuddered.

"Sorry Lou, just thinking aloud."

"What I said was that no one knew who the killer was. He was never found."

"But the killings stopped?" asked Bill, wanting reassurance.

"Yeah, sure," said Phil.

But Lou remained glumly silent at his side.

"Did this guy actually say that?" Bill pressed.

"Kinda."

"Phil, what the fuck do you mean, 'kinda'?"

There was a shocked gasp as Bill spoke. No one had ever heard him swear. He took a moment to calm himself before continuing.

"I'm sorry, but we've got our kids here. We have to know. Phil, what, exactly, did the man say?"

"Like I said, he was kinda evasive."

"We have to find out what the hell's going on," said Bill, "I'm going to get the Cousins in here to give us some straight answers."

Bill stormed out of the room, leaving silence in his wake. Neil raised an eyebrow, but Annie cut him dead.

"Not a word, Neil. Not one goddam word."

From his seat at the window, Dave had paid little heed to

most of what was being discussed. He was bewildered and hurt, his attention still focused on Neil. And now, as Annie snapped at Neil, Dave was dismayed to realise that he still felt a protective response rise within him, even after the way Neil had treated him; after everything he'd said. But as Bill marched out of the room, he momentarily interrupted Dave's view of Neil and that short break, the severance of the visual link, was enough to stay Dave's urge to leap to Neil's defence. Some of the tension went from his body and he sank back into the window recess. Let Annie say what she liked. Neil had it coming.

The thought was liberating, though it came with a small side order of guilt. Dave had to turn his head to the window, staring out into the night, so that no one would see his smile.

Outside, night was falling fast. The entire scene was becoming one of textured blackness save for the light from his window, and that from the others around the room, which were casting irregular squares of waxy yellow light onto the uneven snow of the clearing. Dave saw the rough approximation of his silhouette in the closest square of light and childishly raised his hand to wave, just to see his shadow mimic him. The action was foolish certainly, but he no longer cared. With snowball fights and building snowmen, Dave had today awakened an unsuspected, childlike side to his nature. And hell, if Neil was going to cut him out, then he no longer had to care either for Neil's approval or for his censure; Dave could indulge this inner child to his heart's content and, from now on, he intended to do just that.

Just then something in his view of the clearing suddenly shifted and Dave was instantly alert. Something was out there, beyond the reach of the light from the hotel. Something large.

"Man, did you see that?" he gasped. But no one seemed to have heard him.

He dared not look away from the window to call on the attention of the others, but stared fixedly out into the night, increasingly uneasy, sensing that the thing was staring right back at him. He felt horribly vulnerable, easily visible against the bright light of the room, and quite unable to judge the distance between himself and the hidden observer. He strained to make out more detail but, as before, the more he looked the more ill-defined the form became. Then, even as he watched, it seemed to melt into the surrounding shadows, leaving him unsure as to whether he had really seen anything at all.

"Seen something?"

It was Jeff. Dave shrugged.

"Maybe."

"What? What did you see?"

"I dunno. I think there was something out there."

"Something?"

"An animal maybe."

But, even as he said the words, Dave knew that what he had seen was no animal. He had sensed something more, an intelligence, out there in the darkness, watching him. As the sense of vulnerability came back to him, a wave of fear passed through his body, the hairs on his limbs rising and his shoulders shivering involuntarily.

"Oh, come on Dave," Jeff laughed, "Don't let yourself get spooked by Phil's murder stories."

Still shaken, Dave was unconvinced by Jeff's reassurance. But he good-humouredly suffered Jeff's slap on his back and forced a smile, pretending that he had indeed put the incident from his mind.

"I can't find them," Bill announced, marching back in the room.

"Did you look in the basement?"

"Of course I did. And I can't see any sign of their pickup outside either, not that you can make out much in the dark out there. Who was it said they were back?"

They all turned to one another, questioning. The trail of relayed conversations led back to Jeff. For a moment, he was puzzled. Then he remembered.

"Ree," he said, "She spoke to them down in the kitchen, after lunch."

"You sure? There was no sign of them when we were down there washing up," said Bill doubtfully.

"No, it was after we'd done washing the dishes. Ree went down to look for the dishwasher and they caught her snooping around."

Neil grinned and cleared his throat as if to say something, but Annie hissed, "Shut up Neil!" before he had the chance to form a single word.

By now, Bill was indifferent to Annie's treatment of Neil. He was focused solely on getting to the truth about the killings.

"Rita definitely said she saw them?"

"Spoke to them. And she certainly looked very embarrassed."

"Who looked embarrassed?" Rita had just walked into the room.

"I was just telling Bill that you had an unexpected visit with the Cousins this afternoon."

"Oh thanks for that, Darling."

"OK, so where are they now?" Bill raised his arms, exasperated, "It's not that big a place. Where the hell are they?"

"Who? The Cousins?" asked Rita, "Did you look in the basement?"

"Yes, Rita, I looked in the basement."

"Sorry!" Rita rolled her eyes, "What's the big deal

anyway? Why d'you need them right this minute?"

Phil started to speak, but Bill cut across him.

"There've been child abductions and murders here that started back in the fifties and, for all we know, could still be going on."

Rita was stunned.

"What?" she asked weakly.

"Phil and Lou met some guy when they were outside," said Jeff, guiding her, unresisting, into the chair next to his, "He told them all about it."

"What?" she repeated, completely bewildered.

"What?" Neil mimicked.

Both Jeff and Annie shot him narrow-eyed glares.

"Jeez, lighten up," he muttered, palms raised.

But both continued to stare at him until he shrugged and looked away.

By now Rita had begun to grasp what she had been told. She turned to Lou.

"This guy you met, you sure you believe him?"

Lou nodded mutely.

"Shit," Rita formed the word slowly, letting out a long breath.

"Question is," said Annie, "what are we going to do about it?"

"What can we do? We can't find the Cousins to verify what Spielman said, and the road to town is blocked with more than a foot of snow."

"Bill, we can try to keep calm for one," said Jeff, "We need to think clearly so we can decide what to do."

"Bill's right though," said Dave quietly, "Whatever we might decide to do, we're stuck here: it's snowing again."

Other conversation stopped and everyone turned to the big picture windows.

"Jeez," Bill whispered, "we're stuck alright. And it's getting heavier."

Annie closed her hand around his.

"I don't like this, Honey."

A nod of mutual understanding was the only consolation Bill could offer her.

For a few moments no one spoke.

Then Rita asked, "Where's this Spellman now?"

"Spielman," Phil corrected, weary of having to repeat himself, "He said he lives not far from here."

"Alone?"

"How should I know?"

"Does it matter?" Jeff asked.

"I just thought that, if he lived with a bunch of people, maybe a small logging settlement, we could go to them for help. They might have some skidoos or something."

Then Neil spoke up.

"Unless they're in it with him."

"In what? What d'you mean?"

"Am I the only one who thinks this all sounds rather unlikely? This guy Spielman sees these two out there and spins them some scare story to frighten them off. I mean, we don't know who this guy is, or what his motives are. Maybe he hates the Cousins. Maybe he doesn't like having a hotel up here in his neck of the woods. Maybe he just hates outsiders. Who knows?"

After a moment, Annie spoke in reluctant agreement,

"Neil has a point. We can't be sure how much to believe."

"You weren't there," said Lou, indignantly, "You didn't hear him talk. He wasn't making this up."

"With the greatest respect, Lou, you're very young."

"What's that got to do with anything?"

Rita tried to help.

"I think what Annie means is that you might not have come across as many con men as us old folks have."

"Don't patroness me!" Lou snapped.

Eyebrows were raised, but no one ventured a word of correction, not even Neil.

"And anyhow," Lou went on, "Phil was right there with me and he heard every word."

All eyes turned to Phil.

"Looked to me," he said, "like Spielman was on the level."

They all absorbed this in silence.

"We have to speak to the Cousins," said Bill, "Rita, when you spoke to them did they say anything about going out again this afternoon?"

"No, but I only spoke to their daughter and she's like her mom; doesn't say much."

"A daughter?" Jeff sounded surprised, " I didn't even know they had any kids."

"Yeah, Laura. Nice kid, but quiet."

"So have you actually seen her parents today?"

Rita shook her head.

"OK, so that's why we can't find them; they must've left Laura here when they went into town."

"No, Cousins told us that they were going to church. I'm sure he'd have said something if they were planning to leave Laura behind," said Annie.

"Yeah, that's right," Rita agreed, "And anyway, when I spoke to Laura, I said something about how they must have had a difficult journey on account of the snow, and she didn't say anything like that she'd been here all the time, or that her parents weren't back yet, or anything like that. Mind you, thinking about it, she did seem a bit y'know simple, so she might not have understood everything I was saying."

"How old is she?" asked Lou, "Would she know anything about the murders, d'you think?"

"No," Rita again shook her head, "No, I don't think she would."

"Well that's irrelevant anyhow; 'cause she's not here now."

"What do you mean?"

"She's not here. She's gone. I looked in every room down in the basement and there's definitely no one there."

"She was outside with the kids earlier," said Rita, "Maybe she's still with them."

"What?" it was now Bill and Annie's turn to look perplexed, "Phil, weren't you and Lou out there with them?"

"We were, till Spielman turned up. After that we all came back in, and we told the kids to go play in their room."

"When was this?" Rita asked.

"I dunno. Maybe a half hour ago, forty minutes, before we came in here."

"That's weird, 'cause I definitely saw Laura and the kids out there, but I couldn't see you two."

"We were there; this Laura kid wasn't. OK?"

"Sure she was. She was with the kids. I saw her. She waved up at me."

"If she'd been out there, Rita, we'd have seen her. And we didn't see her, so she wasn't out there," Phil was becoming irritated, "The kids were with us the whole time."

"OK, then maybe the kids went out again, with Laura, after you came in."

"No way, we told them to go to their room and stay there. No way would they have gone out again without our say so."

Annie scrambled to her feet.

"I'm going to go check on them."

Lou jumped up from her chair.

"Me too."

They hurried from the room.

"Oh, well done Rita."

Ignoring Phil's irony, Rita turned and spoke quietly to Jeff.

"D'you want to go check on Em?"

"No, it's OK. We had a talk earlier and she's just getting some rest. She didn't feel too good; ate too much at lunch."

"She's ill? My cooking's poisoned your daughter?"

"No, Ree," he laughed, glad of a break in the tension, "lunch was great. Em just ate too much, that's all. She'll be fine in the morning."

"I'm getting a drink," said Phil loudly, "Anyone else?"

Heads were shaken and Phil left the room, alone.

Those remaining in the lounge shifted uncomfortably in their seats. Small talk seemed somehow inappropriate. Several minutes passed in silence.

Eventually, Rita spoke quietly to Jeff.

"Laura's a bit simple. I really don't think her parents would leave her here and not tell us. I'm sure they'd want us to know she was here so we could, y'know, look out for her while they were away."

In the otherwise silent room, everyone had heard her whispered remark.

"You may be right," said Neil magnanimously, "but if you are, then you do realise what that means, don't you? It means that the Cousins, all three of them, did come back from town, since when they have all vanished. And this while, for whatever reason, this Spielman character is prowling about, trying to scare people away from their hotel. Maybe he really hates the hotel and its owners. Maybe he's got something to do with the Cousins' disappearance. Who knows? But it seems to me that Spielman chose the right people as targets for his scare story. I mean that moron, Phil, isn't going to ask any searching questions, is he? And that educationally stunted jail bait child bride of his probably wouldn't understand them if he did. Spielman could have told them anything and they'd have accepted it. And tell me, Jeff, would you rely on Phil's ability to tell if someone is lying to him?"

Jeff shrugged.

"I don't know what to think," said Rita dejectedly.

Again, the conversation lapsed.

"Just a minute," said Jeff, "Phil said that Spielman was coming back later, didn't he?"

"I don't remember him saying that."

"Yeah, Ree, he did. So we can quiz the guy then, OK?"

"Knock yourself out," said Neil, beginning to tire of the whole subject.

"Jeff, do you really think something bad could have happened to the Cousins?" Rita asked, "I mean, maybe we should take some precautions if Spielman does come back? He could be dangerous."

"Oh please!" Neil sneered, "He's just some ancient, tobacco-chewing, inbred hick who hates outsiders."

"Did you see him?"

"You know I didn't"

"Well then."

"Look," said Neil, trying to sound reasonable, "Phil said the guy was old, yeah? Well, if we're cut off by this snowfall, how's some old timer going to be able to get around? And how's he going to do us any harm? He's one and we're, what, eight? You do the math."

"But you said he might not be acting alone."

"No I didn't."

"You said they might be in it with him."

Neil frowned.

"Who?"

"The people he lives with."

"You were the one who said there might be some community near here. Turn around and take a look at the map on the wall over there. What do you see? Trees. Mile after mile of trees, trees and nothing but more fucking trees. Do you see any villages? Apart from the disused grain depot, do you see any settlements of any sort, until you get to that ghost town, Losien?"

"OK, you've made your point. So what do we do now?"

There was no chance for anyone to reply.

With a shout, Annie burst into the room.

"They're gone!" she screamed, "The kids are gone!"

23

The room was in uproar. Jeff, suddenly pale, was running for the door. With Rita struggling to keep up, he leapt up the stairs, three at a time and hammered on Emma's door, becoming frantic when there was no reply.

"Get back!" he shouted.

He hurled himself at the door, bursting it open. Em's room was dark and still; her bed empty.

Jeff walked over to the bed and sank to his knees, head lowered, his hand resting on the cold pillow. For a moment he was incapable of action; not knowing what to do next. Rita stole forward and took his arm.

"It's OK, Honey, she can't be far. We'll find her."

Jeff remained still, as if he hadn't heard her, and indeed, Rita hoped that was the case; she could scarcely believe she had just uttered such unconvincing and unfounded platitudes. Obviously she hoped that Em was somewhere in the hotel but there was a strong possibility that the headstrong, attention-seeking teenager could well be farther afield. Rita glanced towards the window. If Em had gone out there, how on earth would they find her? Where would they even start to look, in deep snow, unfamiliar terrain and rail tunnel blackness? Rita shook herself to dispel the thought. Her shiver jolted Jeff from his trance.

"I've got to find her," he whispered, "Come on."

Back in the lounge, the scene was now one of aimless panic. Bill had dumped a hastily gathered assortment of jackets and boots onto a chair. Annie and Lou, grabbing at the heap of clothes, were pulling on ill-fitting and ill-matched items with frantic disregard, their anxious faces blotchy and already wet with tears. Dave was pacing the room. Already dressed for the search, he was snapping batteries into a powerful flashlight. Only Neil remained untouched by the hysteria. He looked up from his armchair, catching Jeff's eye as he and Rita rushed back into the room.

In that moment, from across the desperate activity in the room, Jeff took in Neil's relaxed form, reclining comfortably by the fire, lazily stifling a yawn. Evidently none of the panicked, parental anguish had impacted on Neil in any way. As always, he had assumed the role of dispassionate onlooker, observing events while remaining untouched and unaffected by them. In other circumstances Jeff might have ignored the familiar selfishness and insensitivity, but now Neil's calm detachment affected Jeff far more than any of the futile shouting and headless frenzy going on around them. In that instant Jeff felt his distaste for Neil's indifference turn to an overwhelming hatred welling up within him, a cold loathing which he knew would neither fade with time nor be forgiven. Whatever were to happen, however things worked out, Jeff vowed to himself that, when all this was over, he would never again have anything to do with Neil. As far as he was concerned, that arrogant, fucked up, self-obsessed bastard was history.

Jeff felt his hands clench into fists. He wanted to march right over and shake Neil up, force him to show some trace of concern. But he did nothing. Even in his agitated state, the overriding demands of ingrained civility curtailed his outburst.

"Are you just going to sit there?" he snapped.

Neil seemed unconcerned.

"You have a better suggestion?"

The studied lack of concern in Neil's voice pushed Jeff over the edge. Ingrained civility could go hang!

"You shit!" Jeff shouted, "You self-centred prick! Can't you see what's happening here?"

If Neil was surprised, he still didn't show it.

"Yes, I can see," he answered calmly, "but it seems like I'm the only one who can."

Bill looked up.

"What d'you mean? You know something we don't?"

Neil shrugged.

"Only that Phil's mystery woodsman has got you all so spooked that you're proposing to go rushing headlong out into the dark, without even making a thorough search of the hotel. Those kids could be anywhere in this place: in a closet, in the attic, hiding under a bed. You're the expert on kids, Bill, you tell me."

"God, he's right," Bill gasped, sudden hope in his voice, "Come on!"

The realisation that Neil's maddening calm had in fact been a reasonable reaction to events pained Jeff more than he would have cared to admit. He felt foolish, ridiculed, as if Neil had made a specific, personal criticism of his own fevered panic. Perhaps the others felt the same as, quieter now, they hurried to follow Bill from the room, removing and discarding gloves and hats to left and right.

"You not going?" Neil asked Jeff, turning away to warm his hands at the fire.

Jeff had intended to go, but he was damned if he'd go at Neil's sending, so he stood his ground and turned the question back on Neil.

"Aren't you? The search was your idea."

"No," Neil, eased deeper into the cushions, "I'm good here, thanks. But don't let me keep you from doing your paternal thing. You'd better run along though, or someone else will find her before you do. And you wouldn't want that."

"What? What's that supposed to mean?'

Neil made no effort to turn, but continued to stare into the flames.

"Oh come on Jeff, you want Emma to know how much Daddy really cares. Am I right? Or are you really worried that she might have already figured out just how little you do care? Has she seen you for the ineffectual, self-involved, part-time parent you actually are?"

"Fuck you, Neil."

Neil smiled.

"A charming suggestion, but you're not my type dear boy."

Smugly satisfied, Neil turned to witness Jeff's reaction, but saw instead, to his irritation, that Jeff had already gone, leaving Neil's words to play to the empty room.

A thorough, but fruitless search had now been completed and the parents were passing into various states of disbelief, which each attempted to handle in their own way. Bill and Jeff were trying, independently, to organise everyone; shouting orders that met with no response whatever. Annie was clinging to Bill, hindering his attempts to direct matters and quite oblivious to the irritation this was causing him. Lou sat, absolutely quiet, shaking her head and gently rocking. Phil, newly returned from the bar, was bewildered by events and too relaxed by alcohol to react appropriately. Only Rita and Dave seemed to be acting to any useful purpose. Dave had taken the map from the wall and spread it out on the table. Hunched over it, he searched for some clue as to where to start a search of the woods. Huddled next to him, Rita lowered her voice to a whisper.

"We'll need some sort of weapons."

"What?"

"We'll need something if someone's got the kids," she paused, not wanting to think of the terrible possibilities, still less put them into words, "and even if the kids have just wandered off then, OK great, no fighting, but you said Em thought some animal had followed her and y'know, there could be bears out there. Either way, we need some weapons. You got a gun?"

Dave shook his head, appalled at the question. But he began to see the sense in what Rita was saying. The possibility of a bloody outcome to the coming search in the woods was dawning on him. He felt the warmth drain from his face and he shivered.

"You gonna be OK?" Rita whispered.

To this he nodded, hesitantly.

The noise of Jeff and Bill's futile shouting was becoming intolerable.

"Will you both shut the hell up!" Phil bellowed, banging his fist on a table.

Abruptly, Bill and Jeff fell silent and turned expectantly towards him. But Phil had no plan to share with them, no great idea; he had just wanted the noise to stop. Jeff and Bill stared at him.

"Thank you," he said, blinking at them uncertainly.

"You're drunk," Lou said with quiet disgust.

"No way. I just had a few shots, but the bar ain't even locked up. You all should get in there. Looks like you could all do with loosening up. 'Specially you Babe."

Cold fury burned in Lou's eyes.

"If it wasn't for you, Ethan would still be here with me. You made me leave him with Lisa and Mikey, and now he's missing. He's out there, God knows where, in the cold, and you're drunk, you useless piece of shit!"

Still oblivious to her fury, Phil whistled.

"Didn't know you even knew words like that, Babe," he grinned stupidly, "I gotta tell ya, it's come as quite a shock."

Very slowly, Lou walked over to Phil and slapped him, hard, across the face.

The sharp sound of the slap galvanised Jeff and Bill once more, but now they worked to a common purpose.

"We should split up to search. Rita, you come with me. Annie, you go with Bill, OK? Great. OK, Phil...Phil?"

Jeff realised that Phil was completely ignoring him. Still standing, Phil's attention was wholly on Lou as she turned and walked away. He was drunk but even so, he knew he was in big trouble this time. Talking his way out of this would take something special. Of course it would help if he knew what he was supposed to have done wrong. But, though he struggled to replay the last few minutes, his clouded head refused to clear. He shrugged and sank into an armchair.

"There's a map here," said Dave, "Should we divide up the area?"

"Good idea. There are four groups of two. Split the area up into four."

"Whoa, hold it right there," Neil had stirred again, "Jeff, I'm sorry about your kids, but there's no way I'm going out there."

Jeff lunged towards him.

"Wait!" Neil forced himself as far back as it was possible to get in his chair, "Have you seen how dark it is out there? Just tell me how you propose to see where you're going, never mind how you're going to follow any tracks, in pitch darkness."

Jeff stopped. His hands were gripping Neil's collar, their faces just inches apart, but all the energy of his anger suddenly drained away. His decisiveness of only a few seconds earlier gone, he now felt weak and utterly helpless.

Dammit! Neil was right. Again.

How were they going to find their way? And if they, as adults, were likely to get lost, how much worse would it be for the kids? Jeff had never before felt afraid for Emma; he and Julie had always shielded her. But now his little girl really needed his protection and he didn't know what to do. He began to tremble.

"I don't know. I don't know how, but I have to try."

"Come on, Jeff," Bill eased him away from Neil, "There must be flashlights or something useful somewhere. Come help me look."

Bill paused a moment.

"Has anyone called 911?"

Jeff looked uncertain.

"Would they be able to get here in this snow?" he asked.

"They might be able to send a helicopter," said Rita, "But we should ask them to come as soon as possible anyhow."

"Sure, but I left our cell phone back home."

"It's OK," said Dave, "there's a phone in the office. I'll go."

Bill smiled.

"Thanks Dave. Meantime, can I suggest that the rest of you get dressed as warm as you can."

"And take some extra clothes or blankets with you to put on the kids when we find them," Rita added, as much to raise hopes as for any practical purpose.

Dave went through the door behind the reception desk and opened the glazed door to his right. The office was quite crowded, with filing cabinets, cupboards and packing boxes lining the walls and a large desk filling the centre of the room. The phone was on the desk. Dave paused a moment, composing what needed to be said, then he picked up the receiver.

There was no dial tone.

The line was dead.

By the time they reassembled minutes later, Jeff and Bill had found two hurricane lamps and a flashlight. Rita had gathered as many warm clothes and blankets as she could find.

Annie began silently to fold blankets and scarves, tucking them into her backpack. Lou threw some blankets at Phil.

"Fold them!"

Phil did as he was told, but continued to stare at Lou in sullen, silent confusion.

Dave came back into the room.

"The line's down: guess it must be the snow."

The already anxious faces around him registered even greater concern at the news.

Dave walked over to the map.

"OK, there's not a whole lot of landmarks around here, but there is a river not far into the trees. I can't tell how big it is, but there are rapids and pools marked, so we'd all better take care."

"How are we going to manage not to get lost?" Jeff asked, with little expectation of an answer.

"I've been thinking about that, Hon," said Rita, "How about we switch on all the lights in the hotel, I mean every last one of them?"

Neil was scornful.

"That's not going to give you enough light to see by. It's pitch black out there."

Rita was equally scornful in her reply.

"Duh! They're to help everyone find their way back here."

"Hey, that's an idea," said Dave excitedly, "how about we switch on the lights in a different number of windows on each side of the building, like in a pattern, then if each pair searches the area in front of one of the sides, we'll know whether we're keeping to our search area just by looking back at the hotel."

"Come again?" Phil frowned.

It was quickly agreed. The hurricane lamps were lit and the area around the hotel divided up between the searchers. Still, Neil showed no intention of joining them.

As the others hurried out to the lobby, Dave hung back.

"Are you really not going to help these people? They're your oldest friends."

"First answer me this. Have you discounted what the rest of them seem to have ignored; that Spielman has an axe to grind, some grudge against the Cousins?"

"No, not at all, but for all we know, he may have taken his grudge beyond just trying to scare people away from the hotel. If he's taken the kids, who knows what he could do?"

"Exactly; **if** he's taken them."

"Well, if Spielman hasn't got them, then those kids are out there on their own and they won't survive the night in this cold. Either way we've got to find them."

"Find them? Ha! How are **you** going to manage not to get lost yourself? It's dark and icy cold out there, you have no idea even where to start looking and the forest is

259

immense. It's hopeless. You've bought all this fancy gear, but look at you; you're a city boy, right down to your Nubuck boots. You won't last thirty minutes out there."

"Don't you think I know that, Neil? Yeah, I'm scared I'm gonna get lost, or fall in the river, or break a leg and I'm terrified of bears, wolves and God knows what else. And all of that's without the possibility that the crazy old lumberjack could be out there with an axe just waiting to carve us all into little pieces."

Dave paused for a second, appalled at this litany of his fears, so much more real and terrifying now he'd spoken them aloud. Before his nerve failed him, he spoke again, his voice quiet but determined.

"But, fact is Neil, those kids will die if we don't find them. It's that simple."

"So tell me again how it will help them if you all get lost out there as well?"

Dave stared at Neil in disbelief.

"OK, y'know what Neil? I give up. You stay here, safe and warm, with the drunken moron. I'm sure you'll find plenty to talk about; you've got a lot in common."

Phil looked up and managed,

"You talkin' to me? Are you t-?" before a noisy belch overtook him. He grinned idiotically across at the pair of them.

Neil spoke coldly, without even looking up at Dave.

"Get out. And take that moron with you. The cold air should sober him up soon enough."

Dave shook his head in disbelief. An unbridgeable gulf yawned wide between the Neil he once thought he knew and the cold, uncaring stranger that Neil had now so clearly shown himself to be. If Neil's earlier behaviour had distanced Dave, this selfish lack of concern for his friends' missing children shattered whatever remnant remained of Dave's love for him.

He walked away from Neil now with no regret whatsoever.

Jeff took one more look around the faces of his friends in the lobby. He saw fear and anxiety in their eyes and he wished he could say something to reassure them. But he had nothing.

"OK, let's go," he said quietly, "We'll meet back here in one hour. If you find the kids or you want to get everyone back here for some other reason, sound the horn in one of the cars three times. If you hear the horn, head back to the lights as quick as you can."

Jeff looked for Rita.

She was talking quietly to Dave.

"Did you find a gun?" she whispered.

"No. You?"

"No, but I got these knives from the kitchen. D'you think I should give them out?"

Dave shrugged.

"I guess."

Rita spoke up.

"Before we go out, I think we should all take one of these."

She held out the selection of fierce-looking kitchen knives. Annie gasped and turned away, clinging even more tightly to Bill. Lou stepped forward and took one of the knives without a word. Dave and Jeff each took a blade, but Bill hesitated.

"Just in case," Rita prompted.

She held out a knife, but Bill shook his head.

"I don't want one," he mumbled, "I don't think I could, y'know...use it, so there's no point..."

"There could be bears in the forest."

Rita winced, conscious that she might be making Annie even more upset.

"Bill, take it," she continued, "just in case."

Before Bill could respond, Annie turned, her face tear-stained and wild.

"Give me the damn thing!"

She snatched up the knife, gripping its handle in a defiant fist.

"Now can we please go find the kids?"

Jeff opened the door and the anxious search party quickly spilled out into the bitter night, calling over and over for their lost children.

24

Dave, searching alone, had allocated himself the area in front of one of the narrow sides of the rectangular building. To either side, he could hear the others calling out, but ahead there was no sign of life.

He took a fleeting pleasure and some pride in the fact that his new flashlight was working well. It formed a brilliant tunnel of light, sweeping right across the clearing to the tree line ahead. However, beyond that, its light was soon blocked by the densely-growing trunks. In truth, even with this impressive new flashlight, Dave would only be able to see ten, maybe fifteen feet in any direction once he entered the forest.

He walked slowly to the edge of the clearing and, with each step, the reality of the danger he faced weighed more heavily on him. He felt suddenly very cold, but the cold had nothing whatever to do with the fallen snow or the biting air. He slowed to a stop. He knew he had to move, but the courage that had carried him thus far had deserted him.

What was he doing out here? He wasn't the heroic type. He didn't have a pioneer bone in his body. And he hadn't the first clue as to what he'd do if he met Spielman. If things went badly, he'd probably be more of a nuisance than a help to those kids and most likely he'd just become another person for Jeff and the others to rescue. Perhaps he should have listened to Neil and stayed indoors out of everyone's way.

But even as he thought this, Neil's unconcerned sneer came to mind, and decided Dave's course of action for him. He would not let himself become like Neil. If he turned back now, he might be safe and free of harm; he might survive, return to the city and go on to live to a comfortable old age. But he would have to live those years knowing that he had once abandoned five young children to die alone in the dark. What sort of person would be able to live with that knowledge?

Neil, that's who.

As Dave stared into the trees, his first meeting with Emma came back to him. Had Spielman been stalking her even then? Recalling Emma's frightened face, Dave felt a sudden, renewed urgency to find the children. With a roar, that came from somewhere hidden deep inside, he began to run and crashed into the scrub beneath the trees, calling out the children's names.

Lou had been given the flashlight that Bill had found. Its beam was weaker than Dave's, but she didn't care. She didn't want to waste any more time searching for new batteries or looking for another flashlight. She was totally focussed; driven only by her desperate need to find her precious son. Against his need, her own safety counted for nothing. Speed was everything.

Lou led the way across the parking lot and along the track. The snow had drifted into deep banks and, even in the troughs between them, the snow was nearly at her knees; progress was slow.

Phil stumbled along behind her, muttering under his breath. When he cursed as he tripped on a branch hidden in the snow, she rounded on him.

"Shut up! Just shut up! I can't hear anything but your bitching."

"Yeah? Well I don't give a -"

Phil didn't get to finish the sentence. The glare on Lou's thin face, lit by the now distant lights of the hotel, stopped him as surely as if she had again slapped him across the face. Out here in the dark cold of the night, her face seemed unnaturally pale while her eyes burned with a frighteningly powerful intensity. Phil realised that the balance of power and control between them had shifted. For all his size and machismo, he was cowed into submission by that look.

"OK, Babe. I'm sorry," he mumbled.

But Lou had no time for him. She turned away without a word. Phil could keep up or get lost and right now, she didn't much care which.

Jeff and Rita held hands as they hurried from the comparative safety of the clearing into the densely growing trees. Jeff held the hurricane lamp ahead of them, its flame casting flickering shadows that animated everything around them, making it difficult to discern a way forward. Even had they been able to see clearly, the many low, twisted branches and the icy drifts of snow further hampered their progress. As the minutes slipped by, Jeff became increasingly agitated and soon his frustration boiled over.

"Emma! Emma!"

He was shrieking her name. Tears blurred his vision and poured down his cheeks as hopelessness overwhelmed him. Only minutes from the hotel, he was already close to despair.

"Oh God, Ree, I've lost her."

"We'll find her."

"You can't know that. She's gone, Ree, she's gone."

"Jeff, look at me. Look at me. We'll find her. I promise you, we'll find her."

Jeff was not convinced, but he let himself be urged forward and tried, with little success, to blink the tears from his eyes. Rita's hand, firmly gripping his, was now his lifeline, his sole connection with reality; everything else was reduced to a dimly lit and indistinct tangle of blurred tree trunks, his world shrunk to the limit of the hurricane lamp's hissing light.

Annie and Bill shared the second hurricane lamp. Bill walked with the lamp held high in one hand, the other holding Annie's trembling hand. They were fortunate in finding the path's entrance into the trees quite quickly, and were soon cresting the rise that overhung the rapids.

"What's that gurgling?" Annie whispered.

"Sounds like water. We must be near the river. Watch your step."

Bill strained forward, peering into the gloom, but the lamp's glass was already sooty and the light it gave out was failing.

"Just wait here a second, Honey. I'll go on ahead -"

"No way. We're staying together."

Annie's tone would not countenance any disagreement. Bill squeezed her hand in acknowledgment and began slowly to edge forward.

Suddenly he cried out and let go of Annie's hand. He flew away from her, down into the darkness, the lamp somersaulting through the air before smashing onto the rocks below.

Annie screamed.

"Bill! Bill! Where are you? Bill? Please answer me."

For a few terrible, lonely seconds she had no reply. Then she heard a moan.

"Annie, are you OK?"

"Am **I** OK? Of course I am, you big lug. Where are you? Are you OK?"

Bill grunted in reply.

"Where are you?" Annie's tone was anxious, "I can't see a thing."

"Don't move!" Bill shouted quickly, "There's a rockface just ahead of you, nearly vertical and covered in ice. Stay where you are and keep talking to me so I can find my way back to you."

"Oh Bill, my love, I'm here. Up here. Can you still hear me?"

Nothing.

"Bill? Oh God, Bill?"

Only the gurgling of the water.

"Bill, please, say something."

Still nothing.

Annie shrieked, "Bill!"

"What? I'm right here."

Annie spun around, arms out, feeling for Bill. When her fingers closed on his icy, sodden clothing she hung on and dragged him towards her.

"Thank God you're OK," she gasped, "We'll have to get you back to the hotel before you freeze. Come on."

Without the lamp, the journey back was a hit and miss affair, with both Annie and Bill stumbling into tree trunks to left and right as they felt their way along the path. Finally, with huge relief, they saw the lights of the hotel reappearing ahead of them.

"Come on, we're nearly there."

By now, Bill could manage only a nod in reply; his body had been overtaken with violent shivering and his breath was coming in sudden sharp gasps.

As they staggered out of the trees they were startled by a loud blast of sound: a car horn. Frozen or no, Bill was galvanised by the sound. It re-invigorated him with sufficient energy to carry him back to the hotel at something approaching a shambling run. He burst into the lobby, a wild, deranged figure in his soaking clothes.

"Jeez!" said Neil, for once showing his surprise, "What the hell happened to you?"

Bill ignored the question.

"Where are the kids?" he gasped, "Where are they?"

Neil shook his head.

"Then why d'you call us back?"

"I didn't. It was Lou and Phil."

"Have they got the kids? Don't mess with me Neil. Where are they?"

Neil nodded back towards the lounge and Bill hurried away. Annie paused a moment before following him.

"Kept warm and dry enough did you Neil?"

Neil made a slight nod, but showed neither embarrassment nor regret. Annie sneered at him, a look of absolute contempt on her face.

"Neil, you've gone too far this time. I will never forget this. You...you disgust me."

Neil affected nonchalance.

"Sticks and stones, Annie, sticks and stones."

At that moment the doors opened and a blast of cold air rushed in and over them: Jeff and Rita had returned. Undistracted, Annie kept her attention fixed on Neil.

"Sticks and stones?" she whispered venomously, "Don't tempt me, you selfish son of a bitch. Get out of my way."

"Annie, wait up," Jeff gasped as he hurried after her, "Where are the kids?"

Neil looked at Rita who was still standing just inside the doors, impassively regarding his exchange with Annie.

"So sorry you had to witness that," Neil said, with cloying insincerity.

"Forget it Neil," Rita said quietly, "I'm with Annie.

You are a selfish SOB, a worthless, self-obsessed waste of space. If there was any doubt of that fact before, you've certainly settled the matter today."

Before Rita could say anymore, or Neil make a response, the lounge door banged open and Jeff called her to the join the others inside.

A bizarre sight met Rita in the lounge. A large and grizzled old man lay on a sofa by the fire. His arm was bound in a makeshift bandage and his face seemed creased in pain. A bloom of bright red blood was spreading through the fabric of the bandage, growing larger even as Rita stared.

"What going on? Who's this?" Rita asked.

"This is Mr Spielman," said Jeff, attempting a smile of reassurance to Rita, whose eyes had grown suddenly huge with alarm.

"What the hell's he doing here?" she gasped.

Neil came into the room.

"He told everyone he'd come back later," he said, "And when he did, Phil stabbed him."

"That's not the way it happened," Phil cut in. Both Lou and Spielman looked at Phil intently, "We found him in the woods. It was dark, and it all got a bit confused, OK?"

Jeff didn't really care about any of this. He fell to his knees next to the old man.

"Mr Spielman, do you know where our kids are?"

For several, painful moments the old man simply stared at him as if he hadn't understood the question. Then, with aching slowness, he shook his head.

"Don't reckon I do, son."

"It's no use," Bill interrupted, "We're wasting time. I'm getting some dry clothes then I'm going back out to search for the kids. I'll be as quick as I can."

But Jeff persisted. He wanted information.

"Come on, Mr Spielman, you know something about all this. You warned Lou and Phil about the abductions."

"Sure did, son. Was the only thing I could do. Wouldn't have been right else."

"So, do you think our kids have been abducted?"

The old man nodded.

"Why? Why would someone do that?"

"Might not necessarily be a someone, son."

"What?"

"I don't want to frighten the ladies, son, but might be it's not so much a someone as a something."

Jeff shook his head in disbelief.

"What are you talking about? Look, this is serious: our kids are missing, for God's sake If you know anything, anything at all, please tell us."

"Like I told your friends, there's been kids disappearin' for years, always girls an' young kids. An' whatever it is steals them away ain't never been apprehended. Years back, when I was young, I found one of them. She was dead. All laid out on a table, with grasses an' such all around. When I saw her poor face, well son, ma guts turned over; to see her lying there so bruised and dirty. Such a pale, pretty little thing."

He glanced over towards Lou, but she immediately looked away.

"The killer was gonna burn the place down, an' her body an' all the evidence with it. Put wood and dried grass against the walls."

"Walls? A building? Wait, was it here? Did you find the body here?"

"No. No. In a shack, down the river aways. Near some falls."

"He took the girl there? Mr Spielman, could you take me there?"

"No, son. That was years ago. That shack's most likely an overgrown heap of rotten timber by now."

"I don't care. Take me there. Please."

"Can't do that, son."

"Why the hell not?"

Jeff had lost patience with Spielman. He pushed himself to his feet and the old man winced as the sudden movement jolted his injured arm.

Rita moved to calm Jeff, her hand grasping his.

"He's an old man. And he's hurt," she whispered.

She turned to Spielman.

"Mr Spielman, could you maybe draw us a map?"

Spielman's frown deepened.

"I could do that, ma'am, but don't rightly know that I should. There's evil there."

"What d'you mean? Does someone live there?"

"No. But, like I said, ma'am, this ain't necessarily a someone."

Rita thoughtfully regarded the old man. His lined face gave little away. It could be, she supposed, that he was simply senile or delusional; all his stories could yet turn out to be no more than a futile waste of time, diverting them from their search. More worryingly, there was also the possibility that Spielman was neither confused nor unbalanced, but scheming; it was possible that he did, after all, have something to do with the children's disappearance and was now intentionally misleading their parents.

But what else did they have to go on?

"Please draw us the map anyway, Mr Spielman. We've got no idea where the kids might be and they've been out in the cold and the dark for over an hour already."

Spielman looked uncomfortable.

"I don't know, ma'am."

"Please, Mr Spielman, think of the children. I'm

begging you, please."

With great reluctance, Spielman nodded and Rita hurried out to the reception desk to get some paper and a pen.

Bill and Annie were coming back down the stairs. Bill was now in dry clothes, but his face was as pained as before.

"Rita, is everyone ready to go back out?"

"Almost. Spielman's drawing us a map of a possible place where the kids might be... taking shelter."

Sudden hope lit Bill's face.

"A shelter? Where?"

"A shack, somewhere down river."

Bill and Annie exchanged looks. The optimism faltered and Annie's lower lip began to tremble.

"Rita," Bill explained wearily, "the banks of the river are lethal. The rocks are steep and they're covered in sheet ice. I had a lamp but I fell in. And the water's brutal. It's freezing."

Rita understood what Bill was saying; if the kids had wandered off along the river, without lights, they were likely to have fallen just as he had. And, once in the icy water, small children would not have survived.

She looked into Bill's eyes and saw the light there fading as the hope of finding his children died. He looked suddenly old and broken. But still he hugged Annie to him, feigning strength and hope, for her sake.

Rita touched his arm. There were no words.

As he struggled to draw the map, Spielman began to recount his story. He looked at the faces surrounding him. He had their full attention.

"It started back in the fifties, 1957, the poor girl I found and four kiddies, all dead, and they never did find the killer."

For a moment no one made a sound.

The attentive hush was abruptly interrupted by Neil.

"That's not quite true, is it Spielman?"

Neil's voice betrayed no emotion. It was the tone he employed to bewilder trial witnesses into unwarranted and damaging self-contradiction. Here, in the hushed lounge, it worked to good effect on Spielman; the old man looked completely baffled. Intrigued faces turned from Neil back to Spielman.

Spielman searched Neil's face.

"What yuh tryin' to say, son? Yuh sayin' I'm a liar?"

"Heaven forfend," Neil affected hurt and surprise, "No, I'm saying only that you're mistaken. The killings didn't start in 1957. A young woman was killed here, back in 1946. Isn't that right?"

"I...I don't know...I...Oh yeah, I remember now: there was a body found, a woman, near the edge of the forest. But that weren't nothin' to do with this. Heck, there weren't no kids missin' an' no one knew who she was, or where she come from. Most likely she was a drifter, just passing through; there was a lotta folks on the road back then, looking for work, or just a place to be, after the war. An' anyhow, no one knew for sure if she'd even bin killed or just died natural: there weren't a whole lot left of her when they found her. I remember there'd been a bad winter that year. Most likely she just had enough an' up and died, poor girl. But, how the heck d'you know about her, son?"

"I know because, instead of blindly charging off into the night like these others, I have spent the last hour in the hotel office. There's all sorts of interesting reading in the filing cabinets there: newspaper cuttings, police reports, copies of witness statements."

Rita looked anxious.

"What are you saying Neil?"

She backed away from Spielman.

"Does he have something to do with all of this?"

"No," Neil gave Spielman a reptilian smile, which did nothing to reassure the old man, "Spielman here is mentioned, in 1957, but only as the discoverer of the remains of one Suzie Bower."

"She was the girl I told you about. Lyin' on the table, with the grasses...such a pretty thing. Shook me up real bad," Spielman looked wistful, lost for a moment in his past, "Was years 'fore I could go back to that part of the forest."

"Please, Mr Spielman," Rita urged, "the map."

Suddenly Jeff spoke up.

"Dave! Where's Dave? Has anyone seen him?"

They all exchanged panicked glances and shook their heads.

"He was searching alone," said Annie, "Oh God, Bill, something's happened to him now. Oh God."

But Bill was too numbed at the loss of his children to register any additional concern.

Suddenly Annie shrieked.

"Perhaps he's found the kids!".

"If he had, he'd have brought them back, Annie."

"Maybe he can't because...because he's injured or he needs help or something. Come on, Bill, we've got to find him."

Bill shook his head.

"Bill, come on!" Annie was now tugging at his arm, crying, trying to shake off his dazed inactivity. She turned to Jeff for support, "Tell him, Jeff, tell him we've got to find Dave."

Jeff answered, but his voice was flat. Like Bill, he was close to despair.

"Annie, Dave was searching in a completely different direction to where Spielman's map says this shack is. We can't search in both directions; look what happened when we split up before."

"Jeff, we have to split up. We don't know for a fact that the kids are in the shack; they could just as likely be with Dave. If we split up into two groups, no one will be on their own this time. Please Jeff, all of you, come on, let's get back out there."

"I'm going to the shack."

Bill had spoken and, in the short silence that followed, Annie looked uncertain.

"Honey," she urged, "they could be with Dave."

"I'm going to the shack," he repeated.

"Annie," said Rita, "why don't you go to the shack with Bill? We'll look for Dave. Jeff, honey, is that OK with you?"

Jeff was quiet a moment.

"I hope Dave's OK, Ree, but I'm going to the shack with Bill. I don't know why, but I've just got this feeling the kids are there."

Rita could see that Jeff's slender hope for his daughter lay in this conviction that she was at the shack. Without this belief, he would despair. Jeff had to go to the shack with Annie and Bill.

Looking around her at the worried faces, Rita decided to take charge.

"OK Jeff, you should go to the shack. Lou, what do you want to do?"

"I'm going to the shack."

Lou's decisiveness surprised everyone, as she sat grim faced but otherwise impassive.

"You can't search for Dave alone," said Jeff, suddenly frightened for Rita.

"Don't worry." Rita sounded confident, "Neil will be coming with me."

"Odd that I don't recall volunteering. I'm staying right

here, thank you."

Rita moved towards Neil with the coldest look in her dark eyes.

"If you don't move your sorry ass to come help me find Dave," she hissed, "then I will make it my business to see that your reputation, such as it is, is totally destroyed when we make it back to civilisation. There's gonna be a whole heap of media interest and I will tell everyone, in lurid detail, what a low-life piece of crap you really are. I will tell them all that you chose to abandon young children, and even your own partner, because you don't give a shit about anyone but yourself."

"My dear," said Neil feigning a smile, "you forget that I'm a lawyer. That rant would undoubtedly count as a glowing endorsement. I'd be busier than ever."

Smiling his humourless smile, he cast a look around the assembled group, but no one returned the smile. No one was even remotely amused. It was clear that they would no longer tolerate his selfishness. Seeing this, Neil resigned himself to the inevitable. He had no choice.

"So that's how it is, is it? Well don't expect any heroics. First sign of trouble and you're on your own."

Jeff was understandably anxious that Rita would have to rely on Neil.

"Phil?" he asked, "Would you go with Rita and Neil?"

Phil glanced across the room at Lou. She said nothing, but her sullen face made her feelings clear, even to Phil. Lou would be happy to see him choose any direction and just kept on walking, if it took him away from her. Relieved to have an excuse to be apart from her, Phil agreed to accompany Rita and Neil. That eased Jeff's mind a little, but still he leant forward, his head close to Neil's.

"If you do anything to harm Ree," he whispered, "or if you abandon her out there, believe me, you won't have to worry about any killer; I'll kill you myself."

It sounded ludicrously melodramatic and Neil was tempted to sneer but, as he drew his head back, he caught the fierce intensity of hatred in Jeff's eyes and stopped dead. He was startled, realising that this was a very real threat of harm, a threat which, coming from Jeff, was further heightened by its unexpectedness. Neil had long been aware of the antagonism and intellectual rivalry that Jeff felt towards him, but had dismissed it as laughable nonsense. He had very poor regard for Jeff's abilities, and it amused him to taunt and bait him, as he had earlier. But the Jeff he had goaded into shouting at him, before the search, had been hot-headed and impulsive; this Jeff was coldly determined and deliberate. There was icy resolve in the eyes of the usually ineffectual college professor.

Neil swallowed hard and struggled to regain his composure.

"I said I'd go, didn't I? Threats are not necessary."

Rita looked at him in disbelief.

"Oh no? I think they are. You'd happily stay here and leave Dave and the kids out there to face God knows what. Self-interest is your only motivation for anything, isn't it Neil?"

Still shaken, Neil merely turned away.

Speilman had collapsed back onto the cushions.

"Think he'll be OK?" Rita asked.

"I may be old, young lady, but I ain't deaf. I've survived out here in the wilderness since 'fore you were born; I'll be jus' fine. Go find your kids, but please," he grasped Rita's hand, "take real good care of yourselves. There is somethin' evil out there."

With that, the old man eased back into the cushions, his injury clearly causing him some pain. The friends looked unsure. Something evil? What had the old man meant by that? They exchanged nervous glances.

"Come on," Annie urged them, "he'll be OK. Let's get back out there."

"Wait one second," it was Rita, "I have an idea."

She ran to the reception desk and began to rummage around its shelves.

"Honey, what are you doing?"

"Help me look, Jeff. There must be some here."

"Some what?"

"Marker pens, or scotch tape, or string: something to mark the trees so we can find our way back. Once we're deep in the trees we can't see the lights of the hotel."

Without looking up, Rita continued to turn out boxes and rifle through drawers.

"Yes!" she shouted triumphantly, "Here!"

She jumped back up, her face a manic smile. Bemused faces stared back at her. In the frightened quiet of the room she was suddenly conscious of how inappropriate her smile must seem. Apologetically, her face reddening, she held up two reels of tape and a ball of string.

As everyone readied themselves to return to the search, Jeff and Rita kissed goodbye and, for both, this parting was painful. Jeff was torn between his near certainty that he would find Emma in the shack, and the small but persistent concern that he could in fact be wasting precious time, following directions supplied by a crazy old man who seemed obsessed with evil 'somethings' out in the forest. Jeff didn't want to be parted from Rita but, if Spielman's ramblings proved to be unreliable, then she might be the one to find Emma. He and Rita had to separate; time was slipping relentlessly away from them, and with every passing minute the chances of Emma surviving must surely be dwindling to nothing.

Rita, for her part, was anxious not for herself, nor even primarily for Emma, but for Jeff. Would he be able to cope without her, out there in the forest? She knew how desperate he was and her impulse was to be with him, to comfort him, should the worst happen. She wondered briefly why it was that she didn't share his certainty that Emma was in the shack. He, Bill and Lou all seemed so sure. Was it because she could never have the same emotional link to any of the children as did their own parents? Rita wanted to find Emma, as she also wanted to find Lisa, Mikey, Ethan and Laura. But, looking around, she could plainly see the terrible difference of degree between her need and that being endured by the children's parents, whose faces were almost unrecognisable from the laughing, carefree smiles of the morning's snowball fights.

Whatever the reason, Rita didn't share their conviction that the kids would be in the shack, nor could she shake off her concern for Dave. He might be hurt or lost, but he could yet be key to finding the children; he might have caught sight of them, or found some evidence of them. There was even the slim chance that, as Annie hoped, he might already have found them. Rita looked across at Annie, now pulling on her warm clothing and opening the door to the icy dark of the clearing. Why was it that Annie was not convinced, as the others were, that the children were in the shack? Surely, as their mother, Annie was every bit as devoted to Lisa and Mikey as was Bill? Why, like Rita herself, was Annie so hopeful that Dave held the key?

It was time to go.

Rita hastily dismissed her musings. Maybe Annie's very different belief was proof that there was no special parental link to the missing children. Maybe everyone in the room was simply clutching at a possibility, any possibility; each desperate to make their hope a reality, armed only with the force of their own conviction.

25

Dave was forcing his way through the trees.

To distract himself from the realisation that he was now out all alone, at night, in a vast forbidding forest, he tried to focus on how useful his new cold weather gear was proving to be. His hands and feet were still warm, though the snow was more than a foot deep. Dave was congratulating himself on his forethought and feeling almost cheerful, when he caught a sudden flash of light down at his side; the beam from his flashlight had reflected off the large kitchen knife in his hand. This frightening knife, so unfamiliar and unnatural in his hand, once again reminded Dave that he was in very real danger, and all the outdoor equipment in the world could not alter the fact that he was utterly unprepared and unsuited for what he might face.

After walking for what seemed a very long time, his absolute unsuitability for this sort of endeavour was abruptly brought home to him; he suddenly realised that not only had he forgotten to mark any of the trees along his route, but he had also not checked his watch when he left the hotel. He had little hope of finding his way back and no idea when the hour would be up.

The knowledge that he could now add being lost to his list of woes, was more reality than Dave could cope with;

tears began to fill his eyes, blurring his vision. He staggered on, slipping as the ground below him dipped away.

Blindly descending the slope, he was moving quite quickly, almost running, when he slammed into a large branch that had fallen across his path at waist height. The breath was punched out of him by the impact. He dropped both the knife and the flashlight, doubled up and staggered from side to side, gasping for air. Falling to his knees, his struggle to recover took several minutes. Thankfully, the flashlight was still working. It was pointing in his general direction, to his right, so that although his immediate vicinity was in darkness, he was comforted by the nearby shaft of light. Slowly, his breathing became more regular and the sharp pain in his ribs began to subside. Now the only sound he could hear was his own breathing. All around him was cold silence.

Then, suddenly, Dave froze, holding his breath. Something had moved across the beam of the flashlight. Had it gone from left to right, or from right to left: towards him? He couldn't be sure. Whatever it was, it was big; big enough to momentarily block the beam entirely. What was it? There was a scratching, rustling sound; loud and horribly very close. Dave's heart was pounding. He was so desperately afraid; he wanted to be home. He wanted to be safe. He wanted Aunt Sarah. Anyone.

Dave jumped, as, in one sudden movement, the flashlight was swept up and turned directly onto him. He stared wildly into the beam. What was it? He could make out nothing other than the light. What was going to happen? Oh God, let it be over. He screwed his eyes tight shut, not wanting to see what was going to attack him. For a few, terrible seconds nothing happened. Then Dave again jumped in terror; something had tapped his shoulder. In total bewilderment he turned, had a fleeting glimpse of bone white teeth, and taut, pale skin, then took a numbing blow to his head.

He felt the stinging cold of the snow as he hit the ground. Then nothing.

26

Rita, Neil and Phil had the hurricane lamp. Swinging, its light rocked crazily as Rita hurried across the clearing.

"Neil!" she shouted, "Keep up!"

Neil would not run, but he did walk more quickly than was usual for him. He intended to keep near enough to the light of the lamp to be able to see and avoid obstacles, whilst staying sufficiently far behind so as not to appear unduly keen; he was, after all, out here against his will. Phil was ahead of him, walking next to Rita, who was trying to make out a path or at least some way into the tangle of closely-growing trees.

"It's no use," Phil was saying, "There's no way in."

"Forget it Phil. We're not going back to the hotel. Now help me find a way in. Look, here."

Rita and Phil eased their way under a fallen tree that rested, at a crazy angle, against the trunk of another. To Neil, following on behind, Rita and Phil appeared to vanish into the curtain of trees. The lamp's light was soon hidden from him and, although the moonlight was brighter now, through thinning cloud, Neil felt sudden, overwhelming isolation.

"Wait up! Wait up, or I'm going straight back to the hotel," he shouted.

Rita had circled a branch of the fallen tree with the

coloured tape, but Neil could see no sign of any such markers on the trees ahead of him. Peering forward, he could just discern the faintest twinkle of the light ahead.

"I said wait!" he shouted again, "Rita, wait!"

Neil was startled by Rita's reply, so sharp and clear on the cold air.

"For Pete's sake, Neil, we are waiting for you. Will you move it!"

Swearing and stumbling, clumsily, towards the light, Neil joined Rita and Phil. They were standing on the bare ground beneath the spreading branches of a huge fir tree. Only a light dusting of snow had reached the ground here, so they could see clearly that there were two possible paths leading away from them into the trees.

"Glad you could join us."

Neil grimaced, too angry to make a reply.

"OK," said Phil, "so, which way now?"

"I think we should check out both," said Rita, "We could follow them for, say five minutes, then come back here and decide which one looks the most hopeful."

"I'm not going alone," said Neil quickly, "and we have only one lamp anyhow."

Before she had given herself time to decide what she must do, Rita opened her mouth and spoke in an encouraging and confident tone.

"Come on, it's not so dark now; it's a full moon. I don't want us to lose time, so you go with Phil. I'll see you both back here in ten."

Why had she said that? She didn't think of herself as being brave. She didn't want to go on alone, but something in her had taken over. She would do this because she had to do this. There would be time enough later to be afraid.

"No, wait," Neil gasped, "I'll go with you. Phil, you go that way."

"Why me? Why do I get to go alone?"

"Because you're the super fit, All American hero type," said Neil dismissively, "You'll be OK."

Rita stared at Neil. By moonlight and the flickering light of the lamp it was impossible to read his face. Why had he prevented her going on alone? She had expected him to be glad to be rid of her. Could it be, she wondered, that there existed some small trace of the gallant buried deep beneath the self-obsessed exterior? Could Neil be experiencing the same inexplicable calm that she now felt? Had he been taken over by the conviction to do the right thing, regardless of the outcome? The idea fought against all the experience she had of him, but how often had she heard of people rising to unlikely heights of courage and selflessness in the face of adversity? She could be witnessing Neil's finest moment; his triumph over selfishness.

Sadly the truth was more prosaic: Neil was, in fact, merely trying to ensure that Jeff would have no cause to blame him for any harm that might befall Rita. Over the years, Neil's experience in court had shown him, time and again, that people suffering extreme emotional distress could, and frequently did, react with wholly uncharacteristic ferocity. Neil had been thoroughly unsettled by the intensity of the hatred in Jeff's eyes. It would therefore be wise, he thought, to try to keep Rita from doing anything too foolhardy.

Phil, however, stood his ground, his mouth working furiously, trying to formulate an argument as to why he should not be the one to go on alone.

"Yeah?" he said finally, "Well, I ain't gonna."

Rita was losing her patience.

"For God's sake Phil, what's the problem? We'll meet back here in ten minutes. How far apart can we get in that time? If anything happens, just call and we'll come running."

Phil looked dubious.

"Can't say as that reassures me any."

"Reassurance?" Rita sneered, "Oh, come on, Phil. What have you got to be afraid of? What's happened to the macho sports jock? An hour ago, you were even brave enough to attack a defenceless old man."

Phil hung his head.

"I didn't do that."

"What, he stabbed himself?"

"No. It was Lou."

"Yeah, sure it was."

"No, I swear, it's the truth. She went crazy: stabbed the guy just 'cause he was staring at her. And he just stood there, bleeding. Didn't seem angry or nothin'. Like he expected it. It was weird. Fuckin' freaked me out."

Phil's face was unusually pale. Rita thought he looked utterly shaken. He was telling the truth. She and Neil exchanged glances and, in the moment that followed, the hiss of the hurricane lamp seemed to grow louder to fill the silence. Rita didn't know what to say.

"Phil, are you...OK?"

She leant forward to touch his arm, but Phil suddenly pulled away, rejecting her sympathy.

"Oh, save it, Rita! I know none of you give a shit about me, so shut up and just you make damned sure you're back here in ten."

With that, Phil turned and marched off down the left-hand path.

The lamp's hiss continued.

"Well, well," Neil said at last, "life's rich tapestry just keeps on getting richer."

Rita was equally amazed.

"He meant it didn't he? I can't believe it: that baby-faced little girl stabbed the old man."

"Yeah," Neil answered wearily, "she stabbed him. But why are you so surprised? The doe-eyed dumb blondes, they're always dangerous. She didn't fool me with that simpering, 'little girl lost' thing she had going."

"Oh sure. You'd see right through that wouldn't you, what with you being so empathic an' all. Come on, we've got ten minutes."

They set off down the right-hand path. But, after only a couple of minutes, their way became completely blocked by densely-growing scrub which, covered in snow, now had the appearance of irregularly shaped, powdery white mounds, glittering in the moonlight. The pathway simply stopped and it was impossible even to guess how deep was the enveloping layer of snow. The path, if this was a path, was impassable.

"OK, let's get back."

As they waited for Phil, under the large fir tree, Rita asked Neil what else he had discovered in his search of the Cousins' office.

"What does it matter? It's all ancient history. Some of it dates back over fifty years."

"Don't you think it's got anything to do with the kids going missing?"

"Maybe. Hell, I don't know. God, it's cold out here. If Phil doesn't get back soon, I'm going back without him."

"He's only been six minutes. Tell me about the stuff you found. What did you find out about the first killing?"

"The woman in '46?"

"Yeah. Who was she?"

Neil stamped his feet to warm them and reluctantly pulled the scarf from his face to answer.

"As Spielman said, they never identified her, or at least they hadn't identified her in the cuttings I read. There's a couple of newspapers from '46 with stories on the discovery of the body. It was badly decomposed and the only identifying items were a couple of scraps of dress material. She had no handbag or any other possessions. The dailies called her something like the 'Lilies girl'."

"Why?"

"Something to do with the material. Maybe it had lilies on it, I don't know. God it's cold. If he's not back soon I really am going back."

As if on cue, Phil reappeared.

"There's no way through," he said, "How about you?"

"No. No, that way's blocked too."

"OK, so we go back to the hotel?"

"We should keep on looking. There could be another way into the forest. Let's go back to the clearing and try again."

With a great deal of moaning and ostentatious stamping of frozen feet, the two men followed Rita back to the clearing. There they searched back and forth but found no other way into the densely-growing trees.

"That's it," said Neil, "I'm going back. This is pointless."

Rita was equally downhearted, but she was reluctant to abandon the search.

"Don't you care that Dave could be out here somewhere? He could be hurt. Please, let's keep looking."

"Stop with the bleeding heart appeals to my better nature. Hadn't you heard? I don't have one."

"But Dave's -"

"Enough already!" Phil interrupted, "Will you two quit your bitchin'. We're wasting our time here. For all we know, the others could be back at the hotel by now."

"They'd have sounded the horn."

"Maybe they did and we didn't hear it. Maybe they're back there right now worrying about us, wondering where we are. We should go back."

"Truly, we live in interesting times: I actually find myself in agreement with Phil. This has to be a first."

"Please Neil," Rita's tone was pleading, "Phil?"

"No. Face it, Rita, this is hopeless. Give me the lamp; we're going back to the hotel."

Phil made to grab the lamp, but Rita pulled it away and he wisely decided not to force the issue. Rita's face was sullen. She knew she would not be able to dissuade them from returning to the hotel and she hated herself for lacking the courage to search on, entirely alone. With a heavy heart, she trudged on ahead while, with barely concealed smiles, Neil and Phil followed her back to the hotel in silence.

Bill, Annie, Lou and Jeff shared a flashlight.

Bill led the way to the path from the clearing. He was downcast. Resigned to finding only the bodies of his children, he couldn't free his mind of an image of Lisa and Mikey, frozen or drowned, floating, lifeless, in dark, icy water. He blinked to clear his eyes. Annie squeezed his hand. She too was barely containing her tears. Jeff and Lou followed close behind, in silence, both lost in their own thoughts.

Soon they stood on the rise above the rapids.

"Sounds like the water's moving quite fast," Jeff said, "Any idea how we can get down to it?"

"We should walk along the ridge," said Annie quickly, "It's really icy just down there, Jeff, and we can hear where the river is from up here; we won't lose our way."

"Even so, I think we should go as close as we can to the river, just in case."

"In case of what?"

Annie didn't understand, Bill thought, but Jeff, like him, must have accepted that they'd likely find the kids dead in the water. Jeff didn't want to stray too far from the river banks in case he missed finding Emma. Bill felt that same desperate need to lift his dead children from the water and just hold them. They shouldn't be alone, there in the cold and the dark. They needed their Dad. And he needed them. Again, the tears filled his eyes.

"Are you OK?" Annie's face was anxiously looking to him for reassurance.

"Yeah, I'm OK, but I think Jeff's right. We should get as close as possible to the water."

"But you said yourself, the rocks go straight down and they're covered in ice."

"Yeah, but after I fell, I got back up here didn't I? Let me just find that way back down."

Bill shone the flashlight from side to side, looking for handholds or ledges.

"Over there. Look, we could get down there."

With Annie shining the flashlight down on the rocks, Bill half scrambled, half slid down to the base of the rock face.

"OK Annie, it's OK. Now, throw me the flashlight."

Catching the light, Bill turned it onto the broiling surface of the pools and rapids behind him. Scanning back and forth, Bill was torn between wanting to find something and desperately wanting to see nothing but churning water.

"What is it, Bill? What can you see?"

It was Lou. She was leaning out dangerously far over the edge.

"Nothing, Lou, there's nothing."

Bill still felt that mixture of relief and disappointment, but he gathered his wits. He had to focus. He had to talk the others down so they could get on with the search.

"Lou, take a step back. Go to your right some. I'll shine the flashlight for you to see the way down."

Lou followed his lead then, one by one, everyone clambered down to join Bill. Once down, Jeff caught his eye. Bill shook his head and Jeff nodded; understanding.

It wasn't clear whether Spielman's hand-drawn map was to scale, so they had no idea over what distance they would have to struggle along the frozen mud and ice-covered stones of the riverbank. Progress was frustratingly slow and, with many slips and falls, they were all soon bruised, aching and sore, but they pressed on without complaint. From time to time, the moon sped from the cover of racing clouds and cast an ice-blue light on them but, when the clouds once again overtook the moon, the light failed instantly and the four then had to feel their way with outstretched hands.

They would not give up the search, or wait till first light. Where the route became impassable on one bank, they retraced their steps to a point where the river allowed them to cross to the other bank and struggled on there until the terrain forced them to cross back again. Every few feet along their way, Bill shone the flashlight onto the water. There was no sign of the children and Bill didn't know whether to let himself take heart from this. Could he dare to hope that Lisa, little Mikey and the others had come all this way without any mishap? It seemed almost too outrageous a possibility, but he clung to it now; a tiny candle flame of hope in the awful darkness of his former despair.

They edged on downstream.

After another hour they were still moving as quickly as was possible but, by now, that was very slowly indeed. As they became more and more fatigued, their stumbles became more frequent. Tired muscles, unused to exertion on this scale and under these conditions, began to fail. Finally, with a shriek that made the others almost lose their own footing, Annie skidded on the ice. She fell at once, hitting her head against a flat stone and lay very still. Bill fell to his knees at her side.

"Annie, Annie Honey can you hear me?"

No response.

"Annie? Come on Honey, wake up."

Jeff and Lou stood, exhausted, staring down at Annie's inert body, not knowing what to say or do. They were all so tired and, standing still, they were also beginning to register the biting cold.

"Is she OK?" Jeff asked; a stupid thing to say, but he felt he had to say something.

Bill shook his head and wiped his eyes.

"No, I think she's unconscious. She's breathing and I can't see any blood or anything, but she's just not waking up."

"We need to keep her warm," said Jeff, "Here, take one of the blankets."

Bill took off his gloves to unfold the blanket. His hands were shaking. He spread the blanket over Annie and tucked it around her with great tenderness. Tears were now slipping, unchecked, down his cheeks.

"Do you think it's OK to move her? Do you think I could hold her?"

Jeff and Lou exchanged looks. They shrugged.

"I don't know, Bill, but I read somewhere that if someone's in an accident you shouldn't move them unless there's a fire or something. I think maybe we should leave her where she is."

Jeff felt almost cruel saying this; Bill so wanted to cradle his wife in his arms and hold her close. His familiar, friendly face was almost unrecognisable now: distorted by the heartache he was having to endure. And soon Jeff would have to add to Bill's pain. He crouched down next to him.

"Bill?"

Bill nodded.

"Bill, I have to go on. I have to get to the shack."

Bill showed no sign of having heard a word.

"Bill? Can you hear me? I said I'll have to go on. Will you be OK staying here with Annie till I get back?"

Still no response.

Lou was becoming agitated; Ethan was out there. He needed her right now and she couldn't waste time here. She caught Jeff's elbow. He looked up and saw her frown.

"Just a minute," he whispered.

Lou was clearly irritated, but she stepped back and remained quiet.

"Bill, stay here with Annie. We'll go to the shack and get the kids. OK?"

Bill, suddenly animated, grabbed Jeff's arm.

"Get Lisa and Mikey for me Jeff. Get them, please."

Jeff looked into Bill's reddened eyes. It was terrible to see his old friend in such distress.

"I will, I will. I'll get them."

Jeff paused a moment.

"Bill? Can we take the flashlight?"

"Huh?"

"The flashlight, Bill. Can we take the light? There's moonlight here by the river so you should be OK. So, can we take it?"

"Yeah, yeah. Take it."

Jeff and Lou moved away, Jeff pausing to wave to Bill.

"Good luck Bill. See you back here real soon. OK?"

Ghostly in the moonlight, Bill made no response; the sound of his weeping lost in the incessant tumbling and splashing of the river.

Jeff turned away.

27

As Rita had expected, Jeff and the others were not back at the hotel. Spielman was still asleep on the sofa in the lounge but, otherwise, the building was empty.

"We should go out again," she said.

"For what it's worth, I vote we at least warm ourselves first," said Neil.

"There's another first," said Phil, "This time I'm agreeing with Neil. And I think I know how I'm gonna get warmed up," he motioned with his thumb in the direction of the bar, "Anyone?"

The others shook their heads.

"Don't drink too much Phil. We won't stay long; just till either the others get back or we warm up. OK?" said Rita, "While we're waiting I think I'll check out those papers in the office. Will you show me, Neil?"

Neil shrugged. He had nothing better to do and he reasoned that, the longer he kept Rita occupied in the office, the longer he got to stay in the warmth of the hotel.

Phil shrugged.

"Suit yourselves."

He disappeared into the bar.

Rita followed Neil into the Cousins' office and began to flick through the contents of one of the two filing cabinets.

"Wow. I didn't think there'd be so much stuff."

"Yeah. Press cuttings, witness statements, even some pieces of physical evidence. I don't know how the Cousins got hold of those; usually they're held in storage for years, even long after a case has been closed."

"Look here," said Rita, "What are these? Look like medical records, yeah, look there, 'Dr. Beauregard Strange.' What a name! 'Dr Beauregard Strange, Fairfalls County Asylum'."

"What's it about?"

Rita scanned the first page.

"It's kinda faded; a bit hard to make out in parts. Some guy called Henry Boe. Hey, if these are his medical records, we shouldn't be reading them."

"What's the date?"

"What?"

"The date. On the papers."

"September the – oh it's 1912."

"So Henry's not going to be suing you any time soon. What's it say? Read it out."

Rita read:

> "<u>Monday, September 9, 1912.</u>
> <u>Notes on interviews with patient Henry Boe.</u>
>
> Mr Henry Boe : 48, a Caucasian male, enjoying generally good physical health.
> Arrested and put under the care of the County (for observation) for causing a disturbance at St.Vincent's Church, Fairfalls, during the service on the evening of August 11.
> The arresting officers report that Boe became uncontrollable, shouting something to the effect that God was dead and that Satan had triumphed.
> (Regrettably the officers cannot provide verbatim

testimony of Boe's outburst).

Boe was intoxicated and was sent to the cells to sober up. During this time he continued to shout wildly, disturbing not only his fellow prisoners, but also his jailers. Interestingly, he threatened to put curses on them if they did not release him.

(Again, no verbatim testimony).

I was called to give my opinion on him and the sheriff readily agreed to his release into my care.

"Why have the Cousins got this? D'you think this Henry Boe was a relative? A grandfather perhaps?"

"How should I know?" Neil was irritated that Rita had been distracted so soon. Keen to spend as much time as possible here in the office rather than out in the cold, he urged her to continue, "Maybe there's some answers to all this in there. Read on."

Rita looked down and found her place on the faded notes.

> "Since arriving at the Asylum, Boe has shown himself to be withdrawn and easily angered. He has said nothing further of an overtly anti-religious nature and it is my belief that the root cause of his ill-temper and lack of restraint actually lies in his early childhood.
>
> Over the past three weeks I have interviewed him on six occasions. He is very reticent and the following represents all that I have so far gleaned from my sessions with him:
>
> Boe was born in Louisiana, though he refuses to say exactly where. He also refuses to say where he is living now.
>
> (I have had Nancy write the State Authorities in Baton Rouge, but have yet to receive any further information).

Boe refuses to say if he has any living relatives, either in Louisiana or elsewhere.

Boe will not name either of his parents but does say that they were extremely strict and as a boy he suffered many beatings.

In relating the instances of these beatings, Boe becomes noticeably more agitated.

It is my belief that Boe's experiences as a boy caused him to sublimate his feelings. Rather than express his feelings of anger and resentment at the repeated beatings, he turned to the family's maid, a creole woman named Gloria Mercy. As an only child, the boy spent much of his time alone in the family home. Gloria Mercy was his only constant companion. She became his confidant and teacher. I believe that it was she who filled the boy's mind with talk of 'voodoo' (by this I mean the primitive practice of black magic and morbid superstition still current among the negro peoples of the Carribean islands).

The abrupt and, I believe, traumatic end to this destructive and morally suspect relationship came when Gloria Mercy was overheard talking to Henry. Boe is not specific as to the nature of their conversation, but his father thereafter denounced Gloria as a 'Devil-worshiper' and the 'pagan whore of Babylon'.

(Boe claims to remember his father's words exactly).

The maid was immediately dismissed and Boe exacted his revenge on his parents in the way that Gloria Mercy had shown him. He placed a curse on them.

Boe tells me that both parents were shortly thereafter killed in a flash flood. To this day Boe remains convinced that he is responsible for their deaths.

During our last session I attempted to convince Boe that he could not have caused his parents' deaths. I tried to impress upon him the reality that magic and voodoo do not exist. Boe said very little, but I had Nancy take shorthand notes of his responses. The following section is taken from her notes and is particularly interesting. Note that Boe refers to himself in the third person and identifies with his father:

> 'He carved black magic figures: evil, wicked things. Work of the Devil, Ma woulda called them. I knowed he was trying to catch my immortal soul in them, but I stopped him. I stopped him good. I beat him till he was red raw and I burnt them all, every one. See, I knows what they can do. I knows their power. Boys can be evil. The Devil takes them for his own. You mustn't never show pity. Don't matter what he says, nor however much he begs, nor hollers nor pleads; that there's Satan talking through him. The evil one puts lies into the mouth of the boy. You gotta beat that Devil outa him. But I'm wise to him and I beat him good.'

"Poor kid, well, poor guy. I know he's probably long dead, but I can't read any more of this."

Neil reached forward and Rita gratefully passed the document to him. He scanned ahead.

"The doctor came across work, by some Swiss researchers, on 'leukotomy'... sounds like some form of brain surgery. I think old Beauregard was thinking of experimenting on Henry's brain. And, yeah, looks like Henry's come to the same conclusion."

"Why, what does he say?"

"He doesn't say anything specific but, by their next session, Boe clearly wants out. And he's obviously realised that his only way out is to tell the good doctor just exactly what he wants to hear. This entry is only two weeks later, but Boe is apparently already utterly convinced that he is, 'entirely blameless in the matter of his parents' deaths'. And the gullible doctor believed every word."

"How do you know?"

"Because, not only is Dr Beauregard excessively self-congratulatory about his own medical prowess in, and I quote, 'freeing the poor man from the demons of his past', but also this section, here, says it's copied from Boe's release document."

"You don't know that Boe was faking it. Maybe he was cured."

"Get real. In my experience no one discards deep-seated, character-determining beliefs after a couple of unstructured chats with a shrink. And this is 1912, for God's sake. Shrinks then knew even less than the pitiful amount they know today. No, if Henry Boe believed his curse had killed his parents before he trashed that church and met the good doctor then, I guarantee you, he still believed it long after smug Dr Beauregard pronounced him cured, barely five weeks later."

"OK, but I don't see any link with the Cousins. See if you can find their marriage licence. Maybe Boe is Mrs Cousins' family name."

For a few moments they searched quietly.

"Here's another report from the Fairfalls Asylum."

Rita passed the folder to Neil,

"Have a look at it will you?"

With a sigh, Neil opened the folder and began to read silently.

"Well? What does it say? Did Boe end up back at the

asylum?"

"It's a Boe, yes. But not Henry."

"Eh?"

"It's the same hospital. Different doctor though. And it's 1916."

"World War I?"

"No, nothing to do with that. It's Henry's son -"

"How do they know it's his son? Beauregard said Henry wouldn't tell him if had any living family. How old is this Boe?"

"He's a boy. Fourteen. His name is Ezra and it says that the reason for his admittance to the asylum was the sudden death of his father, Henry Boe, a 'man in his fifties'. Odd that they didn't have the detail of his exact age. It looks like this doctor didn't realise that Boe senior had been at the hospital just four years earlier."

"No computers."

"You don't say."

Rita shrugged apologetically. Neil continued.

"Looks like Ezra must have been close to his father. Says here he was grief-stricken, became hysterical and had to be restrained when his father's body was taken from the house. The boy had no other family to turn to, so they thought a week or two under sedation at the asylum might help him."

"And did it?"

Neil read on. Rita was impatient.

"Neil, for Pete's sake, what happened to the boy? Is **he** Mrs Cousins' father?"

"Doesn't say...Let's see. It says that Henry fell down the steps into the basement and broke his neck. The boy then apparently stayed alone in the house, with his father's dead body, for four days before anyone happened to come to the door. The people who collected the body said there was a carved wooden doll and a photograph tucked into the shirt of the dead man...The boy told the doctor that he had no other family and said he'd always lived alone with his father, because his mother had died when he was a baby. But he refused to say anything more about his father."

"Weird family," Rita muttered, "Wait up! If this Ezra was fourteen when Henry died in 1916, and he'd always lived with his father, then he must have been home alone all those weeks when his father was in the hospital back in 1912. And he'd only have been ten years old, poor kid. If there was such a strong bond between them, why didn't Henry mention him and get someone to look out for him?"

"Like you said: weird family."

Rita looked thoughtful.

"What's with the doll and the photograph?"

"Er...doesn't say anything more about that. It says Henry died leaving huge debts, so foreclosure proceedings were begun and the farm was auctioned off. There's an addition here, in different handwriting It seems that, after a short convalescence at the hospital, Ezra was on his own. Initially someone at the the hospital kept tabs on him. It says he drifted from job to job, never staying more than a few weeks, and by the time this extra bit was written, in early 1917, Ezra had left the town and his file was closed."

"Poor kid. A tough start in life. Like his Dad."

Rita looked toward the door and Neil, fearing she was about to suggest going back out to continue the search, quickly distracted her.

"Look at this."

He handed her a yellowing scrap book that he had been reading. Pasted onto its stiff pages were several cuttings from the Losien Gazette, dating from the summer of 1978.

"Wow," Rita breathed, "I don't believe it: the Cousins had a daughter who disappeared back in '78."

Rita flicked forwards through the fading newsprint, "Oh no, that's awful: it looks like they never found her."

"And her name?"

"Yes I see, very weird: Laura. Why would you name your second daughter after one who's disappeared without trace? Is it just me, or is that weird?"

"It's weird, but hey, we've met them; weird is what they do."

"Maybe it was their way of dealing with their grief."

"Whose grief?"

Phil had returned from the bar.

"The Cousins. They lost a daughter."

"Lost? What here?"

"Yeah, back in 1978."

"Killed?"

"Don't know. As far as I can tell, she was never found."

Phil looked suddenly angry.

"If they've lost a kid of their own, then why the hell didn't they say anything? How could they let us bring kids here, knowing the history of the place? And why the hell haven't **they** moved away from here?"

Rita shrugged. She was surprised by the force of Phil's reaction, he hadn't exactly seemed devoted to Lou's son, but he was articulating the questions Rita had been asking herself, and she had no answers. There was an awkward silence.

"Sons of bitches," Phil slurred the words.

Ah, his reaction was not so surprising then, she thought; Phil had drunk too much, again. The alcohol was responsible for his sudden concern for Ethan. Rita tried to calm him.

"OK, Phil, relax."

"Don't you tell me to relax. Thanks to those sons of bitches, I no longer have a woman in my life and I really loved that woman. And now she's out there looking for Ethan, and she hates me, and I don't know why."

Neil was unimpressed.

"D'you think it could have anything to do with you being a drunk?"

Rita frowned at Neil. Now was not the time to provoke a confrontation with Phil. But Neil merely lowered his voice.

"Or a moron?"

"What d'you say?" Phil demanded.

"When?"

"Just now, moron."

"Yeah, that's right."

"What?"

"You said it, Phil, and I couldn't have put it better myself."

"Eh?"

Neil was smiling at Phil. His smile was not pleasant to behold, but Phil was too befuddled to focus properly. Rita shook her head and Neil noted her disapproval but held his smile. After a few seconds, Phil nodded.

"OK then. That's OK then."

As Phil turned away, Neil mouthed the word, 'Moron.' Rita signed to him to stop. It clearly amused Neil to make her anxious. Phil, oblivious to the silent exchange, stared about him at the opened filing cabinets.

"What's all this...crap?"

"Press cuttings and documents about the disappearances."

Phil made to pull a document out of the drawer. The file slipped from his hand, and all its contents fell to the floor. He started to draw the fallen papers together with his foot, but the papers tore.

"Please, Phil, just leave them."

"OK," he stood still, the papers squashed beneath his feet, "What we gonna do now?"

"If we're all warmed up now, I think we should go back out and look for another way into the forest."

Neil spoke up.

"We did that already."

Rita turned to him, her tone weary.

"Neil, it's Dave we're talking about. Don't you care about him at all?"

"I told you before about that bleeding-heart stuff. You're wasting your time. I'm staying here."

"But there must be other ways in. Forest animals must have made tracks and paths through he trees."

"Yeah," Phil laughed, "I reckon a grizzly made the one I was on."

Rita wasn't really interested in anything Phil might have to say, so she responded automatically, as you might to a demanding child.

"I'm pretty sure they don't have grizzlies round here, Phil."

"Well, an elephant then," he giggled, "It's yea wide," he spread his arms, "and it goes on for miles. 'Course, it was dark so I couldn't see that far ahead."

Rita rounded on him.

"What? You told us there was no path, that you couldn't get through."

"Oops!" Phil was giggling again, "Did I really say that?"

"Yes you did, you self-obsessed moron!"

"It was dark," he pleaded, still smiling, "and I was cold...and the path probably doesn't really go on for miles."

Rita was furious.

"Does it?"

307

"Yeah," he belched, "it does. Sorry."

Rita pushed past him, out into the lobby. Neil followed, but with none of her sense of urgency.

"I told you he's a moron."

"We all know he's a moron," Rita snapped, "We've always known it. But what I didn't reckon on was his being a lying moron but, turns out, he is. OK?"

Neil backed off.

"OK. No argument on that one."

"You are coming back out, right?"

"Why do you keep asking?"

"Neil, Dave could be injured out there and I'm going out to look for him," she pulled her jacket back on and began to wind a scarf around her neck, "What will you tell the others when they get back and find that you and Phil have left me to search alone?"

Neil grimaced.

"You'd better make it a good story," she whispered, "because Jeff is gonna take some convincing."

"OK, I'll come. But this time we set a time limit. An hour. No more. Whatever happens we come back here in an hour."

"But -"

"Or I stay here, and Jeff can go -"

"OK, OK, just let's get going. They've all been out there so long already."

As they pulled on their boots, Phil staggered out of the office. He looked at them quizzically.

"What's up?"

"We're going back out."

"OK. Catch you later."

Phil turned to go back to the bar.

"No, stay out of the bar, Phil. You've had enough. We might need you sober."

"No one tells me what to do."

Exasperated, Rita decided to try a different tack.

"You want Lou back don't you, Phil?"

"Kinda"

"OK, then you have to stay sober. In fact, you should come back out with us."

"I don't wanna."

"Lou will be really impressed if you find Dave and the kids. You know how much she loves little Ethan."

Phil paused on his way into the bar. His lower lip trembled.

"Yeah. She loves him more than me."

"No, no, Phil. Lou loves you very much, and just think how much more she'll love you when you find Ethan."

After a moment, Phil's petulant look disappeared. In his drunken state he had already forgotten both the shock he had experienced when Lou stabbed Spielman and the disconcertion he had felt at her unexpected show of determination and power. Lou was now a very different person from the simpering girl she had seemed before Ethan disappeared, but Phil chose to ignore this and, instead, was now completely absorbed in imagining how indebted and amenable she would be when he had rescued Ethan. Lost in his daydream, Phil had also forgotten where he was and that Rita and Neil were waiting on his response. They exchanged glances; Phil was grinning idiotically. In his alcohol-fuelled imagination, he was picturing himself, the hero of the hour, having wildly energetic sex with a very submissive and grateful Lou.

Rita tried to get Phil to focus.

"Phil? Phil, are you coming?"

At this, Phil began to snigger.

Rita frowned; what was so funny?

Phil continued to snigger as they made ready to leave

and was still sniggering as they left the building and stepped down into the snow. The sniggering stopped abruptly, when Phil drew in his first icy breath of night air.

"Thank God for that," Neil muttered, as Phil gasped and spluttered into silence beside him.

They re-entered the forest, ducking under the fallen tree and continued to the fork in the path.

"OK, Phil, lead the way."

Phil was too cold to do more than nod as he shuffled forward to take the lead. The alcohol was producing a monumental headache and he had a powerful and growing thirst. As he walked along, he scooped up handfuls of snow and melted them in his mouth, but this served only to painfully chill his head. He felt utterly miserable.

They struggled on, but made slow progress through the snow-covered tangle of roots criss-crossing the path. The forest around them was a pattern of blue and black shadows, eerily still and very quiet. Apart from their own snatched breaths and the dry squeak of the snow compacting beneath their boots, the only sounds were the occasional slumps of snow falling from branches to the ground below.

"Phil?" Rita gasped, "Has anyone been along this path recently?"

Phil rolled his eyes heavenwards.

"And just how am I supposed to know that?"

"Does the snow looked disturbed?"

"Kinda."

"So, is that a yes? Has someone been this way recently?"

"Like I said, how am I supposed to know that?"

Now it was Rita's turn to look heavenwards. She couldn't trust herself to say anything, but the depth of this man's stupidity was staggering. Behind her, she could hear Neil struggling, unsuccessfully to suppress a laugh.

"Shut up," she hissed.

"I would if - ah!" Neil stopped in mid-sentence.

Rita turned, to see Neil huddled on the ground.

"Neil? What happened?"

"I've broken my foot."

"Are you sure?"

"Well, I don't see an emergency room anyplace, so I'm having to self-diagnose here, but yes," he gasped in pain, "I'm sure."

Rita stood over Neil, impatiently willing him to get to his feet.

"Is it no better?"

He looked up at her, his face a painful scowl.

"What do you think; I'm sitting on my ass in the snow from choice? No, Rita, it's not any better. I have broken my foot," he spoke the words slowly, "This is not getting any better without weeks in a cast."

"OK, OK, I get it. You stay here. Phil and I will go on a bit further. If we don't find anything we'll come right back. Then we'll get you to the hotel."

"No way. You're not leaving me here."

"What choice do we have? You can't walk and we can't carry you any distance."

"Then get me back to the hotel now."

"Come on, Neil, we've already lost too much time, thanks to the moron here."

Phil was too cold and miserable to take offence at this. He merely shrugged and stamped his feet to keep warm while he waited for the others to settle their dispute.

Neil was frightened.

"You can't leave me here. I could be attacked. How would I defend myself? I can't even run away. Shit, I can't even stand up!"

Rita looked around and picked up a length of fallen branch.

"Here. Take this. Now you can defend yourself."

Neil tried to throw the branch back at her. He missed. Rita was unconcerned. Her mind was focused on finding Dave and the kids; Neil's bellyaching was merely an irritating distraction.

"Suit yourself. Sit tight. We'll be a half hour, maybe less."

Neil was becoming desperate.

"I don't care. I won't stay here. Get me back to the hotel. Now!"

"Neil," Rita's patience was almost gone, "Stop being such a baby. We'll be back before you know it."

She motioned to Phil to move on and Neil panicked, realising that she was actually going to leave him here, alone and injured. And she was taking the lamp!

"For chrissake, Rita, leave me the light."

"We need it, Neil. You know we do. Now please, just shut up and sit tight."

Neil's fear exploded into a show of anger. He punched at the snow with both fists.

"You bitch! You fucking bitch! Get me the fuck out of here!"

Rita turned away and Neil's bluster deflated. He turned his attention to Phil and now his tone was pleading.

"Phil? Phil, don't listen to her. Don't leave me here like this. Phil?"

Phil hesitated and Neil seized the advantage.

"Come on, Phil, we go way back. We're friends, right? Get me back to the hotel first. It won't take you long. Phil, I could die out here."

"I dunno, Neil."

Neil tried his last effort.

"I'll pay you. Phil, are you listening to me? I'll pay you to take me back to the hotel. What d'you say?"

Phil looked from Neil to Rita.

"Rita? Maybe we should take him back first," he mumbled.

Rita's last shed of patience vanished.

"Oh, for God's sake, Phil. We're not wasting time carrying him back to the hotel. You stay here with him if you want, but I'm taking the lamp. We've gotta check out this path."

Phil blinked uncertainly at her.

"Jeez, Phil! Try to focus. You stay here with Neil. I'll be back in a half hour or less. Wait here for me, OK? Stay right here. You got that?"

"Uhuh."

It didn't take long for Neil and Phil to tire of waiting.

Phil was stamping his feet.

"I'm cold."

"Try sitting in the damn snow," Neil grumbled, "Here, help me up."

"You should keep off your foot if it's broken. We did basic first-aid at the club. It's how you know it's broken: when you can't bear to put your weight on it."

"Shut the hell up and help me."

Phil lifted Neil upright. At first Neil swayed, reluctant to put his weight on the injured foot, but soon he realised that the pain had lessened. Hesitantly, he lowered his foot to the ground. It was sore, but no more than that. In fact, it seemed that moving the ankle eased the pain. He hadn't broken a bone after all.

"I'm cold," Phil complained.

"You said that already."

"Yeah, well I'm still cold."

"OK, look, we don't have to stay here just because

Rita says so. No one put her in charge. I know I didn't vote for her. And it's not like she needs us either; she has the lamp. I say we go back to the hotel and wait for her there."

"What about your foot?"

Neil adopted a look of patient stoicism.

"It's bad, very bad, but I'll do my best."

"You gonna be able to make it back to the hotel?" Phil asked, "I mean, if we wait for Rita, we could carry you between us."

"For God's sake Phil, we don't need her. We can get back without her and we don't have to stay here, like a pair of school kids, just because schoolteacher says so. No one tells us what to do, right? Especially Rita. I mean, why does that woman have to be so damned dictatorial?"

"Huh?"

"Bossy. She's always bossing people about."

"Ain't that the truth. You gotta feel sorry for Jeff, huh?

"No, not for a second. That ineffectual poseur deserves everything he gets."

"Yeah," Phil bluffed, wondering what an 'ineffectual poseur' might be, "Guess he does."

Neil now chose his words with care. He knew his audience.

"Phil, don't you think maybe Rita needs to be shown that she can't push us around? I mean, she can't tell us what to do. Us men," he paused, watching Phil closely, "I mean, it's just not natural for a woman to be so aggressive."

Phil had a sudden recollection of Lou attacking Spielman. The old man had just been staring at her. Nothing more; just staring. But Lou had gone berserk. She had rushed at him and stabbed him before Phil could react. And then, when Phil had pulled her away, Spielman had said nothing. He just carried on staring at her. It was all so weird.

Phil shivered. In his world view, women should not be capable of attacking people. He had sometimes wondered if Evolution had even made women weaker because they were less stable than men; prone to tears and hysterics. Their problem was their hormones of course; made them unstable. Lou's hormones had probably been in control when she stabbed the old man. If women had been made stronger there'd be fighting all the time. Unstable: biological fact.

Phil had discovered that it wasn't acceptable to express his views these days. People said he was a misogynist. He'd looked it up; it meant he didn't like women but, of course, that was horse shit; he loved women, lots of women. People might not like him to say these things, but Phil knew that the world would be a whole lot better if women went back to being soft and comforting; if they just went back to doing what men told them, specifically, what **he** told them. And he had no doubt that, deep down, that's what women really wanted for themselves. Neil was right; it was unnatural for a woman to want to be in charge.

That was all the convincing Phil needed. He and Neil would go back to the hotel right now. Rita would freak out when she found they'd gone, but she wouldn't try to push them around again, no sir! Phil put his arm around Neil's shoulders and Neil allowed him to take most of his weight as they began to walk.

Moonlight was only intermittently lighting the path and Phil could see no markers on any of the trees but, brimming with his reasserted sense of male superiority and convinced of the innate ancestral hunting prowess that accompanied it, he was supremely confident. They only had to follow a path. How hard could that be? Together they stumbled off in what Phil knew to be the direction of the hotel.

Time had passed and Phil and Neil had not yet reached the clearing. Neil was angrily blaming Phil.

"What d'you mean, there weren't any markers? How were you finding the path till now?"

"I went in the right direction, to the hotel, but it's like the path has taken us someplace different."

"What the fuck?"

Even Phil could see how weak this excuse sounded and he could no longer pretend that he had even the slightest clue where they now were. He abandoned the attempt.

"I dunno, OK? It's hard to see anything with all the snow."

"We should have been into the clearing ten or fifteen minutes ago. We're lost, you moron."

"Well, Mr. Fancy City Lawyer, how come you didn't say nothin' till now."

"I'm injured," said Neil, with a timely wince of pain, "I was relying on you; not the smartest decision I ever made. Turn around. We'll have to retrace our steps."

Phil didn't move.

"What's up? Come on, even you can follow your own footsteps."

Nothing.

"Phil? Can you hear me? I asked you what's up."

"Shh! I thought I heard something."

Neil immediately stopped. Both men were listening intently. After a few seconds, Neil hazarded a whisper.

"I don't hear anything."

"Shh."

Neil was frightened but also angry that Phil was

treating him in this way.

"**You** shh. There's nothing there."

"Shh. There! Did you hear that?"

Neil had heard nothing but Phil's talking.

"Stop trying to spook me, Phil. It won't work. Now can we -"

Neil stopped mid-sentence.

He could hear it now. Something was ahead of them and moving slowly towards them. Neil was suddenly very afraid. Feeling utterly unprotected, he quietly eased back, positioning Phil between himself and whatever was approaching them. They could see nothing, but could hear it, moving towards them very deliberately, not attempting to hurry through the deep snow. Was it stalking them? An animal of some sort. A bear? Neil's mind raced. What was it? It sounded big and seemed to grow bigger in Neil's imagining with every passing moment. A light wind was carrying the sound of its heavy breathing to them on the icy night air.

Neil's body was alert and tense, ready to run at any second. In front of him Phil finally moved: he lifted his hands to his mouth, and shouted.

"Rita! Over here!"

Neil nearly collapsed with shock.

"Shut up you fucking moron! You'll give us away."

As if in response, the sounds got faster. Whatever was out there was coming directly for them.

"Jeez!" Phil hissed, "That's not Rita. Run!"

Years spent in the gym meant that Phil disappeared in seconds. Neil found himself alone. Frantic, he turned and ran for his life. Abandoning all care as to the scratches and thumps of the dense branches, he threw himself into the trees, slogging through the snow with remarkable speed. Why was it following him? Why didn't it go after Phil? It was unfair. It wasn't right; Phil was of no use to anyone: worthless. But he, Neil, had so much left to do. He was brilliant. He shouldn't end this way; killed and eaten by some dumb animal. His chest was bursting with the strain and tears burned in his eyes, but despite his exhausting efforts, he could hear the guttural breathing and heavy footfalls getting closer and closer. It was closing in on him, closing in for the kill.

Suddenly Neil's foot found no ground below it. He gasped. He could see reflected moonlight glancing off icy rocks far below him. His momentum was carrying him forward and there was nothing he could do to stop himself falling into the cold air of the abyss. He shut his eyes and screamed.

In that instant, his pursuer pounced on him and pulled him back from the edge.

Phil had raced away, leaping and tumbling through the snow.

He didn't look back, but he knew he had escaped. It had gone after Neil rather than him. The sounds of pursuit had already faded and Phil was beginning to slow his pace, when Neil's scream rang out. Whatever it was had obviously caught him. Phil tried not to think about what was happening now, but images of Neil's dismembered body kept sliding into his mind. Phil felt bad for Neil, but on the other hand, he was damned glad that it was Neil who had been killed, rather than him.

For an hour or more, Phil continued to push himself through the trees and deep snow. He was hopelessly lost, having absolutely no idea even in which direction he was moving. Also, despite his fitness, he was tiring; his muscles were aching and his nerves raw. He stumbled on until, catching his foot in a hollow concealed under the snow, he sprawled onto his knees. He threw his hands forward to protect himself, and felt a smooth, hard surface beneath the layer of snow. Confused, he brushed the snow away and cleared a small patch of gravel. Fantastic! He was on a road, and the only road he knew of around here was the road into Losien. He was free! He had only to follow the road to be back in civilisation: phones, hot tubs, drinks and, more importantly, no kidnappers, murderers or wild animals on the loose. Revived by this good fortune, Phil struck out along the road with renewed enthusiasm.

An hour later his enthusiasm had waned. It had proved very much easier to walk on the relatively even, man-made surface than it had been to drag himself through the undergrowth of the forest, but the cold was sapping Phil's energy and numbing his hands and feet. He was beginning to doubt that he would survive to reach the town.

Another half mile on, the sky became darker, as the snow clouds returned. In the near total darkness Phil staggered on, blinking snow flakes from his eyes.

More time passed.

Phil was shuffling now, unable to feel his feet within his boots. He knew that, if he gave up, if he lay down to rest, he would probably die of cold out here. His body would be found after the thaw, possibly scavenged by wild animals. He felt nauseous at the thought. The images of Neil returned and this time Phil also pictured his own limbs strewn about, his bones gnawed and discarded on the forest floor.

He had to keep moving.

Suddenly, with a painful thump, he hit something big and metallic that was blocking the road. Feeling the contours under the snow, he realised that he had stumbled across a vehicle. Overjoyed, he felt his way around it. It was strange that the door was hanging open as if the driver had left in a hurry, but Phil paid it little heed. He bent down and peered inside. As far as he could tell there was no one inside.

Hardly daring to hope, he tugged off his glove and felt for keys in the ignition. Damn! No chance of driving back to town, but at least he could get under cover, out of the snow. With a grunt of effort he climbed in and shut the door behind him. Snow, dislodged from the roof, slipped down past the door and fell to the ground as a single mass, the sound muffled and strangely distant.

Phil knew that he was becoming disoriented; sounds were deadened but also, in the unbroken darkness, he was beginning to imagine lights and writhing shades. He had to act. With snow all around him, he would not go thirsty, but he needed food and warmth. Searching, he found some candy. It was old and tasted only of sugar and dust, but Phil ate it greedily. Warmth was going to be a more difficult challenge. The air inside the car was as chill as that outside and, since Phil was no longer exerting himself, the cold crept steadily along his limbs. He began to shiver violently, but made himself move, feeling along every surface, searching for blankets or jackets: anything with which to wrap himself. Dully, in the back of his mind, he realised he was in the cabin of a pickup truck and, hallelujah, there on the floor behind his seat, was a travel blanket.

As warmth began slowly to return, Phil's head cleared somewhat and he finally gave some thought as to what could have happened to the driver. Presumably, he had been forced to abandon his pickup because of the snow. At this, Phil's hopes rose once more; as soon as the snow storm passed, the driver would be back to collect his truck. Phil had only to hunker down and wait for the weather to break.

Soon his eyelids were closing and his head nodding

forward. He was nearly asleep when he found his breathing becoming laboured. He was sweating, taking in huge gulps of air, but it wasn't enough. The air in the cabin was running out. Stiffly, he clambered across the passenger seat and gripped the handle to open the window. Grunting and cussing, he forced the handle to move. Ice had frozen the glass in place and it took all of Phil's remaining strength to wind the window down just an inch. He put his fingers through the gap to loosen any snow that might have built up outside. He could feel none, so he relaxed, collapsing back down into his seat.

Within moments he was deeply asleep.

Winded, Neil flew backwards into a bank of snow.

What the hell had happened? Dazed, he struggled to assemble his thoughts. His body ached and he was in a snow drift, looking up at a night sky, where ragged clouds were tearing across a full, silver moon. As the clouds cleared, the moon was instantly dazzling. Neil had to shut his eyes.

Opening them again, he shrieked. A terrible face, frighteningly close, filled his view, and strong arms were dragging him upwards. Utterly terrified, Neil fainted.

Waking, moments later, he found himself lying on the ground. As a roaring in his ears died away, he stared wildly about. The creature was squatting only an arm's length away and Neil could see that there would be no escape. Instead, as tears began silently to pour down his cheeks at the tragic injustice of it all, he hoped desperately that he would lose consciousness again. But fate was not to be so kind, and Neil remained unwillingly, horribly conscious. He couldn't bear this level of fear. He was petrified: too frightened even to whimper. Screwing his eyes shut, he held his breath and waited for the shock of pain that would surely end this.

As the seconds passed in silence, Neil's body ached with the tension in his muscles. He had attempted to similarly brace himself mentally: searching back for some memory of happier times, but his mind remained a blank. Jeez, that was pitiful: in these last few moments of his life, he couldn't recall a single uplifting event from the whole of his adult life. Neil was not unduly saddened by this. He felt no regret. Life's a bitch. What else was there to know? He just wanted this waiting to end. For chrissake, what the hell was the animal waiting for?

Still, nothing happened.

His lungful of air nearly exhausted, Neil hesitantly reopened his eyes. As he had expected, the creature was still there, but it was showing absolutely no interest in him. Able to do little else, Neil took the opportunity of the bright moonlight to stare at the creature, examining it closely for the first time. It was big, with dark, unruly hair. Its broad shoulders suggested that it was powerful and Neil already knew that it could move with terrifying speed. But what was it? Neil had never exactly made a study of local fauna, but he'd watched nature documentaries over the years and this thing didn't look like anything he'd ever seen on any of them.

Except...

No it couldn't be. Maybe he was concussed. Was he hallucinating? He must be; the only image that he could recall that in any way approximated to this creature was a still from a grainy amateur film, of a dark, hairy figure frozen in mid stride, head turned toward the camera.

Bigfoot!

OK, now Neil knew he was losing his mind. Indeed going mad might be the rational course of action at this juncture; he was, after all, tired, helpless, lost in a forest and about to become a midnight snack for a mythological ape. Who wouldn't go mad? And yet, this thing was sitting right by him. Neil continued to stare at it. For something non-existent, this creature looked, and smelt, very real. But Bigfoot? No way! That film had been a hoax. Had to be. So, what was this thing? What the hell was it?

Neil was becoming addled. Slipping into confusion, he closed his eyes again. Perversely, the very unreality of the situation was calming and oddly reassuring; Neil couldn't feel threatened by a creature that he didn't believe existed. And maybe a protective insanity was the body's way of coping in extremis. Neil relaxed into the madness.

A sudden noise shattered his complacency. His eyes snapped open. The creature was definitely very real. It was now leaning over him, its awful face very close and its foul breath causing him to wince. Neil stared up into its eyes and saw...intelligence. Confused, he searched the rest of the face. It was filthy, had a shock of wild, grey hair and bore a ghastly, disfiguring scar that pulled its mouth into a long, uneven maw; but it was human. Neil stared in utter incomprehension; this was all too much. Would someone please tell him what the hell was going on?

No longer able to cope, he shut his eyes tight and willed all of this to stop.

Jon looked down at the man. Why had he shut his eyes? An old memory came to him; Jon had recognised that look, from long, long ago in his childhood. The man had been frightened on seeing his face.

It was understandable: Jon had long ago known himself to be ugly but, after so many years alone, he had forgotten. Shunning human contact had become instinctive to him and for that reason he had planned to do no more than herd this man and his companion out of the forest. Intending to remain out of their sight, he had stayed upwind of them so that they would know he was there and move away. The two men had obviously been lost and Jon was prepared to help them, but he didn't want to deal with people and he would never have got so close to this one, had the man not been about to fall to his death.

But, now that contact had been made, Jon would have to deal with this stranger and get him to safety. The man still had his eyes tight shut, so Jon poked his arm.

"You must wake. Not safe you here. Evil here."

Neil could not believe what he was hearing. Had he stumbled into a Tarzan remake? What the hell was going on and who was this freak? He stared up at Jon and tried to form words, but no sound came. The night's exertions had perhaps taken their toll; Neil felt an overwhelming urge to sleep. He wanted nothing more than to rest, but the freak was poking his arm again.

"Cut it out," Neil moaned, "Either kill me, or leave me the hell alone."

Jon persisted.

"Not safe you here. Evil here."

Neil drowsily absorbed what Jon had said. Was the freak not intending to harm him then? That was good. But what had he meant? What evil? Realising that he was not about to be killed, Neil began to rally.

Jon saw the awareness return to Neil's face. Now that he had his attention, Jon had to make him understand.

"You must go."

The fear had gone and Neil's confusion and hopeless resignation gave way to an indignant outburst.

"Go? Go where, for chrissake? I'm lost, thanks to that moron, Phil. I have no idea where I am and, believe me, I didn't even want to be out here in in the first place. It wasn't my idea to go for a hike in the teeth of a blizzard, in the middle of the fucking night, to look for those no-neck brats and Jeff's daughter of darkness. And why the hell am I expected to risk my life for the other girl? I've never even met her."

Jon grabbed Neil's jacket and pulled him closer, so that their faces were only inches apart.

"Girl? What girl?"

Jon's tone was urgent, but his impressive halitosis made Neil retch. Jon impatiently shook him, repeating the question, demanding an answer.

"What girl?"

Neil turned his head to one side.

"I don't know. Like I said, I've never met her; never even seen her. The kid's slow, know what I mean? Her parents run the hotel."

Neil stopped. Jon looked blank.

"Hotel?" Neil tried again, "You know, building...big house...many people."

Just as Neil was about to abandon the attempt, he saw comprehension dawn in Jon's eyes.

"You understand that? Hotel?"

"Girl at hotel?"

"Well, like I said: she's from the hotel, that's where she lives, but where she is now? Who knows?"

Jon frowned. This strange man spoke too much and too fast. Jon would have to simplify his question, in the hope that it would elicit a useful answer.

"Girl," Jon said slowly, "hotel?"

"Yeah, I guess," Neil conceded; anything for a quiet life.

With that answer Jon was suddenly galvanised. He leapt up, pulling Neil to his feet.

"We go."

"We do?" Neil gasped, " Where?"

"Hotel."

"No, you don't get it. I don't know where the hotel is. Hell, I don't even know where I am."

Jon ignored him, turned and marched off, dragging Neil with him.

"Whoa! Slow down! I can't take you to the hotel. For chrissake, listen to me!"

Jon released Neil's arm and impatiently turned to look at him.

Neil drew a deep breath then spoke very slowly, making each word distinct and shaking his head to reinforce the message.

"I-do-not-know-where-hotel-is."

"In forest," Jon said helpfully.

"Yes, in forest but I don't know where in forest!"

"I do know."

With that, Jon turned and walked away. Behind him, Neil was taken aback and simply stood, watching him go. Then, all at once, he grasped the importance of what Jon had just said: Jon would guide him back to the hotel. Neil bolted to catch him up and Jon acknowledged him with a grunt. He then pressed on at great speed, making little apparent concession to Neil's ineptitude and unfamiliarity with the forest. Neil was having to work very hard to keep up. In an attempt to slow Jon down, he tried to get a conversation going.

"My name is Neil."

He got no response. Communication was going to be harder than he had anticipated, but he tried again.

"My name Neil. What your name?"

"Jon."

In truth, Neil was a little disappointed at such a commonplace name.

"Bummer."

Jon frowned; not only was this man strange, but he was also, apparently deaf.

"No," he said slowly, "Jon."

Neil bit his lip. Was this guy mocking him? He didn't

know which would be worse: that the freak was ridiculing him, or that the freak might actually think he was stupid. Stumbling along, trying to keep up, Neil had no way of determining the truth of it, so he reluctantly decided to let it go and try another question.

"Jon. Have you always lived in the forest?"

Nothing.

Neil gave it one final try.

"Have you...How long have you...Ah hell, y'know what? Forget it."

They travelled on in silence for over a mile. The deep snow made the going very difficult and, although Jon clearly knew the terrain and was presumably leading him along the least demanding path, Neil was succumbing to cold and tiredness. He wanted a shower and he wanted his bed. He fixed these goals in his mind and trudged on, head down.

They were nearly at the clearing, the lights of the hotel beckoning through the thinning trees, when Neil finally stumbled clumsily and fell, face down, into the snow. While he lay there, Jon studied him closely. It seemed to Jon that this man really did not belong in the forest.

"Why you here?"

Neil raised himself to his knees.

"What?"

"Why you in forest?"

Neil had tried to explain this before and Jon had not understood. He was too tired to go through all that again. This time he would keep it simple.

"I search. Girls, boys gone away."

"Girl gone? Not in hotel?"

"Er...no."

"Gone where? Gone how?"

"Taken."

Jon was aghast. It was all happening as it had before.

That evil was here again, in the forest. He felt sick, overcome with his old fear. The terror of the thing that had leapt at him in the shack, more than twenty winters ago, was still horrifyingly fresh in Jon's mind, undulled by the passing years. But, in spite of his fear, he knew he had to act.

"Must find."

Without another word, Jon grabbed Neil's sleeve and hauled him back into the forest. Neil was furious; to be so close to safety only to have it taken away was too much to bear. He swore and struggled, forcing Jon to stop.

"What?"

"Listen, Grizzly Adams, you can do what the hell you want, but count me out. I'm going back."

Beneath this bravado, Neil was panicking again.

Jon looked confused.

"We go."

Neal's breathing and heart rate were accelerating beyond his control. When he spoke again, it took an effort to keep his voice steady and hold back tears of fear and frustration.

"Go? No, we don't go. You go if you want, but leave me the fuck alone, you freak."

Jon couldn't grasp the notion that Neil felt no compulsion to search for and rescue the missing girl. Instead, Jon assumed that he had again not made himself intelligible to the stranger. Instead of wasting any more time with attempted explanations, he simply grabbed Neil's sleeve and made to move off. But, this time, Neil planted his feet solidly on the ground and wrapped his free arm around a stout tree trunk.

Jon was baffled. He assumed that Neil was father to the missing children and would therefore want to find them. When they did find them, Jon intended to stay hidden, as always; he would need Neil to approach the children and talk to them. But why did Neil resist? Perhaps he objected to being dragged along. Deciding that this must be the case, Jon released Neil and turned to leave.

"Come. We go."

Neil had noticed a branch that had snapped from the trunk to which he had anchored himself. He now saw that it would be easy to snatch it up and hit the freak hard; hard enough to give time to make an escape. In that moment, Neil's fear of Jon and the retaliation that could follow was small in comparison with the dread he felt for whatever terrors lurked, hidden out there in the forest. His decision was made: he grabbed at the branch and swung it at Jon's unprotected head. He struck him a glancing blow to the back of the neck and side of the head. Jon collapsed, insensible.

Without hesitating for even a moment to check on Jon's condition, Neil turned and scrambled towards the lights.

28

Dave woke up.

He had no idea where he was or what might have happened to him. Indeed, for a few bizarre moments, he had no recollection of who he was. He was a blank, with no past and no awareness of the world around him; he could hear, see and feel nothing.

Then there was a rushing noise in his ears, building to a sound like a powerful, buffeting wind. It filled his head and there was nothing but this noise until, abruptly, the volume died away. The sound's texture changed. Was it the sliding and rattling of pebbles continuously washing back and forth on a distant beach? Or was it now the quiet roar that a child hears when he holds a sea shell pressed to his ear? Dave was intrigued.

Against this ebbing flood of white noise, he gradually became aware of another sensation: pressure. He realised that he was lying on his side, on a hard, flat surface and his body seemed gradually to be assuming more solidity and weight. As it did so, Dave's mind too became gradually more aware. He was now conscious of the fact that his left arm was being squashed beneath his body. It wasn't pain exactly, just a tingling discomfort. He tried to free it, but could not. The arm was numb but, more worryingly, Dave was unable to control his right arm in order to help free his left. He was baffled. Why couldn't he lift his right arm? At length, he assumed that he must still be asleep. This was an oddly realistic dream, fascinating in its way, but it had gone on long enough. Dave decided he would wake up.

He opened his eyes.

Nothing. Everything was blackness.

He couldn't see. Could it be that he was still asleep? He blinked and yawned, trying to clear his head. No, he was definitely awake; he could feel the muscles of his face responding to his instruction, and his eyelids were open. That meant, oh God, he was blind! Panic gripped him and the intense emotion seemed to kick-start his remaining senses. A wash of sounds and smells assaulted him. The air was hot, making breathing arduous. Also, his nose and lips seemed to be coated with dust; acrid particles clogging the hairs in his nostrils. He was face down on what must be a very dusty wooden floor, the rough planking dry and reeking of dirt and age. He turned his head to one side, shifting his weight with difficulty; realising, finally, that his wrists were tied together behind his back. His ankles were also bound together. What was going on? Dave could hear voices, at first muffled and unclear. He strained to make out what was being said.

There were two voices. The first was a deep voice. There was chilling menace in its tone. It spoke slowly and deliberately, and it was threatening someone. The second was closer, much younger and female; a young girl. Her voice was loud and forced. Masking fear with audacity, she was forcefully holding her ground.

"What? No way! No fucking way."

It was Emma!

All at once, it came back to Dave that Emma had been lost. People were searching for her. His recollection was still incomplete but obviously, somehow, he must have found her. She was alive and the two of them would have to find a way to escape from this place. Despite the helplessness of his own situation, Dave felt overwhelming relief on hearing Emma's voice; in the muddle of his confusion there was a task to focus on. There was a reason to hope.

The deep voice spoke again.

"You'll do like I tell you, Doll."

"Why? What d'you want with them?"

"I need them, and they want me. They all want to play."

Emma's immediate reply was perhaps foolishly blunt.

"You're one sick fuck."

Dave heard a loud slap followed by quiet sniffing. Emma had been hurt.

The deep voice now dropped to an intimidating whisper.

"You will bring them to me, Doll. You will."

"Drop dead!"

Another smack, then something hit the floor.

Writhing helplessly Dave shouted, "Don't hurt her. Leave her alone!"

His voice was hoarse, chocked with the dirt and dust in his throat.

"Ah," said the deep voice, with evident, malicious enjoyment, "Look, Doll, your friend is awake."

Emma's response was immediate, and disparaging.

"Friend? Him? Don't make me laugh."

That hurt. Dave thought that he and Emma had made some connection when they met in the forest; a shared experience of the teenage isolation that comes with being different. Heck, he remembered he'd tried to help her and he recalled telling someone that she was a great kid. He'd even gone searching for her.

Suddenly, clearer memories of the search for the

children came back to him. He remembered the dark, the cold and, above all, the fear. He had been searching alone; Neil wouldn't help. That's right; Neil had refused to help his oldest friends in the search for their missing children. Tears of revulsion and frustration filled Dave's eyes.

Suddenly, he gasped. He had another flash of memory: the final few seconds before he found himself here: the sharp teeth, the deathly skin and the terrible, empty abyss in the sunken eyes. Dave shrieked and began to struggle frantically, straining at the knots.

"Yeah Doll, looks to me like your friend is wide, wide awake."

The voices continued, ignoring Dave's futile efforts to free himself.

"I told you already: he's not my friend."

"Is that right, Doll? Is that right?"

Dave froze, hearing a weird scratching sound coming towards him. The deep voice was very close now.

"Do you think your friend would like to play. Huh?"

Dave felt something sharp press at his side.

Emma shrieked.

"No! No! Don't!"

Her voice then collapsed to a whisper.

"Please, please don't hurt him."

The deeper voice became mockingly cheerful.

"Now you see how much better that is, Doll? We shouldn't have secrets, you and me. See, now I know that you don't want to see your friend here get hurt. Am I right?"

Dave, holding his breath, heard no reply.

"I said, am I right, Doll."

"Yes," Emma gasped, through her tears.

"Very good. And see now, that's useful to know. You don't want to hurt your friend, and I don't want to hurt your friend, but, if you don't do what I tell you, then I will hurt him. I will kill him. I will kill your friend. Is that what you want, Doll? You want I should kill your friend, Doll?"

"No."

"I don't hear you, Doll."

"No!" Emma screamed, "For God's sake, leave him alone!"

The deeper voice was quietly triumphant.

"God? God don't enter into it, Doll."

Having established his control over Emma, the deep voice was now talking quietly to her. Dave could only catch fragments of their conversation and his concentration was being distracted by the growing pain in his muscles. His entire body was now aching. He longed to stretch, to move freely, but he was so thoroughly trussed up that all his efforts simply tightened his bonds.

Emma had apparently agreed to bring all the other children here. But, putting to one side his certainty that Emma would never willingly bring them to this terrible place, Dave wondered how she intended to find any route through this vast and unfamiliar forest. Most likely she, like him, had no idea where the children were, and was playing for time, as much for his sake as for her own. Dave was sure now that she had earlier disowned him only to try to protect him, acting on the assumption that, if she didn't care about the guy tied up on the floor, then there was nothing to be gained by threatening him harm. But Emma's plan had failed and it seemed that Dave was to be kept alive solely in order to coerce her. He reckoned that his longer term future would look very bleak, and short, if he couldn't find a way of loosening these bonds.

Resting for a moment from the strain of trying to

unpick the knots at his wrist, Dave wondered where the other kids were and how they might be faring. He had no idea for how long he had been unconscious earlier, but it could have been hours, heck, it could have been days, and it was very cold in here, inside some sort of shelter; surely the younger children could not have survived so long out there in the forest.

His thoughts were interrupted; the voices were again coming closer. Emma spoke first.

"I can't bring them back here on my own. I'll need help."

Good girl, Dave thought. Get me untied, then we'll get out of here and just keep running till we get back to civilisation. Then we'll get the Feds to come catch this SOB. Dave had to suppress a smile at the prospect of the capture of his tormentor.

"And I suppose, Doll, that your friend here would oblige. And I'd just wait here for y'all to come back to me? Am I right?"

"Yeah, that's right."

Emma's tone was relaxed, but Dave could imagine the effort that must be taking. She was calmly trying to reason with a psycho. That was one gutsy kid. Dave was seriously impressed.

After a pause, the deeper voice spoke again, sly and low.

"Y'know, Doll, it is a tempting offer."

To Dave, it sounded as if the bastard was smiling and what a terrible sight that must be. Dave was thankful he was spared it. He pitied Emma.

"Yeah," the sly voice continued, "it's a very tempting offer...but, no. Reckon I'll have to decline. Way I see it, you and your friend here might not come back. Once y'all get back to that fancy place, why, you might just forget about me. Shh, I ain't sayin' it's likely, but I just got this feelin' in ma gut."

He was playing with her.

Dave heard Emma sigh. She was losing heart.

"It's OK Em," Dave croaked, his parched throat throbbing with the effort, "Em? Listen to me. You have to go alone, without me. You understand?"

But, before Emma could respond, the deep, wicked voice intervened.

"Go alone? Shoot, there ain't no need for that. What kind of a gentleman would I be if I let a young lady like this go into the forest alone? Shame on you for even thinking such a thing. No, I shall accompany you myself, Doll. I'll be right behind you, every step of the way, till we find ourselves those sweet children. Shh, shh. No, no, shh; there ain't no need for thanks, Doll. Really, no need."

Dave heard Emma quietly weeping. Poor girl, he doubted she could take much more of this.

"And naturally, Doll," the awful voice went on, "if we don't find them, or if you try to run off, why then I'll have to come right back here and your friend, your dear friend here, will get to feel the edge of this pretty blade."

Again, Dave felt pressure in his side.

"No! Get away from him. Please leave him alone."

There was a humourless laugh.

"Get ready, Doll. We're leaving."

"What about him?"

"What about him?"

"We can't leave him like that."

"We can't?"

"No. He won't be able to breathe. Please, pull that back a little."

"For you, Doll, anything."

Dave felt himself briefly lifted from the floor. The tightness of his upper arms relaxed, as his jacket was roughly pulled back. The former total darkness was explained: his thick jacket had been pulled up and forward, completely covering his head and blocking out all light. He was unceremoniously dropped back to the floor, but now there was a line of pale light around the rim of his vision, through which he could feel cooler air blowing onto his face.

Dave was delighted to find that he had not lost his sight. However, before his eyes had time to adjust, the only light in the room was extinguished and the door slammed shut. Dave was alone, with nothing to see or hear, save the chill whistling of the wind through the gaps in the clapboard walls.

Annie had been unconscious for some time.

Bill was sitting at her side, stroking her hand and gently whispering to her; he didn't want her to wake in this darkness and not know who was there with her. Better than anyone else, Bill knew how fragile Annie actually was. Others saw the confidence and the glamour, but Bill saw a wonderful, but remarkably shy woman drawn to performance, always risking hurt and rejection, like a moth attracted to an open flame. Bill's self-defined role in life was to support, protect and care for Annie; to be there with encouragement and reassurance when the flame scorched.

A sudden glimpse of moonlight lit her, and Bill saw Lisa's face in Annie's features. He began to weep again. Where was his little girl? Where was little Mikey? Everything had gone to hell; everyone Bill cared for was lost to him and he could do nothing but pray. Over and over, he begged and bargained that his family be spared and brought safely back to him. As time went by, his whispered prayers seemed to him to blend with the whispering of the river flowing past. Gradually, exhausted and deprived of light and company, Bill was soothed and lulled into a state of dissociated, almost meditative tranquility. He continued to function: stroking Annie's hand, talking to her, tucking the blanket close to her, but his actions were unconscious and automatic. Bill was unaware of both his growing hunger and the intense cold; his mind was elsewhere. He was dreaming that the children were safe. They were playing nearby; Bill could hear them calling to one another.

How long he had remained there in that state he was not sure. One of the children was calling to him now. One of the children needed him and, even in his dreamlike state, Bill was anxious for the child. As the calling turned to sobbing and drew slowly closer, so Bill began to wake from his stupor. With this reawakening came awareness of the cold; he shivered violently. Fully awake now, he could still hear the crying. He shook himself, to be sure he wasn't conjuring the tiny sound from the beguiling murmur of the water. No, this was not his imagination; there was definitely a child crying nearby. For a few seconds Bill felt himself torn between staying with Annie and searching for the child, but, much as he loved his wife, there was really no question: he had to leave her and go to the crying child.

Bill gently kissed Annie's hand before tucking it under the blanket. He struggled to rise, his feet numb with cold and prolonged inactivity. After some effort he stood, swaying slightly and listening intently. Then, hardly daring to let himself hope that it might be Lisa or Mikey, he began to feel his way towards the tiny sound.

Although intermittent moonlight filtered down to the ground in patches by the stream, there were areas of shadow that were in total blackness. No matter how intensely Bill peered into this darkness he could make out no detail whatsoever and, remembering his previous fall into the stream, he was extremely cautious. All the while, the crying was getting closer.

"Hello?" Bill called, "Stay where you are. Lisa? Mikey? Whoever you are, stay there. I'll come to you."

The crying stopped abruptly.

"Talk to me, so I can find you... Please," Bill pleaded, "I need you to talk to me."

Nothing.

Bill stopped. With no sound to focus on, he had no idea where to go. The river's gentle gurgling now seemed intrusively loud; above it, Bill could hear nothing. There was not a whimper, not a broken twig.

Then suddenly, Bill heard a crash to his right; away from the river. It sounded as if a struggle were going on. Heedless of his own danger, he left the river and plunged into the dense undergrowth.

"Hold on," he shouted, "I'm coming."

"No! No Bill, keep away. He'll -"

That voice! It was Emma and she was obviously in great distress.

"Emma! Emma, talk to me."

Breathing heavily, Bill had to stop. He could hear only very muffled sounds, somewhere up ahead. Someone had their hand over Emma's mouth, Bill was sure of that, and the sounds weren't loud enough for him to guess at their direction.

Bill took a deep breath and tried to sound more confident and powerful than he actually felt.

"Listen to me, whoever you are. Leave her alone. Leave her and go. If you hurt her, so help me, I will hunt you down. And I'm not alone: there are others, lots of us, in the forest right now, all around here. They're looking for you and I swear we'll track you down."

Silence.

Bill walked forward, feeling his way, hands

outstretched into the void.

"Emma? Are you still there? Emma?"

Bill peered ahead, but the darkness was absolute. He could see nothing.

Suddenly the scudding clouds cleared and a tiny movement caught Bill's eye. He turned. He was looking directly into Emma's terrified eyes. She was no more than two feet away from him.

Bill followed the black sleeve clamped over Emma's mouth up, up to the face. As he did so, the shadow man's black, fathomless eyes opened and stared down at him. The pale, dry skin drew back and the razor teeth glinted blue white in the weak moonlight. Bill swallowed hard and felt his knees weaken beneath him.

Transfixed, staring up at that deathly grin, Bill peripherally registered a sudden change in Emma; feeling the grip loosen about her face, she had widened her eyes in a warning. As the arm slashed out at Bill, Emma screamed and screwed her eyes shut. She couldn't bear to see Bill's gentle face ripped and torn. She heard the sickening sound, as his body hit the ground, then her mouth was gagged again and she was carried quickly away.

Bill had not been consciously aware of Emma's warning. Her eyes had alerted something more basic and instinctive than consciousness, and that fraction of a second's warning had saved Bill's life. The muscles of his legs had instantly flexed, hurling him to one side, taking power from the blow which now only glanced his shoulder. The bone white hand missed his neck. The wicked nails slashed past him ineffectually.

Bill landed heavily and, before he could get back to his feet, Emma and the terrible creature had vanished into the darkness. Kneeling, Bill slumped forward in despair. He could only imagine what terrors Emma had already endured and the terrible abandonment she must now be feeling. He had utterly failed the poor child. His had probably been the last friendly face Emma would ever see, and he hadn't been able to save her. He would never be able to forgive himself. Bill thought of Jeff, Julie and Rita. How could he tell them? And, having seen the thing that held Emma, Bill also found himself hoping for the unspeakable; that Lisa and Mikey were already dead and safe from that monster's clutches.

Bill lay there on the frozen ground for several minutes, until his mind registered the sound of more crying. This time it seemed to be coming from a different direction, behind him. Revitalised, but cautious, Bill dried his eyes and rose as quietly as possible, feeling his way forward. He neared the river and was fearful that the water would drown the sound, but the sobs were louder now. Bill followed them.

Waking to find herself all alone in the cold dark of the forest Annie huddled deep into the blanket. Her confusion took several minutes to clear. She had no idea where Bill, Jeff and Lou could be or why they had left her here, unprotected and alone. She struggled to think clearly. Surely the others would have left a note, something to tell her where they had gone. By the occasional light of the moon, she searched about her for a message, but found none. They must have left her in a hurry; something awful must have happened. Annie could only imagine what that might have been. Her desperate hope was that Bill, Jeff and Lou were alright and that Lisa and Mikey were now safe. Maybe Bill had found the children and was taking them back to the hotel at this very moment. Annie held onto that hope as a charm to ward off her growing fear of the awful darkness around her.

However, as the minutes passed, Annie's grip on hope gradually loosened. She began to question whether anyone could be left alive; surely they would by now have come to find her. She knew, with a dispassionate, detached certainty, that she did not want to remain alive if Bill and the children were dead. But, at the same time, it frightened her that no one would know where she was, so when she died out here, as she surely would, her body would never be found. It seemed such a foolish, almost selfish, thing to be concerned about that Annie tried to put it from her mind. However, the harder she tried, the more concrete was the image in her mind of her own dead body lying here by the river, year after year; alone and unmourned. Annie couldn't bear the thought that no one would care, or even know for certain that she was dead. Wretchedness overwhelmed her and she began to weep; it seemed all she could do.

Suddenly, there was a sound. Something large was coming towards her. She stopped crying immediately, holding her breath. As she did so, the noises also stopped, convincing Annie that she was being stalked. Pulling the blanket close about her, she drew herself back as close as possible to the rock wall of the narrow river valley. Clouds obscured the moon and Annie willed them to stay put. She stared, wide-eyed, into the darkness, seeing nothing.

After several minutes of silence, the noise began again. Something was slowly moving closer, its progress revealed in the sounds of pebbles slipping and rolling under its weight and in its breathing, which was getting horribly loud. Every muscle was taut, as Annie strained to make herself as small as possible. She hoped desperately that whatever it was could not track her scent; she'd often heard it said that animals could smell fear, and right now Annie was as fearful as it was possible to be.

She shrieked.

"Get off me! Get off me!"

Something had stumbled right into her. Annie lashed out in blind panic and her attacker fell on top of her. Crushed under the weight, Annie screamed again, and he, it was a male voice, shouted in alarm.

Annie stopped kicking.

"Bill?" she asked, incredulous, "Bill, is that you?"

"Annie? Oh God, Annie are you OK?"

They embraced, both weeping tears of relief and exhaustion. As they clung to each other for reassurance in the midst of all the fear and strangeness of the night, Bill told Annie about her fall and explained Jeff and Lou's decision to go on ahead.

"They've gone to get the children. You could tell they felt bad leaving us here, but I told them it was OK. Jeff promised he'd get Lisa and Mikey."

"Oh God."

"It's OK Honey, he'll get them. I know he will. They'll most likely be back here real soon."

Bill wished he could believe his own words, but he had seen the alien thing that had their children. How could he believe that he and his friends could overcome that monster, armed only with kitchen knives and desperate courage?

Annie looked up at him. She knew he was holding something back.

"What is it, Bill? What else did I miss when I was out?"

Bill was at first reluctant to tell Annie what had happened since Jeff and Lou left, but eventually he told her everything; everything, except his despairing hope that Lisa and Mikey were already beyond the monster's power. Bill would never be able to voice such a thought, but the forlorn, brutal hope burned away inside him. Given what they faced, it might be the best he could wish for his darling children.

Annie listened in silence, hardly able to believe his description of Emma's captor. But she knew Bill. He had told her the truth. No matter how bizarre and unlikely this creature she had to get beyond her initial skepticism and accept that they were facing something completely alien

"Was the creature taking Emma to the shack?"

"No. I think they were heading in the other direction: north. But I can't be sure; it's so dark away from the river. I got disoriented. I only made it back here because I heard you crying," he hugged her closer still, "Are you feeling OK now?"

Annie nodded.

"Your head? You don't have a headache?"

"No, I'm OK, really."

"Thank God. I was so frightened I was going to lose you."

"Me too."

Annie forced herself to be positive. Now that she had found Bill, there was hope again and she would not give up while she believed there was hope.

"Come on," she said in a businesslike tone, "We should go on. Jeff and Lou might need our help with the kids."

They helped each other to stand then, hand in hand, groped their way along the river bank, heading down stream.

29

Leaving Jon bleeding and stunned, Neil raced across the clearing and up the steps into the hotel. Once inside, he slammed the hotel doors behind him and frantically rammed the bolts into place before rushing to switch off all the lights in the lobby. With the room now in darkness he went carefully from window to window, peering out into the night, but could see nothing. He kept up his watch for several anxious minutes before turning away. Then, leaning back against the window frame, he slowly allowed his breathing to calm.

Once recovered, he went into the lounge and crossed straight to one of the large windows. Spielman looked up.

"What's out there, son?"

Neil span round. He had forgotten the old man.

"What? Nothing."

Gathering his wits, Neil nonchalantly affected complete disinterest in the impenetrable dark beyond the glass. Walking across the room to the fire, he stood, warming his hands as he tried to think of something casual to say.

"How's the arm?"

Spielman ignored the question.

"Somethin's spooked yuh, son. What's out there?"

"Nothing. Don't be ridiculous. There's nothing out

there. Think I'll have a drink."

Spielman was unconvinced.

"Where are the others?"

"Others?"

"The others, son: yuh friends."

"Is no one else back yet?"

"No," Spielman spoke slowly, watching Neil closely, "only you."

"Yeah, well I guess they're all on their way back now. I need a drink. You want one?"

Spielman raised an eyebrow.

"What happened out there, son?"

"I'm getting a drink."

"I asked you a question, son. What's happenin' out there?"

"I don't know."

"What d'ya mean? Where are the others?"

"We got...split up."

"Split? How?"

"It's dark out there."

"Did you leave that lady out there?"

"What? Who?"

"Rita, her name was Rita. Did you leave her out there, son?"

Neil floundered. He resented this old guy's intrusive questioning, but if he refused to answer, it might look like he had something to hide. For the first time, Neil began to feel something approaching a sense of guilt that he and Phil had left Rita out there, alone. Also Jeff's threat seemed more tangible back here in the hotel. Neil realised that he had to come up with some plausible excuse for his actions.

"It wasn't like that," he began.

He hadn't decided how he would continue so, taking a deep breath, he just said the first words that came to him,

"There's a wild man out there; looks like Bigfoot."

He now had Spielman's full attention.

"You've seen it?"

"Yeah, and he is one scary mother."

As Neil described Jon's mutilated face, his wild hair and the foul-smelling animal skins, Spielman's jaw dropped in amazement.

"Did he have the children? Did yuh see them?"

"Children?" for a few seconds Neil's face was a blank, "Oh...no, no; just him."

"But d'yuh think he's taken 'em?"

Neil had given no thought whatsoever to the children. He cared little enough for them under normal circumstances but, now that his own safety had been threatened, they and their well-being had disappeared from his concerns entirely. He neither knew nor cared where they were. However, he had no wish to attract irritating criticism for this indifference, so he endeavoured to keep Spielman's interest focussed on Jon.

"Do I think he's taken the kids? Well, sure."

As Neil spoke he realised that, in Jon, he had the ideal, inarticulate scapegoat. Jon could assume the blame for anything. Neil warmed to his subject.

"Yeah, he's guilty no question; hiding out in the forest. Why else would anyone live alone out here in the middle of nowhere?"

Spielman pursed his lips, but said nothing.

"Also," Neil remembered, "he was really interested when I mentioned the girls."

Spielman turned his head and spat into the hearth.

"Makes me sick to ma stomach."

Neil was both disgusted and encouraged by the old man's reaction, and decided to embellish the story somewhat and develop Jon into a monster worthy of nightmare.

"He went crazy and attacked me, for no reason; just went berserk. And, believe me, he's strong, really strong. I didn't think I'd make it. Phil ran off, scared I guess, and I...I tried to lead the crazy guy away from Rita. OK, it wasn't much but, realistically, it was all I could do for her. Anyhow, I ran and ran and he was chasing after me, like he was hunting me down. Then he attacked me."

Spielman raised a questioning eyebrow.

"Again?"

"Yes, again."

"And you're still alive?"

"I was beaten unconscious, for chrissake."

Spielman nodded.

"Uhuh. And did yuh find yuh friend?"

"Who?"

"Yuh friend...Dave?"

Neil was irritated by the undisguised tone of reproach in the old man's words, but he felt no remorse at having forgotten Dave. Dave, like the missing children, was a minor player, of little importance.

"No. I didn't find him. The crazy guy must have killed him."

"Uhuh. How d'yuh reckon that?"

"How? Because...he told me he'd killed him; that's how. He was boasting about it, OK?"

Even as he was saying this, Neil feared this might be one lie too many. What if Dave were to walk back into the hotel right now?

But no, that would be OK; Neil could always say that Jon must have been lying to him. His story would hold, so long as Jon was unable to challenge him, and Neil trusted that, with luck, the extreme cold would soon compound Jon's head injury and loss of blood, to produce the desired outcome.

"So, how d'yuh escape?"

"Well...I...I waited till he was looking the other way, then I ran. I ran for my life and I lost him, back in the trees. Then I ran all the way back here."

Spielman narrowed his eyes. It was hard for Neil to gauge his reaction to the story.

"Yuh must be one helluva runner, son."

Neil's anger rose; how dare this old fool doubt him?

"I work out."

"Uhuh?"

"Yeah, most evenings, at least two hours. Happy now? Mind if I get my drink?"

As Neil walked towards the door, Spielman cleared his throat.

"What?" Neil demanded.

"Must have one helluva good sense of direction too, son."

Neil rounded on him.

"Fuck you, old man! You weren't there and you don't know what happened, so get the hell off my case!"

Spielman was unperturbed.

"You're frightened, son. That's understandable. And that's OK. But don't yuh be tryin' to threaten me."

To emphasise the point, Spielman drew the butt of a gun from his pocket. Neil paled. Having made his point, Spielman calmly re-pocketed the gun.

"Now," he continued, "tell me the truth, son. Did yuh lead it here? Has it followed yuh. Is that what yuh lookin' for at the winduh?"

Neil didn't know what to say. As it was quite possible that he had killed Jon, he would have to be careful what he admitted to. On the other hand, if Jon was still alive, it seemed unlikely that he would simply go away and leave them alone. He would probably come here in search of revenge. Neil shuddered. Again, everything would be so much easier if Jon were dead: no one to come seeking vengeance, and no one to contest Neil's version of events.

"Well, son, is it out there?"

"We fought. I think...I hope he's dead."

"Need to do more than hope, son, but don't trouble yuhself. With this here," he patted the pocket containing the gun, "we can put an end to it right now. Are yuh with me, son?"

Neil wasn't sure what the old man was proposing

"Son, are you willin' t'go back out there and kill this sonofabitch, pard'n my french?"

The old fool wanted him to go back out there.

No way!

But after a moment's reflection Neil realised that he would feel a good deal more secure if he had Spielman's gun for himself. With that in mind, he pretended to consider Spielman's suggestion for a moment or two, before sighing, as if accepting a heavy duty.

"OK...Give me the gun and I'll finish this, before anyone else gets hurt."

"This gun don't leave my side."

"Don't be ridiculous, Spielman; you're in no fit state to go anyplace."

"If what I think is out there, is out there, we're both gonna have to take it on."

"You have another gun?"

"No, but you don't need a gun do yuh, son? It attacked yuh two times and yuh survived. Reckon there's not many folks could say that."

Neil was irritated that his own lie had caught him out.

"Why do you keep calling him 'it'? I told you, he's a man. A crazy man, a kidnapper, a psycho maybe, but a man."

"Sure of that, are yuh son?"

"Yes I'm sure. What kind of question is that?"

Spielman turned to warm his hands by the fire.

"How old would yuh say this crazy man was, son?"

"How old? How the hell should I know?"

Spielman waited.

"OK. If I had to guess, I'd say he was about sixty-five. What's your point?"

"And the monster that stole the children back in the fifties, how old would he be now?"

"What?"

"How old?"

"How the hell should I know?"

"If Karen and I are right, the monster who killed those kiddies would be one hundred years old by now."

"What?"

"Yep, yuh heard right, son; one hundred years."

"What? What the hell are you talking about? And who's Karen?"

"Mrs Cousins. She and her husband own this place."

"Oh her? Yeah we've met; had the pleasure of her company over dinner. She's one party animal."

"Don't rightly know what yuh mean, son, but that poor lady's suffered. She dunt want no kids here. She wanted t'cancel the booking when she heard y'all were bringin' children. Asked me t' keep a watch."

"Right," Neil rolled his eyes, "And the hundred years?"

"We reckon as how it must live way longer than other folks. Yuh say it looks sixty-five, but, like I said, it's gotta be a hundred, easy. Could be older. That creature coulda bin killin' for centuries."

Neil wondered how he should deal with this situation. Inside the hotel, he was subject to the ravings of an irrational old fool, who had a gun, while outside there was a crazy wild man who, if he was still alive, would no doubt be after Neil's blood. It was not an ideal set of choices.

"Spielman," he wondered, "did Lou knock you out

353

when she stabbed you?"

Spielman paused.

"Ah. Yuh know it was the little lady did this?"

"Yeah. Phil said she went crazy and stabbed you for no reason."

"Oh, she had her reasons. Reckon I provoked her. She looks so like I remember the poor dead girl I found. I couldn't help but stare. Guess I spooked her is all."

"Spielman?"

"Uhuh."

"When she stabbed you, did you fall and hit your head?"

"No. Why d'yuh keep askin' me?"

"No reason, other than you're talking like a crazy person. You're telling me there's a centuries-old monster on the loose."

"Yuh don't believe me? But yuh seen it with your own eyes."

"I saw an old man who's aggressive and crazy, maybe psychotic, but not some serial killing Methuselah."

"But yuh think it's taken the kids?"

After what he had already said, Neil had to agree, but his tone was guarded.

"Yeah...So?"

"OK, well I reckon it's done this before, but even if yuh reckon it ain't nothin' but human, we should go get it anyhow."

"So, give me the gun."

"You harda hearin' son? This gun never leaves my side. And anyhow, if we both go out there we'll more likely catch it. You go out the front door and I'll go out the back."

Neil was bored with all this, but now saw a way out.

"OK, have it your way. Front door. Got it."

Spielman struggled to his feet, swaying slightly.

"And we'll meet back here in one hour. OK, son?"

"Sounds good to me."

In the lobby, Neil made a show of releasing the bolts and unlocking the front doors, as he watched Spielman walk away down the corridor.

"Good luck, son," Spielman shouted, "Good hunting!"

"Yeah, sure," Neil muttered, "Whatever."

After a few moments, Neil heard the distant sound of the back door shutting.

"About time!"

He pushed the bolts back into place. He had no intention of going back out to face that hairy, foul smelling lunatic. He now had the hotel to himself and could enjoy a drink and then have that shower he'd been promising himself.

Dave had been struggling to untie himself for what seemed like hours, without any success. Indeed, the ligatures were tightening, becoming tourniquets, as he twisted and pulled at them. Dave knew that he was worsening the situation; his frozen hands were becoming numb, the circulation of blood being progressively strangled at the wrist. Despite this he had to keep trying, because he also knew that Emma, regardless of any threats or inducements, would never help her captor to find the other children. She might be able to delay matters, but eventually it would be clear that she would not cooperate, then the death-faced demon that captured Dave would be back to kill him. He had to get away from this place.

Finally, with excruciating pain in his hands and at his ankles, Dave decided to try to get out of the building, still bound. It was a measure of his desperation that he had not considered how he was going to cover any distance once he was outside, and lying in the snow and debris of the forest floor. With no idea of how long Emma and the creature had been away, or how soon they would return, Dave threw himself into convulsive moves that rocked him closer and closer to the door. It was an exhausting effort and agonisingly slow, but eventually he could feel a strong draught of icy air on his face; he was close to the door. He would now have to reach the handle and he paused while he considered how he was going to do this.

As he rested, he heard something above the low wailing of the wind through the gap under the door: there was a scratching at the glass of the window. Something was creeping around the side of the building. It was coming towards the door.

His captor was back!

With feverish speed, Dave devised a plan to trip him as he came through the door. Dave had no clue what he would be able to do after that, but there was no more time; that was all he could do. Lying just inside the door, he lay still and braced himself for the pain of the impact.

Rita had struggled on alone, until the path became impassable with snow and with laden branches fallen to the ground. Reluctant to abandon the search, she had continued until her hands and feet were numb with cold, but now it was time to turn back and, as if to compound her misery, the sky clouded over and snow began to fall.

When Rita finally arrived back at the fork in the path, Neil and Phil were nowhere to be seen. She was furious that they hadn't waited. Cursing at them, the snow and the cold, she stamped off towards the hotel, fully expecting to find them both in the bar. The hurricane lamp lit the markers on the trees and she made good progress until, as she neared the edge of the clearing, a fallen branch blocked her way. She clambered over it, and stepped down onto something soft.

Jon moaned and Rita leapt with the shock of hearing his voice so close. She held up the lamp and scanned all around. When the light fell on Jon, Rita gasped. Her hand went to her mouth.

"Jeez!" she whispered, beginning to back away.

Jon looked up at her and, seeing his large, pleading eyes, Rita stopped. This was no wild animal; it was a man, and one who looked to be in pain. Rita was still cautious, but her natural sympathy came to the fore.

"Are you OK?" she asked, "Your head looks like it's bleeding."

"Man. Gone."

"A man hurt you?"

Jon nodded.

"Who?"

"Him Neil."

"Why am I not surprised?"

Had anyone but Neil hurt this strange man, Rita would have been more wary of the circumstances that might have led up to the injury, but Neil was enough of a bastard to have hurt this man for no good reason.

"Why d'he hit you?"

"Not know."

"Did you hurt Neil?"

"No. I stop him fall."

"You stopped him falling? You saved his life - not necessarily a good use of your time by the way - and the ingrate smashes your head open?"

Jon frowned: he didn't fully understand. This woman spoke too fast, like the man who hit him. She also used unfamiliar words and words that Jon only half remembered from long ago.

Rita could see that he was confused. Perhaps he didn't speak english.

"Heck, I'm sorry," she said, "Too fast, eh?"

Jon nodded.

"Sorry. OK. Me, Rita. You?"

"Jon."

"Great. OK, Jon, where is Neil now?"

"Gone."

"Back to the hotel?"

"Hotel, yes. You must go. Not safe you be here. Must go."

"Come with me."

Jon shook his head. Rita tried to persuade him.

"If you came to the hotel with me. I could clean that wound."

Again, Jon knew that he hadn't understood all the details, but he trusted this woman; she was concerned for him. It was important that he made her understand she was in danger. Jon didn't want any harm to come to her or to her children.

"I go find girl."

"What girl? The children, the missing children? You know about them?"

"Missing."

"Yeah, that's right. Do you know where the children are?"

"No. I find."

"Hold up there, you can't go alone…Wait here…Stay here. I go to hotel. Get help. We all find the children."

"No. I go find now. I go this."

He pointed to the woods on the opposite side of the clearing.

"Is that south?"

"I go now."

Jon rose to his feet. His head was throbbing, but he could see and hear well enough. He would recover fully, given time. He rubbed life back into his chilled limbs.

"Are you sure you won't stay, even just long enough for me to treat that cut on your head?"

As she spoke, Rita moved a step forward. Jon backed away.

"I go this," he pointed again, "You stay hotel. Not forest; not safe."

"I'll get the others and we'll follow you if we can."

Jon looked into her eyes, trying to make her understand. This was important.

"No. You stay hotel. Evil. Not safe. I find children. You stay hotel."

Thanks only to their having the flashlight, Jeff and Lou had seen and recognised the falls and the clump of dense trees shown on Spielman's map. They turned away from the river and soon they were crouched at the edge of an overgrown clearing.

Intermittent moonlight lit the scene as Jeff peered forward.

"There it is: the shack Spielman was talking about."

Lou nodded.

"OK, let's go."

She was already on her feet, but Jeff caught her hand. She turned on him.

"What are you doing? Let go of me."

"Wait. If we go rushing in, the kids could get hurt. Let's do this by the book."

"What book?"

"Sorry. I mean we should be careful; check the place out from here, before we go in."

"Jeff, you can check out whatever you want, from wherever you want, but my son is in there and I'm going to get him. Now."

Jeff gave up.

"OK, but keep low."

They crouched into a run and quickly covered the distance to the shack.

Lou bobbed up and was straining to look through the window, when Jeff pulled her back down.

"Listen!"

"What?" she whispered, "I can't hear a thing."

"Shh."

"What? Can you hear something?"

"No. It's stopped now."

"Then, for God's sake, why are we still out here?" Lou hissed, exasperated, "Give me a leg up."

Jeff supported Lou as she scrambled up to the window. She pressed her nose against the filthy glass.

"It's no use. I can't see a thing. Give me something to clean the dirt off."

"Like what, for Pete's sake? Use your glove."

"Oh, yeah...OK, I can see...something."

"What? What can you see?"

"Hard to say."

She scratched more of the grime from the glass.

"For God's sake, can you see the kids?"

"Shh!" Lou whispered, "It's very dark in there. I can't see the kids, but there's something moving. Could be an animal; a dog maybe. Whatever it is, it's big; we'll have to be careful. OK, get me down."

Jeff didn't enjoy being ordered about like this, but he swallowed his pride and helped her down.

"Listen!" she whispered, "You can hear it moving around."

"If that's a dog, why isn't it barking?"

"How the hell should I know?"

"OK, OK. You didn't see any sign of the kids?"

Lou shook her head.

"No, but I want to get in there and check the place out. Maybe they've been moved on from here," she

360

frowned, "But how are we gonna get past the dog, or whatever it is?"

"I guess we use these."

Jeff brandished the kitchen knife.

"Where's yours?"

Lou turned away.

"Guess I must've dropped it somewhere."

Jeff took a deep breath.

"In that case, we'll go in together, but you stay behind me."

"OK."

With great care, Jeff and Lou crept up to the door but, as the dry planking creaked below their weight, the noises from inside the shack stopped. Whatever was in there had obviously heard them. Jeff tightened his grip on the knife and mentally rehearsed the stabbing movement he would have to make.

Lou was impatient.

"What are you waiting for?"

"Shh!"

"Get on with it, or give me the knife."

Jeff took the door handle and slowly turned it.

Lou was exasperated.

"Open the goddam door."

"Will you shut up!"

He began slowly to ease the door open.

"Oh, for God's sake, give me that!"

Lou grabbed the knife from him and, with a fearsome yell, pushed past him, into the shack. The door slammed open and, peering into the darkness, Jeff heard a scuffle and then a shout. He rushed in and saw Lou standing over a strangely hunched figure on the floor. The figure was arching and stretching, almost writhing. As Jeff's eyes became accustomed to the gloom, he saw that the figure was a man: it was Dave! Jeff rushed over and knelt next to him. Dave's shoulder was bleeding and he was bound, hand and foot. Though hindered by the lack of light, Jeff set to untying the knots.

"Are we glad to see you. What happened? Who did this to you?"

Getting no response, Jeff leant over to look into Dave's face. Dave was staring up, transfixed by the knife in Lou's hand. Lou was standing above him, her face a blank.

Jeff spoke to her, gently.

"Lou?...Put down the knife...Lou?...Lou, can you hear me?"

Lou seemed not to have heard.

"Where's Ethan?" she whispered, "Where's my baby?"

Lou opened her fingers and dropped the knife to the floor. Dave's blood was smudged at its point. Jeff reached up and took Lou's hand.

"We'll find him, Lou. We'll find all of them."

He squeezed her hand and gave what he hoped was a reassuring smile, but Lou shook her head and sank down against the wall. She stared straight ahead, seeing nothing. Jeff turned his attention back to Dave.

"D'you know where the kids are? Have you seen them?"

He struggled with the ties.

"Emma. I've seen Emma; she was here. He took her away."

Jeff stopped.

"Who?"

"Some guy. I don't know; I couldn't see. I think he was wearing a Halloween mask. He threatened to kill me if Emma didn't do what he wanted."

Jeff's throat was suddenly dry. He couldn't speak. A man had his little girl. Jeff's mind was frozen.

"Jeff?"

"Huh?"

"Don't give up, man. She's a real fighter that daughter of yours and she was OK when they left. Just get these off me, then we can follow their tracks and get her back."

Jeff suddenly snapped to and renewed his efforts to free Dave's wrists.

"Shit, these are really tight!"

Lou spoke up, her voice flat.

"Use the knife."

Jeff took Lou's advice, then slid the knife into his belt. Dave was free, and able at last to stretch his arms and legs. But, rather than the immediate release from agony that he had anticipated, his muscles now pained him more. Jeff had to help him to his feet and then support him for several minutes while the searing cramps in his limbs slowly eased.

Lou couldn't bear this delay. Her eyes were hot, but she had no tears. She was totally consumed by her need to find her son. It was alright for Jeff; he knew his daughter was still alive. He could follow her and find her. But where was Lou's poor baby? Where was Ethan?

"Can we please go?" she snapped.

"Sure," Dave winced, tying a rag around the cut on his shoulder, "I'm good to go."

The three stumbled out of the shack and down its steps. Bright moonlight now lit the clearing, sharply defining every contour with deep violet shadows. Finding the tracks should have been a simple task but, while they could see their own tracks leading to the shack, they could find none that led away.

Jeff's frustration exploded

"Damn it! Damn it to hell! Where are they?"

"Dunno man, let's keep looking."

"What's the point? They're gone. Emma's gone. Shit, if we only knew where the bastard was taking her."

"He said he wanted her to get the other kids and bring them to him."

"What?" said Lou, suddenly alert, "The other kids are alive?"

"Yeah. Yeah, I'm sure that's what he said."

"Oh thank God! Where are they?"

"I don't know. Don't think he said."

"What? Think back. Did he say anything, anything at all, about where the others are?"

Dave trawled through his memories, trying to recall the exact words the man had used.

"I don't know. I don't think he said anything. I'm sorry."

"Please, think! He must have said something."

Jeff found Lou's state of heightened agitation worrying.

"Come on Lou, let's try to stay calm."

"Shut it, Jeff! Dave? Anything, anything at all?"

"He did say something about the place being fancy."

"Fancy?"

"Yeah."

"That's it?"

"I'm sorry."

"That's it!" Jeff's voice was excited, "The only fancy place for miles is the hotel. They're going to the hotel! Come on, we've got to get back there."

He turned and started to retrace their tracks back to the river, but Lou remained where she was.

"No, Jeff. Ethan and the others aren't in the hotel. We know that. I'm not going to waste my time going back there."

"But -"

"No, Jeff, no. It's OK for you; you know Emma is on her way back there, but I don't know where Ethan is. He could be anywhere. He could be dead."

"I thought we'd agreed they were still alive."

"Only because the man who has Emma thinks that they are. But he also thinks the kids are at the hotel and we know they're not. No, my baby could be dead, out here, all alone in the cold and the dark."

Lou's voice trailed away into silence and she began to weep, the tears rolling silently down her cheeks as she stared bleakly ahead, seeing nothing. She was absolutely still, as if frozen to the ground and, in the surreal light, her pale skin shone like a statue, her tears like drops of rain running across its marble face. There was an unearthly quality to the moment and Dave could almost believe that Lou had been turned to stone. He shivered and looked to Jeff for reassurance, but Jeff too was unnerved by the strangeness of Lou's stillness. She seemed distant from them both; disturbingly remote, as if she was no longer even aware of their presence. Neither Jeff nor Dave knew how to react. What Lou had said was true; out here in the forest, in bitter cold, it was very likely that Ethan was already dead. And if, by some chance, he was still alive, they had no idea where to begin to look for him. Lou had every reason to despair.

Jeff felt deeply sorry for her; she wasn't much more than a kid herself and she was desperate and heartbroken, on the verge of despair. And she had been right too when she said that they knew only where Emma was. But that was all that Jeff needed. He wished he could comfort Lou, but there was nothing anyone could say to make things right and, all the time they stayed here, Emma was getting further away. He had to go.

He spoke, breaking the spell.

"Lou, please we've got to go."

She wiped away her tears, but she didn't look towards him.

"You go. I'm staying here."

"What? Why?"

"I have to find Ethan."

"Jeez, Lou, you can't stay here. Come on back to the hotel."

"No."

Jeff looked, at Dave, pleading. Dave took a deep breath.

"It's OK, Jeff, you go back. I'll stay here with Lou, until we find Ethan."

Jeff hesitated. He drew Dave aside.

"Are you sure about this? The woman just stabbed you."

Dave shrugged.

"It's OK, man. Go get Emma."

Jeff was hugely grateful for Dave's offer to stay. It was unbelievably generous of him; not only would he be left with Lou, who was clearly in a very fragile state of mind, but he must also know that Lou's hope of finding her son must be a forlorn one. They would have to have the most formidable good fortune to happen across the kids by chance.

Jeff felt bad leaving Dave here like this, but time was pressing heavily on him. He had to leave.

"Thanks, Dave. I can't tell you how much I appreciate this."

He turned and walked a few steps, then stopped. He ought to leave them the flashlight. He had only to follow the river back upstream to the falls. Dave and Lou could be searching new ground. But, what if he were to need the light to find Emma? He was torn with indecision.

"You OK man?"

Jeff couldn't trust himself to look back. He felt terrible guilt, leaving Dave and Lou without a light, but selfishness had won out. He had to find Em, and to do that he might need the light. He waved a hand in farewell.

"Yeah. I'm good. Take care of yourselves."

"You too man. Good luck."

Jeff nodded and began to run away across the clearing.

After Bill's brave but futile attempt to free her, icy fingers closed about Emma's mouth and she was carried away.

Poor Bill. Fixed in Emma's mind, a slow motion sequence was playing over and over: his body crumpling and falling to the ground. Bill must be dead and now she was being taken away by his killer; this shadow man.

Shadowman.

It was a good name for him, Emma thought miserably, as the gaunt, dark-coated figure slipped, effortless as a shadow, over the snow. She didn't like to dwell for too long on who, or what, the Shadowman might be. He was unlike anyone or anything she recognised, and he was utterly terrifying. His initial, superficial politeness had changed as soon as he had control over her; switched, in a second, from charm to threat and from concern to cruelty, until Emma was dazed and uncertain. She took some comfort in the fact that Bill could no longer be hurt by this monster. But it wasn't over for her, or for Dave. Poor Dave, who had also tried to help her, now lay, trussed up, alone in the darkness of that filthy shack. Emma wept quietly for them both.

After some distance, the Shadowman put her down. They stood now, at the edge of the clearing surrounding the hotel, he painfully gripping her elbow.

"You're hurting me."

The Shadowman ignored her. He was intently looking back and forth across the clearing and seemed to be sniffing the air. Finally he twisted her arm, forcing her to turn and face him.

"Now listen to me, Doll, and listen good. You are going back to the hotel and once you have those sweet children you will come right back here. If you don't come back real quick, or if I even suspect you're not coming back; I'll come in and do things my way. That could be very bad and you don't want that, do you, Doll? And if you think to run away, why, I'll go kill that friend of yours."

Emma hung her head and said nothing. The Shadowman shook her to force her to look up at him again.

"And, naturally, you won't say a word to anyone about me while you're in there. You understand me, Doll?"

Emma nodded blankly and he pushed her forwards. Stumbling a few steps, she stopped and waited for him to follow, but he hung back. He was going to remain here, under cover of the trees. Hope suddenly soared within her again; he couldn't know what was happening once she was out of his sight, inside the hotel, and there had to be some way that she could get the children out and spirit them away to a place of safety. Emma knew that saving the children meant risking Dave's life, but she was sure her Dad would figure some way to rescue Dave. How she wished her Dad was with her now as she crossed the clearing alone. Feeling very small and vulnerable, she didn't look back, but felt the eyes of the Shadowman on her, following every step.

Eventually, she climbed the steps and turned the door handle. It didn't move: the doors were locked. Emma hadn't expected this. She turned and scanned the treeline. He was out there somewhere. She could feel his eyes watching her, but she couldn't see him. Panicking now, not knowing where he was and fearing that, at any second, he might appear at her side, Emma repeatedly pointed at the door handle and shrugged exaggeratedly; the Shadowman must see that this was not her fault. What should she do now? And what would he do?

The dark figure emerged from the trees. The face, pale as the snow, turned directly towards her and, although he was some distance away, Emma felt the dark eyes burning into her. He lifted a thin arm and pointed: she was to go around to the back door.

Emma stepped down from the locked door and began to skirt the building. At the back door, she clambered up the steep steps and went inside. The door shut quickly behind her. There was no light.

Suddenly, Emma shrieked. Something had touched her. There was something there with her, hidden in the darkness of the unlit corridor.

"Please! The other door was locked. Couldn't you see? You told me to come round to this door. It wasn't my fault."

She slumped to the floor, covering her head with her hands.

The light snapped on, but Emma, eyes tight shut, remained cowering against the wall.

"Huh? Who're you?"

It was a gruff voice. Not the Shadowman. Blinking, Emma rose hesitantly to her feet. In the harsh light, an old man was standing, his left arm in a sling, his right resting on the light switch panel. He stared at her for a few moments and then, without a word, leant forward and poked her arm.

"Hey! Cut that out!" Emma snapped, "What d'you do that for?"

"Jus' checkin' child, jus' checkin'."

"Checking what, you wierdo?"

Emma hadn't seen Spielman before and she was still breathless with shock. She stared at him.

He was apologetic.

"Yuh alright? Didn't mean to scare yuh."

Still Emma remained guarded.

"Who are you?"

"Spielman, Eric Spielman."

"What are you doing here? And where is everyone? Where's my Dad?"

"Yuh Dad?"

"Jeff Bishop; tall guy, blond hair."

"Reckon, he'd be out, lookin' for you."

"What? Out in the forest?"

"They all out lookin' for yuh."

"Oh no! It's all my fault," Emma burst into tears, "I want my Dad. I want my Dad."

Spielman shuffled uncomfortably from foot to foot. His life had not equipped him to handle this situation with any degree of confidence. Frowning, he wiped his hand clean on his grubby shirt before awkwardly patting Emma on the shoulder. She shrugged him away.

"What am I gonna do? Oh God, what am I gonna do?"

Spielman recognised the fear in Emma's voice. He tried to reassure her.

"Yuh can stay here. Yuh'll be safe here till yuh Pa gets back."

"You don't understand. That Shadowman is out there right now and, if I don't go back and take the other kids with me, he's gonna come after me and he's gonna kill Dave."

"Shadowman eh? Yuh say it's out there now? But I was just out there searchin' and I couldn't see nothin'. Are yuh sure?"

"Of course I'm sure. How d'you think I found my way back here? The Shadowman brought me."

"Why?"

"Why what?"

"Why d'it bring yuh back?"

"I told you: because he wants the other kids."

"But they ain't here."

"What?"

"They ain't here no more. We all thought it, the thing yuh call the Shadowman, had taken'em."

Emma began to shake.

"Oh God, oh God, oh God. What are we going to do? If I don't come out soon, he'll come in after me. We've got to hide!"

"No. There ain't no hidin' from it and we can't take it on alone. We gotta get outa here. Come on."

Emma didn't move. Too much had happened tonight. She knew she couldn't face the Shadowman and everyone else had already left the hotel, so this weird old man was probably right; they too should get out, as quickly as possible. But Emma was exhausted and she knew now that she had made it this far on the hope that her father would be here and he would somehow make everything right. Emma wanted to be a little girl again. She wanted to curl up into a tiny ball and and hide away from all of this. She shut her eyes; she didn't want this nightmare any more.

Spielman looked at her in panic. What was she doing? Was she going to collapse? They didn't have time for this. If this Shadowman was coming to the hotel, they had to get the hell out of here, fast. He shook her shoulder.

"Wake up, wake up. This ain't no time for sleepin'. We gotta go."

Switching off the light, he took up her limp hand and led her to the door. Emma allowed herself to be led; she had, for the moment, given up.

Spielman eased the door ajar and peered out into the night. He could see nothing but the racing shadows of the clouds scudding across the moon. Everything else was frozen, ice blue and black. Swallowing hard, Spielman took a firmer grip of Emma's hand and hurried down the steps.

Behind him he heard a splintering crash as the front doors were broken down. Emma and Spielman had escaped with only seconds to spare.

The Shadowman was in the hotel.

30

Neil had indulged himself with a very long, hot shower.

He was beginning to feel human again, after the rigours of the futile search out in the forest. A glass or two of fine cognac had helped his recovery and he now stood smiling contentedly, eyes shut, with the full force of the shower on his face. He hadn't a care in the world.

Shaking his head to clear his ears, he turned off the flow of water. He was reaching for his towel when he heard a loud banging. What was that? He paused, but whatever had caused the noise appeared to have stopped and Neil was unconcerned. He supposed that the plumbing in a building as old and, frankly, substandard as this one, would be cantankerous and prone to bangs and rattles; maybe some air had been trapped in the system of pipes and cisterns.

Then it came to him that the banging had probably been one of the others coming back to the hotel. Damn! Just when things were going so well. Now he'd have to unlock the front doors to let them in and then deal with all their questions. Why aren't you out there searching like the rest of us? How could you casually take a shower while the kids are lost out in the forest? Blah, blah, blah...Like he cared! He sighed; might as well get it over with.

Wrapping himself in a bath robe, Neil crossed the landing to look down into the darkened lobby. Seeing no one, he was about to continue down the stairs, when a movement caught his eye.

The tall, ragged figure of the Shadowman was standing in the middle of the room. Neil could not yet see its face, but the unnatural thinness, the dark coat and the pale hands with their long, bone white fingers were unnerving enough. Neil began to back away, but his feet, still wet from the shower, slipped on the polished wood and he fell noisily, grabbing at the handrail for support.

The skull face of the Shadowman snapped up towards him and Neil looked down into the depths of those jewel black eyes. Slowly, with menacing deliberation, the Shadowman smiled and Neil blanched at the sight of the sharp, jagged teeth. Too frightened to scream, he suddenly turned and ran, in blind panic, to the nearest room. It was a child's bedroom and, in the dark, Neil cursed with desperate frustration as he tripped and stumbled over discarded toys and clothes. Arms outstretched, he frantically searched for the doors of the closet. Once inside, he pulled the doors shut and held them closed.

His heart was beating erratically and much too quickly. His breath was coming in short, racing gulps. The rest of his body was frozen. He was tense; listening and wildly staring into the dark. Through the closet door, barely an inch from his face, he could hear the sounds of bedroom doors being opened and closed. Whatever that thing was, it was coming for him; searching from room to room.

And the sounds were getting closer.

Neil held his breath for several, tense seconds as droplets of sweat rolled, tickling, down his face and back. His cramped fingers, gripping the handle of the closet door began to tremble. If that thing came into the room now, there would be no hiding the noise of that vibration. Fighting to control his panic, Neil had to use his last reserve of energy to control his shaking hand. Now he could only wait.

Finally, after many minutes, Neil allowed the unbearable tension in his body to subside; the sounds had died away. Ever cautious though, he decided to remain where he was for a few minutes more, listening intently for any sound of the creature's return. After maybe five more minutes of absolute silence, save the tiny sounds of his own breathing, he flexed his fingers and prepared to turn the handle. Slowly, with eyes screwed shut in concentration, Neil eased the door open.

He opened his eyes.

The hollow, black eyes were staring right back at him, just inches from his own.

Neil gasped. He was petrified.

In total silence, the Shadowman leant his head first to one side and then to the other, as if studying Neil's stricken face. He then eased forward, until his pale, lifeless face was almost touching Neil's. Neil stared maniacally back, his breaths now shallow, staccato, his whole body rigid. Like an insect trapped in the spider's web, he knew he was about to die but he was too shocked to do anything.

Apparently satisfied, the Shadowman grinned, pulling back his parchment skin to expose the dagger sharp teeth. Neil now had the choking smell of its breath in his nostrils. He couldn't bear this. He was going to faint.

With a dry, scratching sound, the creature slowly extended its arms. As Neil watched, horrified, the bony hands pulled open both doors of the closet. With an abandonment of all control, urine flooded hot down Neil's trembling legs, soaking into his bathrobe. He registered the sensation almost as though detached from his own body; he was powerless to prevent it.

The Shadowman tilted his head once more and then, inexplicably, stepped back from the door. Still frozen, Neil continued to stare. What was happening? Why wasn't he dead? As he stared fixedly into the glittering eyes, his brain slowly began to re-engage with the situation. Perhaps this thing was blind and, if Neil were able to remain absolutely still, he would seem invisible to it. Yes, all he had to do was to wait the creature out. He could do that.

But, as the minutes slipped by, the Shadowman made absolutely no sound and showed no discernible movement. He seemed not even to breathe. Neil, on the other hand, was increasingly consumed with the pain in his tensed muscles. He longed to grimace, to blink his burning eyes. Most of all he wanted to move his arms and legs. In the awful silence of the room, the pain built higher and higher.

Finally, Neil knew he could bear it no longer. He would have to make a dash for the bedroom door. Perhaps, if he locked the door behind him, the delay might give him some chance of escape. It seemed a very faint hope, but the pain was now such that he would almost prefer to be caught and killed than remain like this any longer. He had only to will himself to move. When he did, the movement would have to be fast. He would have to throw himself towards the door at full speed; any hesitation and he would be dead, no question. Looking into those unfathomable eyes, Neil began silently to count down from ten.

Three...Two...One!

Neil exploded from the closet. Dodging low to avoid the creature, he hurled himself at the bedroom door and grabbed for the handle, but it slipped in his sweating hands. He grabbed at it again, but it wouldn't budge. The door was locked.

Neil was trapped. There was a rustling sound behind him; the thing was moving.

"Fuck!" Neil screamed, rattling the handle.

He was now blinking back tears, weeping at the futility of his attempt to escape and at the certainty of imminent pain and an agonising death. His energy spent, Neil let go of the handle. It was over. Resigned, he let his body relax, his head sinking forward, onto the panel of the door. He closed his eyes and waited for the end.

When no attack came, Neil's sense of resignation turned to confusion. The thing must have seen him. Why hadn't it made its move? Was it playing with him; a cat with a cornered mouse? Or, could it be that Neil was now invisible to it again? He hardly dared believe it but, with the most minute and studied of movements, he slowly turned his head. The creature was still in the centre of the room. It had turned towards him, but its head was down, its body motionless again.

Slowly, very slowly, Neil turned. With his back against the door and no sign of the door-key nearby, he scanned the darkened room for an alternative way out. The window was to the right of the creature and Neil peered closely at it, trying to see if it was locked. Glancing back briefly to the creature Neil saw, to his horror, that its head was now lifted and the dreadful eyes were on him again. It had been toying with him, savouring his terror. Neil froze, but this time there was no doubt that the creature could see him. With a scratching, as of a thousand tiny claws, it moved towards him.

Almost before Neil had realised what was happening, an arm had extended. It held still for a moment, high above him, the bony fingers stone-like and cold, drawing Neil's gaze upward. Then, in a movement that was too rapid for him to follow, the arm slashed down and across his abdomen. Numb with shock, Neil looked down. In the darkness he could see very little, but he could feel something moving, in his guts. Puzzled, he reached down. The sodden bathrobe was ripped apart and Neil's normally taut skin felt oddly slack. His fingers traced the folds of skin and came to a very straight, deep gash. Pressing through the exposed bands of muscle, he could feel the bulging, warm slipperiness of his own intestines. Blood rose in his throat and he coughed involuntarily. With that, the guts spewed out of him, smothering his hands in a tide of hot blood.

Neil collapsed to his knees, nauseous and light headed. He was aware for a few moments of a burning pain, a searing rawness of his nerves. Then a wash of painless calm came over him. He felt detached from everything, cocooned. It was over. There was no more reason to fight.

Neil let go, and died.

Rita could not persuade Jon to accompany her to the hotel. She watched as he limped away, the sight of his dogged perseverance making her even more determined to get Neil and Phil to rejoin the search. She hurried towards the hotel, slogging through the clinging snow. But just a short distance from the building, she stopped. Something was wrong. The front doors were open, hanging at crazy angles from their hinges.

Rita froze.

Listening, she could hear nothing but the gentle creaking of the shattered doors. She looked from window to window. There was no sign of life. Where was everyone? And what could have caused this damage? Rita's mind filled with images of ferocious bears and madmen with chainsaws. Feeling the blood drain from her face, she shivered. She could feel herself beginning to panic.

Rita had to clear her mind so she could decide what to do. Her first instinct was to run away, very fast. But Phil and Neil were inside. And there was the old man, Spielman. They could all be hurt or injured. However, there was the additional concern that whatever had caused this damage could also still be inside the hotel.

Eventually, her decision was made for her. As she stood pondering her next move, the skies suddenly darkened and heavy snow began to fall again. With huge flakes falling thickly and forming a dense wall of shifting darkness all around her, the darkened lobby beyond the broken doors now seemed to Rita to be the less threatening option. Gripping her knife more tightly, she moved cautiously up the steps.

Ducking in through the battered doors, she could see very little and, after some moments of indecision, decided that she would have to get some light, even if it drew attention towards her. Grim-faced, with her back braced against the wall and the knife held ready, Rita clicked on the light. She was at first dazzled by the sudden brightness and then amazed to see that the room was exactly as it had been when she left the building earlier. She had been expecting a scene of chaotic devastation, but nothing was out of place, which Rita found even more disturbing. The splintered wood from the doors was scattered inside the doorway, which meant that the force had been directed inward, from outside, but what had happened after that? Had the attacker simply vanished or had there been no one here to offer any resistance? Perhaps Phil, Neil and Spielman had already escaped, or maybe they had hidden. But where were they now?

Rita dared not call out. If whoever, or whatever, had done this was still inside the building, the light would already have announced her arrival to them; they already had that advantage of her. And while she might hope that they had taken flight on seeing the light come on, she was more concerned that they might still be here. Maybe, even now, they were watching her, alert and ready to pounce. For the moment, Rita remained motionless and silent, not knowing who or what she might face and unsure what she should do next: stalemate, with an unseen and possibly non-existent foe.

She knew that she had three choices. She could turn and run away. This idea had obvious and immediate appeal but, as well as seeming the cowardly option, a glance beyond the wrecked doors showed that the snowfall had not lessened. Alternatively, she could stay exactly where she was and wait for help to arrive, but she had no idea how long it would take for anyone first to realise that help was needed and then to come to her aid. Finally, she could summon all her courage and search the hotel for Phil, Neil and Spielman, with the constant fear that she might find someone or something else, or that it would find her.

It was with sickening dread that Rita resolved to take the third course of action. She would start with the ground floor. Spielman had been in the lounge and Phil seemed to spend a good deal of time in the bar, so she would search these two rooms first. The lounge door was ajar, but again, everything inside was in order. Dying embers of the fire still glowed in the grate. There was no sign of the old man, but also no sign of any struggle. Rita crossed to the bar. She hadn't been in this room before but again, nothing looked disturbed or damaged and there was no one there. The dining room. The large room was reasonably tidy, considering what inexperienced hands had set and cleared the tables. Again, there was nothing untoward or out of place.

Back in the lobby, Rita had a decision to make: should

she go down to the basement, or search the upper floors? It was perhaps the fear of being trapped underground, with no escape route except up via the lobby, that led to Rita climbing the main stairs in order to search the bedrooms first. She went on up to the rooms in the attic and searched each one carefully, thankful that the beds were divans, with no space beneath them to hide an attacker. The closets and bathrooms were also empty and Rita began to allow herself to believe that the attacker had fled the building after demolishing the front doors. She could almost imagine that, at some time in the future, she would look back on her tremulous progress through the hotel and laugh at herself. Almost.

Rita descended to the first floor feeling curiously detached; she was terrified, but nevertheless, here she was, searching an unfamiliar building, alone, with three adults and five children missing and a madman on the loose. It was so unlike her to behave in this way.

She'd always taken pride in having what her mom called 'good old fashioned common sense', but usually that good sense served to keep her out of danger, rather than draw her into it. Where had the courage come from to tackle this? Rita had never had to confront a burglar in her home or a mugger on the street, yet now she had accepted that she might have to deal with a kidnapper and murderer. It was bizarre that this should be happening to someone as ordinary as herself, and equally bizarre that she should be rising to the challenge. Only two days ago, her life had seemed so routine, almost humdrum. Nothing had given a clue as the turn her life was about to take. Perhaps it was the unexpectedness of the situation and its remoteness from her normal life that allowed her to cope. Whatever the explanation, Rita felt herself to be changed; she could, and would, cope with this.

With renewed determination, she began to search the

first floor bedrooms.

Bill and Annie were slipping and sliding along the treacherous rocks at the river's edge, heading downstream. Hand in hand, each drew comfort and resolve from the other, but the cold was sapping their strength.

They had been quiet for perhaps an hour when Annie broke the silence.

"Bill, we've missed the shack haven't we?"

"Yeah, Honey, I think we have. If Spielman's map was anything like to scale we should have got to the clump of trees he talked about, near the falls, way back. But it's just too dark, we most likely went right by and didn't see them."

Annie began to sob quietly.

"Come on, Honey, I could be wrong: maybe we haven't got there yet. We can't know for sure, so we'll keep on looking, OK? We won't give up."

He squeezed her hand and she pulled him to her in a brief hug.

"Sure. We'll keep looking...And we'll find Lisa and Mikey."

Bill kissed her, but couldn't trust himself to speak.

They fell to silence again for some time until, with moonlight reappearing, they could see that the river was dividing into two streams around a rocky outcrop.

"Which should we follow?"

Bill shrugged.

"No idea. I don't remember Spielman showing the river dividing like this."

"Well," Annie sounded very matter of fact, "we're on this bank so I reckon we should follow this stream."

"Sounds good to me, Honey. How're you doing?"

"Hey, don't you worry about me. I'm OK, especially now I can see where I'm putting my feet."

Annie managed a brave smile. She and Bill walked on.

"What's that sound?" she asked.

"I'm not sure, Hon."

A few minutes passed.

"It's getting louder."

"I've got a bad feeling about it: I think it might be a waterfall, and it sounds like a big one. If we lose the moonlight I think we should stop in case we get too close to the edge."

As if on cue, clouds obscured the moon and the light was gone. Abruptly thrown into darkness, Bill and Annie waited, looking skyward to see if a gap in the clouds was imminent. After several minutes, they risked edging forward, very slowly. The noise was becoming a thunder. Fine spray soaked the air.

"I think we should stop."

Annie sounded anxious.

"OK, Honey, we'll wait for the light."

Stopping where they were, their patience was soon rewarded as a veil of thinner cloud skimmed in front of the moon. They gasped and instinctively drew closer together. They were teetering on a wide slab of rock that overhung the waterfall. Looking ahead there was only empty space and looking to the side, their gaze was drawn almost hypnotically down into the plummeting maelstrom.

"Jeez that was close!" Bill whispered through clenched teeth.

Annie was already beginning to move away from the precipice, gently pulling him to follow.

"Bill, come on. Don't look down."

She could see that Bill was becoming transfixed by the water falling away into the mist, far below them. Fringed in waterlogged moss, the rock on which they were standing was itself slippery; Annie and Bill were in great danger. Bill was physically exhausted and had been stressed beyond endurance. He was now being lulled into a stupor by the falling water. Annie had to get him to concentrate on moving away from the edge, but she didn't want to startle him. She had to raise her voice above the din, but she spoke slowly, with gentle insistence.

"Bill? Bill, come on. Come with me."

At this, Bill dragged his attention from the falling wall of water and stared, uncomprehending, into Annie's eyes.

"That's it, my love," she soothed, "Come with me."

Still in a dream, Bill allowed Annie to lead him back into the trees.

Rather than try to retrace their steps, clambering back along the riverbank, with the risk of slipping into the river so near the head of the waterfall, Annie decided to strike out into the trees. She had no idea in which direction she was leading Bill. She knew only that she had to keep going. She surprised herself with the force of her own single-mindedness. They would find Lisa and Mikey, or they would die in the attempt.

With the moonlight still strong and clear, Dave and Lou were making slow but steady progress through the trees.

Since Jeff's departure, Lou hadn't said a word. As she led the way, with Dave following in her wake, her mind was turning over and over. She knew that she had no basis by which to judge which direction they should take, but she walked on, willing this route to be the right one, praying that she would stumble on some clue, some evidence that Ethan was still alive. She had to believe that she would find him; she could not live if she were to give up on her son now. He was her future. She simply had to find him.

Left to his own musing, Dave suddenly had a worrying thought.

"Lou! Lou listen to me."

Lou slowed her pace, but continued walking.

"What?"

"The man who had Emma obviously thought the kids were still at the hotel, so he can't have been the one who kidnapped them."

"Yeah. So?"

"Well, they wouldn't have just wandered off on their own, would they? So someone else must have taken them. We should be careful; there's more than one of them out here."

They both began to look around, scanning the area.

"I wish we had the flashlight," said Dave.

"I wish we had the knife."

Annie was stumbling now. Neither she nor Bill felt they had any heat left in their bodies. The snow was making their movements tortuously slow and the bitter cold was unrelenting. Bill was moving now as if in his sleep; fighting to keep his eyes open, but beginning to lose the battle. His walk had been reduced to a painful shuffle.

They were barely moving and Annie knew that they were not going to survive the night. Her earlier dispassionate conclusion, that she did not want to live if her children were dead, was again in the forefront of her mind, so she was unafraid at the prospect of her own death. She was not alone now; she and Bill would die here together. They would be with Lisa and Mikey soon.

A sense of peaceful resignation calmed her.

"Bill," she whispered, "I think we should rest a while."

Bill turned his drowsy eyes to hers. He was awake enough to know what Annie meant. If they sat down to rest out here, they would sleep and never wake.

At first he thought to argue, but he had no strength left. He was close to collapse. He nodded to Annie and they sank to the ground. They kissed each other for the last time, then closed their eyes. They lay together, in an embrace, waiting for sleep and oblivion.

Travelling alone, Jeff had journeyed upstream without mishap and was now at the foot of the icy rockface.

He used the flashlight, low against the rock, to highlight handholds and ledges, but then had to switch off and stow the light, to free both hands for climbing. After all the night's exertions, his legs trembled as he supported all his weight on his toes. His cold fingers felt numb and awkward as he felt for the holds. He was making progress up the rockface, but it was unbearably slow. Then, just as he neared the top, he heard a crashing, snapping sound above the thunder of the water. Jeff hung on, listening. His fingers were beginning to cramp and the back of his calves were shaking quite violently. He gasped. Unable to support his weight for much longer, he would either have to scramble for the top now, or fall. Suddenly there was something above him: a head. Spielman!

The old man dropped to his knees and hauled Jeff up to the top. Then as Jeff looked up and saw Emma, Spielman clamped a hand over Jeff's mouth.

"Yuh musn't make a sound. It's in the hotel. Y'understand? We gotta get outa here, right now."

Overjoyed in spite of Spielman's warning, Jeff and Emma hugged each other. Jeff kissed his daughter's hair, and wept through his smiles. But, watching their reunion, Spielman was becoming increasingly agitated.

"We really gotta go."

He pulled at Jeff's sleeve and led them upstream, along the top of the rockface.

"I've got a flashlight," Jeff whispered above the noise of the water.

"No! No light. It'll see us. We gotta get away from

here or it'll hunt us down. Yuh gotta move faster, son."

"What is it?" Jeff whispered, "What's in the hotel?"

"It's what yuh daughter here calls the Shadowman. It's killed before an' it'll kill again. We gotta get away. Yuh can hide out in my trailer."

Jeff looked down at Emma's frightened face.

"It's true Dad," she whispered, "The Shadowman killed Bill and he forced me to go to the hotel. Me and Mr Spielman only just got out of the hotel in time. We heard the Shadowman hammering on the front door when we sneaked out the back."

Jeff put a reassuring arm around her shoulders and felt the shudders as Emma tried to stifle her tears.

They hurried on, following the course of the river, until a fast flowing tributary joined it to their left. Here, they turned and followed the new water course into the trees. Where the terrain became too steep, Spielman led them away from the stream, striking out into the forest. Soon, Emma and her father began to flag. The cold chilled them and the rough, snow-covered ground had them stumbling clumsily. Eventually, Spielman signalled to them to stop and rest. While they leant back against tree trunks he kept up a watch, looking back and forth and listening for any movement.

"OK we should go now. My trailer ain't far. I had t'bring yuh a long ways around in case it was lookin' for us."

Spielman led the exhausted pair to a small clearing, in the middle of which stood his trailer. It was essentially a large, battered metal box; not a thing of beauty, and it was surrounded by piles of cut logs, covered with faded tarpaulins and deep snow. Oil-coated components from a variety of partially dismantled vehicles also littered the site. Spielman led Jeff and Emma to the door and ushered them inside.

The accommodation was basic, but after a night spent in the snowy wilderness of the forest, it seemed quite wonderful. Spielman took a pile of clean blankets out of a cupboard and showed Emma where she could sleep. Soon she was comfortably tucked up in a cozy makeshift bed but, before she let herself sleep, she urgently pulled Jeff closer.

"Dad, when the Shadowman realises I've got away, he's going to go back to his cabin and Dave's there. He's going to kill Dave. You have to stop him."

"Shh. Don't worry. Dave's not in that shack any more. Lou and I went there looking for you and the other kids. We found Dave and cut him free. He told me that you'd been there. That's how I knew to come back upstream to the hotel to find you."

"Oh Dad, you're brilliant! I love you."

Jeff could hardly hold back the tears. Emma had said she loved him. She'd called him brilliant. His heart felt full to overflowing.

"God, I love you too, Emma," he squeezed her hand, "Now, you get some rest, OK?"

Emma nodded and snuggled down into the blankets. Jeff sat with her for a few minutes until her hand became limp in his and she began to snore gently. He tucked her hand under the blankets and went back outside to talk to the old man.

"Thank you so much for getting her out of the hotel."

Spielman nodded.

"I'm gonna make me some coffee. Yuh wanna cup?"

Jeff nodded, but watched with increasing concern as the old man made up a fire from some of the wood lying around the trailer.

"Won't the smoke give us away?"

"No, this wood's very dry; ain't much steam. Also, there ain't much wind so what smoke there is should go straight up," he explained, "The gas cylinder in the trailer don't switch on right. Need to get it fixed. Generally, I'd use the generator, but that's one noisy contraption, so I won't be usin' it till things is safe again."

Soon the fire was lit and an ancient black kettle set to heat up over the flames. Spielman shovelled grounds into the boiling water and poured them both a steaming cup of strong coffee. They drank in silence for a few minutes, allowing the warmth to spread through their bodies.

Spielman spoke first.

"It ain't human. That thing in the hotel. We were lucky to get away."

Jeff decided not to address what the creature might be. He had more pressing worries.

"I have to go back."

"No, son, yuh should stay here. It'll kill again."

"Rita, my wife, is going to go back there. She's somewhere in the forest now, searching for Emma and the other missing children, but she'll go back to the hotel sometime soon and she'll have no idea what's waiting there. I have to go back."

Spielman looked anxious. He knew what Jeff would ask of him and he dreaded it.

"Would you look after Emma till I get back?"

The old man looked very worried indeed.

"Yuh shouldn't go. That Shadowman'll kill yuh."

"I have to go back. Rita could walk into a trap. Please, I need you to look after Em."

Spielman angrily cast the grounds of his coffee into the fire. As the flames fizzed and spat, the old man paced back and forth.

"Aw heck! Alright. But yuh get back here as soon as yuh can."

"That's a promise."

Spielman noticed the knife in Jeff's belt.

"I jus' hope yuh know how t'use that."

Jeff tried to look confident, but he couldn't judge from Spielman's expression whether he had succeeded. The old man looked very edgy and Jeff certainly felt very frightened himself.

"Take that path there. It'll take yuh to the track that yuh drove in on when yuh came t' the hotel. Turn left and follow the track, but keep off it. Stay in the trees where yuh got some cover and be careful, yuh hear?"

Jeff's heart was thumping. He was quite terrified, but he managed to control his voice.

"Thanks," he muttered, "I'll do that."

"Good luck, son."

"Thanks for everything. Take good care of Emma."

Spielman nodded and Jeff set off to return to the hotel, alone.

Jon was forcing his way through the trees.

He had wandered this forest in every season, so a covering of snow presented no problem; it could not completely disguise the familiar landmarks. He was travelling, as quickly as possible, back to his cave to get supplies. It was a desperately long journey when the fate of several children hung in the balance, but Jon knew that he would have need of every arrow and knife he owned if he were to defeat the monster he had seen in the shack all those years ago. Even with all his resources, Jon was not wholly convinced that the thing could be killed. But he knew he had to try.

He was nearing the stream that led to his cave when he noticed a disturbance of the fallen snow; something large had crossed his intended path, recently. With sudden dread, Jon faced the possibility that the monster had somehow overtaken him and cut him off from the sanctuary of his cave. Very well; if their confrontation was to be sooner than he had hoped, Jon's best chance lay in catching the creature off guard. With luck, it might not realise that Jon was so close. Jon would follow its tracks, stalk it and attack it, hopefully before it was even aware of him.

Trusting to this plan, and to good fortune, Jon turned to follow the tracks. Fully alert, moving as quietly as possible, he crept cautiously forward, but found the tracks ending abruptly at a mound in the snow. Jon carefully approached it and saw that it was moving very slowly; almost imperceptibly rising and falling.

It was a body, no, two bodies. Jon brushed the light dusting of snow from them; a man and a woman. They were barely alive. The man, was very cold and near death; Jon would have to act swiftly to save him. With a grunt he lifted Bill up onto his back and set off, with as much speed as possible, to the cave.

He scrambled up the rocks and into the hidden entrance, then stopped in his tracks. There, lying together under some of Jon's animal furs were three small children. They were fast asleep, but looked in good health. Recovering from the shock, Jon remembered the man he was carrying. He lowered Bill gently onto the floor and covered him with animal skins. Working quickly, he began to rub Bill's arms and legs and, after much frantic effort, was rewarded by a hint of colour returning to Bill's skin.

Jon tucked the furs around Bill, then hurried off to recover the woman.

Left without even the small amount of heat from Bill's body to warm her, Annie was fading fast. When Jon lifted her, he could feel the lifeless chill in her body. Ignoring his own safety he ran for the cave, with reckless speed. He slid her under the furs, next to Bill and rubbed furiously at her limbs to warm her. For a long time she remained deathly pale, her breathing almost undetectable, but Jon persisted and slowly she began to come back from the edge of lifelessness.

Wearied by the effort, Jon sat back. Wrapping himself in a fur, he took a few moments to survey his home. His possessions were all neatly stowed in their usual places but this familiar tidiness and order seemed completely at odds with the fact that, to his left, two adults were now sleeping under his warmest furs, while three children were snuffling contentedly as they slept under furs to his right.

How had these young ones found this place, one small cave in such a vast forest? Jon mulled over this problem as he made up a small fire. It was inconceivable that the children could have found this place without help. Who had brought them here?

Keeping watch, warming himself by the fire, it suddenly occurred to Jon that the children could have been hidden here, in his cave, by the creature that he had been arming himself to kill. It was possible that the evil he had feared all these years had finally discovered his sanctuary. If this was so, there would be no place of safety and Jon would have to go far away and find himself a new home, if were ever to feel safe again. He had to find out if his dread was justified. The children could tell him who had brought them here, but Jon couldn't face their shock on seeing him. He felt foolish; he was in his own cave, his home, and yet he was afraid to wake one of his uninvited guests for fear of their reaction. He decided that he would wake the woman. She could question the children while he hid his face.

He shook Annie's shoulder and prepared to quickly cover her mouth if she began to make too much noise. Annie opened her eyes.

"Holy shit!"

Her hand went to her mouth.

Jon put a finger to his lips, but Annie ignored it.

"Get away from me!"

Her voice was very loud, reverberating in the cave. Jon clamped his hand over her mouth.

"I not hurt you. Please, not noise."

Annie's eyes were wide and staring at him. She was in shock and though Jon hated to be examined so closely, he gave her a few seconds before trying again.

"I not hurt you. Please you not noise."

He judged it was now safe to remove his hand. Annie continued to stare at him, as he eased back to squat by the fire.

"Who are you?"

"Jon."

"Where's my husband?"

She turned and saw Bill lying next to her.

"Bill. Bill, are you OK?"

Bill stirred, but didn't wake.

"He very near dead. Now OK."

"How did we get here?"

"I carry."

Annie absorbed this and felt contrite.

"Thank you, Jon."

She looked around her.

"Where are we?"

"I live here."

"In a cave?"

Annie had spoken hastily and was immediately concerned that Jon might have taken offence at her tone, but he seemed not to have noticed.

"Yes."

"Really?" she tried to hide her disbelief, "It's...It's lovely."

Annie found her eyes drawn back to the scar disfiguring Jon's face. She very much wanted to ask him about it, but she doubted his vocabulary could frame a useful answer. She turned her attention back to Bill.

"He will be OK, yes?"

"He rest. Be OK."

Annie nodded and leaned over to give her sleeping husband a gentle kiss. She felt the warmth of his face and remembered with a shudder their last kiss, as they had lain down to die. How chill his lips had been then. Jon was right, Bill must have been very close to death. If this strange man hadn't brought them here, they would probably both be dead by now.

She felt oddly ambivalent about still being alive; if they didn't find the children, then she might regret Jon's kindness. As soon as Bill had recovered they would have to go back out to the search.

Jon got to his feet.

"You come please."

Puzzled and a little disconcerted, Annie stood up, but held back. Jon motioned her to follow him and led her to the other side of the cave.

"My God!" Annie shrieked, "Lisa! Mikey! Wake up! Mommy's here."

Annie was simultaneously laughing and crying, overjoyed at seeing her children alive and well. Lisa woke first, rubbing her eyes and yawning.

"Hi Mom."

They hugged as Mikey began to stir.

"Mommy, Mommy, Mommy!" he yelled, throwing himself into her arms.

Disturbed by all the commotion, Ethan began to moan. Annie shepherded the others away so that the small boy could sleep on. As they neared Jon, he stepped away into the shadows and the children, noticing him for the first time, leaned back against their mother.

Annie was about to reassure them and tell them not to

be frightened, that Jon was a good man who had saved their lives, but before the words had formed, a thought suddenly came to her: why were her children here? Was Jon the kidnapper? Had he taken them from the hotel? Straightening, she protectively pushed Lisa and Mikey behind her.

"Jon, tell me, how did these children get here?"

Jon shook his head and Annie narrowed her eyes. Had he not understood her, or was he avoiding her question? She would have her answer. She wasn't afraid of this man. If he had done anything to harm her children, he would suffer for it. Angry now, she spoke the words with cold clarity.

"I asked you a question, Jon. Did you bring these children here?"

"No, Mom," Lisa interjected before Jon could reply, "We came here with Laura."

Lisa looked around.

"Where is she Mom? Where's Laura?"

"I don't know, Sweetie. I haven't seen her."

Annie turned to Jon, her tone now less hostile.

"Jon, where is Laura?"

"I not know Laura."

"Laura...she's a girl."

Jon pointed at Lisa.

"Laura?"

"No, I'm Lisa."

"No, Jon," said Annie, "Not Lisa: another girl."

"Not know. Lisa say Laura find here?"

He was beginning to understand. A girl, called Laura, had brought the three children to his cave. But why? Who was she?

"I not know Laura."

"Her parents run a hotel, here in the forest."

"Hotel? Children missing, hotel."

395

"Yes," Annie said, drawing her children close, "These children. These are the missing children."

Jon was baffled. He could not understand how the girl had led three small children many miles from the hotel, through freezing temperatures and deep snow, to his small cave, in safety. How was it possible?

"We need to get back to the hotel."

"No," Jon was alarmed, "Not go in forest. Evil in forest."

"What d'you mean? We have to tell the others that the children are safe."

"What about Laura, Mom?"

"Yes, yes, we have to find Laura, and Emma too."

"You stay in here...cave. I find Laura and Emma too."

Lisa giggled. Annie nudged her to be quiet.

"You don't understand, Jon. There are other people, our friends, looking for these children. We must tell them that these three are safe."

"Please not. Not go in forest. Big evil in forest. I kill."

Annie gasped.

"No," Jon said quickly, "I kill evil."

With a moan, Bill stirred.

"Annie, Annie? Where are you?"

"Daddy!"

Lisa and Mikey rushed to their father, taking him completely by surprise. He could hardly believe the evidence of his eyes.

"Lisa? Mikey? My God, it's really you!"

With tears pouring down his cheeks, Bill hugged his children to him. Annie joined them and tenderly stroked her children's hair as Bill continued to hug them so tight that they could barely breathe. Annie told him that Laura had brought the children to the cave.

"Why? Why did she take you?"

"It was a game," said Lisa.

"Darling?" said Annie, "Did Laura make you leave the hotel?"

"No, she didn't make us. We were just playing and she brought us here. It's an adventure, like back when there were pirates."

Annie frowned.

"Darling, tell Mommy, did you meet anyone who was mean to you? Were there any pirates?"

Lisa gave her mother a disparaging look.

"I'm eight years old, Mom. It was just a game; there aren't really any pirates."

"Good, good. Mommy's glad to hear that."

Bill looked up.

"Honey, how did we get here?"

"This guy, over here," she motioned to Jon, "saved both of us; carried us here, when we were all but frozen to death."

Bill looked up, but Jon stayed back in the shadows. Annie beckoned to him again.

"Jon, why don't you come say hello?"

"Jon?" said Bill, "Is that your name, sir? I'm Bill and I want to thank you, from the bottom of my heart, for saving my lovely wife and children, and me too."

With some difficulty, Bill stood up.

"Please, Jon. I'd like to shake your hand."

Jon reluctantly edged forward, into the firelight. Bill saw the scar, but his own smile never faltered. He walked forward and took Jon's hand.

"Thank you, Jon. I owe you, big time."

Jon was astounded. No one had ever reacted in this way. Even Suzie had been frightened at first sight, but this man didn't flinch. He showed Jon only sincere gratitude and respect. Jon was dumbfounded.

"Jon, when I was waking just now, you were saying

something about evil in the forest."

Jon picked out a few of the words, but wasn't sure that a question was being asked of him. He frowned and shook his head.

"Keep it simple, Honey, I don't think Jon speaks english."

Bill looked directly into Jon's eyes.

"I speak too fast?"

Jon nodded.

"I am sorry, Jon. Is there evil in the forest?"

"Yes, evil, yes. You stay here. Not go forest. I go find Laura and Emmatoo."

"Laura and Emma."

"Emma," Jon repeated.

"But will evil harm you?"

Jon looked blank, so Bill tried again.

"Evil kill Jon?"

"No. Jon kill evil. Find Laura and...Emma"

Bill turned to Annie.

"He's going to go out there and look for the girls and I've seen what's out there. I've seen the thing that's got Emma. I can't let him face that alone. Will you stay here and watch over the kids -"

"No, Bill!"

Annie could see where the conversation was going and she didn't like it.

"Don't say another word. We both nearly died out there. The kids are safe now and I won't let you risk yourself going out there again. Please Bill."

"Annie, he's going out to look for Emma and Laura. I can't let him go alone. I have to go."

"OK then, why don't you stay here with the kids and I'll go and play the hero out in the forest."

"The kids need their mother."

"Yeah? Well they need their father too and you'll be

no use to us dead."

"I know that, Honey. I won't do anything stupid."

"Going back out there is stupid!"

"Annie, I can't let him go against that thing alone. I couldn't live with myself. It's...it's not like anything you've ever seen. And we have to try to get Emma back, and find Laura."

"Huh! That stupid girl shouldn't have taken the kids out of the hotel in the first place. I don't want you dying to save her."

"Annie, don't talk like that. Rita said Laura's simple. You can't blame the poor kid."

"Yeah? Well I do. This is all her fault"

Annie didn't really mean any of this, but she was very frightened for Bill. The recent memory of his ice cold lips and skin was painfully vivid; she had come too close to losing him already. But, no matter how much she might wish otherwise, Annie knew that Bill would go. He simply could not stand by and ignore someone in need of help. He was always selfless. It was one of his most wonderful and endearing characteristics; one of the reasons she loved him.

"Annie, please try to understand."

Annie understood. She knew that Bill's selflessness could be the cause of her losing him. She knew it, but there was nothing she could do to prevent it.

"Go then. See if I care."

Bill hugged her.

"Thanks Annie, and I promise, I'll be careful."

"You're a stubborn fool, Bill Clearwater. And you'd better take care of yourself, or so help me..."

Bill squeezed her hand.

"Jon," he said, "I come with you. Find Emma and Laura."

Jon looked Bill up and down. A short time ago, this

man had been near death and now he wanted to go back out into the forest. Perhaps he was crazy. He didn't look crazy, but he didn't look like much of a fighter either. Also, he had shown Jon immediate respect and acceptance. No one had ever done that; Jon didn't want to see him hurt.

"No."

"Jon?"

"No."

"Jon, you need help."

"No. You stay here in cave. Not go in forest. I go find Laura and Emma."

"I insist. I go find Laura and Emma with Jon."

Jon shook his head. He was sure that taking this man with him would be a mistake. At the very least Bill would slow him down and, should the worst happen, Bill would be of little use against the evil. But time was pressing and it seemed that he was not going to be able to convince Bill to stay.

He nodded.

"You eat."

Jon took some dried meats and fruits from his food store for Annie, Bill and the children to share. While they were eating, he took containers down to the stream and filled them with water. Returning, he showed Annie where he stored kindling and wood for the fire.

It was time to leave. Annie was trying to be brave for the sakes of Lisa and Mikey, but a tear was trembling on her eyelashes as she and Bill made their farewell.

31

Jon and Bill made steady progress northwards. They followed the stream up a gentle slope and were about to begin a steeper climb to higher ground when Jon raised his hand. Both men stopped and Bill waited as Jon listened, turning his head from side to side, trying to pinpoint the position of something. For his part, Bill could see and hear nothing out of the ordinary.

"What is it?" he whispered.

Jon pointed to the lower ground off to their right. Bill scanned the trees, but still could see nothing. Jon signalled for him to crouch down and, as he did so, Bill heard it: a movement, snapping twigs and squeaking footsteps in the snow, somewhere below them. To Bill it sounded like a large animal, a bear perhaps, but Jon knew it for what it was: two people, following a route south that would take them roughly parallel to the path Jon and Bill had just taken. Jon raised his head and peered down the hill. The sloping ground was rocky, with little soil, the trees consequently sparce. Jon could see quite a distance through the well-spaced tree trunks.

"Bill. You them?"

Bill raised his head and looked to where Jon was pointing. There between the trunks, he could see two figures: one tall and one shorter, struggling through the snow.

"I think I know the tall one, maybe. But I can't be sure from here. Too far away."

Jon nodded and took Bill's arm, pulling him to his feet. "Come."

Jon began to move across the icy rock face with practised ease and at great speed. He had never encountered anyone this close to his cave; it was unsettling. He wanted Bill to confirm that these strangers were no threat to his unexpected guests sheltering back in the cave, and he wanted that confirmation quickly, before these two strayed any closer to his refuge. Bill tried to keep up with Jon, but it was hopeless. On a narrow ledge of smooth ice, he lost his footing and began to hurtle down the slope. He tried to run, but the slope was too steep and he raced downhill in a series of frantic leaps, tumbles and rolls. At the foot of the hill he collapsed onto the snow in front of Dave and Lou, gulping huge lungfuls of air and quite unable to speak.

At first, Dave and Lou were too shocked to react. They recognised Bill immediately, in spite of the furs that Jon had given him to wear over his own gear but, for several seconds, they simply stood staring at him. Then, with a crash, Jon appeared above them. He was scrambling down the rockface, at a hectic pace, prepared, if necessary, to fight to protect Bill. With a final leap, he landed at the bottom of the slope and crouched, protectively, next to Bill.

Dave started forward, hands outstretched in a pacifying gesture.

"Wait up, man! Take it easy. No need for anyone to get hurt here. Let's talk, OK?"

Jon looked up at this tall man. He looked even more out of place here in the forest than did Bill. His jacket was the colour of leaves in the fall, but alarmingly bright;

it pained Jon's eyes to look at it. He grimaced.

Dave, taking this to be a worrying sign, backed away a few steps.

"It's OK man, we don't want any trouble. I'm sure we can talk this through like reasonable people. You don't want to hurt this guy. OK? So let's talk. Let's just all take a breath, calm down and talk, OK?"

Jon picked up some of the words. Why was this man so keen to talk? Did any of these people ever stop talking? At Jon's side, Bill was still breathless, winded from his headlong dash down the hillside. Jon put a reassuring hand on his shoulder.

Dave wasn't sure if Jon's gesture was intended to be threatening to Bill, but he took Jon's baffled silence for progress of a sort.

"If we're on your land," he continued, "if we're like, trespassing, we can go. We'll just take our friend here and go."

Lou had had enough. She pushed past Dave.

"Cut the crap!" she shouted, "Get the hell away from him, right now, you freak, or..."

Lou didn't spell out the consequences, but she had no need to; as soon as Jon saw her pale face and blond hair, he thought of Suzie. Memories of Suzie's pitiful death and his guilt at his failure to save her, spilled back into his mind, momentarily drowning out the reality around him. Forgetting any threat to himself or to Bill, he looked into Lou's wild eyes, seeking some recognition, but he found only hostility. Jon was nonplussed.

Bill, meanwhile, had recovered. Shaking his head and still breathing heavily, he raised his hand.

"Dave, Lou, it's OK. This is Jon. He saved Annie and me...And three of the kids are safe in his cave, back there."

"What?" Lou gasped, "Ethan! Is Ethan OK?"

"Yes, Lou, he's safe."

Lou stood for a few seconds, speechless and immobile, unable to assimilate what Bill had just said. Then, overwhelmed by the news, she burst into a noisy explosion of emotion, laughing hysterically while tears poured down her cheeks. Her son was alive! The instantaneous release of anxiety made her feel lightheaded. Her legs became weak and began to shake. Reacting quickly, Dave caught her and held her as she fell, sobbing onto his chest.

"It's OK girlfriend, you cry all you like. Just let it out. Let it all out."

But the emotion was soon spent and the weeping abruptly subsided. Lou mumbled a brief apology to Dave, pulled herself away from him and briskly dried her eyes. Now that she had regained her self control, she was determined to go to this weird guy's cave immediately but, looking around, she was irritated to see that no one else seemed to share her sense of urgency. Bill and Jon seemed to be chatting.

"You, she go to cave."

"No, Jon, we should all stay together."

She interrupted their conversation.

"What are you talking about?"

"Jon thinks I should lead you back to his cave, but I think we should stick together."

"OK, so let's all get back there. Come on, let's go."

"No, he's saying he'll go on alone."

"So?"

"Lou, the thing that took the kids is still out there somewhere. It's got Emma and Dave thinks it's making for the hotel. Jon's going to try to stop it before it does any more harm."

"So?"

"We can't let him face that alone."

"Will you please get to the point."

"Ethan will be safe back in the cave; Annie's with them and there's food, drink and shelter."

"I get it, you want to go after the madman who took the kids. That's great; you go do whatever you gotta do. Me? I don't care about him. I don't care about anything. I have to go get Ethan, and that's it. Just tell me how to get to the cave and I'm gone. Then you can all go hunt this guy. I don't care what any of you do. I just have to get to my baby."

Bill tried once more to persuade her.

"Lou, if you knew what was out there, believe me you'd want us to stick together. Jon can't face that thing alone."

Dave, who had been quiet for a few moments, now spoke.

"Bill, you know the way to the cave, right?"

"Yeah, I guess. You follow the stream until-"

"OK man, that's cool. How about you take Lou back to the kids and I go to the hotel with Jon?"

"You don't know what we're up against, Dave. I've seen it."

"It?"

"Yeah: it's the weirdest looking...Dark eyes, dead-looking and teeth; shit, they're like, I dunno, like shark teeth, but thinner, really sharp."

"He's filed his teeth?"

"No, Dave. You don't understand. I don't know what it is," Bill paused, "but I don't think it's human."

"What? Get outa here!"

Dave's grin faded. It was obvious that Bill wasn't sharing the joke.

"Are you for real? Not human, are you kidding me? OK, if it's not human, what the hell is it?"

"I have absolutely no idea. It's tall, very tall, and thin

and it's got nails, or claws; they're like blades."

"A bear?"

"No Dave. It's nothing like a bear."

Bill shivered, feeling the hairs on his arms rise. The memory and the fear were both very real, but he steadied his breathing and forced himself to remember the creature that had lashed out at him and taken Emma away.

"It looks like it could be human, or was human, but it's deformed; kinda stretched and dried out. But when you see it, there's something about it makes you think of, I dunno, some huge insect."

"Shit!"

Lou had heard enough. If something like that was on the loose, she had to have Ethan close. She had to be with him. She would protect him, against anything and to the death.

"I have to get to Ethan. I don't need a man to protect me. Just give me the directions and I'm gone. The rest of you can do what the hell you want but, with or without you, I'm going now."

"I'm not saying you need a man to protect you, Lou, and I can't give you directions," said Bill, "I can't explain the route; I'd just know it as I go along."

Jon was also becoming agitated at the delay.

"Bill. She, you go to cave."

Bill was torn.

Taking a deep breath, Dave broke the deadlock.

"Bill, it's OK. You go with Lou. Get her to the cave. She needs to be with her son and you should be with Lisa and Mikey. I'll go with Jon."

Again, Dave was amazed to hear himself. What was he thinking? The creature Bill had described sounded like some undiscovered species of carnivore or some nightmarish H.R.Giger creation. What the hell was he doing, volunteering to go after it? His only skill was the ability to run away, very fast, so he'd be useless in a fight. And, despite all his expensively acquired gadgets and equipment, he was completely ill-prepared for survival out here in the wilderness. His own natural environment assumed the basics of heat, comfort and designer label accessories; he simply didn't belong out here. Yet despite being cold, tired, hungry and frightened, here he was volunteering himself again. He'd heard of snow blindness, maybe he had snow madness!

Bill remained undecided, but Jon could waste no more time.

"Come."

He signalled for Dave to follow and led him away into the trees.

"Take care of yourselves," Bill called out after them, "and keep a lookout for Laura."

Dave waved an acknowledgment and then disappeared into the forest.

Rita had been thorough and systematic. She had searched from room to room, but found no sign of an intruder or of anything that would explain the damage to the front doors.

Now only one bedroom remained to be searched. She reached for the door handle but, before she could open it, there was a noise downstairs. Rita stood absolutely still, the handle half-turned in her hand. There it was again. Someone or something was moving about in the rooms below her. Holding her breath, Rita turned the handle through the final half turn and opened the door just wide enough to allow her to sidle into the room. Not daring to switch on the light, she stood, waiting in the darkness, as the noises came closer.

The intruder was on the stairs.

Now he was just outside, in the corridor and Rita's

heart was beating so loud that it seemed to fill the room. Could he hear it from out there? She knew that he could not, yet she automatically began to back away from the door. Suddenly she was falling; her feet slipping from beneath her. As she fell, the door slammed open and the light snapped on.

Jeff was standing in the doorway, knife in hand. He looked down at her, but not with relief or recognition. His face was drained of colour and he looked horrified.

Rita recovered quickly.

"Jeff," she said, trying to reassure him, "It's OK, Honey, it's me."

Jeff still looked appalled. He bent forward and spoke hurriedly.

"Ree, give me your hand. Just keep looking at me!"

Naturally, as soon as he said this, Rita immediately looked away from him. All around her she saw crazy patterns, splatters of deep red, crisscrossing the walls and ceiling. What the hell had happened here? Rita's hands, flung out in an attempt to break her fall, now lay at her side in some cool, tacky liquid. She raised her right hand to her face. It was slowly dripping crimson; the floor around her was covered in a slick of blood. That explained why she had fallen. And she had fallen onto something soft.

She turned her head, and her own cheek touched the cold of Neil's torn, lifeless face, his bulging eyes lolling towards her own. With an incoherent shriek, Rita leapt up. Panicking, flailing about for support, sliding on the pool of blood, she grabbed for Jeff's hand. He pulled her to him and steadied her as she looked back. She had been lying on Neil's bloodied body. He had been ripped apart and the room around him wrecked; the closet doors wrenched apart, the bed upturned and slashed.

"Holy shit!" Rita gasped, "What could have done

408

this?"

Jeff could do no more than stare about him in silence. Rita squeezed his hand.

"Let's get out of here."

They backed out of the room, closed the door and leant against the wall, both blankly staring at nothing. Gradually, Rita became aware of the cold. Her back felt particularly chill. She reached down to rub her legs and touched the saturated cloth; she was completely covered in Neil's blood, slimy with the spilled contents of his guts. She fell forward onto her knees and retched.

She could not vomit because her stomach was empty, but she remained hunched on the floor of the corridor, staring blankly ahead, at the golden grain of the polished floor boards. Her mind was furiously turning and she now saw her meeting with Jon in an very different light. He had known Neil's name and said that Neil hit him, but maybe that gash to Jon's head had been Neil's dying attempt to save himself. Had she been all that time in the presence of a killer? Jon was certainly powerfully built and was probably physically capable of having caused the destruction in the room and of tearing Neil to pieces. However, against these propositions was the look that Jon had given her, she couldn't forget it, surely it was too intelligent and humane to be that of a ruthless killer? Doubt also rested in Rita's nagging belief that whatever had caused Neil's death would have been drenched in blood himself and Jon had not been.

Looking down at Rita, Jeff could do no more than gently touch her head, as waves of nausea washed over him too. Having seen the mayhem in the bedroom, he was plagued with thoughts of what Em must have seen and endured while she was being held captive. But what completely overwhelmed him was the knowledge that what had happened to Neil could so easily have happened to his little girl.

Rita was the first to recover.

"Are you OK?"

"I guess. You?"

"Yeah," she sighed, "Jeez, poor Neil. Even he didn't deserve that. No one deserves that. I just hope it was quick."

Jeff nodded.

"We've gotta get out of here, Ree," he whispered.

"You think it's still in here, in the hotel?"

"Don't know. I've only been into the lobby and the lounge. They look OK, but the front doors are smashed to hell."

"Yeah. They were like that when I got here. I searched the attic and all of this floor. This room is the only one where anything's out of place."

"Out of place? I call that more than being 'out of place'."

"You know what I mean: in all the other rooms everything looks normal."

"So, whoever or whatever did this came straight to this room? Why? What's so special about this room?" he shrugged, "It was in here and Neil disturbed it when he came in to search the room. It killed Neil and then what, disappeared?"

Rita shook her head.

"I don't know...but I met a man out in the forest."

"What! When?"

"Just before I came back in here. He looked kinda wild, like a mountain man, y'know, wearing animal skins."

"Did he hurt you?"

"No. He was hurt himself. He was bleeding from a nasty cut on the back of his head. Said Neil did it."

"So you think he came back in here and killed Neil in revenge?"

Rita thought for a moment.

"No. When I left to come back here, he went off in the opposite direction, south I think. I came straight here and the doors were already smashed. And whatever it was caused the chaos in there, must have been real loud, but I didn't hear a thing while I was searching the rooms, not till I heard you downstairs."

"So he'd attacked Neil before you met him and Neil hit him in self-defence."

"I thought of that, but he'd been hit on the back of the head. If he was attacking Neil he wouldn't have been looking the other way, would he? And look at me," she turned to show him her blood-soaked clothes, "Whoever did this to Neil would have been drenched in his blood and Jon only had blood around his head wound."

"Jon?"

"Yeah, that's his name?"

"You spoke to him? Jeez, how close were you? Are you OK?"

"Yeah Honey, I'm fine. And y'know, the more I think about it, the more I'm sure Jon couldn't have done this."

Jeff looked baffled.

"If you're right about this guy, and he didn't kill Neil, then who did? And where's the killer now?"

"I don't know, but the only place I haven't checked out is the basement. We should do that."

"Are you insane? We should get the hell out of here. Where's Phil?"

"I don't know."

"What? Wasn't he with you and Neil?"

"No. The path divided and we had to split up. Then Neil hurt his foot and he and Phil must have come back here."

"They left you out there alone?"

Rita shrugged.

411

"Sonofabitch!"

"Let it go. It happened, it's over and it looks like they paid a high price. They both might still be alive if they'd stayed out there with me."

"You think Phil's dead too? Where's his body?"

"Like I said, I haven't checked out the basement. He could be down there. Jeff, we've got to search it."

"No way! We're getting out of here, right now."

"Jeff, think about it; the others will be coming back here, to the hotel, and we have no clue where they are now, so we can't intercept them and stop them. We have to make sure the hotel's safe. If the killer's here and we don't stop him now, he could pick everyone off, one by one, when they come back. We have to do this."

"Ree, you saw what it did to Neil, right?"

"Yeah, that's why we have to stop him. Besides, Neil was maybe taken by surprise and plus there are two of us...Jeff, we have to do this."

"Shit!"

"Jeff?"

"Shit! Alright we do this," he sighed, "But first, in case I don't make it-"

"We'll make it."

"Ree, this is important. I have to tell you."

"What Honey?"

"Bill's dead."

"What? No!"

"Yeah. Em said-"

"Em?"

"Yeah, she's OK. She's with Spielman in his trailer. I came on ahead to check out the hotel before I brought her here."

"She's safe? Oh Honey, that's wonderful."

"Yeah. But she said she was with this guy in the forest when Bill found her."

"Did she say what the guy looked like?"

"I dunno' I think she said he was tall, thin and weird-looking. Does that sound like your mountain man?"

Rita shook her head.

"Anyhow, Em said Bill tried to free her and he was killed. And she saw it all, poor kid."

"You think it's the same guy as did this?"

"Seems likely. We're talking a serial killer here."

"Poor Bill," Rita whispered, "And poor Annie."

She felt another wave of nausea, but quelled it. She had to think.

"Jeff, we have to check out the basement. If it's clear, it would be the easiest part of the building to secure. We could use the reception desk as a barricade and we'd only have one door to guard."

"That's because there's no other way out."

"Sure. But the basement is concrete, even the ceiling, so no one could break through or burn us out and the windows are tiny; much too small for a man to get through. And any shelter has to be better than being out, unprotected, in the snow and the dark, am I right?"

"What about Spielman's trailer? We could go there."

"No trailer's going to be as strong or easy to defend. The basement would be like a bomb shelter. We could all stay there until someone sends help."

"That's assuming help comes."

"Yeah, but that would be true wherever we were."

Much as he wished that he could persuade Rita to abandon the hotel, Jeff couldn't fault her reasoning so he had to agree to search the basement, albeit reluctantly.

"OK. Let's get this over with; after what you've just said, I don't want to leave Em out in that trailer any longer than I have to."

Hand in hand, they crept down the stairs. The lobby was as eerily undisturbed as before and they both struggled to reconcile the normality here with the horror they had just witnessed upstairs. They eased behind the reception desk as quietly as possible. First they peered into the office, then Jeff stood guard at the door while Rita made a more thorough search of the room.

"It's OK it's clear," she whispered, "Here's hoping the rest of the basement is too."

"Amen to that."

They edged down into the basement and stood, back to back, at the foot of the stairs. It was very dark in the kitchen. They would have to turn on the light. With Rita nodding in agreement, Jeff reached out and clicked the light on.

They blinked in the sudden brightness. The large room was empty and its pristine brushed metal surfaces gleamed. There was no indication of anything having been disturbed. Jeff and Rita checked the oven, the cupboards, the store rooms and the walk-in larder in quick succession. There remained only the utility room to be searched. Phil's body had to be in there.

Both Rita and Jeff felt the need to dry their palms and tighten their grips on their knives before Jeff, his hand on the door handle, mouthed a silent three, two, one. They burst through the door, and were confronted with an entirely ordinary room. Boxes of soap powder, fabric softener and general cleaners were ordered neatly on the shelves, while the washing baskets containing carefully folded clothes had been placed tidily on top of the large washing machines.

Where was Phil?

Rita nodded towards the machines. Jeff frowned, then shrugged agreement. With Rita standing at his side, knife at the ready, he opened each door with a flourish. There was nothing inside.

Jeff was baffled.

"If Phil's not down here, where the hell is he?"

"Maybe he's not dead after all. Maybe he escaped, or maybe he went back out to look for me."

"I doubt that. It's not Phil's style. It's far more likely that he just ran away when he heard Neil screaming."

"Who could blame him?"

"I could. He was supposed to be staying with you."

"Don't worry. I'm OK now; I've got you."

"And I've got you, Babe."

Rita managed a smile and squeezed Jeff's hand, but her mind was busily considering their options.

"It looks like whatever attacked Neil has gone," she said, in a quietly matter of fact tone, "So now, how are we going to make this basement safe and keep it that way while we go get Emma and Spielman?"

"You still think this is the safest place to be?"

"I'm sure of it. There's no other stone or concrete-built building for miles and, like I said before, the others must be heading back here as we speak."

"OK, I agree; no need to go through all that again," Jeff paused, "So we'll do like you suggested and barricade the door into the lobby. Then you stay here and I'll go get Em."

"No way. You're not going out there alone. We'll both go."

"We can't. What if he comes back while we're out? We'll have to search the whole place all over again."

"Just the basement."

"Yeah, but -"

"It's unlikely either of us could defend this place alone, so there's no point in one of us staying behind. We'll both go, but first we'll put something behind the reception desk, to block the door, and if that's been moved when we get back, then we'll know someone's been down into the basement. OK?"

415

"OK, OK. Let's get moving."

They wedged the reception desk chair in front of the door so that it would not move accidentally, but only if someone applied a good deal of force to push it clear. Then, with a final look around the deserted lobby, they pulled their collars up and clambered out through the broken front doors.

The skies were clear again and, with the benefit of both the flashlight and bright moonlight, Jeff found his way back to Spielman's trailer with relative ease. The old man watched their approach. He was alert, standing next to a small fire, gun in hand. As they came closer, his face fell.

"Jeepers lady, what happened?"

"Someone killed Neil, back at the hotel. I found his body. There was a blood everywhere and I fell in it."

"There's water heating here on the fire. Yuh can wash some of that off, if you've a mind to."

"Thanks, but there's no time. We've got to get back to the hotel."

The old man looked askance.

"Yuh got a killer there and yuh wanna go back?"

"It's OK: we searched the whole building. He's gone now and the basement is strong enough for us to defend if he comes back."

Jeff was content to leave Rita to convince the old man. His prime concern was his daughter.

"How's Emma?"

"She's asleep. Poor little lady was all tuckered out."

As Jeff climbed into the trailer to check on his sleeping daughter, Spielman turned his attention back to Rita. He looked carefully into her face.

"Tell me, did yuh see it?"

"What?"

"The thing that's doin' the killin'. What the little lady

in there calls the 'Shadowman'?"

"I'm not sure."

"What d'yuh mean? Did yuh see it or didn't yuh?"

"Neil was already dead and the...Shadowman was gone when I got back, but I did see a man in the forest just before that."

"A man?"

"Yeah. He was powerfully built and he had long, wild hair...And he was wearing animal skins and furs."

"Yuh saw him up close?"

"Yeah. I spoke to him."

"Then yuh lucky to be alive. Your dead friend told me it attacked him."

"Neil?"

"Yeah. He came back to the hotel like a scalded cat. Kept lookin' out to see if it was followin' him."

"And was it? Did you see it?"

"No."

"Then you don't know it's the same person."

"He described him like yuh did just now: wild lookin', long hair, animal skins. And, like I said, he said it attacked him and some other guy for no reason. Then it chased him through the forest. He had a fight with it and he thought he'd killed it."

"Neil? Are we still talking about Neil?"

"Yeah."

"Well I don't like to speak ill of the dead, but Neil was no fighter. It wasn't his scene."

"He said he led it away from yuh, t' protect yuh."

"And that's definitely not Neil. No way."

"Well that's what he told me. And now he's dead. So who killed him?"

"I don't know, but I don't think the man I met was dangerous. He didn't threaten me at all and his eyes were so intelligent and gentle. I'm really not convinced he could have killed Neil, or Bill."

"So yuh know about yuh friend Bill? The little lady told us he died; a bad business," he shook his head, "So don't be lettin' no big eyes fool yuh; he's the killer alright."

"Did Emma say that?"

"That little lady's said nothin' more. She's bin asleep since her pa left."

Rita wasn't convinced of Jon's guilt; Emma's description to Jeff of the tall, thin 'Shadowman' didn't sound much like Jon. But she decided not to argue the point with Spielman and, instead, changed the direction of the conversation.

"Will you come back to the hotel with us?"

"No. I've bin safe here all these years. Reckon I'll be safe a few years more."

"Mr Spielman, I saw the devastation Emma's Shadowman caused when he killed Neil. Your trailer won't protect you if he comes here."

Spielman was thoughtful for a few moments.

"I know the hotel's stronger than this here trailer of mine, but I don't believe this Shadowman will come here if there ain't no kiddies here. It's them that he wants."

At that moment, Jeff stepped down from the trailer, carrying Emma. He had heard the old man's words.

"If that's true, Spielman, then we'll need all the help we can get back at the hotel."

Spielman looked embarrassed. Truth was: he was an old man and he was feeling the strain of this awful night. Raw courage and his anger at the killings long ago, had sustained him through hours of searching the forest for the killer, despite having himself been stabbed. The worst, however, had been spending the last hour or so, frightened and alone, watching over a young girl whose very presence in his trailer made Spielman a target for the killer. Now, Spielman was exhausted. He dearly hoped these people would be able to save their children, but he also wished they would go now and leave him to rest.

Spielman wallowed in this fashion for a few moments, until the memory of Suzie's poor, dead face came back to him. His dismay turned back to anger. He couldn't let the monster that had killed her and all those children get away again. Decades from now it would come back to kill again and, next time, he would be too old to do anything to stop it. His mind was made up: no matter how tired his old body, determination would somehow carry him through. He had to try to end this.

"Wait up there, son. I'll get ma ammunition."

He re-emerged from the trailer moments later, carrying blankets which he passed to Rita, and several boxes of bullets. He shut the trailer door and kicked some dirt over the fire. Then together, they made their way back to the hotel.

32

The chair was still wedged in place. Spielman and Rita had to work together to push it out of the way.

Once the door was clear, Rita ducked her head inside while Spielman kept a lookout. She nodded to Jeff and went ahead of him as he carried Emma down to the kitchen. Using some of Spielman's blankets, Rita fashioned a bed on the floor of one of the store rooms. This room had no windows and so seemed the most secure. Jeff laid Emma down and covered her with another blanket.

"Jeff, why don't you stay in here with her while I check the other rooms again?"

"But the chair hadn't been moved."

"Just in case."

Jeff nodded.

Rita went to each of the basement rooms in turn and reassured herself that all was in order. Only then did she let herself relax.

Spielman called from the top of the stairs.

"Everything OK down there, folks?"

"Yeah, everything's fine."

"Then hows about yuh help me block this door again?"

Both Rita and Jeff went to help the old man. They

managed to push the reception desk further back, so that it partially blocked the way to the door. Then Rita took a marker pen from the desk and began to write on the notice board above their heads. She wrote, 'Pinders College, Class of 86', in large letters and drew an arrow pointing to the door. Both Jeff and Spielman gave her questioning looks.

"So the others will know where to find us," she explained.

Once the sign was written and the door locked shut, they dragged the large filing cabinets from the office and wedged them into place behind the door. Then, going down to the basement, they checked all the windows and used blankets to cover those in the kitchen so that the light couldn't be seen outside. Finally, they allowed themselves to sit and have a cup of coffee.

"We should try to get us some rest," Spielman suggested, setting down his cup.

Rita and Jeff looked at the old man. They had been too engrossed in their own worries until now but, seeing his weary, dark-ringed eyes, it was clear to them now that he was quite exhausted.

"I'll take the first watch," Rita volunteered.

"No, Hon. You go get washed up. There's clean clothes in the laundry room. I'll take the first watch. And you get some rest, Mr Spielman."

Spielman was only too happy to take a later watch. He curled up in a corner and wrapped himself in a blanket. When Rita checked on him, moments later, on her way to the laundry, the old man was already fast asleep.

It had taken Rita some time to wash and wipe herself clean, but she felt so much better to be free of the dried layer coating her skin and matting her hair.

Looking through the washing baskets, she found some

clothes that obviously belonged to a woman somewhat shorter than herself. The jeans ended several inches above Rita's ankles, but otherwise the fit was good and she also picked out a shirt and a sweat top. Wearing them she now felt deliciously clean.

She checked on Spielman and Emma. They were still asleep, he in his corner and she in the store room. Rita poured two cups of coffee and took them up the stairs to Jeff.

"Thanks. Hey, you're looking good."

"Yeah, I feel human again. Anything happening?"

"No. It's been absolutely quiet out there, as far as I can tell," Jeff waved a hand over a pile of papers on the filing cabinet, "I've been reading through some of these to pass the time. There's some weird stuff in here. God knows why the Cousins collected it."

"Yeah. Neil and I had a look through some medical reports earlier."

"The Boes?"

"Yeah, father and son. But we couldn't find a link between them and the Cousins."

"Did you read the interviews?"

"What interviews?"

"A whole file of them, going back years. The earlier ones were written by Mrs Cousins, but our friend Spielman got involved later on. It looks like they quizzed any Californian tourists that came through Losien."

"Only Californians? Why? What about?"

"It's a bit obsessive; they wanted to find out everything these people knew about a child killer who went on a killing spree in LA in the late forties. They were interested in the gruesome details: when he started killing, how he killed, how many he killed: his MO. And, as well as the interviews, there are these cuttings, from the LA newspapers of 1950.

The story made the front pages for weeks. It was obviously big news back then and the press milked it for all it was worth. The stories are inventively lurid, as you'd expect, and they seem to have elaborated freely in the absence of hard facts; there's a lot of editorial comment, opinion pieces and speculation. They came up with a catchy name for him though; they called him the Baby Doll Killer."

Rita shook her head.

"Never heard of him. What did the tourists say about him?"

"Well, don't forget that most of them probably got their initial information from the same newspapers that were hyping the story to boost their circulation figures. And, over time, they probably enlarged and exaggerated the stories in the telling. But most of them seem to agree on the basic facts; that over three or four years the killer lured young children to his house and then killed them. They also said that he later kidnapped a young woman and forced her to help him. He got her to approach the kids first, to allay their suspicions.

When it comes to what happened to the kids once he had them, the stories begin to vary. Most agree that, having kidnapped the children, he buried them in his basement. They said that each child was put in a small box and had a carved wooden doll put in with them, and at least seven children had died before the young woman escaped and went to the police. But some said the kids died in the boxes, some said he killed them before he buried them, some said he sexually abused them, some said he tortured them, and one couple said they'd heard that he cut out parts of their bodies once they were dead. Whatever the truth of it, all of them remembered his name, even many years later. He was kinda like a bogeyman; all the more scary for being real and in their own back yard."

"And what was his name?"

"Boe. Ezra Boe."

"Shit! A relative of the Cousins was a child killer?"

"Looks that way. Now we know why they kept all this stuff about him."

"What happened to him?"

"This last cutting is from, let's see, the LA Times, Tuesday, December 12, 1953. It says that Boe was arrested on Saturday, October 28, 1950, when his reluctant accomplice, 17 year old Rosa Maria Lopez, escaped and raised the alarm. On June 20th, 1951, after months of psychiatric evaluation, Boe was pronounced incapable by reason of insanity and committed to life in a secure hospital for the criminally insane. But only two years into his incarceration, he escaped while being transferred to another facility."

"Then what?"

"There aren't any later cuttings in this file, but there's loads of other documents in the other drawers."

There was a sound on the stairs below them.

"There weren't no sign of him for the next four years."

Spielman had heard them talking and was climbing the stairs to join them.

"Karen, that is Mrs Cousins, and me kept lookin' for evidence, but most folks back then thought Boe must be dead. Karen and me, we wrote to the newspapers and had 'em go back through the archives. We got us some press cuttings on missin' children from places between California and Losien. Over those four years there were five kiddies disappeared from towns along that route and ain't none of them ever bin found. We tried to tell the sheriff, but he said that we couldn't prove nothin', on account of how there weren't no bodies and Boe hadn't bin seen. So five kiddies disappeared between California and Losien, after Boe escaped, then in 1957 Suzie Bower and those other kiddies was stolen away and killed right here. Boe didn't die: it took him four long years, walking, but he came back home."

"Home?"

"Yeah, he was born in Fairfalls. His ma died young and Boe was put into a orphanage by his pa. There's some papers from the orphanage in here somewhere, on yella paper."

"Yellow? Oh yeah, I see. St. Hilda's Orphanage. It's an internal memo, from a Sister Veronica," said Rita, reading aloud.

> "Ezra Boe (3 yrs and 7 mths) has been with us since his poor mother succumbed to pneumonia, two years ago. He is a cheerful little boy, rarely cries and is content and obedient at all times. On the 12th of last month, Sr Josephine was approached by the Whitneys who expressed their wish to adopt Ezra. I took it upon myself to notify his estranged father, Mr Henry Boe, of the Whitney's request and I regret to have to tell you that Mr Boe has now removed Ezra from St Hilda's."

Jeff shrugged.

"Well at least Henry loved his son."

"If he loved him why was he in an orphanage?"

"Weren't no welfare, ma'am."

"No, I guess not."

They fell to silence for a few minutes.

"Why yuh reading Mrs Cousin's private papers, son?"

Jeff was surprised by the question.

"I don't know. To keep myself awake I guess, but also as it turns out, because the stuff in these files might have something to do with what's going on here. How long have you known about all this?"

"I lived in this forest near all my life, son, an' I seen an' heard some strange things. There's stories go way back before white folks drove out the injuns. The injuns understood; there's things, ancient things here, spirits an' the like, that ain't got no rational explanation. Things live here that shouldn't. But Mr Cousins, he can't see it, says it's all hogwash. That's why Karen confided in me, an' we worked together to find all this evidence."

"Evidence? Of what?"

"Don't yuh see? Boe's the killer, but look at this...if I can find it..."

Muttering, Spielman started to search through the top drawer of the filing cabinet.

"It should be here."

"What are you looking for?"

"A scrapbook."

"This one?"

Spielman looked dismayed.

"Yuh bin readin' that too?"

"When I was in here with Neil, yeah. Sorry."

Rita couldn't look Spielman in the eye. He took the book from her with reverence.

"This is Karen's private book. It's got all her memories of her daughter. Her daughter disappeared."

"What?" Jeff interrupted, "When was that?"

"Back in '78. Disappeared and they ain't never found her poor body. An' the worst of it, a reason I helped Karen all these years: I was the last person to see that poor girl alive, out in the forest, by that broken down shack. I coulda saved her. I shoulda walked her back home, but I thought she'd be safe away from that evil place. I told her to get. Told her it was private property. I shouted till she ran off and ain't no one seen sight nor sound of her since. So when Karen asked me to help her find evidence I did everything I could t'help the poor lady."

"So she collected all this stuff in an effort to find out what happened to her daughter?"

"That's right, ma'am. John, that's her husband, thought she was losing her mind. He wanted to leave this place, but Karen refused to leave. They hadn't the heart to keep this place open, so John spent years scratchin' a livin' doin' part time jobs in Losien. He used to do some work for me if I had a big timber order come in. But he weren't never cut out for workin' with his hands and he eventually persuaded Karen to reopen this place as a hotel, even had me build a climbing frame for the kiddies. That upset Karen and I damn near refused to make it, but it was so mighty important to John. Karen didn't want no kiddies stayin' here, but John had it fixed in his mind that they had to move on; get on with their lives. Yuh booking was the first they'd had since Laura disappeared. This place bin empty all those years and Karen never gave up hope that their little girl would come back; just walk back in through the door like nothin' happened. She kinda knew that her daughter was dead, but she never gave up hopin' for a miracle."

"So it wasn't that Boe was related to her or her husband?"

"No," Spielman shook his head, "Why d'yuh think that?"

"No reason. I guess I misunderstood. So Karen thinks Boe killed her daughter."

"That's right ma'am."

"But surely he must have been dead years ago."

"That's the point. Look what Karen's writ here."

Spielman pointed to a hand-written scrawl at the side of one of the fading press cuttings in the scrapbook. Next to an article headlined, 'NEWCOMERS' DAUGHTER VANISHES', Karen Cousins had scribbled, '75', underlining it with bright red ink.

"What's it mean?"

"Boe woulda bin seventy-five years old."

"We are talking about Ezra Boe, The Baby Doll Killer?"

"Yeah."

Jeff thought a reality check was overdue.

"A seventy-five year old? It says here that her daughter was thirteen. Surely such an old man would have been too frail, she'd have been able to run away."

Spielman smiled knowingly.

"Precisely."

Rita and Jeff exchanged glances.

"Sorry, Mr Spielman, but I don't know what you mean."

"What I mean, ma'am, is that he shoulda bin too old, but he wasn't. It's like I said: things live on here in the forest that shouldn't."

Behind the old man's back, Jeff rotated a finger at his ear and silently mouthed the word, 'Looney'. Rita frowned at him.

Spielman hadn't looked up, but he seemed to have guessed what was happening.

"Yuh don't believe me? Think I'm crazy? Just read some the evidence we collected. Just read it an' yuh'll understand why Karen wanted to cancel your bookin' when she saw y'all had kiddies. John, her husband, he didn't understand. He said she had to get on with life and stop living in the past. He shoulda listened to her. And yuh should do the same. Read the evidence."

"Yeah. We'll do that. Meantime, why don't you go back and get some more sleep?"

"There bin any action out there?" Spielman jerked a thumb towards the barricaded door.

"No. Nothing."

"OK then. I'll do that. Wake me when yuh need me to take the watch."

"Sure thing."

Jeff and Rita watched Spielman return to his corner of the kitchen and they didn't speak again until they were certain he was out of earshot.

"What's he on?" Jeff asked, eyes rolling.

"Shh. Don't be cruel. He's an old man."

"He's a looney tune!" Jeff laughed, "But what was that about the Cousins' daughter?"

"Yeah it's really sad. There's old pages of the Losien Gazette in the scrapbook. She disappeared the same year they arrived here at the hotel. Her body was never found and, as far as I can tell, no one was ever charged with her abduction."

"Could have been a bear, or a wolf. Do they have wolves here?"

"No, I don't think so. But if it was a bear, wouldn't they have found some of her belongings, torn clothing, something? There was no sign of a struggle. Nothing at all. Like the headlines said, she just vanished. And, by the sound of things, her loss pushed her mom over the edge."

"Well, we saw that for ourselves didn't we? The woman's a total introvert. I don't think she said a single word to anyone all evening."

"Yeah, but the weirdest thing is that, after losing Laura, they had a second daughter and they gave her the same name. That is weird isn't it?"

"Can't have been easy for the second Laura to be her own person. But you said she seems friendly."

"Yeah, she was more welcoming than her mom, but she didn't say a lot more. I told you before, didn't I: she's a nice kid, but maybe a bit, y'know, slow."

They sat in silence on the floor of the office, drinking their coffee.

"You done?" Rita asked, "I'll take these back down to the kitchen."

"Are you tired? Don't you want to see what else we can find out?"

"You need the company?"

"Kinda."

"Sure," Rita smiled, "I probably wouldn't be able to sleep anyhow."

For the next hour or so, Rita and Jeff read through the papers that Karen Cousins had so assiduously gathered together. It was clear that the hunt for her daughter had consumed her entire life from the day Laura disappeared. Her sense of utter despair and loss ran through her annotations and comments, touching Rita profoundly. Weeping quietly as she read on, Rita felt an almost visceral, empathic link with the grieving mother

"Poor woman."

"Who?"

"Karen. Losing her daughter has destroyed her."

Jeff put down the document he was reading and drew Rita close. There was nothing he could say, so he just held her. Eventually, Rita sniffed and dried her eyes.

"I don't know why this is affecting me so much."

"Do you want to stop?"

"No, no, I'm fine. What have you been reading?"

Jeff picked up a yellowing sheaf of papers.

"It's quite interesting. It's the notes from the hospital in California that Boe was sent to after he was arrested," he paused, "Are you sure you want to hear more of this stuff?"

"Yeah, go on," she wiped her eyes, "what's it say?"

"It's mostly about Boe's early life and some of it's in his own words. There are notes from sessions with various doctors over many months," Jeff read ahead, "I'll

431

paraphrase..."

Rita waited.

"OK. It says that, after collecting Ezra from the orphanage, Henry returned to his farm and brought the boy up alone. Ezra had no toys and no playmates. He was very lonely and became increasingly withdrawn. His father had little time for him and even told him that he'd wanted to leave him at the orphanage until he was old enough to be of more use on the farm. He told him that he only took him from St. Hilda's when he did because the sisters were going to give him to a couple who couldn't have kids of their own."

"The Whitneys."

"Yeah, I guess."

Jeff scanned the rest of the page.

"Ah, now this is interesting: to amuse himself, Ezra carved small wooden dolls to keep him company."

Rita looked up.

"Like the ones he put in the boxes, with the children?"

"Don't know. Haven't got there yet. He says that, when his father found the dolls he apparently assumed that Ezra was involved in some kind of black magic."

"That was in something I read with Neil: Dr Beauregard's reports. Henry was brought up with a creole lady who was into voodoo and all that stuff. Henry believed that he'd killed his own parents with a black magic curse."

"Yeah, I glanced through those earlier, while you were cleaning yourself up. Well Henry didn't like Ezra's wooden dolls and he tried to get him to admit that he was trying to catch someone's spirit with them. Ezra says his father beat him and burned the dolls. But it looks like Henry's efforts backfired; Ezra was intrigued by his talk of black magic rather than discouraged from it by the beatings. He tried to get more information from Henry.

Henry was reluctant to say any more, but Ezra says that, occasionally, when his father was in one of his darker moods, he would apparently tell Ezra that the devil and dark spirits were all around them...Yeah, it says here that Henry told his son that he could actually see huge demons surrounding them and watching them, ready to steal their souls."

"Great parenting skills."

"Yeah. Sounds like Boe senior had major problems."

"I'll have to read Dr Beauregard's medical reports again."

"Why?"

"One of the papers I read with Neil; I think I got things round the wrong way."

"D'you want me to go on with these?"

Rita nodded and Jeff found his place again.

"Looks like life on their farm was very hard. The area suffered repeated droughts and the land became too dusty to produce decent crops in sufficient volume. As his farm went downhill, Henry became increasingly remote and given to violent outbursts. Then, one day, Henry just left. He didn't tell Ezra where he was going or how long he'd be away. Ezra only learned years later that his father had gone to the church in Fairfalls and caused a ruckus.

"After that, while Henry was in the asylum, Ezra survived by living off canned foods. Lonely, and without Henry to stop him, he carved himself another doll for comfort. He says he knew that his father would beat him and destroy the doll if he came back and found it, but as time went by he nevertheless began to wish his father would return, as he had no one else in the world. Ezra says there used to be only one photo of his father in the house: a picture of him in army uniform. Ezra took the photo out of the frame and kept it safe, with the doll, under a loose floorboard in his bedroom."

"Why did he take the photo?"

"The doctor's asked him that, but he writes that Boe smiled and refused to answer."

"May be he was just missing his Dad, so he wanted to keep his picture close."

Jeff shrugged.

"Yeah, I guess kids love their parents no matter how godawful they are. It says here that, when his father finally returned from the asylum he was furious that Ezra had eaten so much and neglected the farmhouse and the fields."

"He was only ten years old. Poor kid."

"Hmm," but Jeff wasn't really listening. He had turned over the page, "Weird."

"What?"

"The reason he took the photo. According to a different doctor, in a subsequent session, Ezra actually believed that he had summoned his father back from wherever he had disappeared to, using the doll, the photo and the power of magic. Ezra decided not to tell his father though and Henry didn't notice that the picture was missing from the frame for several days. When eventually he did, he demanded Ezra give it back. Ezra told the doctor that, in retrieving the photo, he was able to keep the doll hidden under the floor boards of his bedroom. And there the doll remained, known only to Ezra, for the next four years.

"So, let's see...When Henry dies, after slipping and falling down the cellar steps, Ezra, now aged fourteen, hides in the farmhouse, with his father's dead body, for four days until a neighbouring farmer happens by. It was Ezra who tucked the carved wooden doll and the photo of Henry inside his dead father's shirt. The men from the funeral home, who came to collect the body, took them out. They discarded the doll and gave the photo to Ezra.

They assumed that Ezra must have loved his father very much because he became hysterical and had to be restrained when his father's body was being taken from the house."

Jeff began to flick on, through the pages.

"Is that it?" Rita asked.

"No. There's a note, referring the reader on to a later session...Here it is...Ezra explained to yet another psychiatrist that the doll was to capture his father's spirit and bring him back from the dead. He believed it would work because it had brought him back before, when he'd only had a photo of his father to make the magic. Ezra apparently couldn't understand why the doll and the magic hadn't worked when he had, not just a photo, but the actual body of his father right there. Ezra said he became hysterical because he realised that his efforts had failed and they were taking his father's body away, so he wouldn't be able to try the magic again."

"So he wanted to bring the old bully back from the dead?"

"Apparently so."

"That was one very confused kid. And the sum total of the help he got was a week or two under sedation before being kicked out into the world to fend for himself."

"Monsters aren't born. They're made."

"Hmm. So you buy what Spielman said?"

"I don't know about Boe kidnapping and killing children around here, but he looks guilty as hell in the Californian killings."

"Does Boe actually admit those killings?"

"Let's see...Give me a minute. I'll go back over the pages I skipped...Yeah. Here's a report of an early interview with police, in January of 1951.

"Boe was asked if he had killed before. It says here

that he at first refused to talk, so they suggested to him that he couldn't have killed before, because he wasn't smart enough to have gotten away with it. Boe immediately became agitated and they were about to abandon the interrogation when he suddenly began talking. Ah, the clumsy psychology must have worked: he told the detectives that he had killed once before. However, Boe said it had been an accident and he stuck to that story. He wouldn't say where or who he had killed. He just repeated, over and over, that he had taken her money and her ticket because she no longer needed them."

"A girl? A child? Had he killed a child?"

"Doesn't say. Maybe Boe wouldn't tell them."

"And what about the children they knew about: the ones in the boxes?"

"That's not in here...Oh yeah, sorry, here it is...Boe refused to admit to killing any of them, in spite of eyewitness statements from Rosa Lopez and the two surviving children that said, from the get go, that Boe was the killer. He just kept on saying that he couldn't have killed them because he wanted to play with them. He said they'd live forever."

"Forever?"

"That's what it says here. He must have meant the afterlife."

"Who knows? The guy was a psycho. He could have meant anything, or nothing. I guess we'll never know."

Jeff looked up from the papers.

"You look tired Babe."

"I am. I'm absolutely dead on my feet."

"Why don't you go get some sleep?"

"I'd love to, but are you OK to stay on up here?"

"I'm fine. Go. I'll be waking you to take over in a couple of hours, so you'd better not waste any time."

"I'm gone already. Love you."

They kissed and then Rita went down to the basement. She put the cups in the sink and turned down the lights, before curling up next to Emma on the storeroom floor. Exhausted, she was asleep within seconds of closing her eyes.

33

Weak daylight was filtering in through the narrow opening in the pickup's window and Phil's breath was clouding and adding to the frozen condensation on the inside of the windshield. He shivered. Try as he might, as indeed he had for the last hour, he could not get back to sleep: he was simply too cold. He would have to get out and start walking again. The exercise would help to warm him, but his legs were achingly stiff; this would be a painful process.

With the dawn light, Phil could see that the pickup was leaning at a crazy angle and he concluded that it must have run off the road and into a ditch where it now rested at an angle of about forty-five degrees. That explained why he had found it so difficult to reach across to open the window last night: he would have had to clamber uphill across the seats. He was amazed that he hadn't noticed the listing of the pickup then; he must have been more exhausted and disoriented than he realised. Last night, he remembered now, he had to stoop to get in through the driver's door, but that hadn't registered as being at all unusual at the time. Now that same door was set in deep snow that had fallen overnight or slipped from the roof; he would have to climb up and out of the passenger door.

Cursing, Phil stretched his arms and legs, pushing down on the dashboard to propel himself up towards the passenger door. Like the window itself, the unlocked passenger door was frozen into place and, in a moment of panic, Phil thought he might be trapped inside for ever. With a roar, he hammered at the door, pounding it with his fists until, finally, the ice seal gave way and the door creaked open an inch. The door was free, but also heavy with the weight of a thick layer of snow; it slammed shut before Phil could stop it. Fearing he would have to hammer it open all over again, Phil threw himself up against it with all his strength. The door shot open, bounced against the side of the truck and slammed shut again, as Phil fell back down into his seat.

By now, Phil was crying with frustration. He was alone, in pain and felt half dead with cold. For all he knew, everyone else in the reunion party could be dead by now, frozen to death or murdered somewhere out there in the forest. Phil's only comfort was his belief that the owner of this truck would be back as soon as the weather allowed; help would come eventually. He had only to stay alive until then. Most pressing was his need to move around, to improve his circulation and warm himself. He had to focus. Wiping away the tears and chiding himself for his weakness, he opened the door for the third time. Calmer now, he used less force, so the door fell open and he was able to climb out onto the side of the pickup. He slid down, through the covering layer of fresh snow and stumbled onto the uneven ground. Behind him, the pickup groaned as it settled back into place. The passenger-side wheels were at his shoulder height and the whole length of the driver's side of the pickup was embedded in the snow.

"Must've been one hell of a smash," he muttered.

As he spoke, Phil realised that his lips were chapped

and painful. It was just another misery to add to his aching limbs and his pounding headache. Life sucked!

He looked about him as he stamped his feet and paced to and fro. To either side, the forest built up, layer on layer, into an impenetrable mesh of snow-drifted trees the bare, tangled branches of which pointed up into the pale sky high above him, blocking out all save the strip of sky directly above the roadway.

Phil looked at the snow-covered track itself and frowned. It was not a flat surface: there was something large in front of the pickup. Phil wandered over to the obstruction. Presumably this was what had caused the pickup to crash. He kicked at it with his foot. It didn't feel as solid as a rock or a tree trunk. Curious now, Phil scuffed more of the snow away. Cloth: a jacket.

It was a body!

"Jeez!"

Phil leapt back and stood, staring at the huddled form, as he tried to gather his wits. Obviously, whoever it was would be dead; they were no threat to him. He was safe. He must control his breathing and calm himself. To this end, Phil took in and let out several deep, slow breaths until his heart rate slowed once more. That done, he edged forward. He had to see the face. With the toe of his boot, he shook the remaining snow from the face.

It was Cousins: the manager of the hotel. His face looked strangely colourless and thin, and had around it a frozen halo of crystalised blood, but Phil recognised him.

Thinking back, Phil remembered someone telling him that the Cousins had left the hotel to go to church in Losien.

"Didn't get to say your prayers did you? You poor schmuck!"

Phil spoke aloud for his own benefit. It was unnerving, being out here alone with a dead person. It was then that he noticed the second heap, at the side of the road. In spite of himself, he felt himself drawn to it.

Phil cleared the snow from Karen Cousin's face, but quickly used the side of his boot to move some back, to cover it again: her pale, glazed eyes were frozen open and looking straight ahead. That was more than Phil could stomach.

He tried to think. The Cousins could have been thrown from the pickup when it crashed, or they might have crawled, injured, from the wreckage, or they might have met with whatever it was that Phil had heard chasing, then killing Neil out in the forest. Either way, Phil had found the owners of the truck, and they weren't going to be bringing help any time soon. He would have to walk to town. He felt in his pockets: he still had a few pieces of candy. With shivering hands he struggled to put one into his mouth. He had to remove his gloves to unwrap it and was amazed at the speed at which his fingers chilled to uselessness. Now he rammed his hands back into the gloves and set off down the track, grim-faced, choosing the direction at random.

Phil soon began to suffer. His legs were shaking with cold and fatigue and his spirits were flagging. He was muttering to himself as he stumbled along, railing almost incoherently against all the unfairness of his entire life to date and bemoaning the cruel twists of fate that had led him to this particularly miserable situation. Someone would be held to account for all his suffering. He would sue and someone would pay.

It was the outburst of a child; self-obsessed and peevish. And similarly, while he knew that it would be a long walk to Losien, he was nevertheless childishly disheartened, having walked barely a half mile, to see no sign of life yet. It simply wasn't fair!

Phil trudged on, loathing the world and every person

in it.

As time went by, Phil's stumbling became progressively less co-ordinated. It was now an effort to remember to put one numbed foot in front of the other. The slowly increasing daylight brought no warmth with it and, if anything, Phil felt colder now than he had when he set out. He had only one piece of candy left. With uncontrollably shaking hands he retrieved it from his pocket. But, in pulling off his gloves to unwrap it, he lost his grip on the candy and it flew away from him, into the snow.

Phil cried out and fell to his knees, scrabbling about in the snow, frantically searching. He couldn't see much, as his eyes were watery, though he was too exhausted and hadn't the energy to cry. And it was all to no avail: the candy was gone. Phil knelt back, raised his face to the sky and yelled, as loud and for as long as he was able. In that yell was all the anguish, misery and hopelessness of his unfairly restricted life; his lack of opportunities and the thoroughly undeserved success of others. It was a cathartic release and Phil expected it to be his last utterance: he was going to die out here. What a waste! What a terrible loss! And yet the world wouldn't notice: no one had ever really appreciated him and he was going to die alone and uncared for out in this wilderness. Utterly forlorn, he let his head roll forward onto his chest.

For a few seconds his mind was numb. Then he registered that, in letting his head fall forwards, he had glimpsed a flash of light somewhere off to his left. He couldn't think clearly enough to imagine what the light might be, so he raised his head again and tried to focus on the light. It was a very faint yellow, flickering, nearly hidden by the close-growing trees.

A fire! Warmth!

Getting to that light became Phil's sole focus. He struggled to his feet and staggered towards the tiny beacon, panicking when he lost it briefly between the trees, and overjoyed when he saw it again. His push through the trees brought him out onto a narrow path. He looked back along it. The path led from the track, but Phil was too tired to care that, had he stayed on the track just a few yards more, he could have turned onto the path directly and avoided all the effort of forcing a way through the snow-covered undergrowth. He turned back and followed the path further into the forest.

There were now fewer trees masking the fire and its growing glow was the most wonderfully welcoming sight Phil could imagine. The path opened out into a clearing in which there were stacks of cut logs, each covered with a tarpaulin and topped with a layer of snow. All around him, the snow concealed many unidentifiable objects littering the ground and surrounding an old and battered trailer, which stood at the centre of the site. The fire was just outside the door of the trailer and was a good deal smaller than the blazing bonfire Phil had been anticipating.

He called out, oblivious to any danger from whoever might live in this run down wood yard.

"Hello! Anybody home?"

The snow muffled all sound and his voice was already weak and uncertain, so Phil staggered to the door and knocked on it as hard as he could. When he still got no response, he tried the handle. The door was unlocked and he gratefully climbed inside. It was very dark until Phil opened the grubby blinds at the windows. The glass needed a clean, but it let in enough light for Phil to look around and see that this place had what he most needed: food and blankets. Not caring that the fabric was stained and smelly, Phil took two rugs off the floor and wrapped them about him. Then he rummaged through the cupboards and selected a tin of baked beans. He opened the tin and spooned out a mouthful of the contents. Even uncooked, they tasted better than anything Phil had ever eaten. But he knew that the trailer must contain some means of cooking them and he soon found the gas stove. He turned on the valve and searched for some matches but, as far as he could tell, there were none. The smell of gas was by now becoming unpleasant and Phil went to turn the valve off, but it resisted his efforts. The smell was really strong now and Phil began to panic; he had no qualms about stealing some food and rugs from the trailer's owner, but filling their trailer with gas might be considered unneighbourly and backwoods people always owned shotguns. With one last twist before he abandoned the attempt, Phil managed to stem the flow of gas. It wasn't off completely, but at least now there was no telltale hiss. Phil reckoned that, if he left the door slightly ajar, the small amount of gas that was still leaking from the valve, would dissipate safely enough.

It was then that Phil remembered the fire outside. He was delighted; he would be able to cook the beans after all. Of course, it would probably be wise to keep the door shut until he'd finished with the fire, but he could open it again before he left, so that would be OK. Phil helped himself to another tin and, within minutes, having coaxed the fire back to life, was placing both tins in the glowing embers. He spooned out the hot beans and savoured every wonderful mouthful.

The food warmed him and made him feel quite positive, almost cheerful. Phil was now in a very different mood to that of only a half hour before. Replete at last, he eased back, tugged the rugs closer and enjoyed the warming glow of the fire. It was only now that he gave any thought as to why someone would have made up and then left a fire burning, albeit very low, so near to the trailer. For a few, worrying moments, he thought that the owner of the trailer might be about to come back and demand restitution, but then he decided it was far more likely that the owner of the trailer had left in a hurry when the snow began to close in. Perhaps they had expected the snow to extinguish the flames. It was just lucky for Phil that it had not.

He wondered whether he should stay here at the trailer until the cold weather cleared, but then he remembered the gas. It probably wouldn't be healthy to stay inside the trailer overnight, so he would have to resume his walk to Losien. With a heavy heart he went back into the trailer for the last time and took several candy bars, stuffing them into his pockets with greedy enthusiasm. He felt a fleeting sense of guilt about the gas, but he brushed it aside, reasoning that old trailers such as this one would surely have hundreds of small cracks and rust holes in their walls; the gas could safely escape through them.

With that thought, Phil dismissed any concerns. He hugged the rugs close and began to walk back down the path.

34

Jeff had dozed off, but he awoke now with a start; something was moving about in the lobby.

Holding his breath, he put his ear to the door and listened. There it was again: a dragging, scratching sound rather than distinct footsteps.

It was back!

The time had come: the thing, Emma's Shadowman, was back inside the hotel.

It had perhaps returned to the broken down shack in the forest, as Emma said it had threatened to do. If so, Jeff could imagine its fury at finding Dave gone. He hoped that Dave and Lou had kept moving away from that terrible place and that they, and all the others were safe, but now Jeff had to concentrate; the Shadowman was here and it was hunting. With that thought, Jeff suddenly panicked: he hadn't arranged any way of alerting the others, asleep down in the basement, without also alerting whoever or whatever was out in the lobby. He would have to leave the door and go down to the kitchen himself. With the most careful of movements, Jeff sidled past the filing cabinets and down the stairs to the kitchen.

He went first to Spielman, still asleep in the corner and gently shook him by the shoulder. With unexpected speed, the old man opened his eyes and had the gun ready in his hand in an instant. Jeff put a finger to his lips and then pointed up to the lobby door. Spielman nodded. Next, Jeff looked for Rita. Finding her in the storeroom with Emma, he very gently shook her awake. The anxious look in his eyes alerted her immediately and she got to her feet, her heart already racing. She retrieved her knife and began mentally to prepare herself to use it.

"It's definitely not one of the others come back?" she whispered, without much hope.

"No way. I don't know what it is. It's big and it makes a weird scuttling sound when it moves. I don't think it's an animal, but I don't think it's a...a person," Jeff replied, shocked to hear himself saying such a thing.

Rita paled but touched his arm, to reassure him.

"We can do this, Babe."

Jeff nodded, but wished he felt more certain.

He crouched next to his daughter. He hated having to wake her. It would be wonderful if he could let his little girl sleep through whatever might follow, but she needed to be awake: she might need to run, to escape while he held her Shadowman at bay. Looking down at her beautiful, sleeping face, Jeff hoped against hope that, somehow, they would all come out of this alive, but the memory of Neil's mutilated body wouldn't altogether clear from his mind. With his hand resting gently over her mouth, Jeff whispered to Emma. She woke without any noise and was almost immediately on her feet and ready. Ready for what? Jeff wondered. None of them knew what the next few hours held and they were all very afraid. But, looking into his daughter's eyes, Jeff saw a centred calm and a maturity there. Emma had probably been through hell in the last twelve hours and, of all those down here in the basement, she had the closest experience of the thing upstairs yet, in spite of this, or perhaps because of it, she was showing the least sign of panic. Jeff just hoped that her calm was born of confident determination rather than of resignation.

There was a sudden, very loud crash upstairs.

"Sounds like the reception desk," Rita whispered.

"Jeez!" Jeff looked anxious, "How big is that thing?"

Emma took her dad's hand. It was a gesture intended to encourage him rather than to reassure herself.

"Don't let it scare you, Dad. It's trying to frighten us. It likes to play sick games, and terrifying people is a big part of the game."

Jeff looked down at his daughter and, not for the first time, wondered what she had seen and endured at the hands of this Shadowman. Jeff would have given anything for her to have been spared all contact with the monster, but he couldn't make it so, no matter how dearly he wished it. He knew he had to channel his hatred of that thing. He had to stop it.

Spielman readied his gun and crept slowly towards the bottom of the stairs. He made barely any sound, but the noises from the top of the stairs which had died away, now suddenly redoubled.

"Get back!" Jeff hissed, "It can hear you."

Spielman replied in a hoarse whisper:

"I'm ready. Y'all get back there. If it gets past the door, I'll let the sonofabitch have it," he paused a moment, before apologising automatically, and somewhat incongruously, given their desperate and extraordinary situation, "Pard'n ma french, ma'am."

Rita couldn't help but smile.

Jeff was not so amused.

"Hell, Spielman, will you shut up?" he begged.

As if in answer, all the noises suddenly stopped. The four in the basement looked from one to another in the silence. Only Emma seemed to expect what happened next.

With a splintering scream, the Shadowman slammed into the door, smashing it and rocking it from its hinges. Jeff and Rita, both taken by surprise, jumped at the violence of the noise and Spielman gasped, working hard to re-steady his gun hand. Emma, her face still fixed and unemotional, began slowly to back away. Rita went with her and put her arm around her shoulders. In her free hand, Rita gripped her knife with fierce resolve: she knew now that she would use it. If she had to. If this thing, this Shadowman, threatened the people she loved, Rita now knew that she would do everything in her power to kill it. Her heart rate steadied. She felt absolutely no fear.

Light from the lobby flooded into the dark well of the stairs. Then suddenly the light was gone, eclipsed by the tall, creeping body of the Shadowman.

In the sudden darkness, Spielman fired his gun blindly. But undeterred, and with deadly speed, the Shadowman lashed out and threw the old man across the room. Spielman skidded across the tiled floor and hit the metal cabinets with a crash. He lay there dazed, but alive.

Jeff could see that the old man was still holding the gun in a wavering aim at the creature.

Another shot rang out. The bullet missed its target and smacked into the wall. The Shadowman's face snapped about, the malevolent sunken eyes fixing on Spielman. The creature began to emit an eerie, hugh-pitched shriek but, as it crouched to launch itself at the old man, a large pan hit it squarely on the head.

Jeff looked triumphant.

"Over here, you bastard. Over here!" He turned to Rita, "Get back! If I can distract him, get her out of here."

The awful screech rose to an overwhelming scream as the Shadowman turned on Jeff. It was in front of him in seconds, moving with incredible speed and terrible grace.

It lifted Jeff off the floor until he was looking, eye to eye, into the baleful, death mask face. He was mesmerised, held in the terrifying depths of the Shadowman's glittering eyes.

Jeff was dimly conscious of the smile forming on the Shadowman's face and of the long, thin arm unfolding and extending upwards. Bone white fingers opened wide, their cruel nails razor sharp. There was a moment, as the Shadowman waited to strike, in which Jeff knew that he was about to die, but he had only two concerns: he wanted to give Emma and Rita enough time to escape, and he didn't want Emma to see him die.

"Go!" he gasped, "Run!"

"Hey, you sick fuck. Leave him alone! If you want me. I'm here!"

It was Emma.

Jeff was appalled and cried out in an incoherent moan: a mixture of disbelief, fury and despair. What the hell did Emma think she was doing?

The Shadowman released him, dropping him to the floor, discarding him as a child might a broken toy. Jeff landed heavily on his arm and he lay there in agony, wincing up at the Shadowman standing over him. Emma had hidden herself and the Shadowman now stood, slowly moving its head from side to side, sweeping across the room, trying to find her.

It moved away from Jeff, to the base of the stairs where, with apparently little effort, it began to push the heavy free-standing metal cupboard across the tiled floor. The cupboard rocked into place, completely blocking access to the stairs.

"Don't want you running away again, do we Doll?"

With the Shadowman occupied, Emma crept from her hiding place. Keeping low, behind the cabinets, she began to pull her father clear. She pulled him into one of the store rooms.

"Get in here!" she whispered.

"Where's Rita?"

"She knows what she's doing," Em spoke brusquely: she had no time to waste on explanations, "Dad, please, get in here!"

Jeff couldn't make sense of what was happening.

He heard Rita's voice. She was calling out to the Shadowman.

"She's here. The girl's in here!"

What the hell was going on?

Suddenly, there was a roar behind him in the kitchen and Jeff looked back, just in time to see Rita darting out of the utility room and slamming the door behind her. She locked the door then helped Spielman to his feet. As she dragged the old man across the room towards him, Jeff rushed to help. Glancing back over his shoulder, he saw the door of the utility room begin to vibrate: the Shadowman was preparing to smash his way back into the kitchen.

"Get back in here!" Rita ordered, "Shut the door!"

Jeff pulled the door shut behind them and watched as Rita and Emma started moving boxes away from the walls.

"Jeff, help us look for it,"

"Look for what?"

"The dumb waiter. It's our only way out. Come on, it's somewhere in here."

With that, Rita moved a stack of empty boxes and saw the wooden door of the dumb waiter.

"How did you know it was here?"

"Laura told me. Somehow."

"Somehow?"

"Yeah. I don't know. It wasn't spoken words exactly. I don't know. Look, there's no time for his now. Come on Em, you first."

Emma clambered into the tiny box of the dumb waiter and Rita pulled on the rope to winch her up. Once at the top, Emma tugged on the rope to let them know she'd arrived. As she began to lower the box again, there was a sudden, shattering crash out in the kitchen: the Shadowman had broken out of the utility room.

"Quick, Spielman. You next."

"No ma'am. Ain't no way I'd get into that there tiny box. I'll keep the creature busy while yuh get away."

"But -"

"Go on, get! Yuh wastin' time we ain't got."

"Rita," Jeff urged, "You have to go. Get in."

"No. You have to go next. You're bigger than me. It'll take both of us to get you up there."

Jeff could see that Rita was right and, with no time to argue, he squeezed into the dumb waiter. Spielman and Rita pulled hard on the rope and managed to get Jeff to the top. They felt his signalling tug on the rope just as the door handle behind them squeaked a turn. They held their breath. Silence: perhaps the Shadowman didn't know where they were. Rita began to lower the box of the dumb waiter as quickly and quietly as possible. It arrived just as the door handle turned again. This was not the squeak of a speculative half turn, but a full blown, angry rattle of the handle: the Shadowman had found them.

"You sure about this?" Rita asked the old man.

It was his last chance.

"I said get!"

As Spielman unceremoniously bundled Rita into the box, she leant forward and kissed him quickly on the cheek. With a look of surprised embarrassment on his face, he pulled down on the rope and sent Rita up to Jeff and Emma. His job done Spielman then turned, aimed his gun at the door and prepared himself.

Jon and Dave had arrived at the hotel.

On seeing the ravaged front doors, Jon signalled for Dave to go round to the hotel's back door. He would go in the front. Dave nodded and moved around towards the back of the building.

With great caution, Jon eased over the broken doors and surveyed the lobby. He had few memories of domestic interiors and certainly life in his grandmother's farm had not exposed him to luxuries such as the sofas and shiny, polished tables of the hotel. For a few moments he stood and stared about him, awestruck by the glamour of the place.

A sudden noise sent him diving for cover. He peered out from behind one of the comfortable armchairs and saw three people hurrying away up the stairs. Jon jumped up. He had recognised one of them. Seeing them disappear up onto a second flight of stairs, he called out.

"Rita!"

Hearing her name, Rita turned. Jeff and Emma had gone on ahead, up into the attic, but she hung back. Had she imagined someone calling her? She scanned the lobby and saw Jon as he rose from behind an armchair. He began to wave up to her, a crooked smile lighting his face, but there was a sudden, deafening crash and Jon froze in mid-wave, his attention taken by something out of Rita's view, his face suddenly deadly serious.

Rita was frightened: she could guess what had happened. She crept forward to the bannisters from where she could overlook the lobby. She didn't try to catch Jon's eye: he was studiously avoiding looking towards her and she guessed he must have good reason for doing so. For a few seconds everything seemed normal then, with a rasping, scratching sound, the

Shadowman moved slowly out from behind the wreckage of reception desk, directly below where Rita was standing.

Even from this viewpoint, the Shadowan was frightening. It moved towards Jon with steady, focused intent, its thin body stooping forward and its brittle arms rising for the attack. Dreading what she was about to witness, Rita gasped involuntarily and that barely audible sound was enough to distract the Shadowman. Its brittle body twisted, the skull white face fixing on her. It held Rita in its terrible gaze as it began slowly to move towards the foot of the stairs.

"Leave her!" Jon shouted, "I kill you."

But the Shadowman did not react. Jon had to think quickly. He wanted to say something more, something that would goad the Shadowman into following him out of the hotel, but he couldn't pull the words he needed from his forgotten past.

Then all at once, when he was on the verge of despair, his brain somehow unlocked a stream of lost words and Jon found them flowing from him as they had not done for years.

"Hey, remember me?" he yelled, "I smash your head with shovel. Remember? Remember?"

The Shadowman stopped. It tilted its head to one side, listening. Rita couldn't believe Jon's sudden fluency.

"Yes. That was me. And you should stay dead in earth, where you belong."

Rita could see the Shadowman's vicious nails begin to dig into the soft wood of the bannister.

"I will kill you!" Jon yelled.

The Shadowman growled, but did not move.

"Scared?" Jon's tone was mocking, "Well, I know where Laura is. I have the girl!"

That was the trigger. Jon had the creature's attention. Looking down, Rita noticed the slightest of movements, as the Shadowman turned back down towards Jon. It was tensing its muscles, getting ready to pounce.

"Run Jon! Get out!"

Her shouted warning came just as the Shadowman leapt back and down, landing only feet from where Jon had been standing. Jon was already racing away towards the trees but Rita knew she had to get him more time. Thinking quickly, she grabbed a vase from a table and hurled it down towards the Shadowman, before ducking down behind the table. As the vase smashed onto the floor, the Shadowman span around. Its death-mask face flicked down towards the floor and the glittering eyes took in the shards of pottery rocking to and fro on the polished wood. It raised its terrible gaze and began to look around the room, searching for the perpetrator. Rita stayed absolutely still, although her heart was again thumping in her chest. She held her breath.

Just then, the final remnant of the front doors suddenly collapsed and fell to the floor with a crash. Seeing this, the Shadowman appeared to lose all interest in the vase. With a monstrous scream it leapt out through the doorway and hurled itself out into the clearing.

Rita let out a sigh, then gathered herself and ran on up to the attic, to check on Jeff and Emma. Jeff was waiting for her at the top of the attic stairs.

"Ree, where have you been? I thought you must have hidden in one of the rooms down there. You had me so worried."

"Dad!" Emma called, "The Shadowman's outside."

Jeff ran over to the window.

"Look," Emma was pointing, "I think it's chasing after the man who ran into the trees over there."

"That was Jon," said Rita quietly, "and he just saved our lives."

Jon ran across the clearing, knowing that he had only a few seconds' advantage on the killer; running for his life.

Not daring to look back, he threw himself down the track and hurtled along it as it swept away to the right. Many years living in the forest had honed his muscles and kept him lean and fit, but Jon wasn't a young man and he wasn't sure how long he'd be able to keep running at this rate. He also had no idea where he should run to, but the directions seemed almost to have been chosen for him. After several hundred yards he darted to the right onto a path leading him away from the track into the trees.

Jon was pounding through the snow, head down, racing along the path. He looked up. There was something strange coming towards him, some way up ahead: not an animal, but a man, wrapped, Jon could now see, in rugs. At that moment Phil looked up, saw Jon and panicked. He turned to run back to the safety of the trailer, but Jon was gaining on him fast. Phil rounded a corner and Jon was upon him. Jon hit him with such force that he lifted him clear off the ground and together, they flew away from the path, landing heavily a couple of yards into the trees. Jon recovered immediately and threw himself on top of Phil, clamping a hand tightly over his mouth.

Phil was horrified. His first thought was that he was about to die at the hands of this madman. But, looking up into Jon's disfigured face, he saw that Jon had little interest in him. Jon's eyes were frantically scanning back and forth along the path, on the lookout for something, something that clearly terrified him.

For a moment Phil looked away from his captor, towards the nearby clearing. He could actually see the trailer from here. Could he escape this lunatic and get back there? Phil was in the process of carefully flexing his muscles, checking that he hadn't been injured in the collision, when he felt the hand at his mouth press down harder. He looked up and followed Jon's gaze.

A tall, gaunt figure was moving smoothly over the snow-covered path. As it moved, it made a dry, rustling sound and Phil noticed then that there was absolutely no other sound around them; this strange creature was moving through an eerily still and absolutely silent world. Phil couldn't look away from it. It was following the path and seemed to pass the point at which he and Jon had collided, without a pause but just a few yards further on, it stopped and began to turn its head from side to side, searching. When it turned to look in their direction, Phil felt the blood drain from his face. He froze and felt Jon duck down lower next to him. The skull-white face moved slowly, the sunken eyes, shiny black and diamond hard, seeming to cut right through him. It had seen them: Phil was sure of it. He closed his eyes; he had seen enough.

"Come here!" Phil was startled to hear a girl's voice, "Come play with me!"

The voice was very soft, not more than a breath, but in the weird silence of the forest, they all heard it clearly.

Phil opened his eyes again and saw Jon looking even more startled than himself. Jon was gazing, open-mouthed towards the trailer. Phil strained to see what was going on. The figure was still facing them but, to Phil's intense relief, the hushed invitation seemed to have distracted the dark terror from pursuing its interest in them.

"Come play," the girl urged again, her voice drifting to them like a gentle breeze, "Come on, I wanna play."

The strange creature tilted its head, as if in thought. Moments later, apparently decided, it began to turn away and Phil saw the bone dry skin pull back to reveal the awful smile, the rows of tiny, dagger teeth, glistening in the pale light. It was so dreadful a sight that, if Jon's hand had not still been over his mouth, Phil would have cried out then and given their position away.

Jon was still staring at the trailer. Phil sensed his agitation; Jon was tensing for a fight, or preparing to move. Suddenly Phil realised that Jon was preparing himself to attack the thing on the path. No! Phil could not let that happen. If this ugly critter gave their position away, they would both end up dead, no question. Phil readied himself as the whisper came again.

"Come on. I wanna play. I'm here. Come find me."

Next to him, Jon began to mutter.

"Where she? Where she?"

Jon was about to move, Phil thought. When the time came, Phil would have to act very quickly to stop him.

Suddenly, Jon gasped.

"She there," he whispered, "She in there."

Now everything happened at once.

The dark creature began to move, with terrifying speed, towards the trailer. Seeing it, Jon jumped to his feet and was about to give chase, but Phil tackled him and brought him crashing to the ground. The two men struggled, until they heard the click of a door handle: the Shadowman was climbing up into the trailer.

Time then seemed to slow to an imperceptible crawl.

Jon opened his mouth in a desperate, silent scream, his eyes huge and filled with tears. Phil turned and saw the fire beside the trailer flare up, its flames licking around the trailer door. In a frozen instant, the entire trailer was engulfed in a huge, broiling mass of fire, the explosion lifting the roof clean off, releasing a ball of dark smoke to slowly churn upwards into the sky.

Time quickened once more as a deafening wall of noise and rushing wind blasted over the two men, and the trailer roof crashed back to earth with a splintering thud.

The main body of the trailer was now a roaring inferno, flames jetting out of every opening and shooting high into the air.

Phil was delirious.

Jon was distraught.

Jon looked across at the man who was lying next to him, laughing ecstatically, and Jon punched him, very hard, in the stomach. Phil stopped laughing.

From the attic windows of the hotel, Jeff, Rita and Emma had witnessed the explosion. They could hear the continuing roar of the flames even from this distance and the dark cloud now hung low over the trees. Jeff and Rita exchanged glances. They had no idea what had happened and knew they would have to investigate.

Rita turned away from the window.

"Downstairs?"

Jeff nodded.

"Ready?"

"Yeah, let's get it over with."

"But we stay together, OK?"

Jeff nodded. He couldn't stand even the thought of being separated from these two again. He called Emma over and, together, they made their way downstairs.

35

Jon and Phil were limping back to the hotel.

There had been little point in staying where they were, as there was now very little remaining of the trailer. Several stacks of cut timber nearest to the ruined trailer were now ablaze, the snow cover melting and hissing away into steam.

Nothing could have survived.

Phil was nursing a pain in his guts and remained unclear as to why Jon had hit him. It was something to do with a girl Jon now claimed to have seen inside the trailer just before it blew up. As they stumbled along the path, Phil explained, over and over, that he hadn't seen anyone at the trailer window and that he'd been inside the trailer not long before and it had been quite empty. But, despite Phil's repeated protestations, Jon remained downcast and inconsolable.

Slowly descending the main staircase, Jeff and Rita were walking protectively on either side of Emma. Jeff had felt uncomfortable passing the door of the last bedroom, knowing that Neil's butchered body lay in there. Down here in the lobby, it was now Rita's turn to feel uneasy.

"It was standing right here," she whispered, "Then it came creeping up the stairs towards me, until Jon goaded it into chasing him instead. He was insanely brave, really amazing, and his speech, you wouldn't believe it. Maybe it came back to him because of the heightened emotion or the stress of the situation, I don't know."

"Weird. Did h-"

"Shh!"

Jeff looked around.

"What is it?"

"I heard something."

They huddled together, listening hard.

"There it is again."

They all heard it: a slow, grating squeak. It seemed to come from somewhere close by and, to their dismay, it was followed by the sound of careful footsteps, creeping towards them. Something was obviously trying to make as little sound as possible on the polished wooden floors. They nervously tightened their grips on each other: the footsteps were getting closer.

Suddenly Dave's head appeared cautiously around the corner of the corridor. Initially he looked as shocked as they were, but then he broke into a huge grin. Delighted to see them all safe, he ran towards them and gave each of them a bear hug. He reserved his closest hug for Emma.

"God am I glad to see you safe, kiddo. Rita, let me tell you, this girl here is just about as brave as it's possible to be. I mean, she stood up to the scary SOB who attacked me and trussed me up like some prize turkey. She was fearless. She gave him hell."

Emma smiled awkwardly, unused to such effusive praise.

"Don't you be shy girl," Dave lifted her chin, "You're a hero. You hold your head up high."

They all laughed with relief and held on to each other until the laughter subsided.

"Did you hear the explosion?" Jeff asked Dave.

"Yeah, what was it? Hey, where's Jon? We came here together, anyone seen him?"

Rita told him how Jon had taunted the Shadowman.

"He saved our lives, Dave. It was so brave, what he did."

Emma looked up.

"Dave, did you and Jon set up explosives as a trap?" she asked.

Dave shook his head.

"I'd like to say yes. It would have been so cool to lure that SOB into a trap, but no; we came straight here. What blew up? Was it a car, or some sort of fuel store?"

"Of course!" Jeff exclaimed. "I must have been disoriented, seeing things from up in the attic. The explosion was at the trailer!"

Dave frowned.

"Trailer?"

"Yeah; Spielman's trailer."

"Hey, where is the old guy?"

Jeff and Emma fell silent as Rita told Dave how Spielman had died fighting the Shadowman down in the basement, buying them time to escape.

"So the old timer was one of the good guys. Poor old Spielman."

They all nodded but, before Dave could ask about remaining members of the party, Jeff spoke up.

"Look, I'm sorry, but can this wait? We don't know what's happened in that explosion. The Shadowman could be back here again soon. He's after the kids."

Rita squeezed Emma's hand.

"But we're not gonna let the bastard even get close, are we?"

"How about you stay here with Emma," Dave suggested, "while Jeff and I go check out this trailer?"

"That's a very kind, if rather sexist offer, Dave, but

we've decided to stick together from now on, no matter what."

"All for one? That's cool. OK, shall we go?"

As they turned to leave, a dishevelled figure appeared in the doorway, silhouetted against the light. It spoke.

"We killed it," the voice was hoarse, but familiar, "Any chance of a drink?"

It was Phil.

Jeff was amazed.

"Killed it? What, the Shadowman?"

"The what?"

"Tall, dark, face like a skull."

"Yup. That's the guy. Blew him to smithereens. Now, how about that drink?"

"Phil, you said 'we'; was Jon with you?"

"Yeah. He's outside."

Rita broke away from the group and went to the shattered doorway to call Jon in. He needed encouragement, but eventually he agreed. At that moment, the door behind the reception desk fell off its remaining hinge and everyone gasped as Spielman emerged from the wreckage, smiling and well.

"Mr Spielman," Emma shrieked, "you're alive!"

"Am I? Well, sure is a comfort t'hear that."

Rita smiled.

"How did you get away from the Shadowman?"

"I don't rightly know, ma'am. I had ma gun aimed at the door, jus' waitin' til it pushed its way in. I woulda shot it fulla lead. But somethin' musta distracted it, cus it jus' upped and went."

Spielman's smile froze when he caught sight of Jon stepping through the remains of the front doorway. His hand closed on the gun in his pocket.

"Ain't that the wild man yuh met in the forest ma'am?"

"Yes he is and he saved our lives, and he's got the others safe back in his cave, so please put away your gun and come say hello."

Once Jon and Phil had convinced the others of the Shadowman's death in the explosion, they all retired to the basement for some much-needed food and drink.

Over steaming cups of coffee and hot chocolate, they swapped their survival stories and eventually Dave asked the question that Rita and Jeff had been dreading.

"Anyone know what happened to Neil? Not that I care, you understand. That boat had definitely sailed."

"He's dead Dave."

"Ah."

Dave fell silent for a moment and, all around the kitchen table, people stared down into their cups, waiting to take their lead from him.

"Was it quick?"

"Yeah, think it must have been."

"You don't know? Was no one with him? He was alone?"

Rita nodded.

Dave again lapsed into silence.

"D'you know where his body is? Would you be able to find it again?" Dave forced a smile, "Because Neil wouldn't have wanted to be seen dead out in the wilderness."

Others round the table smiled sympathetically.

"Dave," Jeff said gently, "he's upstairs; in one of the bedrooms."

"He died in his bed?"

Jeff shook his head.

"I'd like to go see him, to say goodbye."

"I really don't think you should, Dave," Rita said quietly, "It must have been quick; there's a hell of a lot of blood and...stuff," her voice failed her.

Dave understood. He got to his feet. He needed some air.

"Think I'll just take a minute if that's OK."

"Sure," said Rita, "Want some company?"

Dave shook his head and left them. The others watched him go in silence.

Jeff was the first to speak.

"So, is that everyone accounted for, except Laura? Has anyone seen her?"

"Can't say, son. What's she look like?"

Jeff frowned and looked across at Rita. She had raised her eyebrows in a similarly questioning frown, no doubt sharing the same thought: how could Spielman not know what Laura looked like, if he'd really been as close to the Cousins family as he claimed?

"Laura, Mr Spielman," Rita prompted, "The Cousins's daughter?"

Spielman's weather-beaten face creased into deeper, angry furrows.

"This some kinda joke? Cus it ain't funny."

Phil looked from face to face.

"Am I missing something? What's going on?"

"I don't know, Phil," said Jeff, "Why don't you enlighten us, Spielman?"

"Huh?"

"How is it you don't know what Laura looks like? Memory failing you? Or is it that you've not been quite straight with us?"

A worrying thought occurred to Rita.

"Mr Spielman, why didn't the Shadowman attack you, down in the basement?"

"That's a good question," said Jeff, becoming increasingly animated, "It rips Neil to pieces, but you, it leaves unharmed, just wanders off for no reason. Isn't that what you said?"

"I don't like yuh tone, son. An' I ain't answerin' no more o' yur damn fool questions."

Spielman made to rise from his seat, but Jeff grabbed at him and pushed him back down.

"Phil, get his gun!"

Phil paled.

"He's got a gun?"

"Yeah, in that pocket."

"What the Sam Hill d'yuh think yur doin'? That gun don't leave ma side. Give it back t'me."

Rita tried to calm the situation.

"We just need to ask you a few questions, Mr Spielman. We have to be sure, after everything that's happened. You can understand that can't you?"

Held down by Jeff and Phil, Spielman was in no position to argue, so he grimaced and remained silent. Jeff then opened his mouth to speak, but Rita stopped him: she thought it would be better if she put the questions.

"What we want to know, Mr Spielman, is how it is that you don't know what the Cousins' daughter looks like?"

"I never said I didn't. 'Course I know what their little girl looked like -"

"Looked?" Jeff interrupted, "Looked? Past tense? Are you telling us Laura's dead?"

"What are yuh talkin' about? Yuh know damn well she's dead. I told yuh I bin helpin' her poor ma find her killer for years."

"No, Mr Spielman," Rita spoke now in a gently encouraging tone, "we're talking about the second daughter."

The old man was clearly mystified.

"There ain't no second daughter."

"Yes, there is," Rita insisted, "I've seen her. She was

467

here, right here in this room, before all this started."

"Ma'am, I can't say who yuh seen an' who yuh ain't, but I'm tellin' yuh Karen's little girl, Laura, has bin dead twenty-four years an' I ain't never seen no other girl here at the hotel, not in all those years."

"Wait," Rita said, remembering, "there's a picture of Laura on the wall behind the reception desk."

"But -" Spielman started.

"Please let me show you, Mr Spielman. I'll just get it."

Rita hurried up to the lobby. The photo had been knocked from the wall, but it was unbroken, even the glass in the frame was intact. Rita carried it carefully down to the kitchen and showed it to Spielman.

"That's her," she said, pointing, "That's their second daughter."

"No ma'am. That there's Laura: their first daughter, their only daughter, their only ever child. An' I'm tellin' yuh, that poor girl's bin dead twenty-four years."

There was an awkward silence, while everyone tried to grasp what was being said. Then Phil spoke.

"So, do we give him his gun back?"

Neither Jeff nor Rita answered him. They were both too confused.

Jon had been sitting away from the table, below one of the windows. Now he looked up. He took in the baffled faces and the uncertain silence, and wandered over to investigate. He glanced down at the photo, and paused.

"She in trailer," he said sadly.

"What?" Rita asked, "When?"

Phil thought he'd answer on Jon's behalf.

"When we were in the forest, hiding from the the...er"

"Shadowman?"

"Thank you Emma, when we were hiding from the Shadowman...Jon says he could see a girl at the window of the trailer. But I looked and I'm telling you, there was no girl, really, there was no girl in that trailer."

"She in trailer, this girl," Jon again insisted.

He jabbed at the photo.

But Phil was equally insistent.

"I'm telling you, there was no girl."

Jon rounded on him.

"You hear her?"

Phil smiled nervously and that was enough confirmation for Jon.

"You hear her, yes."

"What does he mean, Phil? What did you hear?"

Phil sighed.

"Just before the Shadow guy went into the trailer, there was this weird noise, like the wind. I guess it kinda sounded a bit like a voice."

Jon nodded.

"Voice, yes. Hear voice. This girl voice"

"All the way back here, he kept on and on saying that he'd seen this girl and she'd been calling to the Shadow guy. Kinda luring him to the trailer, I guess."

"She in trailer. Evil go in trailer. Trailer..."

Jon moved his arms up and out, miming the explosion.

"She dead in trailer."

Everyone looked blank, uncertain how to react. Jon was once again overcome with sadness. He went back to his chair by the window and turned his back on those watching him from the table.

Rita turned to Spielman.

"You see? He's seen her too, and now the poor girl's dead."

Spielman decided to try to convince Jeff.

"Look, son, I know yuh say he's saved lives an' all, but I don't think yuh friend over there's altogether right in the head. Know what I mean?"

Phil nodded.

"I'm with the old guy on that."

"Phil! You're not helping," Rita snapped.

"Oh yeah? Well, way I see it, this is the old guy's word against the weird guy's."

"No, Phil, I saw her too. I saw her right here in this goddam room."

"OK, so it you and the weird guy's word against the old guy, and me."

"You?"

"Yeah, I told you: I was there when that trailer went up and I looked at the windows. There was no girl!"

"Can everyone please just chill?" it was Emma, "It's no use you arguing this out now. Wait till the Cousins get back and ask them."

"Emma's right," said Jeff, "We'll wait till the road's open. Everything will get sorted out then."

"Except the Cousins won't be coming back."

"Phil? What d'you mean?"

"They're dead. On the track into town. I found their pickup last night."

"Shit."

"Yeah, both either been dragged out or flung out in an accident. It wasn't pretty."

In the stunned silence that followed, they became aware of a small, stifled squeaking: the old man was weeping quietly, huge tears tumbling down the wrinkled leather of his face, dripping from his chin, to form dark stains on his old, tattered shirt.

To see this old man weeping so inconsolably was awful. Rita felt tears stinging at her own eyes in sympathy. Emma tried not to look at Spielman at all: it was too dreadful when old people cried. She hugged her father close. Jeff let his hand slip from Spielman's shaking shoulders. He returned Emma's hug. Phil turned the act of holding the old man down, into a consoling hand on the shoulder, an awkward gesture of comfort.

They all stayed like this for several moments until Spielman's weeping subsided into downcast silence.

Jon had watched all this and now came over to Rita, drawing her to one side, away from the table.

"Girl in trailer, yes."

"I don't know, Jon. I don't know what to think, but at least we know that the Shadowman is dead now."

Jon frowned.

"Sorry," Rita spoke more simply, "I said we know Shadowman is dead."

Jon looked around to see that no one else was listening. Phil, who had casually watched Rita cross the room, took the hint and turned away. Jon then spoke to Rita in an urgent whisper.

"Many years, long time, I kill Shadowman. He kill girl, I kill him. But him body not stay dead. Put in ground, but body gone away."

"What? You buried him and his body disappeared?"

"Disappeared, gone, yes."

"Shit...Are you sure he was dead?"

"Yes. He dead. I...smash head with shovel."

Words failed him, so Jon mimed raising the shovel and smashing it down again. As he did so, the sound of the shattering skull and liquifying brain filled Jon's head, just as it had all those years before. He felt nauseous.

"Are you OK?"

Jon focused on Rita's face and the awful memories and sounds began to fade. He nodded, but said nothing..

"Was that after he killed Laura?"

Jon looked at her with incomprehension.

Rita went to get the photo.

"Is that her? Did you kill the Shadowman when he killed this girl?"

471

"No. I kill Shadowman when he kill girl not her."

Rita tried to understand.

"Suzie Bower was killed before Laura. Jon, did you kill the Shadowman because he killed Suzie?"

"Suzie, yes. Shadowman kill Suzie. I kill Shadowman. Smash head with shovel. But him body not stay dead in ground. Body gone away."

"Are you sure you killed him?"

"Yes."

"But his body disappeared?"

"Yes."

"And twenty years later he killed Laura. Is that right?"

"Shadowman kill Laura, yes."

Rita didn't know what to say. She looked at Jon. He was sincere; she was certain of that. At the very least he believed absolutely that what he had told her was the truth, but Rita couldn't make sense of it.

Phil called her, interrupting her train of thought.

"So, can we let the old guy go now?"

"Yeah...I guess...Sorry, Mr Spielman."

Allowed to move again, the old man wiped his nose with the back of his hand then wiped his wet hand on the frayed sleeve of his shirt. Ignoring the disgusted looks of the others at the table, he then grunted with irritation, pulled the gun from Phil's hand and rammed it back into his own pocket. Glowering, he pushed his chair back and got up from the table. His face was set in the deepest, most sullen frown: it was clear that he would need some placating.

"Tell you what, Spielman," said Phil, rubbing his hands together, "How about I get you a drink?"

Spielman snorted angrily.

"Don't know if I wanna accept no drinks after I bin treated so bad."

"When I feel that bad, I turn to my friends."

"Yeah? Well I ain't got none."

"No problem. Lucky for you, I have an old friend I think you'll get on with just fine."

Spielman looked dubious and even Jeff and Rita wondered where Phil was going with this.

"Yeah, an old friend of mine," Phil winked, "goes by the name of Jack Daniels."

Spielman looked at him for a few seconds in silence.

"Yur an idiot!" he said finally.

"You want that drink or not?"

Spielman continued to grumble, but he nevertheless followed when Phil went upstairs and into the bar.

Jeff looked across at Rita.

"What are you thinking?"

"That Spielman was overly generous. I'd have gone for moron at least."

Jeff smiled.

"I meant, are you OK?"

"Hmm, yeah, I guess. There's just been too much going on tonight. I can't get my head straight."

"Want to talk about it?"

Rita didn't answer. She looked down at Emma, who was resting her head on her father's shoulder. They both looked so content, that Rita couldn't help but smile.

"What?" Jeff asked.

"Nothing. It's just good to see you two together like that. Em, keep an eye on your old dad for a few minutes will you?"

Emma gave Rita a thumbs up.

"Thanks. OK, think I'm going to get some air. Don't worry I won't go far. I'll probably just sit out on the stoop."

As Rita passed the office, she glanced in and saw Dave sitting at the desk, reading some of the papers.

"Hi."

"Hi yourself."

"Feeling any better?"

"Well I've decided to take your advice and not go see Neil, or what's left of him. I think that's the right decision for me now; I'm kinda confused about my feelings for the man, y'know? I mean, he treated me and, let's face it, the rest of you, his oldest friends, like so much dog poop on his Ferragamos, so I feel mad about that. But he died all alone, and I feel bad about that. I guess the thing that makes me the saddest though, is that no one really cares that he's dead. I'm not blaming you, or the rest of them, but it's sad that no one's really gonna miss him."

Rita rubbed Dave's arm.

"Don't worry," he said, "I'm OK, really I am. But I just can't believe how things have changed so much in just a few days. I mean, I really thought Neil was the one. I'd have done anything for him and I wonder, if we hadn't come here, and all this crap hadn't happened, how long would we have been together?"

"You really wanna know?"

"You're gonna tell me like months, right?"

Rita shook her head.

"Days?"

"I don't know what Neil told you but, Dave, he never stayed with anyone longer than maybe four months in all the time I've known him. Sorry."

Rita turned her attention to the papers littering the desk and tried to distract Dave from thoughts of Neil by telling him what she, Neil and Jeff had discovered in the documents. She was telling him about the Boes and was so involved in trying to remember all the details, that she didn't notice Jon standing at the door, watching her. Rita paused, wondering what he wanted. He surely couldn't have understood what she'd been saying. She waited for him to speak.

Jon waved a hand around the room.

"What is?"

"These are papers to do with the Shadowman and the killings."

Jon nodded, but Rita wasn't sure if he'd understood. Dave and Rita watched him go around the room opening books and examining folders, an incongruous sight, in his animal skins. Rita thought he might be mocking them with his studious air; it was unlikely that he could read any of it. However, when Jon opened one particular drawer, he had no need of reading.

It was obvious that something in the drawer had caught his attention. He reached in and carefully lifted out a small ziplock bag. He held it up to look more closely at its contents. Rita could make out a scrap of material inside the bag. She leant forward and took a cutting from the drawer.

"What's it say?" Dave asked.

"It's a cutting from the Losien Gazette, dated Wednesday, September 18, 1946."

LILAC LADY LAID TO REST

> With still no clues as to the identity of the so-called Lilac Lady, whose badly decomposed body was found near the disused grain silos at Drover's Creek, on June 15, a brief committal service was held today at the Havenlea Cemetery, Losien. Sheriff Mason Daniels, present at the interment, told this reporter

```
          that the file on this Jane Doe
          remains open at this time.
```

Rita showed the cutting to Dave.

"I think Neil must have read this, though I'm sure I remember him saying that the dead girl had something to do with lilies, not lilac."

"Easy mistake. Anything else in that drawer?"

"Scraps of what looks like a brown paper bag, or an envelope."

"That's it?"

"Yeah, there's writing on some of the scraps: looks like 'LPD'."

"PD could be 'Police Department'. It's probably the original bag that they kept that scrap of material in. No ziplocks back then."

"I guess. Wonder why they kept it. Jon, could I see that?"

But Jon didn't reply and when Rita looked up, she saw that he staring at the scrap of material as if it meant the world to him, and he was crying.

"Jon, what's the matter? Jon, what is it?"

But Jon just kept on crying. He couldn't put his feelings into words. He couldn't say how he felt: he wasn't sure himself. But, seeing this tiny scrap of his mother's skirt after more than fifty years, telescoped his life and pulled him back to that day when the ugly, unloved and very lonely little boy watched the pretty lady walk away from him forever.

Rita went over to Jon and, ignoring his pungent body odour, put her arm around his shoulder. Jon didn't react. From the distant look on his face it was clear that he was far away and Rita could only guess at what was on his mind. What did this remnant mean to him? She had so many questions, but how was she to phrase them in words that he could understand? She could see the cloth in detail now. It was slightly faded in one corner, but was clearly a shiny, lilac material: satin perhaps. And it held obvious, overwhelming importance for Jon.

They stayed like this for many minutes, until Jon raised his head. He looked into Rita's eyes, pleading. He wanted information. Rita bit her lip. Should she lie about the cutting? Was it kinder to tell him what she had read, or to leave him with uncertainty? She dragged her gaze from Jon and looked to Dave for advice.

"You have to tell him," Dave said, without her even having to ask.

"OK," Rita took a deep breath, "Here's the thing. Many years, long, long time, someone kill girl."

Jon was looking at her, but said nothing.

"Girl dead, Jon. And this," Rita touched the bag containing the lilac cloth, "with dead girl. Do you understand?"

Jon understood only too well. He reached back into his memory for the words.

"Ma say she go to West, but no. This girl, Jon Ma. Ma dead."

"She was your mother? Oh Jon, I'm so sorry."

Jon straightened and Rita felt he wanted her to let go of his shoulder. He was a proud man; he was going to deal with this in his own way. She dropped her arm and eased away from him.

"I go," he said.

"You want I go with you?"

"No. You stay. Jeff go with."

"Oh, OK."

Rita was surprised and a little hurt that Jon would prefer to have Jeff's support at this difficult time. But it was for Jon to choose and she had to accept that.

"Wait here, Jon. I'll get him for you."

She had explained the situation to Jeff before he came into the room. He couldn't understand why Jon wanted his help; Jeff wasn't someone to whom people routinely turned for support and advice. But then, these last few days had changed so much else, so why not this?

"What can I do?" he asked, "How can I help?"

"We go."

"Right. Where?"

Jon looked at Jeff as if expecting some insight to dawn. When none did, he explained.

"You, Jon, go cave. Children go to here."

Jeff was rather taken aback. So he was still not the person to whom people turned for advice and support, but he wasn't too downhearted; he was now the person to whom people turned when they needed a strong man, an adventurer. He felt rather good about himself and Rita read the smugness of his grin with ease.

"Earth calling Indiana. Come in please, Professor Jones."

But Jeff ignored her jibe; his thrill at being part of some elite could not be dispelled so easily. He had been chosen by the expert, the man who had lived years in the forest, to accompany him on a mission: a rescue mission no less! Now that the threat of harm to his loved ones was over, the danger thankfully passed, Jeff had begun to imagine how news of these last few days would be received by others on their return. Specifically, he had begun to wonder how the students and academics of his college would react. His selection by Jon to accompany him on this final trip played into Jeff's daydream beautifully. He fondly imagined his students bragging to their peers about him, the coolest Prof on campus. And the anticipated envy of Jeff's faculty colleagues would, if anything, be even more satisfying.

"Don't get too cocky," Rita chided, "If you're going,

just walk where Jon walks and do exactly what he tells you. And Indie?"

Jeff nodded.

"Take care of yourself."

"I will."

"You're hopeless."

"I love you too."

It took only a half hour to gather food and extra clothes to take for the children. Jon and Jeff were now ready to leave and were saying their good byes.

"You sure you're OK leaving Emma?" Rita asked, "I'm happy to go with Jon if you'd rather stay here with her."

"No. I know she'll be fine: you'll be with her. And, yes, I do now realise that I was in fact probably Jon's last choice for this trip: he won't let either Dave or Spielman go, because they're wounded, and he won't let you, because he thinks Emma needs you. But I want to do this. Is that OK?"

"Sure. No problem. Go have fun."

"What I can't understand is why Jon didn't ask Phil to go with him."

They both looked across to where Phil, who had spent the few hours since dawn drinking an interesting assortment of spirits, was now slumped in an armchair, snoring loudly, an empty bottle cradled at his elbow.

"No," Rita agreed, "I can't figure that one either."

Rita waved Jon and Jeff to the edge of the clearing and then wandered back into the office. Dave was still reading at the desk, surrounded by mounds of paper.

Rita flicked through the stack of medical reports, but she wasn't reading them; she was thinking over those she'd read earlier.

"Dave?"

"Yeah."

"I've been thinking...Remember Henry Boe, the guy whose shrink said he spoke in the third person and was unconsciously identifying with his father who beat him?"

"Yes, I remember."

"Well, I think they got it wrong. Jeff found Ezra's version of events, in some documents from his asylum on California. Turns out that, in the earlier papers, Henry wasn't talking about how his own father treated him, he was talking about how he, Henry, treated his son, Ezra.

"Here, this is the one," she continued, "Yes, here, Henry says, 'He carved black magic figures: evil, wicked things'. See? He was talking about Ezra. I think Ezra was carving these dolls. And look here, Henry goes on, 'He was trying to catch my God-given immortal soul...but I stopped him. I stopped him good. I beat him till he was red raw.' Ezra was making these dolls and Henry thought it was something to do with Voodoo, so he beat the crap out of the poor kid. Jeez, I can't believe I ever felt sorry for the guy. And something Jeff said, about monsters not being born but created, made me wonder how Ezra would have turned out if his father had treated him better. Henry was horribly cruel to him."

"But Henry was beaten by his own parents when he was a child. His only friend, the maid, was sent away and then he was orphaned. No wonder he was messed up. Doesn't he deserve your sympathy too?"

"OK," Rita conceded, "so Henry was screwed up by his parents. But why didn't that make him determined not to do the same to his own son?"

Dave sighed, put down the papers he was reading and turned his attention to Rita. He smiled but, when he spoke, his tone was subdued.

"You act like people are rational beings, Rita, when

everything I see tells me that they're not. Maybe Ezra only started carving his dolls because he was a little boy who liked dolls and he didn't have a sister with Barbies he could borrow. But Henry wouldn't necessarily have understood why his son was carving dolls to play with; don't forget that attitudes were very different back then. God knows, things aren't that great now, but back then..." he rolled his eyes, "Also Henry had grown up alone, with only the maid -"

"Gloria Mercy."

"Yeah, great name, by the way. She seems to have been the only person to feature in his life but, fantastic name aside, she didn't do young Henry a whole lotta good. She filled his head with superstition and nightmares and it was probably because of his childhood indoctrination that Henry later saw Ezra's wooden dolls as black magic, when, all the time, his little boy probably just wanted to play with dolls."

Rita nodded.

"Yeah, that makes sense. And I guess it wouldn't have mattered how much Ezra might have tried to say that he just liked dolls to play with, because, like Henry says here, 'The evil one puts lies into the mouth of the boy. You gotta beat that Devil outa him.' That must have been one difficult childhood: no wonder Ezra was affected. Even if his Dad hadn't been a voodoo freak, society as a whole wasn't ready to accept difference back then. Ezra couldn't have explained how he felt. He couldn't have made Henry understand."

They fell silent for a moment, then Dave spoke quietly.

"If you are the little boy who likes to play with dolls, believe me, there aren't any words you can use to explain; because you instinctively know that those are precisely the words that your ma and pa don't ever want to hear."

Moved, Rita touched Dave's arm. But he brightened.

"It's OK. I got past my parents not understanding a long time ago. And anyway, I had my wonderful Aunt Sarah. And she was one cool lady...Maybe if Ezra had had someone like her in his life, things would have turned out different. The man's life was a tragedy."

"Oh, come on Dave. I feel real sorry for Ezra the kid, but Ezra the adult? No way. What he did was off the scale."

"No excuses?"

"None...Why? Can you excuse what he did to those kids?"

"God no! I'm not talking about excusing what he did, just explaining, wondering what might have been...Believe me, I'd be the last person to suggest that what Ezra did was the result of his sexuality. Best guess, I think maybe he did what he did because he was desperately lonely."

"Lonely?"

"Yeah, I know it sounds weird, but Ezra must have picked up some of what his father had heard from Gloria Mercy. He thought he could somehow bring his dad back from the dead by catching his soul in a doll...So I think he maybe started out wanting to preserve the children he kidnapped, to keep them as kids, as company for him forever. Anyhow, I'm just saying that, if as a kid he hadn't been so alone, if he'd had someone in his life who gave a shit about whether he lived or died, he might have made different choices and given himself different options. Or, at the very least, someone might have been close enough to him to spot the signs and maybe get him some help, or stop him, before anyone got hurt."

"You think too kindly of people, Dave. There aren't many who could find it in them to feel sorry for Ezra Boe."

"I can only do it because he's dead now. He's no longer a threat to anyone, just a nasty, rather pathetic little footnote in history."

"No. It's because you're a nice guy. You are. I always said you and Neil were an unlikely couple."

Even before she finished speaking, Rita regretted having begun. Now the sentence was out there and she couldn't take it back.

"Sorry Dave. Me and my big mouth."

"It's OK. Neil's someone else who might have made different choices if he'd had people around who cared."

Rita looked offended.

"No, I mean when he was a kid. Y'know, he never would talk about his childhood. Not a word. I don't know what caused it, but I reckon he started building walls against the world when he was a kid and then just forgot how to stop building. And he never let anyone inside the walls."

"Not even you?"

"No. I once made myself believe that he would, but no, Neil was only ever interested in Neil. You saw it with the kids. I just couldn't believe it: he really didn't care what happened to them. It wasn't just that he was frightened for himself. He had absolutely no feelings for those kids. Even if he'd somehow been given an absolute guarantee that no harm would come to him, I think he'd still have preferred to stay inside by the fire rather than go look for them. He'd have been just as happy to have the kids die or get saved; either way, he didn't actually care. It's like other people weren't real to him."

They lapsed into silence for a while.

"Did you come across anything new in here?" Rita asked.

"Yes, I did actually. There's a police report somewhere... Ah, here it is. It's from 1945, so Ezra would have been forty-three. He got himself into some trouble and was questioned by the Sheriff in a place called Ricoh.

I checked the map; it's a small farming community, about fifteen miles north east of Losien."

"What did he do?"

"The Sheriff, a Wilbur Walter Watts writes that, 'Ezra Boe arrived in Ricoh, in late September of 1945'. Ezra is described as, 'tall, pale and unusually thin'. Also he seems to have been sullen with 'an evil temper'. After wandering into town, Ezra took a menial job, working in the back room of the General Store. However, Sheriff WWW writes that Boe stayed at the store for less than a month before being given notice by the store's owner, a Mr Elwood P Hacker. Apparently Hacker's teenage daughter, Joanna, claimed that Ezra stared at her all the time and gave her the creeps. When the owner sacked him, Ezra apparently became violent and threatened both owner and daughter. The Sheriff was called, hence Ezra's mention in the records, and Ezra spent a night in the cells before being told to get out of town the next day. He drifted off out of Ricoh, and the report ends."

"The body of Jon's mother was found near Drover's Creek, just the other side of Losien, in early summer of the following year, 1946."

"It's possible, I guess: Ezra, probably still furious that he'd just been sacked from his job at the store, kills Jon's mom and then, somehow, gets to California and continues killing there. Only there, he's killing children. The only problem with that scheme is that Boe was arrested in 1950 and they reckoned he'd already been kidnapping kids for three years or so. How could he have got all the way across the country so quickly, from Drover's Creek all the way to California, when he had no job and presumably no money?"

"Well, before he left with Jon, Jeff found something about Ezra's first victim. Boe wouldn't give many details, but he did say that it had been an accident and he had taken her tickets and money. I think he meant Jon's mom, don't you?"

Dave shrugged.

"Don't suppose we'll ever know for sure, but it sounds likely."

They flicked through the papers in silence for a while. Rita wanted to talk over what Jon had told her and, as she scanned the papers, she mused over how she was going to raise the subject. In the end, she decided on the direct approach.

"Dave, do you believe in ghosts?"

"I'm sorry. Ghosts?"

"Yeah."

"I don't know exactly. Why d'you ask?"

"It's something Jon told me. He insists that he killed the Shadowman when the Shadowman killed Suzie Bower, which is like the late fifties."

"Right."

"So what d'you think?"

"I don't. I mean, I don't know what to think...Do you believe him?"

"I believe that he believes it."

"But the small matter of the Shadowman still being alive and killing for the forty years after that bothers you, does it?"

"Hmm."

Dave eased back in his chair and thought for a few moments before speaking

"I don't know Rita. Jon is certainly a somewhat strange individual, and his sartorial and personal hygiene standards are, to say the least, eccentric, but he's a very brave dude and he has a good heart. There's no way we'd have made it through the last twenty-four hours without him. So, if he chooses to believe that the Shadowman was some ghost, then I for one am happy to let him think it. The man's been living out in the forest for decades, as far as we can tell, completely alone. Heck, he's forgotten how to speak and he wears animal skins! He's bound to be a bit...different."

"So you don't think I should tell anyone?"

"Like who?"

Rita smiled.

"Good question."

"Yeah, well, hope that helps."

"It does. And you're right; who does it harm if Jon wants to believe in ghosts? His secret's safe with me."

It was still early morning when the snow returned. It began slowly with large flakes rocking gently to the ground, but soon smaller, more determined flakes were twirling quickly down, to add to the increasing depth of snow around the building.

Standing, shivering in the lobby, Rita took a few seconds to collect her thoughts. Only a half hour or so before this, as she waved Jeff goodbye, it had then seemed wildly incongruous to her that the gentle light of early morning was shining so prettily through the ragged, gaping doorway. Now the same view was of a total whiteout, with snow beginning to swirl in through the splintered gap to build up against the chairs and tables.

Rita was suddenly anxious for Jeff; the silly, vain, wonderful man. She could only hope that Jon would take good care of him. She composed her face into a confident smile before she went down to the others in the basement.

"It's snowing again."

"Dammit! Pard'n ma french."

"What's the matter, Mr Spielman?"

"Your friend Dave was gonna come with me to find Karen and John's bodies. I don't like t'think of them lyin' out there. Like t' give them a decent burial. But we need the snow to stop."

"It's very heavy at the moment, I'm afraid. But Mr Spielman, I'm not sure if you should bury them before they've been, y'know, examined for evidence, by detectives."

"Detectives! Huh, they couldn't find shit on their own shoes! Pard'n ma french. I watched them flyin' in their heliocopters. They poked and prodded and measured and wrote their goddam notes in their goddam notebooks, but they did never find the Shadowman, did they? Detectives? Shit!"

Rita wisely avoided the subject of detectives thereafter.

She had a busy morning. With Dave's help, she managed to get Phil back down to the basement from the bar, where the temperature was falling towards freezing. Phil now lay in one of the store rooms, snoring happily under a pile of blankets. Then Rita, Emma and Dave collected all the room keys scattered amongst the remains of the reception desk and went from room to room, emptying closets and gathering everyone's belongings. They dragged the crammed suitcases down to the basement and stacked them in the side rooms.

Seeing all the luggage piling up, Spielman grumbled. The old man had no clothes other than those he had on him; everything else he had owned in the world was presumed to have been consumed in the inferno. Rita found a few items that almost fitted him. She took them predominantly from Phil's suitcase, for the very good reasons that, not only was Phil the closest in size to the old man, but he was also fast asleep in an alcohol-induced stupor that would probably last for some time. Consequently Spielman was now sporting a rather jauntily oversized shirt and trouser combination that Phil had included in his packing against the possibility that the hotel might boast a discotheque. Rita was far from convinced that lime was a shade that flattered Spielman, but she decided not to share her sartorial reservations with him.

After his earlier spirited outburst, Spielman decided that he needed to take a nap. Checking in on him later, Rita was amused to see that the old man had taken the lime jacket off and carefully folded in to one side. He actually liked it. There was no accounting for taste.

The basement was not warm, but there was still gas in the cylinders, so they could warm themselves with hot drinks and food and later on, when the others returned, everyone would be able to bed down here. The thought of Neil's dismembered body in the bedroom nearest to the top of the stairs acted as a bar to all the upper floor rooms. Certainly no one would want to sleep up there.

36

Toward the end of the morning, the snowfall began to lessen. Jon, Jeff and the others were expected back by early afternoon so this easing of the weather was very welcome.

Rita and her assistants: Emma and Dave, were now busy, peeling vegetables and opening cans of food. Rather than help them prepare lunch, Phil decided that he would go back up to the bar, in spite of the cold. Thankfully, he had left the kitchen before Spielman emerged from his side room, resplendent in his borrowed lime green, ready to give helpful advice to the chefs.

It was just before three o'clock when Jeff and Jon led Annie, Bill, Lou and the children back into the hotel. They all stood for a moment, their faces betraying their shock at the state of the lobby.

"Dear Lord!" Annie gasped, "Thank goodness the children weren't here."

Bill nodded and lifted his sleeping son down from his shoulders.

Rita came up from the basement.

"Hi. We're all downstairs well, all except Phil; he's in the bar," she hesitated briefly before continuing, still in a bright voice, "Did Jeff get the chance to explain why we're all staying down there rather than in our own rooms?"

"Yes," said Mikey happily, "Jeff said it's 'cause it's an adventure."

Jeff knows how to handle kids, Rita thought with a smile.

"That's right," she said to Mikey, "So, come on, let's go down and have us a feast. I guess you must be starving."

"Not really," said Annie, "You'd be amazed, but we were really comfortable in Jon's cave. Now that really was an adventure!"

"Oh it's so good to see you, Annie," Rita hugged her, "Come on down and tell me everything."

Rita led the way, but saw that Lou was holding back. She had Ethan asleep in her arms and was looking through the opened door of the bar to where Phil could be seen, leaning against the counter, oblivious to their arrival. It seemed to Rita that the wistful look on Lou's face held an element of disdain with the regret.

"Lou," she called, "we brought all your stuff down from your room so there's everything you need for Ethan. Will you come down with us?"

Lou took one last look at Phil and then followed Rita and the others down to the basement.

Once in the kitchen, food was passed around and everyone chatted, relaxed and happy, grateful to have this time with friends after the awful dangers they had so recently faced.

After an hour or so, the conversation slackened and when Mikey let out a loud yawn, beds were made up in the side rooms so the children could rest after their tiring trek through the snow. The adults then had the opportunity to talk over the worst of their experiences, albeit in hushed voices so as not to disturb the now sleeping children. Looking along the table at the familiar faces, Jeff was initially surprised to see that Emma was still sitting here, with the adults, but then he decided that this was the appropriate place for her. She had endured a great deal and he couldn't now go back to treating her as a child, no matter how much he might wish it were otherwise. Events had forced a change in their relationship and Emma might need to take this opportunity to talk things through. Emma caught him looking at her and smiled back at him. Jeff was immensely proud of her in that moment: she had been though hell and yet could still smile for him.

Rita, Dave and Spielman were explaining what they had read in the papers in the office. Listening, Bill, Annie and Lou were ashen when Spielman told them that Boe had intended to kill their children. As he listed all the deaths for which he blamed Boe, Rita was relieved that the old man neglected to give precise dates, so Bill, Annie and Lou couldn't calculate Boe's supposed age; Rita didn't feel able to have that conversation here and now. It was a subject that she felt should be spoken of only once they were far away from this forest and its ancient secrets.

When Spielman began to flag, the conversation turned to trying to piece together the sequence of events that had culminated in the Shadowman's death in the explosion. It became clear that they were missing some pieces of the puzzle.

"Emma," Rita asked, "How did you and the others get to the cave?"

Emma looked uncomfortable, but Annie replied on her behalf.

"Lisa said they went to the cave with Laura. That's right, isn't it, Emma?"

"I don't know...I wasn't with them."

"I'm sorry?"

"Dad," Emma took a deep breath, "I'm really sorry,

but I did a really dumb thing: I arranged to meet the Shadowman."

Jeff was dumbfounded.

"What? When?"

"I met him in the forest and I so wanted him to think I was mature and, like, y'know, sophisticated. So I told you I didn't feel well and I sneaked out while you were all having supper. He was really cool at first, but that changed when I sneaked out...After that he was horrible to me and he just wanted me to get the other kids for him. Oh Dad, I'm so, so sorry."

Jeff remained quiet for a few moments and Rita was just about to intervene and break the silence, when he spoke.

"Em," he said, "everybody gets to do some dumb things sometime in their lives and you don't need me to tell you that what you did was really, really dumb; you said it yourself. But that's over and done, OK? Learn from it so you don't repeat it, then let it go.

"Dave told us how you behaved when that monster was threatening him, and Bill told me you saved his life. I am so proud of you, I can't tell you."

Jeff had tears in his eyes as he looked at Emma. And she saw in him a new person; rather than the man who tried to act as he thought he should, say what he thought he should, the man busy trying to be the 'good' parent, who planned years into the future, but missed what was happening right in front of him, her Dad had, for perhaps the first time, dealt with things as they were, not as he would have preferred them to be. He had reacted to what was important right now and given something of himself. And he'd actually said he was proud of her. Feeling absolutely elated, she reached across the table to gently touch his hand.

Around the table the adults exchanged smiles and, for

a few moments, no one spoke. Then Bill looked up.

"Just a minute," he said, "Where's Laura?"

At first no one wanted to speak.

"Well? Doesn't anyone know where she is?"

"It's a bit weird," Rita began."

"Weird? What d'you mean?"

"Y'know I saw her here, and then later, from the window, with the kids?"

"Yeah."

"Well Jon is certain that he saw her in the trailer just before it blew."

"What!"

"But Phil was there too," Rita went on quickly, "and he swears she wasn't in the trailer."

"Yeah, well I think I know who I'd believe," Bill was appalled, "How can you all just sit here and not do anything to find out what's happened to this kid?"

"It's not that simple, Bill. This is the weird part; Mr Spielman here says the Cousins only ever had one daughter, Laura, and she died -"

Spielman cut in.

"Twenty-four years ago."

"Let me get this straight," Bill spoke slowly, "Are you trying to tell me that you think Laura -"

"Is a ghost!" Emma cut in, "Cool!"

No one said anything for several minutes. The friends sat around the table, each assiduously avoiding any eye contact with the others. They had no idea how to continue the conversation; it was as Rita had said, weird. It was all too weird.

Finally it was Spielman who broached the subject.

"Round here Folks know about the forest; they jus' gotta feelin' 'bout the place. It's parta their lives. But mostly they keep out, an' they think I'm a crazy man for livin' here like I do," he sighed, "So, if y'all can't take it, then just forget about it when yuh go back t'yuh homes in the city. Yuh don't have t'believe. It's not a part of yuh lives. Yuh can leave it behind when yuh go."

"How can you say that, Mr Spielman?" Annie asked in amazement, "What's happened here has changed us for ever. I know I'll never be the same again. And I just thank God that the kids were taken away from here and kept safe, so I don't care if Laura's real or not; I don't have to believe in ghosts or not. What I know for sure is, that girl saved my kids, and she saved Lou's son, and we will always bless her memory for that."

Bill patted Annie's hand and nodded his agreement.

Jeff looked across at Rita. He couldn't read her face. He had no idea what she was thinking. Come to that, he had no idea what he was thinking himself. He shrugged.

"More coffee anyone?" he asked.

The noise built quite slowly. Jon was the first to hear it. He was immediately alert and Rita sensed his anxiety.

"Jon, what's wrong?"

"Something coming. Something big."

All the adults were on their feet in an instant. All save Lou. She stayed in her seat at the table and began to rock back and forth.

"No more. No more," she muttered, "It's over, you said it was over."

"It near," said Jon, "You hear it?"

Rita strained to hear and there it was; she heard, or rather, she felt it: a low throbbing. As she listened, the vibration built, until the ground was trembling beneath their feet. Looking at one another, they were baffled. Then Emma cried out.

"A helicopter! It's a helicopter!"

The noise was unmistakable now and they all rushed up the stairs, spilling out into the lobby as the helicopter rocked to a stop in the clearing. The whine of the rotor blades died away and a man jumped down. Crouching low, he ran towards the building but, as he stepped up to the remains of the front doors, he paused.

"What the heck happened here?"

He looked in at the huddled group watching him from the snowdrift-filled lobby and it was clear from his face that he was now on his guard. He hadn't been expecting any trouble here; this was supposed to be a routine rescue and retrieval. Rita stepped forward and smiled.

"Hi there," she called, "Sorry about the mess. If we'd known you were coming..."

The pilot frowned for a moment but eventually returned her smile. He looked from face to face. These folks had endured some bad weather out here, and then some, but they seemed friendly enough.

"I've come to get you out of here," he told them, "There's a forecast lull in the weather and the cloud cover's improved, but it's only temporary and we don't have much time before it closes in again."

Heads nodded.

"D'you have any injured?"

Given the state of the lobby he thought he'd better ask and, as he'd been in search and rescue for a few years, he was prepared for Jeff's answer.

"Two injured. Three dead."

But he wasn't prepared for the clarification.

"Murdered: one definitely, the other two, possibly."

The man took a step back, clicked a button on his radio and called for some extra back up.

He was obviously nervous and he signalled to his buddy in the helicopter to stay where he was and, presumably, be ready to lift off again at a moment's notice. That done he now stood, framed in what was left of the doorway, and waited for confirmation from his

495

Control. Jeff decided to ease the tension by engaging the man in conversation but, without thinking, he took a step forward and the man immediately took another step back. Jeff put up both hands in apology, stepped back into line with the others and put on his most winning smile.

"Can't tell you how good it is to see someone from the outside world," he called cheerfully, "How did you know we were here and needed help?"

In spite of his need for caution, the man replied.

"My sister-in-law."

Jeff tried to compose his face, but he really had no idea how to interpret what the pilot had said.

"Right...And she knew, how?"

"She works in the diner, in town. Told my wife that she'd had some outsiders comin' through, on their way out here, just before the snow set in. Said we'd better check on you folks on accounta she had the idea that y'all," and at this point he thought it judicious to modify the terms his sister-in-law had actually used, "maybe weren't used to life outside the big city."

The radio crackled and the man visibly relaxed on hearing the confirmation that additional help was already on its way. He relaxed further, when he saw Lisa and Mikey appear at the top of the stairs. He liked kids; had three of his own, and he couldn't help but smile when Lisa and Mikey caught sight of the helicopter.

"Aw cool!" they shrieked, almost in unison.

They couldn't believe their luck: they'd had the wildest, most exciting holiday ever and now it looked like they were going to finish it off with a trip in a helicopter! Unable to contain their excitement, they began to jump up and down, whooping and laughing, dancing through the powdery snow on the lobby floor. The children's obvious joy, and the thump, thump, thump of the approaching helicopter, finally had everyone smiling. Even Lou joined in the sense of relief; emerging from the basement staircase with Ethan in her arms, into a crazy, but happy scene.

The pilot asked for a list of names and told everyone to gather just their essentials since, even with two helicopters, space was going to be limited. A man from the second aircraft showed them his badge and asked about the presumed murder victims. It rapidly became clear to him that their story was more complicated than he could deal with here.

"Listen up folks," he shouted over the chaos of the embarkation preparations, "The storm will be closing in again within the hour, so we don't have time to question you all here. I'll have to ask you all to remain at the station in Losien while we take your statements."

Dave turned to Jon who was standing at his side.

"This is crazy isn't it? Too loud?"

Jon nodded.

"Many people."

He was finding all this confusion and noise disorienting and frightening. Until now, he had kept his head down but now, looking up to speak to Dave, he was noticed by the man with the badge. The familiar look of revulsion passed over the man's face, then Jon saw him look down, taking in Jon's somewhat unusual clothing. The man's thoughts were clear: here was someone who didn't fit in. The freaky-looking guy would be the place to start investigating the murders. Excusing himself from Jeff and Rita, the man came over to question Jon. But Dave intervened, putting his arm around Jon's shoulders and preparing to shower effusive praise on him.

"Ah, sir, I can see that you recognise a hero when you see one. This is the man we have to thank, the man of the moment, if you will. He saved our lives and kept the children in safety in his cave until the danger had passed.

This man risked his own life to save ours and, let me tell you, none of us would be here now if it weren't for this man. I will certainly be using my contacts in the media to ensure that this great American receives the Nation's grateful thanks and recognition. He's a regular hero and I just know you're gonna want to thank him officially."

Jon only understood some of what Dave said, but he could see the immediate effect Dave's words had on the official-looking man. He stopped and gave Jon a rather embarrassed salute, before retreating quickly, to oversee the take off of the first helicopter.

Dave smiled broadly and patted Jon on the back.

"That was fun!"

"Thank you Dave."

Behind them, the first helicopter rose into the sky. In it were Phil, Bill, Annie, Lou and the three children. Lisa and Mikey waved excitedly from the windows.

As Dave waved back, he spoke to Jon.

"You're not coming with us, are you?"

Jon shook his head.

"I go."

"I understand. I know the others will be really sad that they won't get to thank you properly, but they'll understand too. But please, Jon, take this."

Dave took off his jacket and draped it over Jon's shoulders. It was wonderfully warm.

"And these. They're guaranteed waterproof."

Dave took off his new boots and presented them to Jon.

"In fact, here you are, have the lot. I'll just take the rubbish out for you."

Dave took any electrical gadgetry out of the rucksack, and rammed all his remaining clean clothes into it.

"There!" he said triumphantly, "Enjoy."

Dave lifted the rucksack for Jon, and was showing him

how to adjust the straps when Jeff came over.

"We're just going to show them where Neils' body is," he shouted over the din, "Then we'll be ready to leave. OK?"

As Jeff hurried away, Dave looked down at Jon and smiled.

"Goodbye Jon."

"Goodbye Dave."

Rather then go out through the noise and hustle at the front of the hotel, Jon left Dave and headed for the rear door. He stepped out, and paused for a moment, savouring the smell of the trees and enjoying the chill bite of the air. It felt so good to be free of enclosing walls and hard, angled surfaces. Jon was back where he belonged. He took off Dave's orange jacket. It had been a kind gift, but it was far too bright and it made far too much noise. Jon folded it carefully and left it on the doorstep. The boots, socks and other clothing were a different matter: Jon would keep those.

With a smile on his lips, he stepped down from the door and strode away across the clearing.

Jeff and Rita had led the man upstairs to the bedroom. They opted to wait outside as he entered the room. He came out again directly, they thought, because of the unpleasantness of the scene.

"Is this some kind of joke?" he asked them, angrily "You say you're from a college. Is this some student prank? Huh? Because, if it is, I'm warning you now, you will all be up on charges for wasting police time."

Jeff and Rita were shocked. What was he talking about?

"I don't understand," Rita muttered.

She took a deep breath to steady herself then reopened the door. The blood splatters still patterned the ceiling and walls but there, in the middle of the floor, where Neil's destroyed body had been lying, there was nothing but the desiccated pool of brown blood.

Neil's body had gone.

Hearing Rita gasp, Jeff followed her into the room. Like her, he simply stood open-mouthed, utterly baffled. The official looked from one to the other, quizzically. He scratched his head; this would take some sorting out, but there was no time to do anything more now. The radio crackled again: the snow was closing in. They had to leave.

Out in the clearing, Jon looked up and waved to the fast receding helicopter. He was happy; life would resume its pattern now. He would go back to his cave to ride out this storm but, after that, he thought he might look for a new home, deeper into the forest; he was keen to return to his familiar, solitary life.

With a contented smile on his lips Jon walked into the forest.

But Jon was not alone. A dark shape moved at the edge of the trees. Watching the helicopter leave, the tall gaunt figure leant its head to one side and sniffed the cold air. It had a thin, prominent nose and with it, had caught the scent of someone it recognised, someone who had angered it. Someone it hated. With a scratching rasp, it unfurled its brittle limbs and began to move purposefully across the open clearing, its pale face frozen in a leer of eager anticipation, its jewel black eyes glittering and its sharp teeth glistening in the failing light.

Acknowledgement

I'd like to thank Deirdre, Debbie, Sarah-Jane, Dorothy and Ella for their encouragement; Sue, who's had to wait a year for the second half of the book, for her patience; Raff for her continued support; and Hugh, Alex and Peter for their splendid proof reading.

I've really enjoyed writing this. I hope you've enjoyed reading it. Don't have nightmares!

Alison Buck, May 2007

Alnpete is an exciting, innovative independent publisher.
Read the previous title from Alison Buck:

Devoted Sisters

Alison Buck

Elderly sisters Lizzie and May live quiet, ordered lives in the house in which they were born; their self-imposed seclusion and the unchanging predictability of their lives shielding them from the changing world beyond.

But the day comes when this protective isolation is broken; the world outside forces its way in. A stranger appears, unsettling them, bringing with him the threat of danger, upheaval and violence.

Fearful and alone, with all semblance of comforting routine wrenched from them, Lizzie and May are driven to desperation. Dark memories emerge from their buried past as the sisters gradually slip from reason into their own confused realities, within which even their former carefully regulated world seems only a distant memory.

ISBN 978-0-9552206-1-6 pb 224pp £9.99
Read an excerpt at www.devotedsisters.co.uk

Visit the Alnpete Press website www.alnpetepress.co.uk
for the latest information on our titles, authors and events,
to read the blog, or to place a order

Alnpete is an exciting, innovative independent publisher.
Look out for the next title from Alison Buck:

Female Line

Alison Buck

Angela sits in the darkened kitchen, the knife in her hands. Looking down at the blade, she feels nothing. She absently reads the name on the cold metal and then closes her eyes again, lost in thought.

He'll be back soon.

But, for the moment, the silence of the flat is unbroken.

She carefully touches the side of her face. Her teeth are jarred and sore, but she looks down again at the blade and still she feels nothing.

He won't be long now.

As Angela waits, she dreams. She is, in this moment, detached from all of this; from her life with him, from the pain, from the failure of all her dreams, from life itself. This is not revenge. It's too cold for revenge. It's an ending, that's all.

A key rattles in the lock.

He is home...

ISBN 978-0-9552206-5-4 pb £9.99
Spring 2008
Find out more at www.femaleline.co.uk

Visit the Alnpete Press website www.alnpetepress.co.uk
for the latest information on our titles, authors and events,
to read the blog, or to place a order

Alnpete

Alnpete is an exciting, innovative independent publisher.
Check out the first Peter White mystery from Simon Buck:

Library of the Soul
a Peter White mystery
Simon Buck

For years the CIA have been using a poison designed to cause a heart attack and then disperse without a trace. Now a batch has gone missing.

On a visit to Rome, Peter White is recruited by his old friend Costanza into the oldest secret society in the world, in order to help her solve an urgent problem. Cardinals and other clerics around the world are dying of unexpected heart attacks. Police authorities are not interested as there is no evidence of foul play. But Costanza believes someone is using electronic cash and a betting website to fund and coordinate a campaign of murders that will ultimately lead to the assassination of the Pope. She and Peter must track down the killer before any more people die. Using the world's largest supercomputer, deep in the Secret Archives beneath the Vatican Library, they lay an electronic trap and wait. But when the Library itself becomes the target of an audacious plot to steal a 2000 year old manuscript, the problem suddenly becomes much more personal.

ISBN 978-0-9552206-0-9 pb 312pp £9.99
Read an excerpt at www.libraryofthesoul.co.uk

Visit the Alnpete Press website www.alnpetepress.co.uk
for the latest information on our titles, authors and events,
to read the blog, or to place a order